D0821295

I WENT TO SEE MY FATHER

ALSO BY KYUNG-SOOK SHIN

Violets
The Court Dancer
The Girl Who Wrote Loneliness
I'll Be Right There
Please Look After Mom

I WENT TO
SEE MY FATHER

A NOVEL

KYUNG-SOOK SHIN

TRANSLATED BY ANTON HUR

ASTRA HOUSE ⋀ NEW YORK

Copyright © 2021 by Kyung-Sook Shin
Translation © 2023 by Anton Hur
All rights reserved. Copying or digitizing this book for storage, display, or
distribution in any other medium is strictly prohibited.

Originally published in the Korean language as 아버지에게 갔었어
(*I Went to My Father*) © 2021 Changbi Publishers.

The translation of this work was supported by a grant from the
Literature Translation Institute of Korea.

For information about permission to reproduce selections from this book,
please contact permissions@astrahouse.com.

This is a work of fiction. Names, characters, places, and incidents are products
of the author's imagination or are used fictitiously. Any resemblance to actual events,
locales, or persons, living or dead, is entirely coincidental.

Astra House
A Division of Astra Publishing House
astrahouse.com
Printed in the United States of America

Library of Congress Cataloging-in-Publication Data

Names: Sin, Kyŏng-suk, author. | Hur, Anton, translator.
Title: I went to see my father : a novel / Kyung-Sook Shin ; translated by Anton Hur.
Other titles: Abŏji ege kassŏssŏ. English
Description: First edition. | New York : Astra House, [2023] | Summary: "In the wake
of a personal tragedy, a novelist goes back home in the Korean countryside to take
care of her gentle father and learns, through the testimonies of his loving
family and friends, how his lifelong kindness belies a past wrought in
both private and national trauma"—Provided by publisher.
Identifiers: LCCN 2022047568 (print) | LCCN 2022047569 (ebook) |
ISBN 9781662601378 (hardback) | ISBN 9781662601385 (ebook)
Subjects: LCGFT: Novels.
Classification: LCC PL992.73.K94 A6813 2023 (print) | LCC PL992.73.K94 (ebook) |
DDC 895.73—dc23/eng20230106
LC record available at https://lccn.loc.gov/2022047568
LC ebook record available at https://lccn.loc.gov/2022047569

First edition
10 9 8 7 6 5 4 3 2 1

Design by Richard Oriolo
The text is set in Bembo Std.
The titles are set in Trade Gothic LT Std.

CONTENTS

I WENT TO SEE MY FATHER

Some time ago, when I told my father I would write about him, he replied: But what have I ever done with this life?

You've done so much, I said.

I've done nothing at all. He sighed. All I've done is live through it.

CHAPTER 1

IT'S BEEN A LONG TIME SINCE I'VE SEEN YOU

When my mother set out with my younger sister to be taken to a hospital, my father was left all alone in the old house in the city of J——.

If I hadn't heard from my sister that Father wept at the gate as Mother left home, I wouldn't have thought to go down to J—— and stay with him. It had been over two years since I'd been there. My siblings used to take turns visiting our parents in J—— on the weekends, cutting Father's hair or buying groceries, stocking their fridge with enough food to last a week— the filial duties they'd been fulfilling for years. Duties I'd been exempt from so far. In the group chat the youngest started, where he announced whose turn it was to go down to J—— and on which weekend, I simply lurked in the background. After I lost my daughter, the relationships I'd depended on had either shattered or crumbled away. The first thing I did was minimize contact with my parents. I didn't want them to worry; they would instantly pick up on the sadness in my voice or the slightest shade of gloominess on my face. I had too much travel coming up, I would just keep telling them. I'd say that there was simply no way I could make it down to see them for a while. And now my protectively frozen heart was cracking at the news of Father's tears. *Ever since I left my hometown, Father has been calling me back*—is what I almost wrote just now, but that isn't quite right. Father has never asked me for anything. Whenever I heard from my mother or siblings that something was off with Father, I called him or got on a train to go and see him. Because if I didn't do that, my thoughts about him would grow to the point that I wouldn't be able to concentrate on anything else. After a sad silence at this news that Father had wept, I asked, Why did he cry? And my sister answered, I don't know. What with my asking why he cried and her replying she didn't know—we both sighed in unison. Mixed in with my silence was a wisp of this thought: Why didn't you suggest Father come with you when you picked up Mother? But, unprompted, my sister answered: It only occurred to me to ask him to come when I realized he would be left all alone.

—Oh, unni. I feel like I've left a child behind on a riverbank . . .

Her voice trailed off before she spoke again.

—When we were at the gate I asked, Father, will you come with us? And he said he wouldn't. Even as he was crying.

What could he have been feeling, watching my sister take my sick mother up to Seoul? Annoyed by the theatrics, Mother had reportedly said, Why are you crying? Am I going off to die? I'm coming back, aren't I? So why don't you finish up with your dental work while I'm gone? My sister initially thought she was consoling him, but Mother was in tears as well. The scene was so clear in my mind that, before I could stop myself, I sighed again. My little sister blurted out:

—You'd have thought I was ripping them apart for all of eternity.

Mother was to check into the hospital tomorrow. Even if I never went down to J— or hardly ever called my parents, I always knew what was going on because of the family group chat. Because my siblings and I were used to it now, discussing things that were happening to our parents. Including my little sister, who dropped off Mother at my eldest brother's house and called me on her way back home.

—But unni, they all do that, apparently.

—. . . What?

—The sister-in-law at eldest oppa's house said they all do that.

—They all do what?

—When I mentioned Father crying, she said all fathers did that and I shouldn't feel bad about it. She said she took her own mother to a hospital in Seoul when she got sick, and her father cried.

Our sister-in-law's father passed away two years ago.

—I guess all fathers are like that. She said I shouldn't take it too much to heart. I really shouldn't have called you, unni.

My sister liked to square away things that bothered her, but it didn't seem to be working very well in this case because her voice cracked when she said, *So don't think too much about it.*

—Father is getting dental work done?

She didn't answer my question. It was probably a silent admonishment for my recent lack of concern for my family. My youngest sibling had mentioned Father going to a dentist in the group chat. The dentist in town evidently told him to bring a spouse or a child to escort him next time. Father ended up taking his sister's son who lived nearby. "His sister's son" makes our cousin sound like a child, but he's actually well past sixty. Father had wanted his dental treatments to be kept a secret even from Mother, but our cousin ended up calling and telling the youngest about it. Even as my other siblings went on about Father's treatments, I could only stay out of it and wonder, Would he be able to bear it? while feeling too disconcerted to participate. Since that discussion had happened a mere month ago and I'd forgotten already, there was nothing I could say in my defense about my neglect. My little sister, perhaps sensing how she'd struck a nerve, said, You were going through a lot back then, it's understandable that this stuff slipped your attention, and abruptly ended the call. *This stuff* . . . My sister's words left a weight that pulled me down into my chair. After two hours of sitting in utter helplessness, I booked a train ticket to J——, packed up my laptop, and left a message in the group chat saying I was going to see Father. That I would stay with him while Mother was in the hospital. Perhaps surprised after my years of silence, the entire family merely read my messages yet made no reply. And as I waited for the taxi that would come and take me to Seoul Station, the new doorplate on which I had engraved my daughter's name caught my eye. I stretched out my hand and brushed my fingertips over her name and the blue salamander design I'd found in her sketchbooks and had cut into the bronze.

Father wept . . . This wasn't the first time I'd heard those words.

After I graduated from middle school and left J——, Father was said to have wept for four days. When Mother came back from seeing me all the way up in Seoul, she saw that Father's eyes were swollen, and the swelling didn't go down for four days. He would weep as he dipped a gourd into makkeolli rice wine. Weep as he got onto his bicycle with the large rack on his way to the wholesaler in town for more cigarettes. This was back when Father ran a general store by the tracks at the edge of town. *Father had what . . . ?* The news that Father had wept after sending me off left me stunned. It was unimaginable; Mother had said it was the first she had seen him cry as well. *That little thing, that half-grown thing*, he reportedly kept saying, meaning me. When I heard about it, I joked that I had finished growing in middle school, and that 163 cm wasn't little at all.

This was the second store he had ever managed.

Who owned that store by the train tracks? About the time I was in second or third grade, Father took over that store and then gave it up, but then managed it again when I became a middle school student. Calling it a dry goods store might make you think of the supermarkets or convenience stores that are so common these days, but it wasn't anywhere near that size; it was what we used to call a "little spot," which was just a narrow, modest little space in a country village. The displays held an inventory of bubble-gum, bread, caramel candies—things that were there mostly for display and could be inventoried in five minutes. Its real source of income was cigarettes. There was also a big earthen jar buried inside the store that stored makkeolli delivered from a rice winery, and it was always surrounded by the smell of fermented rice with a measuring gourd made of firwood nearby. Father would scoop up the wine in the gourd ladle and pour it into a kettle before handing it over to customers. The customers were mostly people who lived in the village or those who had to go farther in toward Jinsan-ri, Samsan-ri, or Cheonan, to get home. Around sunset, the people who had worked in the fields all day would come to Father's store and drink makkeolli, and during those hours, it was hard to tell who was the customer and who was the shopkeeper. Often there would be yut traditional board games late into the night and the men would bet on soju. A random memory I suddenly recall is of a bunch of long, black rubber bands hanging on the door of that store. The black strands spread like the branches of a willow tree. Whenever I had an errand from Mother or needed to get money from Father, I used to wind the bands around my hand and call out, Father! It wasn't easy asking him for money, which often led to me pulling at those bands for ages without saying anything. People occasionally bought them. On sunny days, the villagers would open the lids of their doenjang or gochujang earthenware jars, covering the mouths with linen. The bands were used to keep the linen from flying away in the wind. The store was that kind of place. It sold things someone might need immediately and spare them a trip to town, all sorts of country life accouterments displayed on shelves or inside glass cases. When I left J—, the store was where I went to say goodbye to Father. And just as always, I wound the rubber bands around my hand and called out, Father! But just then, the bus going to the train station pulled up right in front of the store. It was night; if I missed that bus, I would have to walk all the way to the station. And even if I could walk it, I would probably arrive after the last train had left. Anxious, I kept calling into the dark store, Father! Father!

For all my life, whenever I've had to part with someone, I would hear an echo of my own voice from that time.

Whenever I think of what I left behind in that place, I remember my father standing there all alone as I finally shouted, Father, I have to go, and ran for the bus. The bus had stopped, Father was still inside the store, and I shouted, Father, I have to go now . . . And there I was, climbing on board. Before the doors shut, I leaned out to look one more time at Father's store. Inside, I tried to open a window, but they were sealed shut. With one palm pressed against the windowpane, I stared out to where Father stood in the dim light. He had rushed out of the store, a slipper on one foot and a shoe on the other, standing stock-still, too upset to even wave goodbye as he stared after the bus that was taking me away from him. I had let go of the rubber bands so abruptly that they were still swaying next to his silhouette. The light coming from inside the store cast shadows and blotches on the dark expression on his face. The bus began to pull away before I had a chance to shout goodbye to him. I think about that moment from time to time. About how long he must've stood there after the bus had left. About what he must've felt staring down that dark road, long after the bus had disappeared. About how long he must've waited before going back inside the store. All throughout my city life, when I think of how he must've gone back into that run-down little shop and wept, my hand goes to my forehead, my heart calms down, and I feel a kind of patience and endurance in the face of most things I may be dealing with in the current moment. The old bench inside the shop where people sat to drink makkeolli, the gourd ladle that bobbed around in the jar, the beer bottles he kept cold in the summer in a barrel filled with water . . . and inside the dark backroom of that store, his buk drum, his drumstick, and—

An almost black wooden chest with a lock.

Inside the chest was the money Father made from running the store. The 100 won bills with King Sejong's face, laid flat and stacked over each other, the king's face as flat as the bills. There were a couple of 500 won bills from time to time, and maybe even a 1,000 won note. And the coins.

I first saw the faces of Admiral Yi Sun-sin and the philosopher Yi Hwang along with the armored geobukseon turtle ship on those coins. When I went to get spending money from him before school—for all those little things children needed to buy—Father would mop the floor of the shop before asking how much I needed. Saying the amount made my face go red and my heart beat fast. Regardless of my blushing or my beating heart, Father put the coins in my hand. He never bade me to be careful with it or to study hard in school. If he was wiping things down, he would dry his hands on a towel, open the chest, take out the amount I needed, lock eyes with me as he put it in my hand, pat my head—and that was it. He made that wooden chest with his own hands when he first started working at that store in his thirties. It was just big enough to hold about five books. He was much younger than I am now. What was on his mind as he crafted its sides and hinges and lock? The chest, which I could sit on, aged beautifully as time passed. Admiring every detail including the neatly attached lock, I almost couldn't believe Father had created it himself. Once he passed over the store on to someone else, the chest just lay around the living room for a while. I was once surprised to find a dead bird in it—one of my older brothers had put it there. The chest must've been used by my siblings from time to time to store things. But it was generally thought of as a useless object, with one person moving it here and another moving it there. It was waiting to be made use of until it became mine one day. I put my crayons inside to claim it, or I'd put early windfall persimmons so they'd ripen faster, or I'd store dog-earred books borrowed from school. Sometimes, I'd put my diary in there after clasping the lock shut with a satisfying snap. When Father went back to running the store, the chest that had briefly been mine went back to being his cash chest again. It's occurred to me now that the two times he stepped in to run that store were times when my family needed money the most. When his six children entered middle and high school, one by one. When Father gave up the shop a second time, did the chest return with him as well? That would've been after I had left home. I never saw that chest after he quit the second time. The person who succeeded him would need someplace to store their money, so perhaps Father left it behind.

Some objects just disappear like that. Not thrown away, not taken out, not donated or destroyed, just lost in time at some point and then they slowly fade from our memory. Leaving behind an echo of *It was like that, it was like that back then . . .*

Father was born in our house in J— in the early summer of 1933. He wasn't always the eldest son. He had three older brothers and two older sisters—he was the sixth, in fact—but an epidemic one year took away his older brothers and he became the eldest son. Of a head family, no less. My grandfather, not rumored to be a great physician but a licensed doctor of Eastern medicine nevertheless, was so filled with fear from having lost three sons at once that he forbade my father from attending school. Keeping him at home, he taught him *The Four Books* and made him memorize sayings from *The Mirror that Lights the Soul.* Father can still recite the things he learned from my grandfather. *When one sleeps one does not sleep slanted, when one sits one does not sit uncentered, when one stands one does not lean on one's left foot . . . The ears must listen not to bad tidings, the eyes must see not the faults of others, rotten wood cannot be sculpted, and a wall of rotten clay cannot be plastered . . . One must not find oneself precious and others beneath oneself . . . If it is not a good seat one must not sit in it, one's eyes must not turn to flashy colors . . . Teach others, sprinkle water, sweep, be hospitable, know how to withdraw, love one's parents, raise one's teachers, keep close one's friends . . .* Once he started to recite, it was like unraveling a spool of thread, and I would ask, How can you still recite all of this? And he would answer, Because my father taught me, and would pause in his recitation to say, I wish he'd sent me to school instead, briefly revealing his resentment toward his father. If my grandfather had not been cowed by the fear of disease and sent Father to school, would Father have lived a different life? Would he have been able to leave home one day? I tried to console Father by saying, If you had gone to school in those days, you probably would have had to change your name to a Japanese one. But Father did not go to school. He went out into the fields instead. He turned the loam and planted rice. When he was fourteen, there was another epidemic in the village. And my grandfather, who had prevented my father from going to school because of disease, caught the disease himself. If only he had not visited family then, Father often said when he talked about my grandfather. My grandfather's eldest uncle had caught the disease, and my grandfather himself came down with it after having gone to his home with medicinal herbs to treat him. My grandmother, who had nursed my grandfather, also became infected. That summer, Father lost both his parents in just two days.

Father was working in the fields on the day he lost his father at fourteen.

I was sharpening my plow at the Yeonjeong-ri field when Father suddenly appeared before me and came wading into the rice paddy water, saying I shouldn't be using the plow like that. And he fixed the way I held it and he pressed my shoulder and said that in these times, we needed to learn how to properly handle the ox and plow if we wanted to survive. And after this advice, he waved his hand and suddenly disappeared. One moment he was saying I should take care of the ox, and the next, I blinked and he was gone. He was quarantined at home. I had barely seen his face there, and it was strange that he had come all the way down to the field. I had a pain in my heart about it. I put the plow down in the water and ran home, but Father had spurted blood from his nose, splattering the very ceiling and . . . They said if you lived five days after getting that disease, you would get better. There were so many people who didn't last five days, got covered in straw mats, and then carried away on wagons. Father had just one more day to go, and we were already thinking he'd made it. We were hoping for time to pass. But on the fifth day, he went just like that. Father died, my mind went dark, I couldn't see a thing.

What was I to do now? How am I to live? I cried out to the land and the sky, Why do you do this to me? But my eldest aunt hugged me and said she was not going anywhere, that she would live with me, that I should not fear or cry. I still hear her saying that to me to this day.

At the beginning of every semester I wrote "farmer" on the form where they asked for my father's occupation, but he didn't seem like a farmer to me; whether he was growing rice sprouts in the seedbeds or heading to the rice paddies with a shovel during droughts, there was something awkward about him. As a child I must've thought so because Father did not seem to really concentrate on farming as other fathers did. Not only did he manage a store but he also built stables for cows and hunted birds with a shotgun when there was no farming work to be done. Sometimes, he left home for entire winters saying he was going to get work. I have no idea if he managed to save up any money then, but he always returned when seeds needed planting in the seedbeds to be sprouted for rice. It could've simply been the case that farming wasn't enough to survive and he had to take on whatever work he could to pay our bills, but in my child's eye, all I could see was that he didn't really seem to be a farmer. Perhaps it was also because his face wasn't darkened by the sun but was rather pale. Or that, unlike the other strong-legged fathers who dug up wheelbarrow loads of sweet potatoes from mountain fields, my father was bedridden from time to time. Or that he sometimes wore a leather jacket, put pomade in his hair, and burned rubber on a motorcycle. These memory fragments of my father were impressed upon my mind as him not farming very well and his heart belonging elsewhere.

Father spent his entire life on that lot in J—, knocking down the house twice and rebuilding on the same spot. Any mention of the year 1933 gives me pause as Father was born in that year. That's how I learned that the Korean Language Society's announcement of the "Draft for Standardized

Korean Orthography" happened in 1933, too. It was right in the middle of the Japanese occupation. My heart swells—how extraordinary that people would publish such a document in times of violent oppression! But then comes the realization that simultaneous to this achievement were the clear-eyed, objective perspectives and the shunning of sentimentality by writers like Hemingway in America, which disconcerts me. But not only that. To think that Picasso, whose work still feels fresh to this day, had already realized much of his artistic vision by that time makes me fall into a void of helplessness. Some people are born into love and attention and support from their parents, live their lives in this world expressing everything they want to, and leaving behind their immortal names. Then others, like Father, are born in a completely ordinary farming house far from the then town of J—, in the middle of nowhere in southern Korea, prevented from setting foot in school and never leaving home except for survival itself, living a life of dust. Not to mention having his young daughter turn away from him for no apparent reason.

Whenever I think of Father, I always think of a certain bridge in my hometown of J—. More accurately, I think of when I was a middle school student and looked away from my father on that bridge.

Our home was about four kilometers from town. I walked the ten li distance to my elementary school on a road through clouds of dust and pebbles kicked up by my feet. Nowadays there's a straight, paved road three kilometers long. J— is a city now, but at the time when I bumped into my father on that bridge, it was merely a town. The bridge connected the two major neighborhoods and was called Daeheung-ri. Who knows why it had such a name; I looked up the name's origins one time, but I found nothing. The bridge was in Namsan-ri, not Daeheung-ri. J— didn't even have a place called Daeheung-ri. The only information on the bridge was that it had been constructed during the Japanese occupation. I remember people saying, The bridges those Jap bastards built are the sturdiest. Homeless people lived in tents under it, and anyone passing by the bridge could see how they lived. They washed potatoes in the river, put pots on fires, defecated into the river, and when it was hot, took off their clothes and bathed there. We could see them in the fields when the harvest was over. They scavenged for potatoes that had been missed and rice stalks that had been dropped. When it was dark, they came out from underneath the bridge, sat around a fire on the riverbank, and sang songs. You could smell the smoke while walking across the bridge. You couldn't see them in the winter when they would wear everything they could bear to wear, covering themselves in whatever they could find and never emerging from their tents. They rendered themselves invisible from the bridge. In the spring, a market for selling ducks and chicks would open on the riverbank, and they would finally come out to get some sun. One spring, I saw one of the women had a swollen belly, and eventually heard a baby's cries coming from under the bridge as I crossed it. Around the time I left J—, a public landscaping project left the space under the bridge paved flat. The homeless no longer lived there. Whenever I see city people on the news protesting about another forced relocation, I wonder about the people who had to leave. Where could they have moved to?

At first, the only bridge across J—'s long river was Daeheung-ri, but later on there were two more built upriver nearby the high school and two downriver in Yeonji-dong and by the train station. Despite the landscaping, the river still overflowed during heavy rainstorms and the bridge would look as if it were floating. Sometimes, the rough waters even threatened to overwhelm it. The bridges that were built later would often be submerged or collapse. People would say, The bridge has disconnected. Spring rains disconnected the bridges upriver and summer monsoons disconnected the ones downriver. Embarrassingly enough, only Daeheung-ri, built during the Japanese occupation, withstood any and all amount of rain. Some would praise it as the best little bridge in the city of J—, while others would remark snidely that it was clear evidence the Japanese had every intention of holding on to our land forever.

I ran into my father on that bridge.

The bridge connected the edge of town on this side to downtown on that side, and the middle school, fire station, crossroads market, administrative building, police station, and courthouse were on that side. The village I was born in was about four kilometers away from the outermost edge of town. The children of our village attended elementary school on the edge of town and most of us walked there. There were many paths to school; once you went past the twisting alleys leading from our front door, there was a bit of road you could either keep following or take a detour into a path by the Irrigation Association offices. When I didn't have much time, I would follow the road, but if I had a few minutes to spare, I took the detour that led me to the Irrigation Association dyke route. Beneath the dyke were rice fields. In the spring, in the masses of weeds by the dyke road, morning glories would bloom with heaps of wild strawberries scattered in between. I would thrust my hand through the tangles of dew-laden morning glories to pick the fruit. Putting my bag down on the dyke, I reached so far down that my shirt rode up my back, and I'd stretch my hand toward the strawberries that were just beyond my grasp—which sometimes earned me a bleeding scratch or two from thorns—and manage to grasp a red berry, a joy I could taste only on the way to school. Some weren't ripe but looked like they could be the next morning, and those I'd pull closer toward the road and hide so other children could not spot them from the dyke, sometimes marking the spot with an extra tangle of morning glory vines. Once I got off the Irrigation Association road, my trousers would be heavy with dew and dust. On that up-and-down road was yet another detour that led through rice fields to the first road and a low hill and some burial mounds. The mounds were the midpoint between the school and the village—a place where children would stop to rest on their way home.

Even while "resting," the children could barely stay still as they chased or pushed or ran away from each other, climbing over the mounds and sliding down so often that the sod could not grow grass because it was constantly trampled. Most of the children were freed from this path once they entered middle school, which was deeper into town and better reached by bus or bicycle. And the only way to get downtown was, of course, across Daeheung-ri Bridge.

Which season was it? Father was neither wearing short sleeves nor thick layers, so it must've been past spring and early summer, or past summer and early fall. Was it a market day? There were many people on the bridge. It teemed with the crossing paths of those going downtown and those leaving it. For whatever reason, I was on my way downtown coming from this side while Father was coming from the other. At first I wasn't sure it was him until I stopped in my tracks, thinking, Wait, is that Father? I looked at the man coming toward me again. It was him. It's such a strange feeling to meet family outside the home in an unexpected place. Frozen still, I continued to stare at him. In his prime, Father was of an adequate build and taller than average height. He had fair skin that didn't look like a country person's complexion and a prominent nose that balanced out his facial features. Father, unlike other fathers in those days, never raised his voice. When he was with others, he spoke so seldomly that it almost seemed as if he were alone. Despite this, he had many friends. My siblings would call his friends "ajeh"—the guys. Buksan ajeh, Daesung ajeh, Naechun ajeh, or Gomso ajeh. Whenever we ran into them, they treated us like they were our Father. If they were on bikes, they would let us hop on the back. If they bumped into us in front of a store, they would press treats into our hands. And when there was someone who didn't know us, they'd mention my Father's one-syllable name and announce that we were his children. In their voices was a kind of joy and trust that they were living in the same world as Father. But the man standing on that bridge seemed nothing like that; he seemed like a completely different person.

Sagging shoulders, covered by a shabby jacket and a crumpled shirt tucked into loose trousers . . . His head hung down at first, deep in thought, and as he raised his head, our eyes almost met. I quickly turned my head the other way. I saw the flowing water and the sunlight dancing across its surface. The fact that I had just looked away from Father surprised me, and I was swallowed up in shame. I turned my head again and looked for him. Still lost in thought, Father was bumping against the shoulders of other pedestrians as he crossed over to the other side. His back was a sad sight to see as he disappeared into the crowd. How he seemed to shrink until he looked so small and pitiful. As if he were being left behind, unable to keep up with everyone else. Father's posture remained slouched and low as he crossed that bridge. I followed him with my eyes as long as I could, standing on tiptoes to see over the crowd. He had a slight limp, as if the heel of one of his shoes had worn down more than the other. Then sunlight, people, noise, shadows, and strange blotches filled my field of vision. Father disappeared from view.

And as he did so, the thought that I had turned my eyes from my humble father planted guilt in my heart.

As the train announced that the next station was for J—, I could hear the words: Mommy, we're here, spoken by my daughter in my ear. I closed my eyes and opened them again. It felt as if my daughter was tapping my shoulder. I closed the book in front of me. Despite wanting to read it, I was still on the exact page I had been on when we pulled out of Seoul Station. This train will arrive at J—, please make sure you have all your belongings with you when you disembark. Thank you. Listening to the announcement repeat itself, I took my bag down from the overhead shelf when I almost fell backward. I heard my daughter's voice again: Be careful, mommy! A passing train worker took the bag down for me and placed it on its wheels. Trains are getting better and better these days. I always think this whenever I take one. This time around, when I had taken my coat off at Seoul Station to place it on the shelf, I'd noticed there were coat hooks by the train windows. They were not too big and not too small, neatly placed, just right. The announcements weren't as noisy as they used to be, either. Mindful of sleeping passengers, the voice is soft and almost lilting. Which was why Father, when traveling with Mother to Seoul to see their children, had once missed J— on their way back. I took my coat off of my new discovery and looked out the window as I put it on. How long has it been since I'd been in this station . . . I tried counting but I couldn't remember. Nothing but old memories of J— flashed by my mind's eye. As the train entered J— Station, even those faint scenes were dispelled from my mind.

J— Station was no longer the modest stop where the turnstiles led directly to the platform. Conductors did not walk around with a hole puncher in hand, punching holes through the tickets that the passengers held out. Back then, you could pass through the turnstile as soon as your ticket was punched. And until the train arrived and left, the people seeing off the passengers stood by the turnstiles as the ones leaving looked back from the tracks or waved. J—'s spaces that remain in my mind are generally from the time before I left J— to live in Seoul. The courthouse, the Jaeil Bank branch, the firehouse, the elementary school on the outskirts, and the riverbanks under the bridges I crossed every day to get to the middle school downtown. In the spring, mung beans and boat orchids would sprout green leaves on the riverbank before blooming into yellow blossoms. Having left behind my parents and younger siblings in J—, I would return often until I passed forty. Because I had left before any wounds could form, it was always a place of innocent longing for me. Even after the youngest left J— for university, I continued to go back often. For a long time, "home" meant my parents' home in J—. It was the same for my siblings, and whenever we said things like we'd gone "home" or to "our house," it meant our parents' house. Even by the time J— was administratively elevated from township to city status, our home's village was still not even really part of a town, much less a city. The elementary school was four kilometers away by foot, the market where Mother bought food for jesa ancestral rites was four or five kilometers away, and my middle school was about five kilometers away. Most children who grew up in our village walked to the elementary school and learned how to ride a bike to get to the middle school. I was no exception. Since I moved to Seoul, I learned to make my way back home by train from Seoul or Yongsan Station. It took three or four hours, and then I'd disembark at J— Station, walk down to the station plaza and to a nearby bus stop, take a bus to Ipam or Jangseong or Gochang through the winding mountain roads, and get off at the entrance to our village. Whenever I'd missed the bus and had to wait or had arrived late at night or had much to carry, I would take a taxi from the taxi stand near the train station.

Back when Father rode a motorcycle, he would come to the train station to pick me up when I told him I was coming into town.

When I would go down to the station plaza, he would be standing beside his motorcycle, wearing sunglasses and carrying a helmet. His free hand would shoot up in the air to greet me. I'm here among the crowd, his gesture seemed to say. Every time, I found my father's sunglasses strange, and only when he waved a second time would I approach him. He brought me home like this over several years and must've worn many outfits, but all I remember now is his indigo jacket. There must've been other seasons as well, but all I remember is late spring moving in to early summer. An indigo jacket, neither light nor dark, with a zipper going up to the neck and pockets on either side to put your hands in. Father would put my bag in the basket attached to the front of the motorcycle and have me sit in the back, and we'd noisily zoom toward home. I would put my hands in his jacket pockets and hold on to his waist as the motorcycle wove its way through the traffic by the station and into the roads by the rice paddies and fields. All around, I could hear birdsongs and smell the clear water of the freshly planted rice paddies and see the sky full of fluffy, white clouds. When I would hold Father's waist, he'd say, Hold on tighter, as he accelerated. There was a faint smell of oil in the air. The motorcycle passed J—'s electronics store, bicycle store, and shoe store, and soon came to the road to our village. On the way home was a path that led to a graveyard from where

I'd been told since I was young that a barefoot child would emerge and walk to the village to see his friends. That, sometimes, you could hear the cries of a woman pushing aside the dirt to crawl out of her grave. Why were the characters in these chilling stories always children or women? My older brothers, when they passed the cemetery, would quicken their pace and I would fall behind. Wait for me! I would shout as I ran after them, and when that didn't work, I'd plopped down on the ground and cry. I'd feel a hand touching the back of my neck—I shouldn't have shouted after my brothers no matter how bad they were being, I never should've given up and started to cry . . . Regrets I still have to this day as I look back. When they learned I was scared of the cemetery, my brothers made fun of me every time we passed it. Now even that fear and suffering are bittersweet memories. Riding behind Father on his motorcycle, I would look in that direction and ask, Is there still a cemetery there? Then, It's still there, he would answer every time, until the day he answered that the plot was to be redeveloped and the cemetery had been moved. Even then, my head would still automatically turn toward the cemetery whenever I passed. My hands inside Father's jacket would grip a little tighter. Holding on to his firm waist, we passed the old cemetery grounds. Hold on . . . I liked Father's voice as it carried over the wind. As his speed continued to increase, I leaned into his back and watched the rice paddies and fields and the other faraway villages and hills, my eyes half-closed. My flying hair whipped the helmet he wore. The magpies sitting on the fields would take flight, surprised by the sound of the motorcycle, showing us their white bellies. When the wheels bounced across the bumpy roads, my hands in Father's pockets would grip even tighter. But his waist felt so firm in my hands, so I never for a moment felt afraid or endangered—just felt a sense of liberating relief that weighed on my eyelids.

This house has two entrances.

Father, as if he were on his way out or had just come in from an outing, was standing in the courtyard, dressed tidily. You have to take the alley by the Nonghyup Bank's warehouse, following its twists and turns until the end where the front gate is, or on the road before reaching the warehouse, then walk toward the irrigation ditches where the old nettle trees stand and then you will reach a smaller gate. At the ditch, I get out of my taxi and drag my luggage to the house. No matter which gate you enter, there's nowhere to go once you're in the house. It's the true center of the village. The two gates are always open. Neighbors who live near the road and want to go to the ditch come through the main gate, cross the courtyard, and go out the small gate. And those who live on the other side and are in a hurry to get to the road come through the small gate, cross the courtyard, and go out the main gate. Father was lost in thought, standing in the courtyard as I entered through the small gate. I let go of my luggage so the noise didn't disturb him. Once the wheels were stilled, silence descended around us. Father wasn't lost in thought, but he was concentrating on something in front of him. What was he looking at? I left my bag behind and approached him. In the middle of the courtyard was a little garden surrounded by stones, with a hydrangea in full bloom that a butterfly was fussing over. Father was watching the butterfly's movements in total stillness.

—Father?

Only then did he take his eyes off the butterfly and look at me. His face was so gaunt, his cheeks sunken, and it looked like he was blinking at the sunlight. Father was crying. Tears fell on his dry cheeks. The sight of his tears felt like someone had hit me on the back of the head—a ringing shock like my head had split open. Father, beside himself, wiped his face with the back of his hand like a little boy. His wet eyes were not focused on me, but they were searching for something. Pretending not to have noticed his tears, I spoke in a bright voice:

—What were you looking at just now?

I hugged his waist.

—Is it you, Hon? You've come home?

Despite standing right in front of him, Father looked at me like I was a specter.

—What on Earth were you looking at so closely?

—A butterfly.

—That butterfly?

I looked again at where Father had been staring. A white butterfly flew up the camellia tree and sat on it. Perhaps it was only a camellia tree by name, though, because it hadn't bloomed all winter. But was well underway now, its buds a deep, deep red in the sun. There was already a pile of fallen blossoms on the ground.

—Underneath that butterfly . . .

Father tried to say something but didn't finish his sentence.

—What's underneath that butterfly?

When he pointed down, the butterfly fluttered from the camellia to a pile of stones by the hydrangea. A cairn? There were no other piles of stone except that one, stacked with care. Why on Earth are you crying because of a butterfly? I wanted to ask, but I suppressed the question and said instead:

—Why is there a pile of stones here?

—I buried him there.

—. . .

—Chammie is buried there.

Chammie.

Someone in my family had told me that Chammie had died; I guess that was his resting place. I stared down at the cairn and the butterfly that had landed on it. Father must've stacked the cairn to mark where he'd buried Chammie. The butterfly, sitting on the memorial, was flapping its delicate wings.

When my daughter was still with us, I had had a habit of taking things that had become burdensome down by train or car to my parents' house to lay down at their feet.

Here you go, this is your home now—and with that, I would return to the city alone. Two cats, two puppies, and a parrot. Father made a space in the toolshed for the cats, putting down mats and fashioning a little house for them. My goal was for the cats to move in with my parents, but I failed at that. My father was country folk through and through; if he let the cats live in the house, Others will mock us, he had said. Hence the woven straw mats on the floor of the shed for the cats to stretch out on and scratch. The cats liked climbing, so he put up ladders and tied bits of rope here and there. But the cats didn't stay put in the toolshed, despite my father's wishes. They slipped out and walked about on the courtyard walls or the roof. They napped in the fields or climbed the persimmon tree. It was impossible to tell who owned them as they would freely go in and out of everybody's homes. I urged Father to feed them cat food instead of rice or banchan side dishes that people ate, but he replied, What, are they cows? Why do they need a separate feed? Nevertheless, he served them dry cat food in their bowls at the right time along with some fresh water. Saying he had bought cow feed before but not cat feed, he would zip downtown on his motorcycle to get more of it when he ran out. Mother, fascinated by this new habit, would poke her head out and half-teasingly say, Going out to give the kitties food? Mother said the only reason he did anything was because I was the one who asked him to. Think about it, she once said. If I'd suggested it myself. Cats, what cats? That's what he would've said . . . Your father, he does everything you tell him, right? When Mother needed to nag Father about something, she would call me up in Seoul. Tell your father to drink less, tell him the roads are dangerous so he should give up his motorbike, tell him to stop going out to the music hall downtown for a while . . . Under orders from Mother, I called him to tell him. Blah blah blah, I would go as instructed, and Father would listlessly say, Oh, really? OK, I will. Father and the cats got along relatively well. The cats wandered around freely, and when they were hungry they came to the toolshed and ate their cat food, and at night they slept in their houses. Still, seeing them go half-feral since leaving the city and settling in the country, I couldn't quite decide if I'd done the right thing or not. Some years later, the cats disappeared completely. The dogs did not do well in this house, either. When I brought them here, I had thought they would at least be able to run around to their hearts' content. But the fact that the dogs were off their leashes scared the people who cut through our courtyard to go to the irrigation ditch or the big road. I'd wanted the cats to live in the house and not a toolshed, and the dogs to live off their leashes, but I only learned later on that this was much more difficult to do in the country. When I left the cats or the dogs at my parents' place, I would call Father every morning for a month or two, checking to see whether the cats used their litterboxes or whether the dogs' leashes were too short.

Father would say, The cats are clever, they cover up their business with sand. I think we need to name one of the dogs—what about Maru? Father always answered each and every one of my questions. A few months would go by and my thoughts would stop drifting to the dogs and cats I'd left behind in the country. I didn't call Father as often after that.

The parrot Father had buried in the garden was one I had gotten from the market. Saying that I got it probably isn't correct. The parrot followed me. The Tong-in Market is half an hour from my house in Seoul by car, and there happens to be a shop where I occasionally buy fresh fish. The reason I drive all the way to that shop is because they have herring and flatfish and freshwater fish—the likes of which are not sold at my local supermarket—and not only is everything fresh, the owner is very generous and often throws in a fistful of sea squirts for free. One day I went with my daughter to buy some sole and a display of mugwort happened to catch my eye, so I bought a bundle and slipped it into my shopping tote. I was about to move on when I saw a parrot walking around the market. A parrot? In pictures or books, parrots are normally yellow or green or white, but this one was dark and gray, even its face. I thought it must have an owner somewhere, but it seemed to be alone. A parrot, how odd. I walked on toward the fishmonger's shop and the parrot hopped along after me. Like a puppy! It maintained its distance though, so I assumed it would eventually tire of this game. My daughter exclaimed, Mommy, the parrot is following us! She loved it. At the fishmonger's place, we bought a nice big sole and a codfish and the parrot came right up to my feet. It followed us even as we were leaving the market.

—Go!

I was so annoyed that I shouted, Go! Go away! as if I were scolding a person. The parrot stared at me like it had something to say, but it didn't go anywhere. Even when we had reached our car that was parked in the alley behind Tong-in Market, it followed us. The parrot keeps following us, my daughter said between laughs. I walked right back to the store where I'd bought the mugwort, the place I'd first seen the parrot. What am I going to do with this parrot, it keeps following me! The old lady who had sold me the mugwort *tsk-tsked*. The parrot had apparently been wandering around the market for four days. It couldn't have escaped on its own, said the lady, so the owner must've abandoned it. The old lady looked up at me and said, I suppose you're the owner now? She told me that it did follow people around the market from time to time, but if any of them approached, the parrot would bite and turn aggressive. It seemed calm and friendly toward us. But why? I stared at the gray parrot. I had to go home. I couldn't keep carrying the sole and codfish while being followed around by a parrot bodyguard. I tried shaking it off my trail when it seemed momentarily distracted, but when I turned around, it would be there again. The parrot is Mommy's copycat, my daughter said as she caught up with us. I tried running away all the way to the electricity pole at the end of the market without looking back at all, but it still followed me. Go away! But even shouting at it felt pointless. My daughter and I ducked into the butcher's shop or pretended to buy mallow in a vegetable store. We'd sneak out the other entrance, but it was all for naught. How strange it was to be the target of a parrot . . . It all felt rather pathetic, and when I opened the car door for my daughter, the parrot hopped into the car before my she could get in. This parrot was Chammie.

—It's strange. Not a single sick thing about him but when I woke up, he was dead. He ate well the night before . . .

Father got along well with the gray parrot. He was the one who named it Chammie. From saying the parrot "cham maleul jal handa"—meaning, that parrot sure can talk well. Obviously, it could only learn whatever words Father taught it, what was this about it talking well? But I didn't voice my thoughts and went along with calling it Chammie.

—You miss him?

—We were friends.

Father's voice sounded so empty. When I had first brought Chammie to Father, he had laughed about the fact that I was offloading a bird that time.

—But it's not an ordinary bird, Father.

—If it's not ordinary, then what is it?

—It speaks.

—It speaks?

—I'm telling you. Teach it. It can learn to say things you want it to say instead of you.

Father, who had been so against bringing dogs or cats inside the house, for some reason hung Chammie's cage indoors. No one in the village had ever kept a parrot, and while everyone had seen magpies or sparrows or woodpeckers or ducks or bulbuls or broad-billed rollers, no one had ever seen a parrot before, he must've thought. And he considered himself less likely to be mocked if he kept the parrot out of sight.

Father cared a lot about, and was greatly influenced by, what people said.

When Father hears something and says, People are saying . . . This means what people are saying is wrong and he doesn't believe in them. And so, I left the gray parrot behind and again began to call him every morning. Over the phone, I could actually hear him teaching the parrot how to speak. By the time it could call Father appa—dad—the parrot refused to spend a moment away from Father's side. Appa? When I first heard the parrot say that, I scoffed. How dare this parrot use this informal term of endearment I myself never got to use with Father! Appa, indeed. Father got rid of the cage and set up a peg for the parrot to sit on, but it preferred to perch on Father's shoulder. Sitting there, the not-insignificantly-sized bird would say, Hello! and Welcome! to anyone who visited. Father ended up having to take the parrot to his weekly physical therapy sessions. One morning, when I called Father, the parrot shouted in a cheerful old man's voice, Long time no see! I almost fell off my chair.

—Why is it saying that?

At my question, Father burst out laughing. The sound of his laughter was unexpectedly clear and pure. Well, as long as it makes Father laugh, that's that. As if determined never to lose anyone again, the parrot that had traveled from Tong-in Market to the city of J— stuck right by Father at all times. When Father lay on his back in bed, it sat on his stomach, and when he lay on his stomach, it sat on his back. When Father got up and had to hammer a nail or something, it would slide down his arm like it was a playground ride and sit on the back of his hand. And whenever I happened to call, it wouldn't forget to shout in its cheerful old man's voice, Long time no see!

Father still looked deflated; so I put my arm through his and changed the subject.

—Did you just come back from somewhere?

Not really listening to me, he said, Yes . . . Come inside, and led the way to the steps leading up to the front door of the house. He seemed to have forgotten he'd been crying just a few minutes ago. Going up those eight steps to the front door took eight minutes. He put his left leg up first, his right leg on the same step, then his left leg on the next one, then his right, and so on. I stood behind him and carefully followed up the steps one by one, almost falling when I missed a step. As I wobbled and tried to regain my balance, I felt as if a hand had grabbed my arm from behind to pull me back, which made me turn. Long time no see! From the cairn where the gray parrot that would always surprise me with those words was buried, the white butterfly took flight and fluttered once more to the camellia blossoms.

At first, I thought it would be nothing. Even when my sister told me Father had cried, even when I got there and saw Father staring down at where the parrot was buried and crying, I thought it was just a passing mood—nothing more.

Father said he would skip dinner. Since he couldn't chew anything, he told me not to make any food unless it was for myself. The fridge was filled with banchan Mother had made before leaving the house. Two whole bottles of soy milk in front of the water cask, egg-fried tofu and eggrolls, agar, knuckle broth in stainless steel containers. Little soybean curds filled the lower shelf of the fridge, and mashed potatoes also filled a picnic container. They could all be eaten without teeth or poured into a cup to drink. The sight of the food really brought home that Father had begun his dental work. His hair, which he no longer dyed, was as white as snow, and the gauntness of his face made his jowls stand out. He looked older than ever before. When he refused to eat, I begged him not to take his medicine on an empty stomach; he pointed to a shelf. There was acorn powder there.

—Then will you make dotorimuk?

—If I make dotorimuk, will you eat it?

He nodded. Dotorimuk, of all things . . . I took down the powder mix from the shelf, a little concerned. Not only had I never set dotorimuk acorn jelly before, I had no idea it even came in a powder. The packaging assured me that the powder was from 100% Korean acorns and there were illustrated instructions to make it. Having no other choice, I followed the instructions. I found a pot, poured six cups of water into one cup of powder, and turned on the gas. Boil it on high and keep stirring? I had no idea what high meant, which made me hesitate, but I bravely turned the knob all the way up and continued to stir with a wooden spoon. The solution began to congeal like glue. It said to throw in a bit of brown rice oil and coarse grain salt and continue stirring for five minutes until it turned chestnut brown, but I couldn't find any brown rice oil so I put in soybean oil instead. The dotorimuk mix quickly turned gelatinous in the pot.

I looked for a square container to cool it in, but Father brought over one of the bowls that had been turned over by the sink to dry and told me to set it in there. As soon as the mix was poured, he used a spoon to stir it and feed himself. Without even letting it set and turn into jelly. It looked more like gruel than jelly—I suddenly realized I'd forgotten the salt, but he didn't even ask for soy sauce.

—What does it even taste like?

Father seemed unsure, and simply replied that it went down well. Curious, I took a spoonful of it myself, but spat it out when he wasn't looking. To think that I had asked him what it tasted like; bitterness rose inside me. It had no flavor at all. That was his dinner, and after taking a whole fistful of pills, he called Mother: Doing all right? Mother's voice: Came here to do all right, did I? Father laughed. Mother said, Laughing, are you? Well, said Father, what else can I do but laugh? I couldn't help smiling at their silly conversation. My laughter would've been awkward, so I kept my mouth shut. What did the doctor say? Father asked, tears running down his cheeks again. That's tomorrow, said Mother. Are you crying again? Father said, Didn't the doctor say my tear ducts don't work right? My mother, who was staying in the big city at her eldest son's house before checking herself into the hospital tomorrow, was trying to console my father all the way in J—. The older we get, she said, the stronger we must be. What will people say if you keep crying like that all the time? How will the children feel? I'm sick now, so you be the strong one. Father replied, sounding weak, You're right. Mother asked if he had taken his medicine. Sure, said Father. My name suddenly issued forth from Mother's lips: Don't you follow Honnie around like you do with me and get in her way, she said. I won't, Father said. She's so sad— and then Mother stopped herself. I could sense her urgency, despite how she'd stopped in time. Mother asked him to put me on the phone and sighed deeply. She told me not to sleep on the floor of the little room but to sleep on her bed in the master bedroom. When we were about to hang up, she called out my name one more time and said, I'm grateful for you.

Father lay on his bed in the living room and turned on the TV.

When exactly Father had brought his bed out to the living room and started sleeping there, I have no idea.

I opened the master bedroom door and looked down at Mother's empty bed. When I used to visit with my daughter, the three of us would lie on that bed and talk about Father. My daughter would listen to Mother's stories about Father and ask, Is that true? It's like a story out of a book. She loved listening to those stories. Just like Father's farming tools are neatly arranged and displayed in the shed, the little room of the house had a shelf that took up a whole wall. It was full of the books I'd sent Father. Like the dogs and cats and parrot that I'd offloaded when I couldn't handle them, I would send boxes of books when the piles grew too tall. Father had built the large wall of shelves in that room and neatly arranged my books there. This was the room that my siblings and I would stay in when we visited. Not everyone was a reader, but none of us particularly hated books. And as for me, having a whole shelfful there precluded the need to bring reading material when I visited. The thought that there were books waiting for me at home was oddly reassuring. After spending two years living in New York, I started sending my books over by truck. At some point, my eldest brother had made scrapbook panels of my newspaper interviews and essays and placed them in front of the shelves. This was something he'd wanted to do, so I couldn't stop him. A newspaper had commissioned me to write an essay titled "My Father," and Eldest Brother had made a panel of that as well. With a big smile on his face, he told me that he had read aloud the essay for Father. I actually wish my family did not read my work. It's hard for me to explain why that is but I suppose I'm embarrassed. To restore a time we had together in my own words and put them out in public—it's embarrassing to imagine what they might think of it. And frightful. That time that no one would cares about has been compiled and will continue to exist in essays that I've written. I asked with grim acceptance, What did

Father say? Eldest brother replied, That you remember all sorts of silly things. Silly things. There was a time when I would re-read what I had published just to see what Father was talking about. Whenever I slept in the small room, I had to turn the panels around so they would face the shelves. It felt like the photos of me were staring right at me otherwise.

I couldn't fall asleep, so I took down a book titled *Those Days* and went over to Mother's bed. The sound of the television coming from the living room was loud. I was about to ask Father to turn it down, but instead I closed the door, sat on Mother's bed, and stared down at the words "Those Days" printed on the book cover. That fateful day, when I was frantically writing against a deadline, was my daughter's birthday, something I realized only in the evening. My daughter, on her birthday, opened the door to my study and said, You can do it, Mommy, smiled, and left without breakfast. This happened often. If I hadn't realized that evening that it was her birthday, I wouldn't have gone to where she was studying. If only I hadn't realized it.

Willy Ronis was saying he had a memory for every photograph he took, and wrote about how the ones in his book came about. This book, which I had intended to skim before going to sleep, ended up drawing me in completely. I stared long and hard at one photograph of a young factory worker in the Alsace region of France, who was kneeling before a thread-spinning machine. The thread had snapped while spinning, and she was on her knees trying to fix it. The photographer must've visited the factory intending to photograph what was going on inside. As he listened to the factory owner's explanations about the facility's history, he must've discovered the woman on her knees, trying to reconnect a thread, and asked the owner to wait for him as he went down and took the photo. He said this was because the moment was one he absolutely did not want to miss. A moment that would never appear before him again. Just as he had written in the book, this woman laborer in the textile factory was indeed beautiful and her gestures elegant, like a harpist sitting before a harp. I couldn't take my eyes off her, and my gaze lingered on that page for a long time. I wondered what this place—Alsace, in France—must be like. Was that factory still there? What became of the woman kneeling before the machine mending the broken thread? These thoughts lulled me to sleep, or perhaps my father fell asleep before me—I have no way of knowing.

It must've been around three o'clock in the morning.

I woke and immediately thought that this was Mother's bed and that what had woken me was perhaps the sound of the television, which was still on in the living room. I also needed to go to the bathroom—was Father still watching television? I got up. *Those Days* had dropped by the side of the bed. I picked it up and put it on the nightstand. Thinking I would go to the bathroom first, I opened the bathroom door across from the master bedroom and glanced toward Father's bed in the living room. The blue light of the television screen illuminated the empty bed. Thinking I was seeing things, I took my hand off the bathroom doorknob and called out, Father? and approached the bed. The television was on the home shopping channel, which was having a sale on powdered barley sprouts. Wondering if he'd gone to the bathroom, I went back there and knocked. There was no answer. I pressed the light switch on the wall and looked inside the bathroom. Toothbrushes and a tube of toothpaste in the cup by the sink, a towel with a J— Nonghyup Bank logo stamped on it that was almost about to fall off the towel rack. The showerhead, which had fallen on the tiled floor and was facing the ceiling, and the toilet, silently sitting with its lid open. But Father wasn't there. I glanced at the stainless steel bar next to the toilet seat. Did Father use it to get up from the toilet? Father wasn't there—all that greeted me was a damp smell. I opened the door connecting the living room and the kitchen calling out, Father? He wasn't in the laundry room behind the kitchen, either. And he wasn't in the small room or the closet room where we stored our clothes and bedding. The clock on the wall had passed 3:00 a.m. now. The thought that Father was not here at this hour made me panic, and I went out the front door without putting my shoes on. Into the cold night air, I called out, Father! But it was all silent around me. I went back inside and turned on all the lights in the house, making it bright all around. A sweet brier blossom by the well in the courtyard that I had not noticed during the day shone bright red in the porch lights. Barefoot, I stood in the courtyard and called out, Father? Father! The persimmon tree, the camellia tree, the front gate, the parrot's grave—all silent. Anxiously I looked all around, but all I could sense was cold air.

I discovered Father in the shed, which used to be an ashery.

Father was crouched down beneath the farming tools hanging on the walls of the shed. In the shadows of the rakes, hoes, sickles, hand cultivators, weeding hoes, scrapers, pickaxes, and shovels.

—Father?

He didn't move.

—Father, what are you doing in here?

My initial relief at having found him made me rush to his side, but then I stopped. Father was crying. The sight of his tears made the heat in my body from running around looking for him disappear like I'd been drenched with ice water. I came to my senses and gently turned the light back off in the shed. Thinking Father would want to stay as he was for a moment. What was Father looking at in this place? In the dim shed, I went back to him and crouched by his side, looking where he was looking. Farming tools. Father had retired from farming, but the walls of the shed were still hung with the different hoes used for potato and sweet potato harvesting, as well as scythes for cutting grass. Five or six shovels were hung separately on a pipe. There were also two rakes that looked like tridents.

Father was very strict about putting those tools back in their proper places.

His idea was that if the next person couldn't find the tools, they wouldn't be able to do their work properly. The one who was always scolded about this was my second older brother. Second Brother liked to procure sweet briers or roses and plant them in the empty plot next to the well. He planted so many flowers that the plot soon became a garden. Second Brother also liked to do things like dismantle radios and put them back together again. Father, who hardly said anything when Second Brother took apart a wall clock and broke it, would berate him if he ever left the shovels or hoes he had used lying about. All objects have a purpose and the most important thing to do with them is to put them back in their proper places, he said. Then everyone could find them again quickly, but if someone else didn't put the tools away properly, the next person could waste half a day looking for them. No one was exempt from Father's rule when it came to organizing the farming tools. The thing Father did on the last day of every lunar calendar year was to return borrowed farming equipment and money. There's neither a single piece of farming equipment Father ever borrowed and didn't return nor a piece borrowed from Father that hasn't been returned to him. Father, who didn't seem like a farmer to me in my younger days, now truly does not farm. All that's left are the tools hanging on the walls of this shed like ancient relics.

—Father, let's go inside now.

Afraid he would stay out here all night, I got him on his feet as he leaned on me like a child would. Stepping out of the shed, the cold morning air swirled about our faces.

—Hold on to me, Father.

As we went up the steps to the front door, I grabbed Father's thin arm and had him hold my waist. I didn't know if the fragrance in the air was roses or camellias, but the scent made me feel that it wouldn't be easy for me to return to the city.

The first sentence in my debut novel was *Where did I put them?* *I couldn't find the gloves, even after rummaging through the dresser with the four drawers* are the lines that follow. Ever since losing my daughter, I stopped going to J——. Now, I suddenly remembered writing this work, and so

I took out the book again. My first job out of college had been at a publisher named Eumsa in Seoul between Seodaemun and Ahyeon-dong. It's gone now. Every morning, I would walk down the narrow alley in Yeokchon-dong where Eldest Brother's house was and take a bus on the main street to get to work. Walking down the alley and getting on the bus, my head would stay deeply bowed. I almost never raised my head or smiled. The city was in an almost constant state of mass protests, and the teargas made the air sharp. If I happened to have some business at the school I'd graduated from, a phalanx of policemen would look through my things before allowing me to enter the school. My third older brother had ruptured a disc while studying for his civil service exams and was hospitalized. The publishing house was on the third floor of an old three-story building, and the wooden steps creaked as I ascended them. Whether they were sounds of the seams coming back together or slipping apart, I had no idea, but whenever I heard the sound, I would stop and look back down at where I had come from. There were the few steps I had just come up and the feel of busy passersby. The flat black shoes of the men, the high heels of the women, the sneakers and slippers and low-heeled shoes mixed in with them. I would look down at my own shoes on the wooden steps. Going down these creaking steps again and pushing open the glass door would bring me to the street. I imagined my own feet among all the others walking about that busy morning. If I could get out of here, where would my feet go? To the crossroads where Hwayang Cinema was? The pedestrian bridge that began right before that? If I crossed the road in the opposite direction, I would pass a ChongKunDang branch, and if I didn't cross, I would reach the Ahyeon-dong street where handmade furniture pieces were put out on the street to be sold. But every time, my feet would not go anywhere but up the steps to the third floor. Listening to the creaking sound, I would reach the office and carefully open the door to the room with three desks, put down my bag on the one that was mine, and change into slippers. This changing of my shoes would put an end to that morning's fantasy of walking off somewhere else. My pulse that quickened at the thought of escape would quickly settle down as I adjusted to the mood inside that office. Sighing deeply, I would stretch out a hand to the pile of manuscripts on my desk. Had there been a book in that pile that I actually enjoyed reading, perhaps I would've come to work with a lighter heart. Perhaps I wouldn't have imagined going back out the door I had just come in through to head somewhere else. Right up to the day I quit, that publishing house never put out a single book I'd wanted to read, which is why I'll never know what that other life would've felt like—surely I wouldn't have felt as bored. Doing work I couldn't find meaning in felt like my fingers were disappearing one by one, and I would sometimes put down the pen I was editing with and massage my right hand with my left. My job was to gather manuscript sections that different people had translated and edit them into one cohesive voice for each book. Since these books were translated by five or six different translators who had no idea what happened before or after the chunks they were tasked to translate, the place names and dates and numbers would differ and the same episode would be referenced differently. Every time I had one section under control, the next would feature yet another different set of idiosyncrasies—a process that both overwhelmed and exhausted me. My desperate efforts to herd the chaos into some sort of order, lining up the flashbacks and times and place names, would go on day after long day, giving me splitting headaches. Spending so much time bent over at my desk, my tense shoulders were all the way up to my ears by the end of the day.

Whenever I left work, I would think that things could not continue as they were. That if they did, I would die.

One day, in an effort to save my own life, I took a copy of Lee Heeseung's 1961 edition of *The Great Korean Dictionary* after work to a rented carrel in Yeokchon-dong. Taking up a cubicle there, I spent every day writing and erasing ad nauseum. Then, one day, I wrote the line, *Where did I put them?* I did not erase it. The line, *I couldn't find the gloves, even after rummaging through the dresser with the four drawers*, followed. Once I started going to the carrels with Lee Heeseung's *The Great Korean Dictionary* after having dinner at Eldest Brother's—where I lived—I no longer had to contend with the compulsion to turn from the creaking steps and run away from my job. Once I saw that going to work was a necessary condition for my going to the carrels in the evening, I could calm myself down and go into the office. With patience, I persevered through the chaotic mess of translated manuscripts and continued to contextualize the edits as best as I could, relaxing the tension in my shoulders and stabilizing my once dramatic shifts in mood. There could be no end to such work. Whenever I thought it was complete, I'd open to a random page and a typo would jump out at me. If I took care of that, another one jumped out. When I fixed one spot, another spot had to be fixed because of the first fix. Even so, I sat at my desk in that third-floor office and continued to fix the manuscript for as long as I could. Ever since writing that line—*Where did I put them*—my footsteps picked up and I became quite diligent at all things. I ate my dinner, went to the carrels, and added more words to the words I'd written up to the evening before. This was a time when we used wongoji, the manu-script paper with red grid lines. Some days, I would write just one page, and on a good day, seven. Even on days I couldn't write a single line, that eve-ning time—in contrast to the daytime—would pass by as quick as a flash and it would be nearing dawn in no time. On the first floor of the building with the rented carrels was a place that made tteok. They manufactured tteok in bulk for bulk buyers, but also sold some at their store to passersby, and their tteok machines would start grinding away around three o'clock in the morning. In that hour when everyone else was asleep, the machine that sliced away at garaetteok and injeolmi bean powder tteok would be whirring away. One night, when I came out to the hallway for some air and looked out a window, I saw the shadows of the gingko trees swaying over the empty street. There was so much wind that leaves were whirling and scattering all over the road. The streets at dawn were dead silent. But hearing, around three in the morning, the sound of the tteok machine going shh-shh, my hands automatically gripped my elbows, my arms crossed in front of me. I walked back to my carrel like that, sat down as I released my arms, and wrote the line: *Life has ambushes*. And over my desperate heart that looked down at the shadows of the trees and the fallen leaves tumbling over the empty streets at three o'clock in the morning, my future flashed before me.

I had a vague feeling. That my incompleteness would continue—that wherever I was, I'd be writing and erasing, writing and erasing. That even after writing the last period, I would be endlessly refining the words I had written.

Since discovering Father with the farming tools, every night I wandered around searching for him crouching down in front of something and crying. Sometimes he was next to the well and sometimes beneath the persimmon tree, and once I found him among the large earthen jars in the corner of the courtyard. In the morning, Father would have forgotten all about it and would call Mother in the hospital or suggest he and I go buy sannakji. Live octopus? Father was getting dental work done. He would hardly be able to chew octopus, but assuming he knew what he was doing, I followed him to the market.

—You want to buy sannakji for me?

At that fishmonger's in a downtown market in J—, I stared into Father's face.

Father had suddenly suggested sannakji because of me. He thought I liked sannakji. How did this notion embed itself in his mind? By my memory, he was the one who enjoyed sannakji.

There was one early summer when my Mother had gone up to Seoul to help my younger sister with her newborn. I was also alone in the J— house with Father. He had lost his appetite and would poke with his chopsticks whatever banchan I prepared for him and put them down.

I called Mother, who suggested I go to the market and get him sannakji instead. Sannakji? Mother said it always helped him find his appetite. Which is why I took the bus to the market by the five-way intersection and went looking for live octopus. No matter where I looked, they only had already dead ones. Mother emphasized that it absolutely had to be a fresh, living octopus. I went into every fishmonger's and asked, to no avail. Giving up, I was waiting for the bus back at a nearby bus stop when I suddenly noticed, right next to me, a hwe restaurant tank with live octopuses. I'd never been happier to see sannakji in my life. The restaurant owner scooped out an octopus for me and put it in a black plastic bag. On the bus ride home, the little octopus was so fierce that the bag jerked around in my grasp. I remember being so nervous it might jump out of the bag that my head almost burst. Father took a silent look at the octopus I'd bought for him, took it from me, and without a word, went to the kitchen. He placed it on the cutting board, flipped it on its head, and deftly took out its guts with one hand, removing the beak near the legs as well. Father's movements were almost cheerful. Despite having lost its guts, the suckers on the tentacles still squirmed. Father dipped the whole head in some chojang red pepper vinegar sauce and chewed it. As I stood there watching, Father laid out the washed tentacles on the cutting board, chopped them, sprinkled on some sesame oil and seeds for taste, and pushed the board toward me, bidding me to eat. Just as Mother had said, Father's appetite came back immediately thanks to the sannakji. He ate it so deliciously that I took up a piece but was startled when I felt my cheek being bit from the inside. I spat it out. How odd that this man with such strange tastes would be my father, I thought as my stomach began to turn. As I tried to spit out all the salt and sesame oil still in my mouth, Father asked, Not to your liking? I said, Well, it's still wriggling. Father boiled a bit in hot water and served that to me instead.

I have never eaten sannakji since that day, so how was it that Father remembered me as having liked it? But I didn't want to take away the rare light of pleasure from his face as he set out to the market to buy sannakji with me, so I said nothing and simply watched him choose and pay for an octopus. The fishmonger didn't put it in a black plastic bag but prepared it and put it in a clear plastic container. They weren't a hwe restaurant but nevertheless included sides of raw garlic and chojang sauce. At home, I put the sannakji in a bowl, washed some lettuce from the garden and put it on a plate with the garlic and chojang, and served it to Father, saying, But you won't even be able to chew this. Father said, I wanted you to eat it. Where had his memory gone wrong? Father really did think I liked sannakji. If it's the nature of memory to go wrong, is it all right for me to keep believing in the things I thought were true? Lost in my thoughts, I stared down at the segments of sannakji that were still squirming on the plate. Thinking that the business of living is comprised in part of misremembering and misunderstandings. It was because we can misremember and misunderstand that we can endure certain moments in life. Afraid that Father would stare at the squirming chopped tentacles and start crying again, I said I would boil him some octopus jook rice porridge, and quickly got up from the table.

At night, I gave up trying to sleep in Mother's bed, and instead spread a futon by Father's bed in the living room.

Surely, he would be up and about again, and I would have to go look for him. And I did at one point wake up to find him sitting up in bed, very still. I watched him from the darkness below.
—Sleeping?
—Yes, Father.
—Sleeping, but replying to me?
—Right? Go back to sleep.
Father sat for a little while longer and lay down again. He turned to face a wall where there was a row of portraits of my siblings, Eldest Brother to the youngest, all wearing graduation caps. In the dark, Father was probably staring at each of our portraits, starting with Eldest Brother's. From

behind his back, I also looked up at that photo of Eldest Brother. Next to his was Second Brother, then Third Brother, then mine should've been next but there was an empty space. Followed by one of my little sister, then my youngest brother . . . When he rebuilt this house in 1994 or 1995, the first thing Father did was hammer nails into this wall and hang these portraits. There must've been countless things to commemorate between those graduations, but these were the only photos he had. Gazing at the portraits made me think my siblings never aged, that they went on to exist as is. But Eldest Brother is retired now. I couldn't understand why Father had hung those photos in the most visible part of our house. In the old house, which doesn't exist anymore, he had put up Eldest Brother's graduation portrait, and I assumed it was because having his eldest graduate university was a monumental achievement, but then my brothers' graduation portraits also appeared on the wall every few years. He hit a barrier with me, his fourth child. When it was my turn, I refused Father's request. I didn't want my photograph taken. The school did make me take a photo for our graduation album with me wearing my cap and gown, but I didn't want to blow it up and send it to him. Why on earth would he makes such a fuss, I thought at the time. All visitors would immediately see these photos, and I didn't like that. Indeed, visitors always commented on them. The things they said about having a good batch of children or which child resembled which parent—I hated all of it. Whenever Father would ask for my graduation photo, I would pretend to have forgotten; one time, I simply blurted out, Why do you want to hang that stupid thing? I assumed he would eventually forget, but Father tried his best to get that photo of me. Father was a man of few words. Even now, when someone mentions how little he talks, an uncle and a cousin on my mother's side who had visited for a month would mention with a laugh that during their whole visit Father had only said, Oh, you're here, and when they were about to go, Oh, you're going. And that was it. That was Father, who in his efforts to convince me to send my graduation photo would suddenly transform into a chatterbox. There were things I learned thanks to this. That my elementary school graduation photo was the second photo of me ever taken, and that the first was my 100-day baby celebration photo with my family. In that photo, Father is holding on to Third Brother, who looks like he was about to bounce off somewhere, and next to him is Mother, who had used a fine-toothed comb to give her hair some volume, wearing a traditional jeogori jacket and holding me in her arms. Eldest Brother and Second Brother are solemnly flanking my parents. If that photo had never been taken, the one in my elementary school graduation album would've been my first. In those days, it wasn't easy to have photos taken, and Father spoke of walking to the photography studio in town to take that 100-day photo like it happened yesterday. It is, truth be told, surprising that a 100-day photo of me should exist. Because my older brothers don't have such a photo. Father said he was sorry. That since photos were so expensive back then, my 100-day photo was not just of me but of the whole family. As if telling me a secret, he said, Once you were born, I thought we shouldn't have any more children. Three sons and a daughter were just right. Father said it so seriously that I replied, Father! Are you saying that Ippy and the youngest were mistakes in your family planning scheme? And I laughed. Ippy— meaning cutie—was our nickname for my sister. Father told me not to say that so loudly and furtively glanced around us. Looking very worried that Ippy and the youngest might overhear. Anyway, according to Father, the reason we had our family photo taken for the first time that day was because having three sons and a new daughter made him very satisfied, and he had wanted to commemorate that. He said, I was so happy you were a daughter, I didn't want for anything else in life. This wasn't the first time I had heard this. Mother also would say, on occasion, that the happiest person at my birth was Father. That when people asked him whether he had a boy or a girl, his whole face would light up as he answered loudly, A daughter! That the reason they had put my brothers in new clothes and my mother had puffed up her hair in front of the mirror on my 100-day celebration and we had all gone to a studio to get our family photo taken was because I was a daughter. Father said whatever he could to get my graduation photo, but he couldn't move my heart. One time, I told him it was because I'd graduated from a two-year polytechnic school and didn't have a real bachelor's degree. Which meant Father would make me look like a fraud by putting me up with my brothers. This stumped him for a moment before he suggested I transfer schools to a four-year college. Hearing the term "transfer schools"—pyeonip—from my lifelong farmer Father surprised me so much that I took a step back to look at him incredulously. To think he knew what pyeonip meant. Despite this, I still didn't send him that photo, and my sister and younger brother ended up graduating in the interim. Father, upon hanging their graduation photos, refused to give up on mine and left a space for it. For over a decade after I graduated, he would remind me of it when he visited Seoul or when he heard I was visiting J——. Eldest Brother couldn't stand it anymore and gave me a long lecture about giving in to the old man, seeing how much he wanted it. He really laid it on me for deflecting Father and pretending not to remember his request. He said, Isn't that the essence of Father's life in the end? How could a writer like you know so little of the human heart? What kind of books are you writing if you can't even understand your own Father . . . ?

Father's life? Those photos of us wearing graduation caps?

That's when I finally realized why he was so insistent on hanging those photos in such a visible place, and the realization exhausted me. I did go to a photo studio, years after having graduated, combed my hair neatly back, and took a photo with a borrowed cap. But I stuffed the photo away somewhere and never sent it to him. Why on earth did I make such a fuss over such a thing? When I lost my daughter, everything in my life became a blur. Funny things, annoying things, precious things—they all became meaningless. Today, tomorrow, yesterday. They were all just one lump of time that was passing by. That photograph was tucked away somewhere. I never threw it out, so it was probably gathering dust. In the dark, I looked up at the place where my photograph would've hung. The pain of not having given Father something that he had so wished for washed over me. Perhaps by denying his wish, I had wanted to withdraw from the old things of this village and this house. Just like Father on his bed, I lay on my side on the living room floor. Father stared at the wall and I stared at his back. It felt like we were lying on different steps. Had he finally run out of strength to nag me about the portrait? In the dark, the side of Father's back looked like it had caved in.

As if he could hear me sighing behind his back, Father spoke in a low voice.

—Go to sleep.

—You, too, Father.

Despite his entreaty for me to go to sleep, he called out my name again.

—Hon.

—Yes?

—How is it going, that thing you so wanted to do?

The novella I had written in that carrel, page by page, won a competition for emerging writers—deungdan—and marked my debut as an author. Only on the last day of submissions did I go to the post office, punch a hole through 300 pages of wongoji paper, and tie them together with black string. I hadn't decided on a title until the very last moment. Just before I handed it over to the post office clerk, I scrawled on the title: *Winter Fable.* I was twenty-one. I didn't want to use my office line for my contact number, so I wrote in Eldest Brother's home number instead. Every afternoon at four, I called my sister-in-law and asked if there was any news. She would answer back, every day, What news? And then one day, she said, A literary . . . something called, they want you to call them back. Cradling the phone on my shoulder, I wrote down the number on my hand. When I called Father in J— with the news of my deungdan, he did not understand the meaning of the word and asked me if it was good work. Was it good work? I couldn't answer him immediately. It was back in the days when calling people on the phone wasn't easy. There was one phone the entire village used in the village head's house. Those who had moved out to the city would call the village head if they had urgent business, and the village head would get on the PA and announce the call. The whole village would know who was calling whom. Father would've been feeding the chickens or, because it was October, harvesting the fields, or perhaps he had been in the cow stables and come running to pick up the phone. Not understanding the word deungdan and asking me, out of breath, if it was a good thing—this made me stop in my tracks. I had to answer him quickly because I could already sense from the sound of his breathing that he was worried this would be an expensive phone call for me. I stood in that telephone booth in the noisy city, switched the receiver to my other ear and practically shouted into it: I don't know if it's a good thing, but it's a thing that I really wanted to do, Father.

Since then, I don't think I've ever talked to Father about my feelings.

When I didn't answer, he asked again.

—Not going well?

His voice was clearer than it had been until now. This was not the man who would disappear in the middle of the night and upset me by showing his tears.

—It was good to see you doing what you wanted to do.

He was about to say something else but sighed deeply instead. Father wanted to talk about my daughter. How I had put up a wall so no one in my family could even mention the topic. But I couldn't let it down. Even after my daughter left us, I still set a place for her at the table. I bought shirts in her size at stores and hung them in her wardrobe. No matter what I was doing, I was with her. I would learn about travel destinations and wish I could go there with her. My hands would itch so much from wanting to braid her hair that I'd have to clench and unclench them repeatedly.

—Even if every day feels like you're going to die, a different time will come.

—. . .

—Planting seeds makes one wonder if they'll ever grow into tall grasses for harvest, but days flow by quickly, and the summer comes, then the fall . . .

When will sleep come? I chewed on Father's words like a cow, trying to hear his words, spoken in a low voice, until I heard his faint snoring. But the next moment, I opened my eyes and found him gone. Surprised, I turned on all the lights in the house and called out, Father! Father! I opened the toolshed door, went to the earthen jars, and the well, but Father was not there. Then I remembered hanging a cell phone around his neck before going to bed and so I ran back into the house and called him. The ringing sound came from the small room. As I had never found Father inside the house during his wanderings, my instinct had been to run out of the front door, but here was the phone ringing from the small room. I followed the sound and opened the door to it. Father was lying on the bare floor next to the desk. The panel with the essay I had written about him lay on his chest. The cell phone around his neck rang but he lay there motionless. From the moment we built the new house, this room was called the small room. In the winter we fermented soybeans in the warm part of the floor, and hammered nails on the wall or brought in a tree with many branches to hang up meju soybean bricks for fermentation, covering them with a cloth. The house I had spent my childhood in was gone, but when building both houses, Father had made similar decisions about the orientation and structure. I knew this because, when I stood by the window in the small room, I could almost see out the front door. Being in the small room made me feel like this was the old house. The size and position of the windows were the same as well, and standing at the window automatically took me back to my childhood. The time I slid my feet onto the warm part of the floor underneath the covers where the soybeans were fermenting, peeling sweet potatoes, falling asleep. I'd woken from my nap with mashed sweet potato caked into my hair and I was trying desperately to get it out but ended up having to cut off that part of my hair. The thing I did the most, lying on my stomach over that warm spot, was read books. We didn't have that many books, which is strange because when I think of that room, the first thing I always remember is myself reading. When I looked up from reading, I would sometimes see snow. *It's snowing . . .* I would go right up to the window and look out at the snow falling on the courtyard. Watching the feathery snow pile up made me think each snowflake was a letter of the Hangul alphabet. The whirling letters settled on the courtyard and made lines, which were sentences, and layered into books. Was that the reason why I felt that the snow, which fell for four to five days once it started, felt warm and safe instead of cold and dangerous? The puppies living under the porch would come out and leave footprints in the snow, and I also went out to lie on the newly fallen white blanket and took pictures. After the snow, the winds would blow and the temperatures drop, and the snow on the roof would freeze in place. When the snow fell again before the icicles hanging from the eaves had the chance to melt, the long cones of ice would thicken. These icicles were so large and sword-like that we called them sword icicles. Boys in every household would snap these off and pretend fight with them. No matter who won, the only thing left would be messy footprints and water in their hands from their melting swords. But the fights were brutal. When the snow and sword icicles on the roof began to melt, that was a sign spring was coming. The small room was where I would listen to the dripping of water as it ran down the eaves and onto the courtyard.

And now, in this room where my siblings and I would lay down to rest when we came to visit, was my father.

I hung up my phone, and Father's phone also stopped ringing. Moving over to him, I picked up the panel and leaned it against the shelf and looked down at Father's face. He was crying as he slept. With his hand on his forehead. New tears flowed over dried tear tracks, following his cheekbones and rolling down past his nose and the side of his mouth. All strength leaving my body, I mumbled, Why are you crying? The words scattered meaninglessly into the air of the room. If I hadn't been thinking of how small he'd become, I would've shook him awake and said, You can't go on like this! I put over him one of the blankets from the stack in a corner and slipped a pillow under his head. I stared at his thin, hunched shoulders. Was there something inside him that made him cry—something he couldn't talk to anyone about? As I tried to lower his hand from his forehead, he put it back to where it was in his sleep. Father's shin bumped against my knee. His shin was just skin and bone. I'm sorry, Father. The emptiness and fear that deluged me in the dark made me place my hand on my forehead, just like he did.

CHAPTER 2

WHEN YOU WALK INTO
THE NIGHT

Why was it that whenever I arrived in J— and opened a laptop on the kitchen table or the desk in the small room, I felt as if I'd come back from a long trip?

My memories of Father exist in disparate and elusive fragments like the sound of the wind on some days, of the war on some days, of the flying bird on some days, of the snowfall on some days, and on some days, of the determination to keep living. And what of all the things suppressed within him, never expressed, disintegrating in silence, unspoken?

I stared at the note I had written for myself the night before and deleted it. The only thing I could manage to write after my daughter left me were these little notes. Even these I would often end up deleting. And then I'd sit before my laptop again, hunched over like I was trying to breathe life back into a smoldering spark. Last night, I briefly wondered if I had come to take care of Father or for me to be taken care of, which made me so anxious that I lingered for a long time before my old books shelved in the small room. Sometimes, I would find inscriptions of where and when I had purchased the book and which friends I had been with at the time. Names of friends I had fallen out of contact with—I had no idea how they were doing. A few days ago, while trying to fish out a thin book that had fallen behind the shelf, I poked around with a feather duster, Father's cane, and a long umbrella. The book that finally emerged, complete with dust bunnies, was Pascal Lainé's *A Web of Lace*. I could hardly remember what it was about but I did vaguely recall the protagonist's name was Pomme. And that it meant apple. Pomme, red apple, red apple, pomme . . . The memory was faint, but I think I had loved her. I think Pomme had also influenced me somewhat. A memory of pitying Pomme, who had aphasia, to the point that I walked out to be under the twilight evening sky, sadness overwhelming me. I wiped the dust off the book, flattened the bent pages, and made a space for it on the shelf. I could almost remember the words Pomme had tried to speak despite her aphasia, but my memory failed me.

Whenever I returned to J—, my body was conditioned to taking the smaller gate to the ditches side at dawn and walking to the fields or taking the main gate to the alley and following the road around the village. As I was walking by the nettle trees and wondering if there were any nettles left, looked up at the branches . . . I heard the sound of a machine. I walked toward the sound. In the bluish dawn light, someone was using a tractor to turn the earth in a rice paddy. Wondering who could be working in the fields at such an early hour, I glanced at the tractor and was about to turn away when I saw, on the paddy opposite the tractor, a flock of white herons standing daintily in the water. That many herons? I had never seen a flock of them on a rice paddy like that, which made me forget about the farmer as I stared at them, gracefully flapping their wings. The paddy didn't have any rice planted in it yet and was full of water, which reflected each heron and made them appear doubled. How diligent of them to come to the rice paddy at this hour to feed. When they took off, the still waters shimmered from falling water droplets. The colors of the water and the herons blended into each other on the water's surface. I was completely absorbed in this sight when the farmer turning the earth stopped his tractor and climbed down. It really is you, nuna? he said. It was Isak. What are you doing here, nuna? Isak looked happy to have bumped into me, but I was a little taken aback by how grown-up he had become. It made me laugh awkwardly.

—What are you laughing at?

—I almost didn't recognize you.

Isak smiled, the edge of his big eyes crinkling.

—You know, farmers grow up fast.

He added, But nuna looks the same, which made me laugh again. Isak was the same age as my youngest brother. His eyes were particularly big, like a child's. My cousin's wife gave birth to him in the field when she had gone to pick stray rice grains—"isak" in Korean. So many things have faded away in the annals in my mind, but I still remember the fuss that late autumn day when Isak was born. How my cousin's wife had had no time to run home, pulling down a tall stack of straw on that just-shorn field so she could lie down on it to give birth. Despite having a different official name, people called him Isak because he was born in the field. When he was a boy, everyone became enchanted by the deep shine of Isak's dark eyes. It made him irresistible, making us all pinch his cheeks in passing, and the eyes that once cried with pain back then were now surrounded by laugh lines.

—Why are there so many herons on the rice field?

Uncertain about how I should treat grown-up Isak so early in the morning, I changed the subject to the herons. The white birds on the rice paddy water had made an impression on me, but Isak grumbled that wild animals made farming difficult. There was only so much land, more and more people were leaving the countryside, and the animals were only multiplying. The herons, so elegant to my eyes, had become so numerous that the trees they lived in were dying from their droppings. Isak told me that he had to cut down many ancient pines on the hill behind his house for this reason.

—There used to be scores of them. Now there are hundreds.

As if they'd heard him, the herons that were in the rice paddy water around the tractor flew up in unison and moved on to another field. When we were children, the whole village treasured herons. Father would say that if a heron came to your rice paddy in May, that year's harvest would be bountiful. He carefully avoided startling the one or two that had landed in the fields by taking the long way around. The herons searched for food in the rice paddies and at night flew to the pine trees in the hills and folded their long legs and white wings as they went to sleep. *The herons slept there*, I would think as I gazed at the pine forests in the mountains in passing, and even after they had flown away for the winter, my heart would shine bright.

—And it's not just the herons.

Isak turned toward the nettle trees and nodded for me to look.

—So many birds here these days. The whole neighborhood is noisy. You don't hear people at all, just birds.

I followed Isak into a plastic greenhouse on a field. Despite my expectations, the inside of the greenhouse seemed not only sturdy enough to withstand typhoons but they were spacious, too. There were over twenty hens in there as well as a chicken coop. The hens were a variety of colors, and I spotted some black-feathered silk fowl. At the sound of footsteps, the hens rustled their feathers and a dog emerged from its doghouse next to the chicken coop, wagging its tail at Isak and barking when it saw me. When I froze at the sound of its bark, Isak smiled and said, Nuna has become a scaredy-cat. Don't worry about the dog, it won't bite if I'm here.

—What's that?

There was a row of unidentifiable farming equipment inside the greenhouse.

—A plow.

I gazed at the object Isak called a plow and stretched out my hand to sweep off the clumps of dirt on its blade. This was not in the shape of the plow Father would yoke onto an ox when he needed to borrow its strength. With my eyes on the circular steel blades on the plow, I asked Isak if farming was difficult these days. He replied in a low voice, What work isn't difficult these days . . .

—At least machines do most of the work now. Hooking the plow on the tractor makes turning the fields and rice paddies easy, and it can work so much that you could do every field in this neighborhood in two days.

His thoughtful expression turned a touch regretful.

—Last year, I hooked the plow on a cultivator and tried to dig up sweet potatoes with it but they got all smashed and I had to throw them away.

—Isn't there a machine that can harvest underground crops?

—Of course there is. It's called a harvester, but I couldn't borrow it so I was experimenting with the plow. It didn't work. With no harvester, gathering sweet potatoes takes time and a lot of effort. Because you need a pitchfork or you use your hands.

—You could harvest them after it rains?

If only you could time the rain to when you need to harvest, he replied. I was remembering how my brothers and I would go out to the sweet potato patches in the hills and how it was as fun to us as knocking persimmons off branches. Father would pull up the vines and the potatoes would pop right out of the earth in chains. I would be so absorbed in hoeing the earth and seeing red sweet potatoes jump out that accidentally piercing any with the hoe felt like injuring the back of my own foot.

—That's a tractor.

—That's a planter.

When I pointed to another tool, Isak explained that it was a seeder that sprinkled seeds or a dehydrator that dried chilis. When I asked him where the yoke was, he replied, Yoke? No one uses that anymore. Farmers used to use a yoke when they worked with oxen, but now the plows are attached to tractors. The oxen were so powerful that they could pull away even arrowroot. Hearing him talk, it occurred to me that the yoke hanging in Father's toolshed was as long forgotten as the ox it used to be fastened to. But the sickle and hoe and forked scraper were, as in Father's toolshed, present in Isak's greenhouse as well. I said, You have all these new machines but I guess you still need these scrapers. And he replied, Because they're basic things. Basic things—I gazed at the hoe and sickle and shovel for a long time. The inside of the greenhouse was like a wide courtyard. In addition to the chicken coop and doghouse, there were garlic bulbs and onions airing out on one side, and in another corner that had running water connected to a hose, seedbeds took up a wide space. Rice sprouts grew dense like pine needles on the seedbeds. As I moved on from the tools and looked down at the sprouts, Isak said he needed to plant them in two weeks.

After I left Isak and arrived home, Father said to me, Isn't your aunt here?

—Who, Father?

—Your aunt.

At a loss for words, I stared down at Father sitting on his bed.

—My sister is sick, perhaps? She hasn't visited this morning.

Father's older sister, my aunt, visited this house every morning until the second to last day of her life. Even in the rain, or with flowers falling, or persimmons dropping, or snow melting. Aunt, even after she had left this house, came back to it as soon as she woke up in the morning every day for her whole life. She walked through winds, snowstorms, and rain at dawn while listening to the birds. Father left the main gate of the door open because of her. Aunt would clear her throat to announce her arrival, take a look around the courtyard, close the door to the shed that the wind had blown opened during the night, fill the bucket at the well with water, take a detour around the earthen jars in the backyard, pick the squash she didn't want to see grow too big, pit the leaves of the butterbur she didn't want to thicken too much underneath the walls, clear her throat again, and walk right back to the main road toward home. Whether Father was there or not, Aunt's dawn patrol would happen without fail. Until the day I left the house, I would think, half-awake at dawn, *Aunt is here*, and fall back asleep. Father, Mother, and my siblings must also have sensed Aunt's presence. Because if one day she happened to not come by, everyone somehow knew.

Aunt quietly left this world eight years ago.

One morning, when my fully grown cousin opened the door to my aunt's room at dawn, it was evident she had smoked before passing as there was a couple of drags' worth of ashes on the cigarette perched on the edge of her ashtray. Her very straight back faced the door as she lay, making my cousin think she had risen in the night and was deep in thought. This image of her formidably straight back flashed in my mind. Truly she left the world just as she lived it, I thought. Briskly, and with no regrets, determined never to return. Aunt was a fair and decisive person. She drew a clear and straight line against whatever she disagreed with. After I became an author, the family member whose reaction I was most anxious about was Aunt. Whenever I wrote about anything that featured a family, I could feel Aunt's gaze following me. If there was something she did not like, she would wait until I visited J— and sit in front of me with her legs crossed, rock slightly back and forth, and ask with her eyes narrowed even more, What is it that a writer does? This was not a question but an interrogation. What was it that I did . . . Aunt's interrogation was merciless. *When she was alive*, I was about to add, and suddenly I missed her terribly. Even when I felt like she was interrogating me. During the Saemaeul Movement, the thatched-roof houses had been razed to make way for slate-roofed ones. Father's house was lost to history then, too, and a new house was built. I think this happened when I was in the third or fourth grade. The day the thatched house my siblings and I had been born in was razed, clumps of earth rained on the ground and the birds nesting in the straw of the roof—some of which had laid eggs there or hatched chicks—came flying out, surprised by what was happening. When an earthen wall was broken down, a snake that lived inside it escaped and slithered away into the forest. All sorts of insects crawled out of the ruin and frantically took cover in the dust. This wasn't just one or two houses, which meant every day was filled with cries of birds losing their nests and my arms and legs and cheeks were bitten by bugs that had escaped. At night, my little sister and I went to Aunt's house to sleep.

Aunt's voice had so many layers. A born storyteller, Aunt would tell us—well, to be honest, she said that to her favorite, my sister—endless strange and uncanny stories from times unknown. That she had followed Grandfather to the mountains to forage for medicinal herbs when she met a man, who was said to have lived a hundred years, and she said deer would kindle fires in ovens and snakes were twisting straw into ropes, and she had eaten dinner with a Buddha with ten hands.

—He had ten hands?

—Yes, I saw them with my own eyes . . .

My eyes widened with surprise and she laughed, which sounded bright and clear. Aunt, the storyteller. In that old story when Grandfather ran a medicine shop, Aunt lived in a big house with a black tile roof, and our thatched-roof house we were pulling down now was occupied by people who had come from afar to learn medicine from Grandfather. Back then, the family had owned all the land from here to all the way over there, so much land . . . I still remember her stories, which was why whenever I visited J— I would stop at the place where Aunt always said our land used to begin and look around thinking, *This was where our land started?*

—But why do we live in thatched-roof houses now?

Seeing my perturbed expression, Aunt replied it was because of Cha Cheonja—or "Son of God," the other name for the religious leader Cha Gyeongseok. Back during the Japanese occupation, she said, there was a man named Kang Ilsun . . . A man who could call forth the wind, the rain . . . He opened a medicine shop called Gwangjaeguk on Moaksan Mountain, and my grandfather was one of his followers, and he is the reason my father and grandfather came to establish medicine shops of their own. The Cha Cheonja Aunt spoke about was born in Gochang and was a disciple of Kang Ilsun. When his teacher died, Cha Cheonja established Bocheonism in Ipam township's Daeheung-ri of J— from where he expanded his influence. People from all over the country gathered like clouds to Ipam, said Aunt as if she'd seen it herself. The Donghak Peasant Revolution failed, she said, and we lost our country. What else could we lean on back then? We thought Cha Cheonja would help us climb out of that pit—that's why we clung to him. It wasn't just a phenomenon in Ipam's Daeheung-ri. There were sixty parishes across the country, and hundreds of people followed Bocheonism. It happened over there, said Aunt as she gestured toward somewhere under the night sky. As if it were close enough for us to walk to. They started calling the man the Son of God one day, or some called him Your Majesty. Look, their lives were hard and dry, they were dreaming of a new world, the only thing they wanted was that . . . Her voice trailed off, and Aunt rolled herself a cigarette and placed it between her lips. The dream of a new world. She said, A new world looked ready to unfurl before us, but the Japanese police had a warrant for his arrest. He escaped to someplace in Deogyusan Mountain and held a ceremony to give his new country a name . . . Well, they say he brought lumber from Baekdusan Mountain itself to build a home for his congregation—what more can anyone say about his reach . . . Aunt, speaking as if relaying someone else's words, said that Cheonja failed to ascend. She stopped there and straightened her back as she exhaled cigarette smoke. Even if the Donghak Peasant Revolution and this other movement to create a new world had failed, this land has that kind of power inside it, said Aunt once as she stroked my sister's hair. Take on that power, the two of you, and bask in it. Cha Cheonja had started to build a large worship hall in Ipam's Daeheung-ri and distributed official seals and certificates to his believers. Aunt said, Such ridiculous objects . . . Aunt cleared her throat and unfolded her legs as she shifted in her seat. That silly seal and certificate. People sold off their rice fields for it, and they came from all over to Ipam, kicking up dust. When Aunt said this, I could almost see the dust clouds rise in front of me. She said, They believed those useless things were guides into the new world, that junk. But when you have nothing to lean on, it's human nature to cling to anything, even junk . . . She told us that the house shrunk after Grandfather died, shrunk even more after the Korean War, and all that remained was that thatched-roof house. Aunt continued to tell us stories until that old house was no more and a new one with a slate roof was finished.

In the wall between the main room and bedroom of Aunt's house was a built-in closet.

One day, a hen in a chicken coop laid two large eggs that were transferred to this closet, and from those two large eggs hatched a pair of tigers that live in the walls to this day. In times of war or any other strife, those tigers will emerge from the closet and save us. I still wonder why Aunt told that story about the tigers. Perhaps she meant to reassure us that help would always be there, but it only made me think the tigers would jump out of the closet and maul me, and this made me want to wet myself. Listening to Aunt's stories lulled my sister to sleep, but even after Aunt dozed off, I'd lie in the dark with my ears on alert. All because of the fear I felt from Aunt's stories. I always wished for the fascinating fairy tales to never end. To the point where I looked forward to sleeping over at Aunt's house and listening to the next one. Until I began reading books, I was caught up in the throes of Aunt's strange stories. This storyteller Aunt let go of her strict sense of fairness only when it came to my father. Ever since we were little, I had an inkling that my sister was her favorite because she was the one who most resembled Father, and it was she who gave my sister the nickname Ippy. To this day, I call my sister Ippy-ya, but there's a shade of envy at her family nickname, thinking that Aunt adored Ippy more than me. And in all things, big or small, until the day she left this world, Aunt stood by Father's side.

Father rebuffed all protestations that no female family member who had married outside the family could be buried in our family cemetery. He arranged for her to be buried next to his own plot.

Yesterday morning, Father was looking for Aunt, and this evening he suddenly asked, Where is Chammie?

When Father had asked about his late sister, my surprise had struck me speechless; now, at this abrupt question, I simply pushed the chicken jook I'd made for our dinner in front of him. I'd decided not to let Father's behavior

disturb me, which is why I said in the calmest way possible, Father . . .
Chammie is dead.

—Chammie died? When?

—You know better than I do when. Think.

Looking at the chicken jook, he thought for a moment.

—The fourth month. The sixteenth day. That's when he died.

—See?

—But it feels like he's sitting right over there.

—Where did you bury him?

—In the courtyard . . .

—See, you remember everything.

I was trying to keep my tone light, but my heart ached.

—I know. Think I don't remember? I was just wishing he was alive.
Chammie liked this.

He pointed to the chicken jook I'd boiled for him. A parrot that ate
chicken? I glanced down at the jook.

When I reported Father's condition to my sister, she said it could be
delirium brought on by his arduous dental procedure and insomnia and
recommended I take him to a hospital in J—. That she herself would make
the appointment by phone. As she had predicted, the doctor declared, Most
elders are like this, as if it were nothing. When Father went to wash his
hands, I told the doctor that Father kept having crying jags and wandered
around at night like a sleepwalker, and sometimes even asked after people
who were long dead. The doctor carefully asked how old he was.

—Well, memory loss is natural in folks his age . . .

When Father came back, the doctor asked him what his name was.
Father replied with his name and asked, Why are you asking me that? And
how many children do you have? asked the doctor. Four boys and two
girls—why do you want to know? Father answered each question the doctor gave him, demanding each time why he was being asked that. The
doctor smiled and asked, Where did you go yesterday? Father seemed to

tamp down on his rising anger and replied, They were saying it was going to rain soon, so I visited our family cemetery in the mountains. Had Father gone to the mountains the other day? I stared at Father. He added, without being prompted, that he'd forgotten to take his evening pills and had woken in the middle of the night to take them. Father clearly stated his address and phone number when asked, and when the doctor inquired how much was seven times seven, he promptly answered forty-nine. After stating the precise date and day of the week, he said he was tired now and wanted to go home. The doctor said he seemed to have no cognitive problems and if the tears were too unsettling, he could book a psychiatrist for him. A psychiatrist? Mindful of the fact that Father had fallen completely silent after his interrogation, I said I would call again after consulting with our family. The doctor said that if he sleeps a lot during the day he wouldn't be able to sleep at night, which meant we should use our daytime wisely and take walks or have a lot of conversations. That tears could be connected to depression, but sometimes, this subsides once we've unloaded all the things we've kept buried deep inside. I took a photo of the prescription and sent it to my sister, asking if the medicine seemed appropriate for Father. She told me to hold off getting it because Father was taking a prescription from the dentist with his usual medicines, and there could be a bad interaction. She told me she would look for something that would help him sleep at night.

When we left the hospital, Father looked as if the visit had taken everything out of him. We couldn't even visit the dentist and took a cab home instead.

—Do I do strange things?

I immediately denied this.

—Father, young people go to the hospital when they're sick, too. I go to the hospital when I'm sick.

—You want me to get examined for Alzheimer's?

I felt he'd read my mind, and my face turned red.

—I already was. It came out negative, but I've put a patch on. Doesn't seem like there's a thing to do about it. Living without knowing what I'm doing isn't living.

Hearing Father had already been examined for Alzheimer's on his own made my heart sink. No one in the family had mentioned that. To think that he'd gone to the hospital by himself for the test.

—Living isn't always about going forward. Sometimes, when looking back is better, you can return to that.

Did he mean me? Tired, Father tried to lean further back in his seat, so I had him lean on my shoulder instead. He closed his eyes and murmured.

—Six years already. Since a calf slipped while suckling and broke its leg, and it forgot to learn how to walk. Don't hold on to things. Don't let it simmer, let it flow away. When my mind is gone, I will forget that I ever told you this . . .

I held back the tears that threatened to spill out. I gathered my index, middle, and ring finger, repeatedly running them over my forehead to my nose. Father, who seemed exhausted a moment before, managed to rally enough to tell me that the business of living did not necessarily mean I had to just keep going forward. That if I looked back and saw that it was good, I could return to it. That I should not hold on to things, that I should let things go.

Most of the work I did after becoming a writer was editing and revising what I had written. Although it was not a translation by several different translators, I kept discovering a lot of gaps and mistakes in my writing. But once I was done with my edits, I would think, *This is worse than what I had before* . . . Even after my books came out, I'd find myself poring over them for mistakes. When Father had asked me if the work I had so wanted to do was going well, I'd almost answered, I don't really think I know myself. Father, I don't think I write because I want to write—I write because I want to live. The sorrow that poured out from not having distanced myself enough, everyone else's mistakes that occurred because I couldn't bear to share my burden, the personal resentments that had come from a failure to connect. Having failed to delete or correct them in the file, I had no recourse to begin again. I would open the smashed fragments of writing every day and read them over and over. I probably hoped there was something to salvage, that I wouldn't have to start from the beginning. Which was why I insisted on reopening the files and spending inordinate amounts of time editing. Not even touching the big chunks, just changing particles and the occasional pronoun and words like "field" to "meadow." But the more I did, the more desperately I realized that no matter how I refined the fragments, I could never begin again. The fear that I could never begin again made my very eyelids tremble. Father, I am shattered and fragmented. As you described it, I'm someone who writes about silly things. Things that are nothing. But I have to keep those silly things close if I am to live.

Father lived by his own father's dictum that if one knew how to plow, one knew how to farm.

Having lost his older brothers to an epidemic and becoming the eldest son at fourteen years old, Father then lost his parents to the same disease and took it upon himself to learn one-ox plowing. He wanted to learn two-ox plowing, but he only had the one ox. Sorry for Father who had become an orphan in the space of two days, his mother's family invited him over one day and put the reins of a calf in his hand. Father's maternal grandfather bade fourteen-year-old Father to raise the calf and learn how to make a living. Every day at dawn, the young boy took the calf to the grass by the stream. So the calf could drink and graze there. The boy did not leave the calf's side for a single moment. He measured the growth of the calf's torso and legs by wrapping a single straw around them. Hoping the calf would grow quickly, he would boil some grass jook and pour it into a trough for feed, and sometimes he slept by the calf. The sound of the calf licking its lips, finishing the jook and breathing its heavy breath was like a lullaby to Father.

He thought that it was his own father who he saw on the rice paddy one day—not a specter. That it was his actual father visiting the paddy before leaving this world, giving a plowing lesson to his young son who would need it to lead the household on his own.

—Couldn't even carry his coffin.

This was something Father always added whenever he spoke of Grandfather. *Couldn't even carry his coffin.* Because of the epidemic, people were too scared to hold proper funerals for the dead. Forget proper burials; in those days, even waiting until the darkest hour of the night to bury the dead was hard enough.

—This was back when my uncle in Yongsan was still alive. In the middle of the night, he and my uncle in Jeonju rolled Father's body in a straw mat and carried him on their shoulders to bury him in our family cemetery, and I followed them . . . They kept telling me to go back, but I kept following them . . .

This was the point where Father always sighed.

—The terror, when a big ball of fire in the night sky swooped in front of me, threatening me, stopping me from following . . . Whenever I got up to follow him, the fire would push me, make me fall . . . I couldn't follow. They say it was Father trying to get me to forget him. To scare me so I wouldn't miss him, wouldn't be sad for him—that he had became a ball of fire to stop me in my path.

The fourteen-year-old was scared of the fireball that swirled close enough to singe his hair and could not keep up with his father's younger brothers. Father, Father . . . Left alone in the darkness, all he could do was cry until all the water was gone from his body. Two days later, when he lost his mother, the fourteen-year-old boy did not have the strength left even for a sob. The boy sat with his legs hanging from the porch as he watched the shadows—his uncles—roll her body in a mat and carry her out the gate in the middle of the night.

—Sitting there, feeling empty . . .

Father talked of a laundry line hanging in the courtyard. That as he sat there, drained of emotion, he heard a chittering of magpies. That the only thing he had done that night was to move his gaze fixed on the gate to the laundry line. As I listened to him talk about the magpies, I thought of how I would cling to Father's casually spoken words to get me through times when life seemed to crumble underneath my feet. His low voice. You see, he said, no matter what had happened in the night, the day would come . . . The day would always come. Sayings like that.

—The magpies that hatched their chicks under our eaves were sitting on the laundry line, chittering. I was looking at that for a long time when I saw the mother magpie fly to their nest underneath the eaves to teach her chicks to come outside. There were four or five chicks and the mother kept flying to and from the line, chirping noisily and encouraging them. The chicks came out one by one and would fly for a bit and go back into the nest and fly a bit and go back in . . . I just sat there on the porch and stared at what those magpies were doing. By the time the sun rose, the mother and chicks were all sitting side by side on the laundry line, chittering. My, they were noisy . . . And soon enough the babies were following their mother and flying up, kicking the air, one by one. They couldn't go far at first and would come back down on the laundry line to sit by the stragglers, and the mother magpie looked like she was trying to scold them into the air . . . They kept flying and sitting and flying, and suddenly, the laundry line was empty. I didn't have any strength left and kept staring, but I can never forget it, the laundry line that morning. I kept remembering it, wondering later if Mother hadn't been sitting next to me that morning . . .

I'd always thought Father was awkward at farming, but despite my impression, Father had raised that calf at fourteen and by fifteen was using it to become a true master at plowing. That's when he finally put a ring through the calf's nose—it was on its way to becoming a fully grown ox. Father remembered that day well. As it grew big and strong, the calf would often wrest itself from Father's control. When he took it to the riverbank, it kept trying to trespass into the yards of others or head to the railroad tracks in the opposite direction where there was more grass, and handling him took more and more effort. The once obedient calf was beginning to run, and the boy found himself unable to catch up. Father's maternal grandfather, who took pity on Father, gave him a ring made from the wood of the darae vine and taught him how to pierce it into the ox's nose. Father took it, returned home, and stared at the calf. The quickly growing calf blinked its huge eyes as it greeted Father. The end of the ring was so sharp that it looked like it could pierce through anything. Father touched the nose where it would go. The flesh between the nostrils was soft. Guilt flooded his chest. Once the nose was pierced, the calf would have no choice but to follow Father. Just as his household had no choice but to depend on him. Feeling they shared a similar fate, the boy extended his hand and rubbed the calf's nose. For a while, he hung the nose ring on a doorknob and only stared at it. One day, the muscly calf saw ducks playing in the water and jumped into the river. Never having heard of a swimming calf, Father followed it in. The calf swam better than Father could. Father was not pulling the calf out of the water but the calf was forcing him in deeper. As the threatening water came up to his neck, Father let go of the calf and swam out alone. Why was the calf trying to follow the ducks? The surprised ducks beat their wings and maneuvered themselves into a faster current that swept them away quickly, and the calf, flailing, followed them down the river. Father anxiously ran after it along the riverbank. Some neighbors working on the fields nearby had been watching, and they ran up and helped him pull the calf from the water. The next day, Father took the nose ring down from the doorknob. One of his uncles tied up the calf so it couldn't move, and the boy looked down at the nose ring in his hand. He looked at the wooden yoke that would be hoisted on either side of the ox's head using straps made of ropes, which lay on the ground. And the white salt in the tin basin. He imagined this hard thing piercing the delicate flesh of the calf, the dripping blood. After the ring went through, the yoke would be slung on the ox and fastened there with the straps. The tied-up calf stared at the boy with its large eyes. The early morning light made its eyes seem teary. As the boy approached, the calf's breathing grew rough. When the boy turned, he saw his sister and younger brother staring at him, and he told them to go inside the house. He didn't want them to see the calf's septum being pierced. The boy figured he would have to do it in one precise move to minimize the animal's suffering. Having sterilized the tip in a fire, he hesitated, making his uncle step forward and offer to do it instead, but the boy did not give it to him. It was his calf, and he was determined to do it himself. The boy opened his eyes wide. He walked forward, firmly planting each footstep with more strength. He held the sharp end of the nose ring in the calf's septum and pushed. As it made it out the other side, his hands trembled so much and he had involuntarily closed his eyes; when he opened them, he saw blood dripping from the calf's nose. The struggling calf splattered drops of blood on Father's face. Father took a handful of white salt and sprinkled it on the calf's wound as his grand-father had instructed. Pained by the salt, the calf kept trying to kick its legs as it brayed. The sound rang in Father's ears as he threaded the wooden ring through the calf's septum, slung the yoke around its neck and tied it firmly with the straps. When Father would tell me this story of how he managed to put the ring on the ox, his voice would falter at the end. This thing that I did, he said, to a beast that cannot speak.

Afterward, the ox obediently followed Father wherever it was led.

After losing both his parents at fourteen, Father was, by the time he was fifteen, plowing the nearby fields alone. He also plowed the fields and rice paddies of others and gave his wages to his aunt. Even when he hadn't been asked to do it, he would go around plowing the fields that seemed to need it. I asked, Even without permission? Father replied, If you want rice to grow, you need to turn the earth, anyway . . . But Father, what if they didn't pay you? Father said, That wouldn't happen. Maybe they wouldn't be able to pay me right away, but sometimes they'd give me some money after their harvest. They would always pay me. Judging from Father's expression, I suspected there must've been someone who hadn't paid. I asked,

Did anyone not pay? Father replied that he didn't remember. He seemed to remember, but he did not tell me. He said, Everyone knows I lost my parents in the span of two days . . . When I went to plow their fields they'd ask me to do a good job. They never said anything like, Who told you to plow my field? The world wasn't so mean and cunning as it is now. And if they didn't pay, then they didn't pay. There was nothing I could do about it.

Aunt, who had been arranged to marry into a family in Julpo, had promised my Father as he cried over Grandfather's death that she would continue to live with him, and she did. There was a wedding, but it was agreed that she would move to Julpo a year later.

A long time ago, in this house, Aunt would cook the meals for her two younger brothers and plant squash seeds by the garden walls and dry the washing on the laundry line. On cold winter days, she woke up at dawn to fetch water from the well, boil it in the iron rice pot, and mix it with cold water while checking the temperature with her elbow before setting it up in washbasins and placing the frozen shoes by the kitchen fire to warm them. At night, the three siblings made shadow puppets with their hands in the lamplight. They made dogs that barked, eagles that flapped their mighty wings, and horses that ran the wide plains. When the night deepened, Father and my little uncle slept with Aunt in the middle, their backs to each other. Father, at fourteen, stared at the dark wall and thought how he was the eldest son and would never be able to leave this house. Father was the eldest son of an eldest son. On jesa days, Father's uncles, aunts, cousin, and his cousin's wife would gather at Father's house with bowls of rice and make dotorimuk and tofu, fry up jeon savory pancakes, kill a chicken and serve it boiled and trussed, and offer this food to our ancestors at the jesa table. Father, having inherited the mortuary tablet from his father at the tender age of fourteen, would place it on the table and conduct the ancestral rites. Whenever he did so, he thought of the braying of the calf as it cried when he pierced its nose. He thought of how this house had similarly pierced his own nose with a ring because he was forced to live as his family duties dictated. Did the calf really cry? I asked, and Father said that its eyes were so big that the tears were even heavy.

In the end, Father's sister, my aunt, couldn't bear to leave her younger brothers all by themselves, which is how her husband, the man from Julpo whose face I have never seen, came to live in our village. One time, after I'd just learned to drive, I managed to bring a car all the way to J— and took Father out for a ride. We were entering Gyeokpo by a dusty beach when we saw a sign that read Julpo. What we call Gomsoman Bay today used to be called Julpo Bay. Wherever you happened to stand in Julpo, you can see jagged mountains. The waters near the mountains were deep, too, which prompted a fishing port to develop around it. Fishermen caught croakers and shrimp, and when the catch was good, they made fish preserves from the leftovers. As I drove through it, I asked, Father, is this Julpo that Julpo? One of the things about family is that you can jump into the layers of your shared narrative like this without using too many words. Father replied, Right, this Julpo is that Julpo.

When I think of him, my mind grows silent.

The Julpo man, whose face I have never seen. This uncle was half fisherman and half farmer.

There was once a man. Born in Julpo with its thick rushes and nasturtiums and wide mudflats that were the habitat of great bustards, he moved to J— when the woman he married lost her parents and found herself unable to leave behind her two young brothers. The people of Julpo fish, and the people of J— farm. Having built levees in Julpo, he came to the township of J— where there was no seawater, preserved fish, sea breams, cutlassfish, or salt fields, and took up the role of the eldest daughter's husband in Father's house . . . Eventually he moved his immediate family to a newly built home, which two years later, caught on fire. He ran into the house shouting, Fire! Fire! He rescued his wife and two children from the flames, but he himself did not survive.

Some facts are so fantastic that they don't feel real no matter how much time passes. Were they ever facts? I wonder with suspicion and skepticism. How could such a thing have happened? These facts seem too coincidental or manufactured to fit some formula, making fiction seem factual in comparison.

If Father had had two oxen, he would've diligently mastered two-ox plowing. Because the pebbly, clumped earth of the mountain fields needed two oxen to turn it. For a while, plowing was a source of income for Father. My young aunt felt ill at ease over the plowing wages my young father would give her. Father would drop a crumpled bill around Aunt who would be hanging the laundry or bringing up water from the well and tap her back and say, Nuna . . . Look, someone dropped money here! and run away. In that gloomy house with no adults, the siblings would suddenly fall into a game of tag between the drying clothes and collapse into fits of laughter. My young aunt would accidentally grab Father's trousers and Father would plop down on the ground to stop them from dropping, and when Aunt would try to sit down, too, Father would get up and run away again. And Aunt, about to sit down, would run after him shouting, Hey! As the siblings chased after each other, barely managing to stay out of each other's grasp, the chickens by the coop would flutter about in surprise, the dog sitting on the fence would get up and move out of the way toward the shed, the squash hiding in the vines by the garden wall would crash to the ground, and the pig trapped in the pigpen would observe the chaos in the yard with its black eyes and twitch its ears.

Before the war, there were many days like that in this house.

When the war happened, Father was seventeen, I wrote before feeling something strange. In my own childhood, I heard the phrase *The war happened when I was young* many times from Father. There was no way for a little village like this to avoid the war. The people of the village usually got along, but if ever an argument broke out, they would bring up things that had happened during the war. How this ingrate who would've died if I hadn't hidden him in the closet that time is resenting me for this little thing! How so many people were dragged away because of that armband-wearing traitor, who never apologized for snitching to this day and walks about with his head held high! Father, when he mentioned the epidemic that took his parents and the war, used the word "mayhem." That it was "mayhem" and that it was a miracle any of them had survived. That having survived the mayhem, every day after that seemed like a bonus, a gift.

The village was about ten li away from the center of the town of J—. Unlike the town, where most people were office workers, civil servants, businessowners, or other people in commerce, the village was mostly people who worked the land. Farming methods were very different back then, and all the planting and harvest work could only be done cooperatively, which meant everyone knew everything about each other's fields. *Even when the war began . . .* As I was about to write that phrase, I hesitated. Until now, it wasn't a phrase that gave me pause. But now that I'm about to write about it, I'm suddenly wondering if that verb, "to begin," is the best way to describe a war. To use my father's expression, the "mayhem" was so vast that every day after it felt like a blessing. It shouldn't be described the way I'd write *The tears began* or *The bleeding began*—something about using the same verb feels strange to me.

Despite this, I continue to write: *Even when the war began.*

Even when the war began, the people of the village continued to work in the fields. They planted rice sprouts in the rice paddies, cultivated the mountain patches and planted perilla, and broke apart clumps of earth for the chilis to grow. Father said, It didn't really feel like the mayhem had begun. But I didn't feel liberated when Liberation happened when I was twelve, either. They divided us at the 38th parallel line then, and we started hearing that we couldn't cross it to go to the north. We couldn't hear from those folks up there, we couldn't go back and forth—Liberation business felt a little uneasy. When I was little, my friends and I made a promise that we would go hunting for tigers together at Baekdu Mountain someday. I asked Father, You mean, with Daeseong ajeh and Buksan ajeh? Yes, Father replied, they call this place the granary of the Honam Plains but it's not like I've got lots of land and nothing grows here besides the rice and what we farm . . . As a child we'd heard there were many bears up north as well, so we decided if we couldn't catch a tiger we could catch a bear, sell the spleen, and use the money to move to Seoul . . . Father laughed bitterly. I laughed, too. Because I could imagine the boys dreaming of catching a tiger, and if not that, a bear. Had these boys even seen a tiger or a bear? Father, do you even know what a spleen looks like? He answered, What do you think, I've never even been up north—not that you even could go there back then . . . We were just frustrated, we needed that dream just to have a dream. To think if we went somewhere, we could do something . . . Just thinking that made living easier. But one day, first thing at dawn, the North Korean army pushed in from the north and the south side lost Seoul in just four days . . . We were in the southern part of the South and could only hear about lots of rumors. We had no idea there was mayhem going on, we just assumed it was some business up at the 38th parallel and went on doing the things we were doing the day before . . . You know, Seoul was just a place in stories for us. So far away that we never had occasion to visit, like it was another country . . . They made that border at the 38th parallel so we'd stay on our own sides, but once it broke down, there were fighter planes flying in the air every day and it was rumored the president had fled Seoul and Seoul people had packed up their bags and left. But none of them were coming to our town, so . . . we didn't feel it was happening at first . . .

Not a month into the war, J—was completely taken over by the North Koreans.

When he talks of the North Korean army in the war, Father calls them the Sixth Division. That once the Sixth Division invaded J— in July, people started to change. That the Sixth Division's goal was to trample J— on their way to Gwangju, and Janseong was on the same path. His mentioning this division by its exact name was a little odd, so I asked him how he knew they were the Sixth Division, and he answered, How could I forget it? When they killed so many people in their wake? One of my uncles was a police officer . . . Wait, I said, Jeonju Granduncle? No, said Father, there was one more above him. One more brother younger than my father. A police officer in Sunchang, but he was dropping in on us to make sure we were safe because it was just us three in the house, but someone told on him and a group from the Sixth Division . . . Father went on to say that they entered the courtyard, and my granduncle, who I never met, slipped out the back gate, passing the jars and hiding up in a mahogany tree— almost in one breath. I said, And then what happened? What happened, Father? He hesitated. They knew somehow, he said, that he was hiding in the mahogany tree, they shot the tree until I heard the sound of his body falling into the sesame field . . . I heard it from the jars, where we hid . . . the three of us hiding for our sin of being the family of a police officer . . . When I think of that day, it is strange to think of myself as still living and breathing now. Life feels like a dream. In the middle of the night, they had my Yongsan Uncle and me and some people from the village stand by a rice paddy and said they would count to ten and we needed to jump into the paddy and keep running. So we jumped in and they kept shooting at us . . . I heard gunshots as I ducked in the muddy water, and when I opened my eyes, it was dawn. Everyone was dead except me, and I crawled out of the mud and ripped off the leeches all over my body . . . In the mayhem, I lost my uncles, and the only one who survived is your Jeonju Granduncle . . . They didn't waste bullets on us later on. They made us sit around the

nettle tree near the irrigation ditches and with bamboo spears they . . .
The whole village was screaming and stank of blood and eyeballs bursting
and stomachs bursting and intestines bursting . . .

Father said that those who lived through it had lived through it. On jesa
days, my grandaunt would steam a skate in a big iron pot and deliciously rip
shreds of it to place on Father's plate—I learned that the long scar on her
neck was from the bamboo spears. Whenever she drank a bowl of makkeolli, the scar would turn bright red, a line starting at the nape of her neck.

Deep into the war, Father received his conscription notice. His surviving uncle, who we refer to as Jeonju Granduncle, tried everything he
could to stop him from going. Jeonju Granduncle, my grandfather's youngest brother, was a detective. Whenever Father was given notice, my
granduncle found away to send Father back home. Conscripts were defined
as "Any man at least twenty years old, whose birthday falls between September 1 and August 31 of the following year," and Father was sixteen,
after all. Furthermore, he was the eldest son of an eldest son, which meant
he had to survive for the sake of the household. This is what Father said to
me in his low voice, the voice that would vanish completely someday, the
voice that I've recorded in my notes: For the sake of what household? There
was nothing left . . . Whenever Father thought about his uncle's words,
he smiled bitterly. All they had left was one ox . . .

When Father was once again given notice and called to the police station, Jeonju Granduncle told him to go to a certain shrine and to do what
a man there named Keunbong—big peak—told him to do. Keunbong was
deaf and mute, and I remember him as a man with a big head. He had no
name and no people, and someone had named him Keunbong because of
his big head. *Why is he called Keunbong?* was a question no one asked when
they saw him because his head was that much bigger than everyone else's.
Especially when he stood next to Father, who has a particularly small head.

A vagabond with no roots, at some point he settled under the family's mountain ceremonial shrine by the tombs and raised chickens. There was an occasional black goat well. Keunbong's most important work was to clear the growth from the cemetery around spring and the Chuseok harvest festival before ancestral rites. As Jeonju Granduncle had instructed, Father went to Keunbong, who silently led the boy to the shed of the shrine and locked the door from within. Keunbong rolled a towel into a blindfold and wrapped it around the boy's eyes. He made the boy make a fist with his right hand and extend his index finger and put it on something cold. The chill was brief, and something swept past the middle of Father's index finger. *What are you going to do to me?* Even if Father had asked that question, Keunbong could not have answered. Keunbong, placing the unsuspecting boy's index finger into a straw cutter, quickly brought down the blade. It happened in a flash. Father told me that there hadn't even been time to scream. That when he took off his blindfold, Keunbong was trampling on the cut finger and mashing it into the ground. That he had no idea why something like this was happening and he was so afraid of Keunbong that he couldn't speak. That when he wrapped the cut finger in a towel and ran out of the shrine, he wasn't even bleeding from the cut. Aunt, who had learned to handle medicine from my grandfather, put a thick herbal plaster on his stump. That's when Father could release his fright and burst into tears as Aunt patted his back. Telling him that now that he couldn't pull the trigger on a rifle, he wouldn't be wanted by the military. Keunbong had mashed the finger so it would be impossible to reattach. Live as if you never had it, Aunt told her younger brother as she buried the finger next to the well.

When did I first hear this story? Who told it to me? When I later heard that Father's mind had trouble stilling enough to fall sleep, I would think of the moment Father's finger was cut off during wartime. Because it seemed like those were the kind of moments that would prevent Father from falling asleep.

Whenever I saw Father's stub of a right index finger, I felt an odd sense of sadness. And when I heared the story of how he lost it, I resented Jeonju Granduncle for a while. On winter jesa days when he would come from Jeonju with a box of tangerines and everyone would be greeting him, I would stand off in the corner and seethe. Even when he handed out the pink tangerines, which you couldn't get in J—, I did not accept them. Not accepting his tangerines was the only resistance I put up against Jeonju Granduncle. Only when Aunt would glare at me for my rudeness would I reluctantly hold out both hands and accept one. But I would then throw it into the snow. A pink tangerine rolling on the white snow. The odd sadness that came to me when I saw Father's finger stump. Odd is the only word I can use to describe that incurable sadness. Whenever I felt it, I'd put out my hand and interlace our fingers together. His hand being big and mine small, the interlacing would be awkward, but I would still call out, Look, Father! and wave our hands in the air. I once asked him, Are things difficult for you because of your finger? Father looked down at his stump with no fingernail and mused, Not at all. This kind of thing, it's nothing at all. Which made me wonder what kinds of terrible things he endured since that time he was blindfolded, not knowing what was about to happen, that would render such an experience "nothing at all."

The more I learn about Father and the war he experienced, the more I learn about a certain mysterious name.

For a long time, whenever Father heard someone had come from Jangseong or lived there, he would stare at this person for a long time. Then he would ask them whether they knew someone named Park Muleung after the mayhem. Who was he? I wrote down this name that I had heard from Father so often since I was a child, thinking I should look for him. That chill lingering in his face whenever he asked Jangseong people whether they knew Park Muleung. Who was this man who could cause my Father's face to make that expression? Father never told me who he was. And I could only discern, judging by Father's expression when I mentioned his name, that he hoped Park Muleung was still alive.

Jangseong is where North Jeolla Province, where J— is, and South Jeolla Province meet. Until I started middle school in downtown J—, there used to be a bus headed for Jangseong that went through the main road of our village. Did that bus route still exist? It had signs saying Ipam, Cheonan, and Jangseong, and it drove through once in the morning and once in the evening. Ipam and Cheonan are in Northern Jeolla Province, but Jangseong is part of Jangseong County of Southern Jeolla Province and the Noryeong Mountains. From the railway of the village or the mountain fields, we could see the great peaks no matter where we looked. One of them looked close enough to reach by bicycle—Jangseong's Galjae Pass. Father said the Galjae Pass was not so easy to get to. It looks nearby, but once you set out, you will find yourself walking endlessly without getting any closer. Not to mention how steep the mountain is, which makes it unpopular among climbers, and how every trail is overgrown and a chore to hack through. There is also a swamp where a single misstep can end your life if there isn't anyone around to pull you out, and even if you did somehow survive, you'd find yourself lost and unable to tell which way to go—not to mention the poisonous snakes. Father knew a lot about the Galjae Pass. He spoke as if he'd been there, remembering the pheasants that would flutter up from its forest of rushes to the sky. When I asked him how he remembered the Galjae Pass so well, he would reply, How could I ever forget it?

After three months, Seoul was reclaimed for the South in the Battle of Incheon. The South Korean and UN troops continued north all the way to Amnokgang River, but J—, deep in the south, was in a bigger mess than even at the beginning of the war. The South Korean army and the North Korean army kept taking and retaking the village from each other to the point where the South Korean side would possess the village in the day and North

Korean soldiers would occupy it in the night. Father said this was because the village happened to be right next to Jangseong's Galjae Pass. When I first heard of the Galjae Pass from Father, I wondered where it was, so I looked it up in a book. Called Noryeong during the Japanese occupation, the Galjae Pass got its name from its abundance of rushes. Rushes on a mountain? I imagined they meant silver grass. The Japanese called it Noryeong in an attempt to rename the mountains of the Korean peninsula using Kanji. As if to mock me, an explanation followed that the place was called the Galjae Pass because of all the rushes, but they weren't really rushes, they were silver grass. The fact that it was silver grass didn't change anything about the stories set there. I can't tell the difference between the two plants myself anyway. I only know that rushes grow by the sea or by riversides, while silver grass grows on mountains. Still, if this had been known back then as well, they would've named the place with "eoksae" after the silver grass instead. I still sometimes find myself calling silver grass growing on the mountains rushes. Or the rushes swaying in the wind by the river silver grass. The Galjae Pass probably got its name as people kept calling the silver grass growing there rushes. I read a designation somewhere that said: "Galjae is the path between South Jeolla Province Buki township's Moklan Village and J—'s nearby Ipam township's Gunryeong Village." Father's memory was correct. He said that during the Joseon Dynasty, the only route connecting the Jeolla provinces and Hanyang—old Seoul—was the Galjae Pass, and scholars had to use this route to go up to take the civil service exams. And to this day, in the village, there's a bridge that was named Gwagyo, or the Bridge of the Exams. A bridge that would take me to our village, which is why the sight of it made me happy. When the rains came, the water would lurch wildly—*kwal kwal kwal*—and I would pause on the bridge to watch it. When the heavy summer rains ceased and the water stilled, I would gaze at the clear stream flowing below me on that bridge, filtering through the grasses on either side of the river. At the last line of defense in Busan, where the South Korean troops were victorious at the Battle of Nakdong River, the North Korean army was forced up into the Jirisan and Deogyusan mountains where they launched guerilla counterstrikes. The North Korean army and their partisans also hid along the Galjae Pass, which looks down on our village. As they entered the region, they killed anyone they thought was related to the military or police.

At night, the North Korean army came out from hiding in the Galjae Pass grasses and into the village. The thing they needed most was food to survive in the mountains. Each house was robbed of its provisions, every chicken's neck twisted and carried away, and even the dried corn stalks hung from doorknobs to be planted the following year were snatched.

Father was determined to protect his ox. When the sun set after he worked the fields with the ox, he would lead it across Gwagyo Bridge and over the hill with the shrine and head to the guard box at the end of Daeheung-ri Bridge. He would put the ox to sleep next to the guard box, and he slept on the ox's stomach. At daybreak, he led the ox back to the village, harnessed it once more, and set out to work.

—There was no mayhem like that mayhem . . .

As the village was occupied by South Korean troops by day and North Korean troops by night, the loyalties of the villagers, who until then had all been good neighbors, split in half. During the day, South Korean soldiers checked to see if anyone was consorting with the North Koreans, and at night, the North Korean army decided unilaterally who was on the other side and executed them. Father said, I couldn't make heads or tails of how to survive. The very thought of those days makes him slump his shoulders and hunch over in agony. Father told me it was the first time in his life he was that afraid of people. That he had no idea what terrifying intentions they hid in their hearts—that was what frightened him most of all.

The North Korean army hiding in the Galjae Pass came down to the village at night and dragged off anyone who looked useful. Even though Keunbong had cut his finger cut off to help him avoid conscription, Father had to take measures not to end up in the North Korean ranks. In the evenings, he was often seen leaving home with his ox to hide. One day, he had tied the ox up and returned home for a moment to get something when North Korean soldiers approached. Father said, Your aunt made me climb into the salt sack in the other room and had just thrown something over it when the soldiers broke the door down and threw a big bamboo spear right into the sack. They stuck spears into anything that could hide a person— it just missed my ear. A villager from Ssangun had become an armband-wearing partisan, and he spotted me once in a line of men being taken away. He told his men to let me go because I was a poor boy who had lost his parents and was trying to survive on my own and to let me have my ox, too. I'm still alive today because of him. Later, Father said, I learned he had once carried his sick mother on his back to my father's medicine shop, but he didn't have any money for medicine . . . The old woman was so sick that my father treated her with acupuncture anyway and gave her medicine. Ssangun was the neighboring village where the irrigation ditch began. After surviving the mayhem, Father went looking for the man in Ssangun, but people said he had disappeared into the Galjae Pass one day and no one knew what had become of him.

There's a photo of Aunt as a young woman.

In it, she has her hair fastened into a bun with a long pin, and she is holding a black skirt that falls from her white jeogori in one hand. Beneath her lifted hemline are those white, rubber slip-on shoes called gobaeksin. She wears no beoseon, or traditional socks. Aunt is looking out the corner of her eye into the world, her other hand clinging to Father. What year was this? Father had left home and returned for his parents' jesa rituals, which were only two days apart, and they'd had this photo taken—the first one in Aunt's life. Her voice, which I'd heard since I was a baby, is clear in my memory. Mother sitting on one end of that thatched-roof house porch and Aunt in the center of it, rolling a cigarette and placing it between her lips. Aunt was head of this house. When she sat on the porch she took the center, and at the table she sat across from Father, which is normally Eldest Brother's seat. Aunt was always on Father's side. As Father left home that spring and hadn't returned by summer, Mother automatically began to lament his waywardness. As she does in the photo, Aunt would give her a sideways look. Aunt said, Tiger's father is just frustrated. It's all the war's fault, he means no harm . . . You know he went to the conscription office, but his uncle made them send him back because he was the eldest son of an eldest son, and that labeled him a dodger for life. He gets no peace from that. "Tiger" is the baby nickname for my own eldest brother, too. Which makes Father "Tiger's father." Aunt cleared her throat one more time, looked around the courtyard, put another rolled cigarette in her mouth and took a long drag. She said, Later when he wandered around, trying not to get caught by the North Korean army, he slept in the dew with his ox. He's not doing this because he doesn't like you, he's doing it because he caught the wandering itch back then. Mother then said, If you say that one more time, it'll be the thousandth! The end of Aunt's sentence faded away at this outburst. Mother shouted, Who asked him to become a farmer! I told him I could do it myself! We don't even have that much land! I'm scared the children are going to learn from him, if this man they call their father keeps wandering away from home. Aunt sat there, blowing out a long plume of smoke. Aunt said, There's a jesa soon, he'll come home. He always comes home for jesa.

Aunt was never wrong.

Wherever Father was, he would always return home for jesa days, kill the chicken to put on the jesa table, whack the chestnuts off the trees, and write up jibang paper tags to take the place of the ancestral mortuary tablets that had been got lost in the war. Jeonju Grandfather, along with my cousin and uncles, would perform the rites at midnight and dole out the food to the rest of us waiting up until then. My favorite was the boiled eggs, cut in half with a corrugated knife and stacked on a plate. Father, when he saw me eyeing the eggs instead of the dried persimmons he was handing out, would put one of the eggs with their visible yellow yolk in my hand instead.

A delivery courier walked quickly into the courtyard.

I was opening the curtains to the small room. The man had placed his package on the steps going up to the front door and was turning away when he spotted me and gave me a quick bow.

—Is Grandfather not in today?

That must be what he called Father. Ever since we visited the hospital, Father pretended that everything was fine in front of me. His mood seemed to lift as well. This morning, when I served up soft tofu for breakfast, instead of soy sauce I placed pollack roe and a dot of perilla oil on top. He kept saying how delicious it was. It was the first time he said anything about my food since I came down to J——. After breakfast, he looked at the calendar for a long time and called Mother in the hospital. He had circled today's date in red and asked Mother if she knew why he'd done that. The calendar, compliments of Nonghyup Bank, had letters so big you could read it from a hundred paces away. I was wondering how Mother could ever know why Father would've circled a date on the calendar when she answered that it was the day he was supposed to have lunch with the gukak folk music people, that he was supposed to go with Mr. Baegun, who was going to pick him up around half past eleven, that he just had to wait at home for him. Then she added, Do you really have to go? Father, who hadn't even remembered this lunch appointment until now, answered, I've got to. To do what? To Mother's question he said, Nothing special, but if I miss another appointment, they'll think I'm dead. Although he knew Mr. Baegun was coming for him at eleven thirty, Father was in a rush to be ready by eleven and wanted to stand by the road for half an hour. But rain started falling and I suggested, Perhaps you can take a rain check? Father gave one look at the sky and said, It'll pass soon. As if it were answering, the rain, having carried the smell of trees and earth into the courtyard, ceased. I smeared some sunscreen on his face but he complained it felt greasy and wiped it off. But Father, this sunscreen is the non-greasy kind, I said as I reapplied it, and apparently tired of fighting me off, he sat glumly as I finish putting it on. He was still when I put a hat on him as well. I also gave him a cane, but he left it at the door when he walked out to the alley. He was so thin that the jacket over his shirt and his trousers were all loose on his frame. And the gate he had pushed himself through had been the one the delivery courier had entered just now.

When I said to him through the window that he could leave the package on the steps, the courier hesitated and said, Well, Grandfather always accepts it himself. He doesn't want Grandmother to know . . . As I stared at him uncomprehendingly, he reluctantly left the box on the steps and went out the gate. Not before turning around one more time, though. What was in that box? I went outside and looked at it. I hadn't noticed from the window, but it was fairly large. A frying pan set from a home shopping network. Had Mother ordered it? I thought about opening it but suddenly didn't want to bother, so I placed it on a platform in the toolshed and gazed at the spot where Father had been staring before. The farming tools were still up on the wall. Slowly, I pushed open the side door in the shed.

One winter, the roof of the cement house, built in place of the thatched-roof house, had caved in because of the snow. When spring came, Father had fixed the roof, but that winter, it collapsed again under the weight of snow. Once more, Father waited until spring before fixing it. The next year, the roof collapsed not just in one spot—almost half of it came down, making the house quite precarious to live in. Around the time I was serializing my first novel in a newspaper, Father built the newest iteration of our house. It had a front door that led into the living room. Father made some calculations and installed electricity and an oil-burning boiler. They bought a sofa for the living room and a bed for the master bedroom. It was a new house, but Father had designed the positions and shapes of the room according to the old one. The house still faced west, and the position of the gates remained the same. The only difference was that the house no longer needed a kiln, which also meant that the ashery, where the ash from the fires was stored, could be eliminated to create more room for the toolshed and a doorless shed enclosure that faced the courtyard. Father parked his motorcycle in this other shed. In the summer, the platform in the courtyard would be moved to the toolshed, but as time passed, the platform just stayed in this shed. Stuff started piling up on it that didn't quite belong in the house. Bundles of unpeeled garlic, long boots needed for the rice paddies, bamboo rods to pick persimmons, that kind of thing. People who were dropping by would sit on the platform to chat before moving on with their day.

Later on, Father installed a door and shelves upon Mother's request so they could store more things in it. Soon, the place became Mother's personal storage space. She put a refrigerator in there and a big container of mul-kimchi, or water kimchi, and little ones full of sticky rice gochujang red pepper paste. I liked perilla leaves, so she kept some food made of perilla leaves in some containers just for me. Perilla leaf kimchi, boiled-down perilla leaf jorim, perilla leaves preserved in doenjang. I went inside and opened the door to see it was still full of gochujang and doenjang containers. There was one particularly large one in the corner filled with mul-kimchi.

Ah, this is that mul-kimchi.

The sight of the container made me remember an argument my sister had with Mother. As Mother couldn't use her leg like she used to, my sister had boiled cow's feet for a broth and brought it to J—. Mother was not pleased. She said, So much trouble just for me . . . Perhaps Mother found it difficult, having made and ferried so much food to her children all these years, to have her daughter bring her food this time. Mother didn't like the broth, either. She had a few meals of it when my sister ladled it out, but later she just had rice and mul-kimchi. My sister shouted, Mother! And Mother gave her a look that asked, *What?*

—Are you really going to do this to me?

My sister was so resentful that she was getting teary-eyed over Mother refusing to eat the broth she had made for her.

—You're really just going to eat mul-kimchi?

Well, Mother had replied, mul-kimchi is nice and cool. This made Sister burst into tears and sit down right there on the kitchen floor.

—There's no nutrition in mul-kimchi! Eat the broth I boiled for you! I stood in front of the stove for more than ten hours to make it but you're just eating your mul-kimchi!

Mother recovered from her shock and retorted, Why can't I just eat what I want? Which made my sister stretch out her legs right there on the floor with tears running down her face as she screamed:

—I'm going to grab that mul-kimchi container and dump it out in the field!

As I listened to my sister's recounting of this argument, I interjected at this point: And? Did you throw out a whole barrel of mul-kimchi into the field? My sister said, I was making a point. Do you really think I would've done such a thing? My sister did not, however, laugh as she said this. Surely she was embarrassed about having thrown a tantrum over Mother not eating the broth she had made for her. She had probably gone into the small room and sat in there for a while. When I said this, my sister gave me a quizzical look.

—Wow, unni, how did you know that's what happened without having been there?

Because I'd done the same to Mother. Last year, Mother had been frying up some maesaengijeon seaweed pancake on a camping burner as she squatted on the kitchen floor, but she found herself unable to get up from her sitting position. Third Brother had to take her to an orthopedics hospital in Gangnam and even after her surgery, she had to spend two months recovering in hospice care. Even now, Mother needed a walker to get about. Even as she went to my sister who was crying in frustration in the small room, she was probably leaning on her walker. Mother claimed her stomach had been aching for the past few days, but the broth my sister had brought her had made her insides warm and comfortable, consoling her. As my sister wiped away her tears, Mother confessed she hadn't been able to exercise and was afraid eating so much meat would make her fat, which was why she had eaten the mul-kimchi. *Oh no*, I thought as I listened to my sister's story. So, I asked, what did you say to her? Apparently, my sister doubled down on Mother, hard.

—What fat? That's why you're only eating mul-kimchi? Mul-kimchi is full of sodium, it'll make you fatter if anything! Why on earth would you think I would've brought you something that was bad for you, where do you get these ideas . . .

My sister asked, sobbing, Unni, why am I doing this to Mother? Why am I speaking to her like this? This isn't who I am. She was right—I might've shouted at Mother, but my sister never would've. I'd been to see her when she ran a pharmacy in Seoul's Gil-dong neighborhood. There were several people there waiting to get their prescriptions filled. The pharmacy had a little room attached to it. It looked like she would need some time to finish, so I went into the little room to wait. I could hear the conversations she was having with her customers. At first, I thought she talked an awful lot with the people who were there to get their medicine. *What was she talking about?* I listened closely. My sister was telling her customer that medicine was just emergency relief, that they needed to not depend on pills but to eventually allow their bodies to regulate themselves, and explaining to someone who had stress-related indigestion what their disorder entailed. There was a man with a deep voice who thanked her for the last time he had come to her. He made a living carving wood seals and said that he had a special seal made from the wood of a lightning-struck jujube tree. He wanted to give it to her as thanks. An old woman came with her husband saying how her husband was never home when they were young but now all he did was follow her around, and here he was, tagging along on her prescription errand. As she *tsk-tsked* her husband, my sister gave her a nutrition supplement drink to give to him. I waited for my sister to be done with work and listened to the sound of her voice pleasantly conversing with the people who had come to fill their prescriptions as I leaned against the wall and fell asleep.

It's only because you were worried for her, I was about to say, but then wondered if it were indeed all right to shout at one's mother just because one was worried—instead I said, Shall I read you a poem?

—A poem?

—Yes.

—What poem?

—Brecht's poem.

When she died, they buried her in the ground
Flowers grew and butterflies flew over her.
She was so light she barely pressed the soil.
For her to be light—how much suffering had she known?

It was a poem my daughter would recite to me.

My sister heard me to the end and asked:

—What's the title?

—"My Mother."

Hearing this, she sighed deeply.

—But do people really get fat from drinking broth?

—I don't know, but I think so?

My sister said, Even you're against me, but her voice was without conviction. I asked, Did Father like it? And she said, Yes . . . He ate bowl after bowl and had to spend the next day in the bathroom. Her voice was listless. Mother and Father, she said, their muscles are decreasing, they really ought to eat more protein . . . My sister's voice felt almost like she were next to me. I stroked the mul-kimchi container and gently closed the refrigerator door. What was this house to me? What was it about this place that made me fall into such reveries? It was true that the stories of this house and village were more about storing things than fighting over something.

I glimpsed a bicycle in the corner of the shed. A new one, with the plastic shrink wrap still on the seat. Why was there a new bicycle here? I approached it and touched the bell: a clear, bright sound. I touched it again. The ringing . . . Here, in Mother's refuge, in the house where Mother was absent, the bell sounded sadly in the emptiness.

From the shed, I walked out the small door. I wondered if Father had made it to his gukak people meeting. I'd offered to go with him but he made it clear that I shouldn't. And when I insisted, he refused it straight out. Why was it all right to go with Mr. Baegun but not with me? I thought of walking out the side gate to the alley but I tapped the cement street just outside the gate instead. There used to be a well there long ago. Walking down the alley, one had to pass this well to go through the side gate. Our house had a private well in the yard, but other homes shared this one. Back then, we didn't have a gate here but a wall. Since we pulled down that wall and installed this gate, we would use this outside well to wash the sand off our hands and feet or the dust off our faces.

Why did we fill up the well?

I looked at the wall where the side gate was. Inside the wall was our house, and outside of it was our next door neighbor. Our next door neighbor would think the opposite. My sight followed the wall and stopped at a certain point. Was it there? Where the walls used to not connect. I couldn't discern exactly where that was. The house next door wasn't the same house as back then, which made it even harder to tell. Such useless, utterly useless memories. We didn't always have a gate here. One of my uncles used to live next door. His wife told me that right after they'd married, they lived with us in our house and built their own house in the next field and moved there. They had tiled the roof and built the wall together, and they had built a wall with a gap to connect our uncle's yard with our side yard, which had four big persimmon trees. My cousins and I were always going through that gap. In the fall, we would climb on that wall to pick persimmons. Spaces that now exist only in the memory. We could see our uncle's kitchen through that gap, too. His wife kindling the fire of the kiln, tasting the mallow doenjang stew with a ladle, putting little potatoes with the soaking rice to cook them together . . . her doenjang stew was especially tasty. When I asked Mother why Little Aunt's doenjang stew tasted different from hers, Mother retorted that if I liked Little Aunt's doenjang so much I could go live with her next door. Little Aunt's secret to her doenjang stew was simple. She added a spoonful of flour, which added thickness and umami to the broth.

That's how some memories set. When I have no appetite, I remember Little Aunt's doenjang stew and place a clay pot on the stove, pour in the tangleweed broth, slice the squash—and as if it had just occurred to me, add a spoonful of flour.

And summer nights.

To this day, Father doesn't eat any food made of flour save for noodles. Especially sujebi, those hand-pulled dough bits in clear broth. Father, even during the war, and certainly after, always had to eat sujebi. Almost every meal. At some point, the mashed-up sujebi came back up his esophagus and filled his mouth. Once that happened, he would taste flour for the whole day. Flour was a precious commodity back then, and they would forage for mugwort or pine or elm bark, with only an occasional spot of sujebi floating among the bark. We had to eat whatever we could to survive, Father would always add. Since Father refused to eat flour, Mother naturally shied away from making sujebi or kalguksu noodle soup. Little Aunt made sujebi often on summer nights. Kalguksu was a lot of trouble, but sujebi was easy enough. Little Aunt put flour in a big tin pot and added water little by little as she mixed it in, making me so wild with anticipation that I'd already be waiting among my cousins for my share. When Little Aunt opened the pot lid and dropped in dollops of the dough into the broth, my mouth would start to water. I'd be so excited that I'd unfold the table and set the utensils without being asked. I may have been the only child waiting for the sujebi to come out of the kitchen, though. The grumbling voices of my cousins as the dish made its appearance: Sujebi again? There were no banchan on the table, just the main dish. Perhaps Little Aunt cooked it so often because it was the only thing you didn't need side dishes for. I always wanted more of her sujebi, this dish Mother never cooked. That clear broth, the thick doughy bits, the clean and simple taste. I regretted the disappearance of the sujebi from my bowl so much that I ate it sparingly. Pouring my cousins' leftover broth into my own bowl. You like it! Little Aunt would say as she ladled me some more, and I would whine, I'm full, Little Aunt, but eat it up anyway. Spiced only with a little ground garlic and salt, the sujebi was even good after it went cold. Those days of sitting on the straw mat spread out in their yard, slurping up the sujebi with my cousins: Hyong-e unni, Jungshik oppa, Seonsook, Jungah, Minja, Wanshik . . . The table put away, we'd lie on the straw mat, our full bellies revealed to the night sky and play around, tickling or kicking and giggling, Stop that! Stop that! we cried out, rolling off the mat as we laughed. This was before the village had electricity, which made the night darker than ink and the stars shine especially bright.

It was my fault that the gap disappeared.

It was the time when I always used to carry my baby brother on my back. I must've been eight years old. The baby was my responsibility. He seems to have forgotten it now, but when he was a baby, he was stuck to my back whether in tears or good spirits. His second word after "umma"—the word for mother—was probably "nuna," for older sister. When the baby called out to me, Nuuuna . . . I was so astonished that I remember the moment clearly to this day. How the littlest baby, who had been try-ing to form words for a while, said his first word to me. The joy and excitement drenched me like falling rain, and it was like the moment years later when I wrote the first line of my first work. Long after I had to leave my eight-year-old baby brother behind in J—, I still remember the moment he first said a real word to me. This memory would make my shoulders—hunched for whatever reason—straighten again. During times of dread and loneliness in Seoul, I would recall the moment the youngest went, Nuuuna. Then the longing and the heart-swell I thought had abated would rise up again. There was a time when I would deliberately remember that moment to stop myself from falling over the edge of despair. It was like a light that still flickered in the darkest part of my heart.

—Call me that one more time.

I had turned the baby I was carrying on my back to my stomach and was coaxing him. The baby blinked his eyes and said, Nuuuna . . . Even when the baby had fallen asleep on my back, I would turn him to the front again and say, Call me nuna again, and the baby burst into tears. Through his annoyance, he still managed to say, Nuuuna.

I wonder if it was in the middle of summer. Seeing as I was at home, perhaps on summer vacation. It was one of those times Father had wandered off somewhere. Having seated my baby brother, crying from the heat, on the sack, my goal as the eight-year-old nuna was to drag the sack past the gap through my uncle's yard to the shade of the nettle tree by the irrigation ditches. I was passing through the yard when my uncle, who'd been napping on his porch, got up and shouted at me. For kicking up so much dust. When I looked back, I saw that indeed the sack I was dragging my brother on had created a cloud of dust in its wake. Even in that dust cloud, the baby was still facing me. I was so frightened by my uncle's shouting that I sat down right there and burst into tears. My brother, who did everything I did, burst into even louder tears. My mother came running out, wearing a towel on her head, asking why we were crying. I was too scared of my uncle to speak, which is why I kept crying. And my brother, crying even louder in sympathy, made the yard of my uncle's house completely chaotic with our combined cries. Mother turned to my uncle.

—Why are the children crying?

My uncle looked chastened. In a louder voice, Mother demanded once more, Why are the children crying?

—They were kicking up dust, so I said something to them.

—What . . . Our Hon is only taking her brother to the irrigation ditch because of the heat, and you, their grown uncle, can't tolerate that?

—What . . . So you think dragging a child on a sack making all that dust, in this heat, is normal?

—You take one look at Hon's back. She's been carrying the baby so much that the sweat is making welts on it!

Mother grabbed the baby, gave my uncle a withering stare, and marched back to our house. I left the sack in the yard and followed her, still crying. For a while after, our cousins weren't allowed to come to our house, and my siblings and I couldn't visit them, either. Because Mother continued to be angry at my uncle. Aunt went back and forth between Mother and my uncle, trying to get them to make up, but it was futile. Finally, as Mother continued to fume over what my uncle considered a trivial matter, uncle closed the gap in the garden wall between our houses.

When he came back, Father looked at the wall and scoffed.

—Blessed times are these, that such a silly thing can turn into a fight.

Upon these words from his older brother, my uncle made a gate in the wall near the well and told me that if I wanted to go to the irrigation ditches with the youngest, I should go through there. And thanks to that, the people living on the side of the ditches could walk through our courtyard to the main road. Eventually, my uncle moved away to open a rice shop in town, and another neighbor moved into that house. Since the garden wall between our houses would never have had a passage through it if my uncle's family hadn't been there in the first place, we soon forgot how a gap had been there connecting the two properties. As if the wall had been whole since the beginning.

Because that well was filled in, a car could now drive all the way into the side yard. Was that why Father had it filled in? There were several public wells dug all over the village. The first thing to be rendered obsolete once running water was installed were these wells. People no longer gathered at the well to have conversations as they washed rice or potatoes or prepared radishes, but the well still had water in it. There were two public wells on the way from the main road through the alley. From time to time, I found myself looking down into these wells that were abandoned after the village got running water. Sometimes there are persimmon leaves or unidentifiable motes floating on the surface. Dropping a stone into the stillness makes rings dance on the water. Later on, they covered the wells and then filled them up. J— had so many wells that the Chinese character for well is in its name. Its water was always clean and plentiful. Sometimes, I wonder, Where has all that water in the wells flowed to? And I wonder whether the private wells have also been filled in. Father installed a motor and a tap and fitted a hose so Mother could use the water for various purposes. When the tap is turned, there's a whirring sound, and out comes the well water. It's used to water the rosebushes or to wash the dirt off our feet. When I come to the house in J—, I sometimes go up to the well and lift the lid and look down into the bottom, fascinated that the well still holds water.

I stood in the spot where the well was filled in and stomped on it.

Was there still water down there under the cement? Since it was filled in, I would mumble to myself whenever I passed this spot, There used to be a well here . . . Fewer and fewer people know what I mean by that. *Yes, there was a well here*—someday, no one will be able to give me this answer. When I stand there on the spot where the well used to be, I remember being a child, leaning against the ledge and staring into it. This well seemed deeper than the one at home. I could hardly see any water, only darkness. It was so deep, and the water was blacker than black. Like anyone who fell in would never be able to return. There must've been a fear of that darkness. I never dropped the dipper down there myself. I was afraid I would be pulled in there by the rope. Still, whenever I passed it, I wanted some water and would circle around it. Father once saw me doing that and asked, What are you doing here? I said, Water! And pointed to the gourd dipper.

—You can have water in the house.

Despite saying this, Father lowered the dipper into the well, waiting for the sound of the splash. It was too dark to see that far down, but the splash allowed us to know there was water there. The dipper returned with clear water dancing inside. A water so clear it dispelled any dread the darkness of the well had inspired. Father handed me the dipper filled with water like it was nothing, then strode through the gap and into the house.

What had they filled such a deep well with?

Has all that clear water vanished? I stood where the well had been for a moment and walked toward the ditches. The midday air was alive with the scent of rain, which made me look up at the sky. Clouds were swooshing across the sky. Was it going to rain? Father had gone out without an umbrella. I gazed toward the vegetable patch. In the middle of it was the abandoned cattle pen where Father had raised cows. I applied pressure to the wooden fence, and it gave way easily. There were hooks on either side, but it was just for show. The vegetable patch had lettuce, mallow, and mugwort growing all over the place. Butterbur leaves crept up the wall and scallions grew in their deep greens in a corner. She's planted her seeds again; this was Mother's territory. Mother can't even walk properly anymore, but she hasn't given up on gardening. She's out here, pushing her walker, planting the seeds in spite of it all.

I went inside the patch and looked in the pen.

At one time, this pen used to be filled with cows Father raised, each in their own berth. As per government policy, Father took out a loan to raise them. Mother was reluctant to go into debt, but Father presumed that the government wouldn't rip them off. That, at the very least, they would take responsibility for whatever went wrong. Even if they'd been acquired through debt, Father's heart swelled with pride at the sight of his cows. For the first time since he lost his parents at an early age and was given a calf by his grandfather to raise, he felt liberated from poverty. Father was out before the sun rose, opening the gate and waking the cows. They would be sitting there on their hind legs and recognize his footsteps. As Father entered the pen in his rubber boots, the cows would moo in greeting, wuu—holding out their pink tongues. Their breath made the inside of the pen hot. The energy flowed from Father as he busily fed the cows breakfast and the chewing of the animals of their cud. Their hoofs made regular tapping sounds on the ground, echoing within the pen. The cows did not swallow their feed all at once. They chewed it up, spat it out, and licked their lips. Their mouths never stopped moving. Father ripped open a new bag of feed every morning, poured it into dozens of troughs, and mixed it with fodder. Then he poured fresh water for them, and scraped dung from their hind legs, stacking the piles in a corner. Every morning, Father smelled like cattle.

For a while, Father's smell of cow dung became our college tuition. At the end of summer and winter vacation, Father went to the beef markets to sell off the cows for cash. He would sit on the porch and, with his hands smelling of dung, divide up the money saying, This one is for Third, this is for Hon . . . In case we should lose the money on our way to Seoul, he wrapped it in a cloth waist pouch and fitted it around our waists. Going to the train station at the end of vacation with the money tied around my waist made me feel as solemn as if I were headed off to war.

Father called only Eldest Brother and me by our names. He called Second Brother "Second," Third brother "Third," and instead of calling me "Fourth," he used my name like he did Eldest Brother. My sister was called by her nickname and the youngest was called "Youngest." Of all his children, he clearly relied on Eldest Brother the most. Everyone in our family knew this. When Father called him, it didn't seem like he was call-ing for his child—one could feel friendship in his voice. The words Father said to Eldest the most were, I'm sorry. The second most were, That should've been my job . . . When Father called my name, I would imme-diately uncross my legs or sit up straight. I unfolded the backs of my shoes and my hands patted down my hair. Because I wasn't Fourth but the inde-pendent entity "Honnie." I don't remember when exactly he started calling me that, but it was a little after I had left home. We shouldn't worry about Honnie or Honnie keeps her promises or If Honnie said so, then it is so. The effect of his words was not insignificant. I honestly tried to live up to his expectations of not being a reason for worry. I tried to keep all of my promises, even when they were difficult. And because Father said so about me, I tried not to, at least deliberately, say the wrong thing.

In the cattle pen, the feed and the water troughs fashioned from cement look like relics from a bygone era. I can still hear the smacking mouths of the cows and the sucking of the water as they stuck out their tongues. All that's in the troughs now are dust and hay and pieces of plastic. And lots of spiderwebs in the rafters. Their funnel shapes have a rainbow shine. Spider-webs cling to my face and arms. Across the skylight's wooden frame is tattered cloth. No doubt the cover was from the wind in the winter, which was too cold for the cows, but it's still up there—forgotten.

As I was walking out of the pen, I glimpsed an abandoned house near the fence. Back when Father was raising cows, that house was where Oong and Mr. Nakcheon lived. It had only one room with a kitchen attached, and when Oong and Mr. Nakcheon successively lived there, the place had been filled with warmth; now it looked as if it was about to collapse. The kitchen door was gone, providing a view of the interior and the fence on the other side of the house. There was the kiln where Oong used to cook sweet potatoes and the occasional sparrow he had caught under the awning. Mr. Nakcheon used the iron pot to cook jook for the cows. The two men had only one thing in common, which was that they listened only to Father. Oong was as large as a mountain, could not hear well, and did not know his numbers while Mr. Nakcheon was small, white-haired, and walked with a slouch. Neither of them listened to Mother. Oong, especially, would find someplace to nap if Father did not happen to assign him anything to do. In the fields, in the paddies, and once on the roof, which made his face red. I'd forgotten his face until now. I cleared my throat. To think that I still remember the first time he entered our gate. Oong was around Third Brother's age. Mother's face when she was told he was to live with us. Mother asked, You're saying Oong, the very Oong we know, is coming to live in our house? When she was informed that indeed this was the very Oong she knew, she sighed.

—I can't believe it. Don't you know what kind of child he is?

Mother's face was red from rage as she tried to talk him out of it, but Father stayed silent.

—He can't understand a word we say, what are you going to do with him?

Father didn't answer, and Mother raised her voice.

—Tiger's father!

Only then did Father mumble something.

—So what if he doesn't understand a word or two?

—. . .

—He's a strong boy.

—. . .

—I owe his family that much since the war. And that's that.

—Do you think anyone will care about your debt?

—This isn't because someone will care. I was asked by his grandmother herself, I can't ignore that.

—You should forget things that ought to be forgotten. What is this fuss with remembering every little thing and, on top of it, repaying it?

—Does this look like something that can be repaid?

—. . .

—I'm just doing the things that I can do, that's all.

When Oong's grandmother came through our gate holding Oong by the hand, Oong stood behind his grandmother and didn't say a word. Even when he was standing behind her, he was so big that all we could see was him. You listen to this man from now on, all right? Oong only stared at Father. He didn't look like he planned to listen to him at all. When Father patted his back, Oong only scratched his head.

—Please look after my Oongie. If I could see him living like everyone else, I would have no regrets if I died tomorrow. I can't close my eyes without knowing he's taken care of. He's only lived at home, I don't know if he'll do . . . If he doesn't listen and won't be of help, I'll come and get him, but please, keep him for a while and show him the ways of the world.

What could I teach him about that? Father asked as he took Oong to the cattle pen. Was it because the old woman had told him to listen to Father? Until the day he moved away from Father and to the house in town where they made seals, Oong did everything Father told him to. He followed Father everywhere, taking care of the feed, making fodder, fetching water, and scraping the cow dung with Father. From time to time, Oong took a piece of wood and carved people's names into them. Mother asked what on earth Father had done to him that made Oong listen to everything and Father replied, Nothing, I just told him that one of the calves was his from now on. I pulled open the door to the abandoned house.

It was this room.

Where Father had taught Oong, who was illiterate, to write "Oongie's calf." Father could've written it himself, but he got a sketchbook and sat Oong in front of it and made him write "Oongie's calf" over and over. And he made him read it. Oong, as if reciting the *Thousand Characters Primer*, would recite "Oongie's calf" as he went about his business. The day finally came when Oongie could write the phrase without looking at anything else. Father cut down a piece of wood, sanded it down, and guided Oong's hands to carve out the words there. Once Oong poured ink into the lettering, the phrase stood out clearly like on a sign. Father had Oong punch holes on either side of it, put a blue rope through the holes, and hang it on the neck of his calf. Oong's face lit up as he followed Father's instructions. Father pointed to the sign and told him to read it. Oong stated in a loud voice, "Oongie's calf," clearly and correctly. And so, one of the calves became his. The carving became a hobby of Oong's, and aside from his work of following Father as he helped with the feeding and the fodder-making and the watering and the cleaning away of the droppings, Oong often sanded down wood and carved people's names in them. Father would write them down first in Hangul or Chinese characters. He also taught Oong Hangul. Later on, Oong would be reading *The Four Books* that Father's own father had taught him. Father told Oong that if he ever wanted to leave the village and live in town, he had to know how to read. That there were many jobs in town, and if he worked hard, he could make money and buy a house.

Oong moved on, and a man we called Mr. Nakcheon arrived. His family name was Kim, but we called him Mr. Nakcheon in a manner that was familiar yet deferential to his age at the same time. A deference Mother did not feel at first.

—That Nakcheon man is coming to live with us? What can he possibly do, that useless man!

—. . .

—You're telling me to clean up after that Nakcheon man—of all people!

This was someone even the neighborhood children disrespectfully called "Nakcheonie." He was always drunk and would be lying about anywhere at all, asleep. It was perhaps understandable that Father wanted to bring him into our household.

Father reassured her that Mr. Nakcheon hadn't always been like that. When the people who lived under the town's bridge were banished during the riverbank landscaping project, Mr. Nakcheon had been the only person who stayed behind. He had drifted into the village like the spring breeze and survived doing work for others in the fields or running errands. He never stayed long in one place. Mr. Nakcheon would live in this place and then that one for a year, and sometimes leave the village and not come back for years. No one ever knew where he went. Eventually, he stopped working completely and, like an outcast, drank all the time and slept anywhere he could lie down. He was drunk not because he drank a lot but because his body had become so frail, just a shot or two got the job done. He must've had family he stayed with when he was away from the village, but no one knew for sure. Father defended him, saying that Mr. Nakcheon's soul was heavy with resentment. Resentment? I remember hearing Father use this word when I was in middle school, and looking it up in the dictionary. A feeling of shame and heartbreak. Mother said, If you're going to hire someone, hire the strong, young ones, but you're always getting . . . But when Father stared silently at the courtyard or gate or persimmon tree, Mother added, Even the smallest hen you bring into this house ends up being my responsibility, that's why I'm saying this. But she relented. Father promised her that he would take responsibility for Mr. Nakcheon. During the mayhem, when he was afraid of his ox being stolen by the North Korean army, he had taken his ox to the police station in town and Mr. Nakcheon had been by his side under the bridge on those nights.

—The mayhem again?

Mother, sick of hearing about it, put her towel on her head once more and went away to the backyard, signaling her acceptance of Mr. Nakcheon into the household. He came in where Oong had left, and a sign was hung not from a calf this time but an ox with the name "Kim Nakcheon." When Oong or Mr. Nakcheon fed the cows, they would often be found standing in front of the ones with their "Oongie's Calf" or "Kim Nakcheon" signs hanging on their necks. When I would go to the pen to fetch Oong or Mr. Nakcheon for dinner, Oong would smile brightly, point at his calf and say, That's mine, but Mr. Nakcheon would only give his ox a meaningful look. After about two years with my father, Oong was apprenticed to the seal-maker in town. Saying the country was running the beef industry to ruin. Having made farmers go into debt to build pens and buy cows, the government was now allowing foreign beef to flood the market, precipitating a drop in prices. This was when Father's face, which had been filled with light when he first started with the cows, aged a decade in one fell swoop. The seal-maker was a friend of my father's. Seeing Oong's propensity for carving names into wood, he wondered if that would be a better profession for him. It was important to Father that Oong become a useful person somewhere. Father, who had had no education, never taught anyone until he taught Oong.

The day Oong left our home, his grandmother repeatedly said, Thank you, thank you so much, thank you for everything. Oong held the sign that said "Oongie's Calf" in one hand and the bridle to his cow in the other. Father bade Oong and Oong's grandmother not to sell the cow yet.

—You won't get anything for that cow if you sell it now.

He advised them to sell when things got better. Until Oong left the gate with his cow and stopped looking back at Father from the alley, Father stood there and watched him go. Oong, who would roast sparrows at the end of a stick in the kiln and unexpectedly offer one to me and make me fall backward in surprise, would shout a greeting whenever he saw me in town. Hon! The featherless sparrow he had teased me with would be blackened but its form still discernable, and it made me gag every time. Afraid he was going to stick another roasted sparrow at me, I would jump whenever I heard him call my name and quickly walk away.

The "Kim Nakcheon" sign hanging around the cow's neck was not effective in making Mr. Nakcheon stay. He had surprised us all when my little sister got married because he showed up to give her thick winter blankets with pretty dangling flower embellishments as a wedding present, but then one day, he disappeared from the little house next to the cattle pen. Without giving a word of warning to Father. This was when up to 80% of the price of cows was slashed in the markets. The villagers, who had turned from rice farming to cattle raising, protested to get compensated for the difference. Whenever Father went on the cultivator with the other villagers headed for the protests at the municipal offices, Mr. Nakcheon got on as well. When Father draped on a cow one of the banners that read "Stop the Pressure to Liberalize American Beef Imports" that the vanguard had distributed, Mr. Nakcheon fastened it to the other end. When Father and the villagers headed out to the protests outside of J— to Jinan, Mr. Nakcheon also took up a placard that said "Compensate Now" and went with him.

—I had no idea I would end up there as well . . .

Father, having experienced war, was deathly afraid of moving and acting in groups.

—We were so desperate, we needed to say something. But even then, I couldn't bear to stand with that vanguard.

He was protective of the cows they brought to the protest. After they were done, he hired trucks to ferry them back to their pens. Still, Father could not withstand the losses, and except for the one with Mr. Nakcheon's sign on its neck and seven others, he had to sell off his cows at a 700,000 won loss each. Father's back bent dramatically then. He lost the straightness in his back, and one of the other protesters in the village was so enraged that he ended his own life. After the sale, the pen was quiet. Mr. Nakcheon fed them every morning, took a look around the empty pen, and one day, vanished. There were only eight cows in the pen, which meant Father could easily handle work on his own. But Father asked around everywhere for him. Just like he did when Third Brother failed his high school entrance exams and ran away from home. Mr. Nakcheon's whereabouts never became known. Father said, staring sorrowfully at the sign on Mr. Nakcheon's cow after coming back from a day of searching for him, He should've at least taken his cow . . .

My hand still on the door, I peered inside the abandoned house.

The room, which I thought would be empty, was filled with discarded things. There were spiderwebs here as well. The force of the door being opened made them tremble. One spider, at the end of a long thread, was making its way to another part of the ceiling. A few dried-up insects lay tangled in the webs. Feeling the webs on my face, I brushed them off. Through the webs I could see stacks of unopened boxes. What were these? I was about to reach for one when a wall of invisible webs blocked me and I stepped back. Mr. Nakcheon, who had lived here for a long time after Oong's departure, had left behind his raincoat and boots, which were still here underneath a thick layer of dust. There were spiderwebs across the openings of the boots. They say you could make clothing out of spider-webs . . . The ones that stuck to my hair were tough anyway. The dust seemed impenetrable, and I couldn't take my hand off the doorknob to step inside. When I closed the door, I heard rain falling. The smell of rain hitting the earth lunged at me before I could even turn around. Getting out of the rain, I reopened the door and stepped inside the abandoned house.

CHAPTER 3

INSIDE THE
WOODEN CHEST

What were all those boxes doing in here?

Stumbling inside to take refuge from the rain, I noticed a pile of boxes stacked in a corner. I swept cobwebs off my face as I approached them. Insects that were stuck on the webs, detecting my movement, struggled once more with urgency in their traps. The boxes, upon closer inspection, were mostly home deliveries. Most of them were intact and carelessly placed. They came in all sizes.

Why was there a stack of unopened boxes here?

Puzzled, I picked one up. Shampoo. Another one: vitamin D supplements. And this one? Protein powder. DÖHLER. Made from German peas, apparently. Did Father know what he was ordering? I found myself crouching before the boxes and looking at each item. Sneakers, coat hangers, an iron, a toothbrush holder. I recalled the hesitation of the delivery courier who had come after Father had left for his gukak people meeting. Not to mention the box with the frying pan set. Were these the deliveries Father had also insisted on receiving himself? The ones Mother was not supposed to know about? How was it possible to have all this delivered without her knowing? The sheer number of boxes stacked in the room was dizzying.

Was Father really . . . ?

Feeling like I was standing in front of a closed door, I tried imagining Father ordering these products, but all I could do was blink. Why did Father order these things only to toss them into a room filled with cobwebs? I couldn't understand, which made me reach out and touch the boxes again, just to make sure they were real.

This one is hand sanitizer, I said to myself. I ripped it open, and there was another box inside with the hand sanitizer container. It looked familiar; the brand was the same one at my house in Seoul. I ripped that box open, too. There were two big bottles, marked 1L, and two smaller ones, lying side by side. I picked up one of the big ones and gazed at it before reading the label. Used for sanitizing hands and skin, as well as keyboards and desks. 99.9% effectiveness. 62% ethanol. This product is eligible for exchanges or refunds according to the consumer arbitration resolution standards made public by the Fair Trade Commission. The words felt empty to me.

One night, back in Seoul, I'd woken up in the middle of the night and gazed at a home shopping host hawking hand sanitizer on TV. The host squirted and sanitized her hands countless times on camera, explaining why we needed it. Jabbering on about all the viruses our hands could spread. The host, enthusiastically presenting her product to people she couldn't see in the middle of the night. Listening to her made me feel incredibly lonely. About half an hour before the ordering window closed, I called the number on the screen and ordered hand sanitizer. And here in J— was an exact copy of the box that had been sent to my house two days ago. Perhaps Father had been watching the same program at the same time. I don't even remember where I put that box in my house.

I don't remember if I saw this in the newspaper or read it in a book, but I was reminded of what had happened to an old woman living in a elder care facility in America. She had a bank account that had a bit of cash and received her pension. When she first moved into the facility, her family and friends would visit often, but that soon petered out and she was left alone. Days of sitting by the window without speaking a single word. Then one day, someone called her on the phone. It was a telemarketer. The old woman, not quite understanding what the telemarketer was saying, listened to the end of his spiel. Feeling sorry for taking up his time, she bought whatever it was he was selling. This made the telemarketer call her whenever he had something new to sell. The old woman would nod and say a few words and at the end of the phone call, she would buy the product. This relationship went on for years, and the old woman's room filled up with this stuff. Her phone would've continued to ring if she hadn't passed away. After her death, they found her room almost bursting with unwrapped boxes of the things she had ordered.

Imagining Father watching the home shopping channels on TV at random hours of the day or night, pressing the numbers the program hosts told him to, made me feel depressed. Like stuffing rice without any banchan into my mouth. What could I possibly have to say for myself? For the past few years, I hadn't even called my parents regularly. Especially my father. And they couldn't come to see me, either; I wouldn't allow it. We'll meet some other time, some other time, another time . . . That's all I'd ever say. I'd already known. That someday I would regret every moment I didn't spend with Father when I had the chance. He never wanted anything special. He only wanted to be by my side. He wanted to see me and eat with me and fertilize the persimmon tree at my house for me, but I just kept saying, Another time. I no longer went down to J— to take a hike with him or go down to the town to shop for crabs or ride bikes with him to the ancestral cemetery. Or be there to listen when he took down his old drum, swept the dust off of it, and accompanied himself singing, The flowers they bloom on this hill and that . . .

There it is.

Amid the cobwebs and my disconcertion, I noticed that behind a box on the shelf was the wooden chest that had been in Father's store years before. Pushing aside the box in front of it, I tried reaching for the chest and bumped my head on the edge of the shelf. A sharp, unexpected pain. I was holding onto the chest with both hands so I couldn't rub the painful spot. I could feel my scalp beginning to swell. *Here it was all along,* I thought as I waited for the pain to subside.

Whatever it contained, the chest was heavy.

Whenever I thought about Father, I would think of this wooden chest. I had not seen it since I moved to the city, so I thought Father must have left the chest behind in the store when he had sold it, but I never got around to asking him. To think the chest was here all this time. I managed to get it down safely to the floor when the door to the cattle pen burst open and heavy rain pelted down. The rain so heavy it seemed about to pierce through the butterbur leaves in the vegetable patch.

This was the wooden chest Father used to keep his cash in when he ran his store. Sometimes there were just two 500 won notes in there, and once in a while, a 1,000 won note. Plus all those coins. The reason why I sometimes think of this chest is because of my memory of having fooled my Father when he had that store at the edge of the village. I'd think up things Father didn't know about and lie to him about needing them for school. Not notebooks, pencils, and crayons—things everyone knew about—but other things. The little girl crossing the railroad tracks think- ing of what odd thing she could ask her father for must've had a pretty determined look on her face. She'd blurt out she needed to buy cellophane or a book with a title that was hard to pronounce, and her father would give her a long look and open the wooden chest to give her the amount she needed. If the father had asked her about the thing or questioned if she really needed to buy it or said she had to treat it well and study hard, this chest would be forgotten by now. Whether he could tell the little girl's face was red from lying and her heart was pounding, the father would get up from washing the moonshine jar, wipe his hands on his shirt, and hand the girl the money she asked for. He would look into her eyes again, pat her head, and told her she would be late for school if she didn't run. What did the girl do with the money she'd received through lying? Did she spend it in a manhwabang reading manhwa comics? On dalgona toasted sugar candies made on the gas fire in front of the stationery store?

I couldn't remember what she did with it, but the guilt of having lied to my father remains. The lie refuses to disappear and I keep thinking about it. The fact that it wasn't just any lie, but ones based on the fact that Father never had the opportunity to go to school, makes the guilt heavier. I confessed this to a friend once, but she scoffed at me for being naïve. I hadn't expected that; my friend asked me if I really thought Father didn't know that I had lied. You mean, Father gave me the money even when he knew? I'd never considered such a possibility. My friend insisted Father had known all along. That most fathers in the same situation would've pretended to be fooled. That if our fathers were really that foolish, what would the world come to? My friend went on to say that it was simply the role of fathers to pretend to be fooled. And I found this idea that I hadn't really fooled my father oddly comforting.

The chest still had the hinges Father had fastened onto it. Also, the place where a lock could be slipped on. This chest had been here all this time— blackened by wear and time. I opened the lid. There was a lock placed on top of a pile of letters.

To think that the chest that had disappeared after Father had quit the store was full of letters. I took out the heavy lock weighing down the letters and placed it on the floor. The letters were divided into two bundles and tied together with rubber bands. I extracted the first letter from the pile and examined the envelope. It was addressed to Father in a thick felt-tip pen. A familiar, energetic handwriting. The address, written in the old style, was blotted in spots. I looked at the return address: Tripoli. In Libya? I knew I'd seen this handwriting before. It was Eldest Brother's.

These were letters Eldest Brother sent when he was stationed in Tripoli. I took a measure of the letters—what a great many he had sent to Father. I had had no idea. Eldest Brother and I had also corresponded a lot back then, which was why his handwriting was familiar. While he worked in Libya, I would drop by his company's overseas affairs office near Seoul Station every other week. I think toward the end, I was dropping by every week. My sister-in-law, who was busy raising their children, would have me pass on her parcels and letters to him and bring her his that had come to the office for her. Anything that wasn't meant for Seoul would've been sent by the office. The family of the company's workers who lived outside of Seoul would've sent their things to the Seoul office, which in turn would've given them this mail. The letters made me remember that during visits to J—, Mother would also give me parcels to pass on to Eldest Brother's company. I examined the other bundle of letters. These were the ones Father send to Eldest Brother. They had the address of the Seoul office and the old-style address of this house. The addresses were now faint on the envelopes. Father had written so many letters to Eldest Brother. Why were these bundles here? Did Eldest Brother gather them to return them to Father? Or perhaps Father himself brought them back when he visited Eldest Brother? There were other letters in the wooden chest aside from these two bundles. Mystified, I kept turning the envelopes in my hands until I finally remembered how Eldest Brother had returned my letters to me as well, secured with a rubber band like these bundles.

—Why are you returning these?

I had taken back my letters, feeling odd about the whole thing. Eldest Brother said he couldn't throw them away because they were too precious. Also, he added, you're a writer so you might need them someday . . . This was when I had managed to publish my debut but wasn't being commissioned for anything new, making my situation the same as before or after my deung-dan debut. Or not—when I applied for a job in Seulleung-dong at *Girls High School Times*, I was able to write that I had deungdan. Not that I had any idea if it helped me get the job. Where were my letters now that Eldest Brother had returned? He hadn't been wrong. Later on, while cleaning out my drawers, I read the letters he had given back to me and wrote a short story titled, "The Mountain Moves Farther Away." The story of when Eldest Brother worked at the Tripoli office, and he had gone on a business trip to the Waw Al Kabir Airport construction site. He wrote he had taken a plane from Tripoli to Sabha and gone 500 km by car to Waw. His driver was a Thai man, and Eldest Brother sat in the passenger seat. The whole route was through a desert, the same view in every direction. Sunlight refracted on the sand to create mirages. The repetitive view, he wrote, was soporific. Then, a sandstorm hit, and he was squinting through it when the car suddenly lurched forward. The Thai driver and my brother lost consciousness. There was no way to know what happened after the car flipped over. The reader could only know that when Eldest Brother opened his eyes, the sun threatened to pierce his vision. He remembered the exact make of the car he was riding: a Prince 3.0. He managed to get to his feet and stare out at the endless sand. Once he gathered his wits, he saw that the car had rolled three times over the sand and that it was standing on its side, broken beyond repair; the desert was so vast in every direction that it was impossible to tell where they had been coming from or where they'd been headed. The Prince 3.0 was completely wrecked except for the frame, but miraculously, the Thai driver and my brother were all right.

—It made me believe in God . . .

Thinking back to that moment made my brother's face look solemn. Eldest Brother, who would follow his wife to mass every Sunday and doze off, became a model congregant once he came back from his posting. I switched the Thai driver to a Bedouin who lived in the desert and changed my brother to a man named Yun. This was a story based on my brother's account of how the Thai driver, right before the car flipped, had said they were about 10 km away from their destination. But the sandstorm had covered their tracks, and they'd become disoriented. They only had a wireless transmitter for communication, but it had been jettisoned in the crash and was buried somewhere in the sand. The wild dogs would come at night, once the sun set around five o'clock. But worst of all, the temperature was set to drop precipitously. The car was a mess, they had no way to communicate, and time was running out—and then, Eldest Brother wrote, a miracle. Unbelievably, they saw a car in the distance, driven by a farmer. A spot at first, it came closer and closer, and Eldest Brother joked that he had fully expected Jesus to be sitting at the wheel. The farmer took the Thai driver and my brother to a police station in Waw, but I wrote the opposite of what actually happened. I had them right the car and flip a coin to determine which direction they would go, and that they would keep driving in that direction even if the landscape didn't change. By the end of my story, the characters ended up right where they started.

I was going through Eldest Brother's letters to Father as the sound of the rain grew louder. Rain, all of a sudden. I looked outside the house. The rain came down so hard that it sounded like the waves. I called Father, worried that he hadn't taken his umbrella with him. It kept ringing on his end but he didn't pick up. Hanging up, I stared out at the intense rain and opened the letter that was in my hands.

For the eyes of my father

My gaze lingered on these words written over two rows at the top of the old-fashioned, black-lined letter stationery. *For the eyes* . . . I hadn't read this expression in ages. A bygone phrase, I thought as my heart ached. Long ago, in a city named Tripoli, my brother's shoulders hunching over as he wrote these words on this stationery—I could almost see him. Eldest Brother wrote in large letters that took up two lines, then skipped another two lines to continue writing.

I hope this letter finds you well.

I arrived here safely, two days ago.
It took twenty hours by plane. We took off at Kimpo Airport,
then stopped in Alaska in America for three hours, flew to Frankfurt
in Germany, and waited there for six hours before arriving at the airport in
Tripoli. Even without the waiting time, we spent twenty hours on the plane.

Never even having been to Jeju Island, the thought of spending twenty hours on an airplane to come all the way to Northern Africa had seemed impossible, but it has happened.

This country is named Libya, and the office I am working in is in a city called Tripoli. Libya and Tripoli—these aren't easy names for us to pronounce, I know. Things are completely different here. Sandy deserts stretch across the entire country. There is no farming on the sand. Think of it, Father. A country where almost all of its land is unfarmable. Their farmable land is only 0.19% of their country. Unimaginable for someone from our country. But Father, deep beneath this sand, there's oil.

Does that make it even less imaginable?

I am attempting to explain to you where I have ended up, as I imagine you are wondering about me, but honestly, I don't know much about this country either. Since I am to live here for some years, I suppose I will have the chance to get to know it. Whenever I learn something new about it, I shall share it with you. Try to imagine it as best you can. Tripoli is the Seoul of Libya. This country's capital.

My life here is simple and so is my work, which is why I foresee I'll have more free time than I did in Seoul. I shall write to you often. So don't think of me as being far away. In Korea did I not live in Seoul and you in J—? Shall we say things have not changed much since then? Think of me as being just a little farther away than before.

Or this, perhaps: Somewhere in the world, there is a country called Libya, and your son is on a trip there, and he will come back soon. Nothing should be different just because I'm not in Seoul.

And Seoul still has the children's mother, Hon, and your third child. We worried about my wife living with Hon and Third Brother without me, and we discussed the issue. That she can rent out the house and stay with her mother if she wanted. My wife thought about it for a bit and said she was fine as things were. That, having been married as long as we have, it would be awkward to stay with her parents now. She added that the home would feel unbearably empty if Honnie and Third Brother were to leave, too. That their aunt and uncle leaving wouldn't be good for the children, either, having just been separated from their father. Financial reasons may be the biggest reason Honnie and Third Brother can't leave, but my wife did not put it that way. We have already taken out all the loans we possibly can to buy that apartment. How silly of me to trouble you with such details. But I'm only telling you because you seemed concerned that I hadn't discussed the current arrangements with my wife. In any case, there's no need to worry on that front.

What I hope for most is that you and Mother do not worry so much about me. This may be a faraway place, but I believe it to be where I belong for the time being. I shall do my best to serve in my role, and the only thing I ask of you and Mother is to stay as healthy as you have always been.

There are many things I wish to say, but I shall stop for now.

The office in charge will send out this letter on a plane flying tomorrow. I shall write to you every week in this manner. You do not have to answer them, Father. As long as these letters make you feel I am near, that is enough for me.

Take good care of yourself.

April 1989
Your son

P.S. Oh, and Father . . . The name of this country—Libya—a new colleague told me the other day that it means "the heart of the sea." I am, in other words, in the heart of the sea. Isn't that splendid?

Is that what Libya meant? I stared for a long time at his last words on the page: *Isn't that splendid?* Have I ever heard Eldest Brother say such a phrase? To say something was splendid was not part of his vocabulary. Eldest Brother, in his words and appearance and lifestyle itself, eschewed the ornamental. Having worked for forty years as a public servant and at a conglomerate, I had never seen him decorate himself with so much as a necktie pin. Because of the fold in the stationery, some of his letters looked split. There were yellow spots where the writing had gotten smudged, and the felt-tip pen was smeared here and there as if drops of water had been wiped away.

Droplets?

Ah . . . I felt my knees give way. Thinking they were Father's tears as he read the letter. I passed my hand over the places where the letters had been wiped. It was like seeing a photograph of a person's emotions. Imagining how long ago, a young man working overseas in a strange country, lying on his bed or the floor as he wrote a letter with a felt-tip pen to the father he left behind in his home country—somehow, this broke my heart. Which had until that moment been a forest of dried rushes, now scattering away in the wind and showing me the back of a young man. And his thick fingers holding his pen as he scrawled, *Isn't that splendid?*

I half-collapsed into a sitting position amid the dust and cobwebs of that abandoned house. Looking through the letters in the other bundle, I found the first one my brother would've received in Tripoli, Libya. It was easy to find; the envelopes were in chronological order.

Read this Seungyeop

How is your health

Glad you arrived safe
How tired you must be to be on a plane for so long
Don't worry about us here, your mother and I are fine
Wanted to write you back so I found this paper in a stationery store I visited
    for the first time in town
Never bought this before so I bought the same one you have

Reading Father's letter, with words spelled exactly as they sound, made me feel I was standing right in the heavy rain. I remembered his writing from the ledgers when he ran the store.

9 boxes of cigarettes.
7 sweet bean buns.
2 bottles of makgeolli

Father wrote letters only to accompany numbers. The only other time I would see Father's writing was after I'd left J— and was living with Eldest Brother. Father would post a parcel of rice for us and send us a telegram.

SENT RICE

Having lived with Eldest Brother since before he married, I was often home to receive many of Father's telegrams until we finally got a phone-line. The telegrams always were single sentences.

SENT KIMCHI
RECEIVE PERILLA
DUG SENT SWEET POTATOES

Father bought the same color felt-tip pen and stationery as Eldest Brother, and like him, used two lines at a time to write, spelling his words phonetically.

I am always splendid

Since becoming your father I have not been your strength only your
burden

But you were always splendid

Your place is where you are now

As you always have done your best in your place and I know very well
you will do fine

If only we could do more for your wife who takes care of your children
and Honnie and Third

I always knew she has a gentle soul but still

We are grateful to her always respect her and try hard and be loving
to her

Nothing more I would want

April 18, 1989
Your father

Before he left for Libya, Eldest Brother visited J— with his family. To
say goodbye to our parents. I was with them. As soon as he arrived in J—,
he visited Father's favorite butcher and bought three geun of beef divided
into three packets of a geun each. My sister-in-law was also born in J—.
Whenever she visited, she would see our parents first, and then try to slip
in a dinner or spend a night with her parents and return the next morning.
That day, we had a going away party for Eldest Brother at our house, and
before it got too late in the evening, she took their children to spend the
night at her parents'. The boisterous mood of the house immediately quieted
down. Even this far south, snow can fall as late as April when the pear blossoms bloom. It was a night when a wind too early to be called a spring
wind blew. There were probably new buds on the persimmon tree in the
courtyard. While Mother and my sister-in-law made dinner, Eldest Brother

helped Father and Mr. Nakcheon feed the cows. This was when Father had sold almost all his cows save seven and the cow with the "Kim Nakcheon" sign hanging around its neck. Mr. Nakcheon could manage the job on his own but Father and Eldest Brother were assisting him anyway. Eldest Brother handled the hose, Mr. Nakcheon spread out the feed so the cows could eat it easily, and Father pushed the cow droppings with a scraper to pile on one side. I watched Elder Brother silently. Because he didn't look like someone who had just come down from the city, he looked like a farmer who took care of cows. His silhouette moved busily in the dimming twilight. Has Eldest Brother always been so good with cows? I thought. The cows that would bray and take a step back if I ever approached them were chewing the feed that he had spread, tonguing the water he'd poured, and blinking their lashes as they allowed him to approach. Occasionally, Eldest Brother straightened his back and tapped the backs of the cows.

After my sister-in-law left for her parents', Eldest Brother took the beef he had bought in J— to our uncles' and Aunt's and went to the master bedroom to sleep. After I had done the dishes, I peeked in and saw Mother spread a blanket for him on the floor. I wiped my hands and went to the small room and eventually fell asleep as well. I don't know how much time passed. Something was knocking in the night. What was it? I wanted to open my eyes, but I was just too tired. Voices moved close then far away, making me wonder if I was dreaming or whether someone was visiting. The voices continued to come and go. They sounded like a lullaby, and I fell asleep as they drifted away and half awakened when they came close again, with occasional laughter, and as my eyelids were so heavy, I tried to go back to sleep until I realized, Wait . . . it's Father. And the laughter was from Eldest Brother. The house was open in all directions, which meant sound could enter not just from the doors or gates but from the courtyard, the side yard, and the backyard. Father and Eldest Brother were walking from the courtyard to the side yard to the backyard and around again, having a conversation. Whenever they passed the small room their voices would be louder, and when they turned the corner their voices would grow softer, then fall silent when they were in the backyard, and then come back when they entered the courtyard and passed the small room's window again . . . That's what they were doing. Awake now, I caught my father's low voice. He was saying, to his son who had come to say goodbye as he was going overseas for work, Can't you not go? This question surprised me so much that I sat up and approached the window to hear their conversation better.

—Why, Father?

—Thinking you won't be here makes me afraid.

—It's not as if I was living with you. Why would you feel afraid?

—This is different.

Father's voice had no strength.

—You won't be in the country.

—. . .

—I can't sleep.

—I'll be back in a few years, Father.

—I'm sorry.

—For what?

—If I were a richer father, you wouldn't have to go so far for work.

—This is company business. I'm going because I got a posting. It has nothing to do with how much money you have. It's not like I'm going there to do manual labor.

It wasn't. Eldest Brother had applied for the position in Libya because it would double his salary. He was planning to earn enough money to buy a place in the city. As long as he had a house, he'd be able to survive—that was his thinking. The voices went to the side yard and faded away. I waited for the father-and-son pair to come around again, keeping my ears open. The more I listened, the more it felt like their roles had been reversed. Eldest brother reassuring Father, and Father saying, How could I live without you . . . Their conversation went around in circles that night.

Eldest Brother must've written his many letters to lessen Father's worries. As reticent as he normally was, his efforts must've been a great comfort to Father.

Eldest Brother's letters always started with, *For the eyes of my father.* And his greeting was invariably, *I hope this letter finds you well.* Just those two lines made all the letters seem the same at first glance. Father's letters always began with, *Read this Seungyeop.* His greeting was always, *How is your health.*

Read this Seungyeop

How is your health

    Went to the bookstore today
    Never thought I would need to go to one in this lifetime but the books smelled good
    Wanted to know what this country Libya looked like maybe in a book
    No books there about Libya
    You said it was a place in the heart of the sea but to me Libya sounds like the name of a flower like salvia

    Asked Honnie to send me a book on Libya
    Just wanted to know what the country you live in is like

    Your mother often cries
    I think she misses you
    She says things I don't understand
    She says after crying the world is bright

    So do not worry

April 24, 1989
Your father

For the eyes of my father,

I hope this letter finds you well.

Life here is busy with me adjusting to things. Which is why I couldn't write you a letter last week. I found myself falling asleep as soon as I got home.

I kept thinking about you saying you went to a bookstore because of me. In J—, the bookstore I went to most often was Jeil Books in front of Honam High School. Was that the one you went to? I was imagining you inside.

Since turning thirty, I haven't been going to bookstores as often.

Hearing that Mother has cried worries me. Please tell her that I am doing fine, and she doesn't need to worry.
All I care about is that both of you stay healthy.
Be well . . .

May 6, 1989
Your son, Seungyeop

There's also a one-line letter sent by Father:

Read this Seungyeop

How is your health

Sowed the rice in the seedbeds today

April 29, 1990
Your father

Read this Seungyeop

How is your health

I have something to tell you

In order to write proper letters to you

I have been learning Hangul

Focusing on writing

It has been some months

A Hangul class was set up next to the agri high school and college students teach there for free, three Hangul classes a week

Such surprise

People younger than me who cannot read learning from scratch

That saying about looking at a sickle and not seeing the gi-ok character is real for them

The college kids surprised at my Chinese characters, ask me what they can ever teach me and why was I there

They said they had nothing to teach me so I told them about you and that I needed to write to my son but I don't want to make spelling mistakes

They had me sit apart and teach just me and gave me a book to learn

They say my reading is very good and I thought that is all thanks to my father

I learned *The Mirror that Lights the Soul* and *The Four Books* from your grandfather and recited them to them

It is fun

Asked your mother to join me but she said why learn something, what use was it now

That she lived fine without it

I said if she could write she could write you and that made her interested but she did not answer

I will keep talking to her

Your mother said when you were all learning to read she knew nothing and she is sad to this day she could not help all of you

Now she says there are no little children to help learn and so no reason to learn writing

Nothing more I would want

April 14, 1990
Your father

Read this Seungyeop

How is your health

Your mother heard from someone that Libya is hot enough to cook a chicken on a rock
    Wants to know if they have misutgaru powder there
    That you liked misutgaru in cold water on a hot day
    Wants to know if we send you misutgaru can you get it

Nothing more I would want
As long as you are healthy somewhere under this sky

June 5, 1990
Your father

For the eyes of my father,

I hope this letter finds you well.

I don't know where the time goes. While I'm supposed to have more time to myself than I did in Seoul, the week flies by and soon I'm told it's letter-collecting day. Last week, I had all sorts of business which made it difficult to write to you, but this week I am determined not to become lazy about it. I am sorry I skipped a letter despite having promised I would write every week.

You must be done with the spring planting?

Mother was probably busy bringing you meals at the rice paddy and your face must've gotten very tan standing in the sun, setting down the lines of seedlings.

Since I was a child, I've always liked planting season. It was fascinating to me how when we were done, the rice paddy would be a lush green. When I saw people in the morning lined up in the water getting ready to plant, I would wonder when they would finish with such a wide field . . . But when I came back from school, the vast rice paddies would be neatly planted. That's how I learned what surprising results can come from people working together. If only all efforts by a gathering of people, working without rest for a set time, would have outcomes as clear—how satisfying that would be. It didn't even have to be our rice paddy. Standing with the Irrigation Association in the middle and green rice paddies stretching away on either side would give me strength, a feeling of safety and satisfaction.

As I told you before, this land is 98% sandy desert, and there is no place here for the kind of rice farming that you are used to.

Please tell Mother she needn't send the misutgaru.

You don't have to worry about food.

There are many Korean workers here.

We live like students in a dormitory. Cooks from Korea were also sent with us. They make us three Korean meals a day. We're eating as we would eat in Seoul. The set times for waking up and lights out also remind me of my military service days. It's still a bit odd for me, which is why I sometimes find myself wide awake for a while after lights out, but I'm sure I'll get used to it. I feel that this regular routine is going to be excellent for my health.

Father.

I know I am far away, but if something happens at home, don't hesitate to tell me.

You don't have to keep it in your heart all to yourself.

I shall write you again soon.

June 12, 1990

Seungyeop

As I read Eldest Brother's letter, I recalled the green rice paddies stretching far on either side of the Irrigation Association dyke. I had been so preoccupied with the morning glories that had bloomed after dewfall or seeing whether the strawberries hidden in the bushes had ripened yet, but Eldest Brother had gazed into the distance, feeling like he held great strength in his hands—to think we had such different thoughts while looking at the same scenery. Father, upon learning Eldest Brother was to live in a country called Libya in central Northern Africa, collected facts about the place and made them his own, like he would carefully plant seed potatoes. These feelings, which I hadn't known about until now. This is why Father had asked me all those years ago to get him books about Libya. When I was getting these books, Father had been attending classes taught by volunteers to learn how to write proper Korean. Perhaps this was why the sentences in his letters, which used to be short and simple, began to have more complex structures, and punctuation appeared.

Read this, Seungyop

How is your health?

Joyful news

A cow had calves yesterday

Triplets
This is so rare I did not even expect it
I've raised many cows but this is the first it's happened
We've had the occasional twin
The cow had a strange pregnancy shape so I wondered if it would be twins
But triplets were unexpected
I'm writing to you to tell you right away

They were born one by one, a half-hour apart
Smaller than a single newborn calf but all three are healthy
Still overwhelmed because triplets are a first
But as I write this, I find I am overjoyed

Calves as soon as they are out can walk
The triplets did so too
They are like deer
Before the mother could lick away the afterbirth they stood up
Wobbling walk
Each of them spreading their leg to get up made me burst out laughing

Oh Seungyeop
I haven't forgotten what you told me when you married
    You bought me seven cows and said you would not be free when you're
married and that I should raise these cows to help with the tuition of your
siblings. You said it was money you saved while working in the
neighborhood administrative office by day and going to college by night
and right before entering your big company

I raised my head. Eldest Brother bought Father cows when he married? I felt a ringing in my head, which made me move my gaze from the
letter to the outside. Thunder rolled over the sound of rain. The rain itself
was so loud now that it felt like the vegetables in the patch were chattering.

Things I hadn't known about until now. Looking back, Father had indeed started raising cows right after Eldest Brother had married, and to think it never occurred to me to question how Father suddenly came up with seven cows. I felt like a butterbur leaf in the vegetable patch being hit by the relentless rain. Was this why he kept those seven cows even after the fiasco with the beef prices? How could I have realized so late that deep inside Father's guilt toward Eldest Brother were these seven cows?

I do not feel good about it

You were born to a poor father, left home at an early age, settled in a strange city where you made your own rice and raised yourself, and if that wasn't enough, you were so worried about us even as you were about to start your own family

It breaks my heart to think of you so and I am sorry

The only thing I could do was not shrink the number of cows

I tried very hard not to have fewer than the seven you bought me

That's why I rode on that cultivator with Mr. Nakcheon to go to the rallies

I tried to do everything I could to keep the number of cows you gave me

Even if I couldn't have more I tried at least not to have fewer

Now that the triplets are born your cows are not seven but ten

If you ever feel lost or angry over there, think of that

That you have ten cows here

Their eyes open wide and shining and waiting for you

I hope this can be a comfort to you

As I always say

Nothing more I would want

As long as you are healthy somewhere under this sky

September 4, 1990
Your father

For the eyes of my father,

I hope this letter finds you well.

I was very surprised at the news that a cow has given birth to three calves. How extraordinary that such things happen in this world. After reading your letter, I asked around and apparently it is difficult to get triplets from a cow even after implanting fertilized eggs. You must've used artificial insemination methods on them like usual, so how did you end up with three calves? It makes me happy just imagining them staggering to their feet and taking their first steps. And your joy is so palpable, I feel it as my own.

Father.
Aiding the birth of one calf is difficult enough, but to think you received three of them—I am so proud of what you did.
But Father.
The cows in the pen, they are not mine. They are yours.

Thinking of the cows multiplying in your pen gives me strength and encouragement. I know how it was always your dream to have all of us obtain university degrees. When you sold your field on the mountain to pay for my college tuition, I took that money and made a vow. That I would help in any way I could to obtain your dream.

Father.
You are right. I am the eldest son of a country farmer with five younger siblings I did worry much when I married. As you know, the concept of money in a place like Seoul is very different from what it is in the country, and I could not afford to set up Honnie and Third Brother separately. Thankfully, my wife is also an eldest daughter from the countryside with many younger siblings, and she was understanding about having the two of them living with us.
Father, you do not have to be sorry.

By gifting you the cows, I had freed myself from the obligation of having to pay for my siblings' tuitions. With just a few measly cows. You had no idea I had such a selfish scheme in mind.

Father.

The reason I could do so was possible only because you were my father. In J——, people would occasionally ask who my father was because they wanted to know which family I belonged to, and I would say your name and they would all go, Ah . . . And treat me as politely as they would treat you. Seeing everyone turn extra polite and friendly when I mentioned your name was something that always made me proud you were my father. I knew that such a father would admirably raise those cows to achieve his dream. And that's how I liberated myself. You built the pen on the vegetable patch, you got a government loan to increase your herd by the dozens, and morning, noon, and night you held your scraper and put your boots on and worked in the hot breath of the beasts and their droppings. It made me worry, whenever I visited, that I had brought you into a life of hardship because I had recommended this work. I know how hard you work, Father. There were times when three of your children were in college at the same time, but you always gave us the money on time, and I was always awed by this. You've fought so hard for those cows—how could you say that they are mine now.

I spend my days not in the worksites themselves but in the offices in Tripoli. Most of my work here is contacting the Seoul office and keeping them informed, nothing too strenuous, and I'm adjusting well. So please don't worry about me.

September 8, 1990
Seungyeop

Read this, Seungyeop

How is your health?

Only a few days until Chuseok
Cold at dawn now, which made us take out thick blankets
The summer birds are busying themselves, ready to leave for other places

No matter what you say, those cows are your cows
Sadly one of the calves is blind
It wasn't able to walk forward and kept bumping its head on the wall so I looked and it can't see
Because it can't see it can't latch on to the mother and while the three were born at the same time, it already is smaller than the other two
I keep worrying because it can't see and the mother must also worry because it keeps licking the blind one more than the others, it will still grow quickly
Just like you all

Nothing more your father would want
Be healthy wherever you are under this sky
And come back soon

Your mother wants to know if you can eat songpyeon for Chuseok
Your mother says not to worry at all about here and rest easy about us

September 12, 1990
Your father

For the eyes of my father,

I hope this letter finds you well.

Today I wanted to share with you some happy news.
Our CEO has informed us they've successfully opened a weekly airline route between Seoul and Tripoli. Until now, landing times for airplanes have been all over the place. The CEO has promised us that if the airline company

does not have airplanes flying at least once a week between our countries, he will charter a plane if necessary. A flight from Seoul every week! The reason everyone here is overjoyed is not just because the materials we need will be sourced easier but also because of the prospect of fresh ingredients for Korean food coming in every week. It may not be enough to be truly satisfying, but we are happy about the variety of Korean food to come.

I contacted the overseas affairs office at the company today, and he assured me they will send over songpyeon this Chuseok. A feat made possible because of the new airline route. My colleagues who've been here longer tell me I'm a man of good fortune to eat songpyeon on Chuseok. They say it won't arrive on the day, but perhaps a little before. Frozen, but the cook here will heat them up. So do reassure Mother that I'll be eating songpyeon here as well, and she needn't worry about me.

Father.

Now that we've mentioned food.
I am supposed to make bibimbap for my colleagues on a Sunday next month. The cook, who's been here for two years now, has never seen downtown. We told him we'd take care of ourselves on that Sunday while he takes in the scenery. Being the newbie, I ended up volunteering to make a bibimbap lunch for that day. I picked the dish because I have great memories of eating your bibimbap, but then I realized, I had only eaten it but never made it myself. Not to mention this is a hot country, and they don't have the variety of vegetables Korea has. Writing this makes my mouth water from remembering the radish bibimbap you would make us. Having made a promise before assessing the material realities of the situation, I now feel a bit sick.

Was there a special method you used in making your bibimbap?
I just laughed writing this letter.
The things I ask my father for.

I am doing fine, so don't worry about me.

I hope you take care of yourself.

September 16, 1990

Seungyeop

Read this, Seungyeop

What a powerful man your boss is

    To make an air route appear where once there was none

    The thought of a Seoul plane going once a week to where you are

reassures me

    That the plane will also take songpyeon makes me think

    What wonderful times we live in

    Bibimbap is easy

    Your mother lets me use the sesame oil only when I am making

bibimbap

    Sesame oil used to be precious, just one drop filled a room with savory

fragrance

    Sesame oil these days isn't the same

    The way they make it is different perhaps

    If you want to make good bibimbap

    Good sesame oil is essential but do they have it there?

I put down the letter I was reading.

It was true. When we were young, Father often cooked for us. He made jajangmyeon black bean noodles, or marinated pork and roasted it on the grill. Occasionally, at mealtimes, we didn't have enough banchan, and I think Mother may have persuaded Father to make bibimbap. Mother said the same thing as Eldest Brother. That when Father mixed the rice, it was more delicious than any other bibimbap. Mother would place the biggest pot in the house in front of Father and over the rice, he'd place inside lettuce in the spring, young radish in the summer, sweet potato sprout kimchi in the fall, and aged kimchi in the winter. Father silently mixed the rice. He spooned in gochujang paste, sliced hot chili peppers, some strong doenjang paste if we had it, and used chopsticks if he was afraid of damaging the radish too much, carefully stirring the ingredients together. Yes, that was what he'd do. Father's bibimbap was especially tasty, and we would hurriedly scrape at the pot before it disappeared on us altogether. But that was all because Mother would break out the sesame oil only when Father was making the bibimbap.

Had it been a dream? But I remember looking up at the clock just a few nights ago, noting that it was two in the morning. I lay in Mother's bed and came out to the living room to lie by Father's bed, then went to the small room and sat at the desk and came out to the kitchen to stand about, and then opened the fridge door and took out the container with the dotorimuk. For Father who didn't want to eat anything, I'd made dotorimuk with the leftover powder from my first night back in J—, but Father hadn't even touched it, pouring it into this container instead. I put it on the table and regarded the living room where Father was. He looked peaceful under the nightlight. With a spoon, I tapped the dotorimuk. It had gelled and was cold. I only remember taking up a spoonful of it. The spoon was left on the table—I was eating the dotorimuk with my hands. The tabletop was getting messy and clumps of dotorimuk clung to my clothes. Then Father was reaching out with his stub-index finger hand, wiping my mouth, putting the empty container and spoon into the sink, wiping the tabletop with a cloth, and quietly sitting down next to me. When Father reached for my hand, I whipped it back from the tabletop, thwarting him. My fingers with their crushed, chestnut-colored dotorimuk. Father sat there next to me, hunched over. Until I came back to my senses and told him, Please go back to bed, Father.

I remember a certain winter night.

In the winters, snow would fall for four straight days on J——. Since becoming a writer, I've written many variations of this line. That J—— was a city where snow fell for four straight days in the winter. Winds blowing from the fields would follow the railways and dykes and over the rice paddies and reach the courtyard and porch. Sometimes I woke to the sound of our window-panes rattling in their frames. Winter nights where the shadows of the falling snow scattered across my room door as I watched from under my blanket. The kind of night where Father's covered rice bowl was wrapped in a blanket and placed on the warm spot of the heated floor, the rest of his meal prepared on a separate foldout table. Taking out the sesame oil when Father made bibimbap wasn't the only thing Mother did—roast seaweed wafer appeared on the table only on nights when Father came home late after socializing at gatherings with the other men of the village. Father, when he was young. In a good mood, slightly drunk, he came through the gate and took a moment to bend over and push the shoes that were being snowed on under the porch, sweep the courtyard of snow, and only then enter the house, accompanied by cold air. Even as Mother complained of his coming and going late at night, she would draw back the protective screen over his meal and get his rice from under the blanket over the warm spot on the floor, serving up a plate of roasted seaweed later marinated with sesame oil and cut into flat rectangles. The savory fragrance wafted through the house and we would gather silently around Father's table. Only Eldest Brother, who was treated as an adult ever since he was a child, did not come to him, sitting alone in the small room instead. Father would place some rice on a piece of seaweed, roll it, and feed it to us one by one. When Mother scolded us for eating food meant for Father, he assured her he already had dinner. Which Mother probably knew already. Despite this, Mother would always prepare a meal with roasted seaweed for him on late cold winter nights.

I've written about this several times—snow on a late winter night, my father having come home and wrapping rice in seaweed, feeding us one by one as we sat in a circle around his little foldout table. The simile used was different every time, something to the effect of woodpecker chicks being fed by their father in an oak tree. I still remember the delicious taste of that roasted seaweed in my mouth as I waited for my turn again. A magazine interviewer asked me once if I thought of myself as happy, and the question triggered that memory, so I replied that receiving Father's seaweed-wrapped rice had made me very happy. Eldest Brother made a scrapbook panel out of that interview, showed it to me, and then stood it with the others against the shelves in the small room. Father read it and asked me, You were happy then?

—Yes, Father.

He laughed. Of that moment I'd said was a happy moment, Father said he had been terrified. That it frightened him as a young man to watch his children eat.

—Frightened you? Why?

My mystified expression made the smile fade from his face.

—You think it can be explained?

As Father retreated, Mother tried to help.

—Think of what appetites you all had. How long has it been since we didn't have to worry about food? At the time, we ate today while worrying about tomorrow. I'd open the rice jar to get rice for dinner and see the bottom of the jar—feeling my heart drop in my chest. To see more and more of the bottom of that jar, and six children with good appetites running up to you. Who wouldn't be frightened . . .

When Mother tried to explain Father's thoughts, she often perked up as she unburdened her own fears.

—But we couldn't be frightened all the time—where's the life in that? Sometimes you would frighten us, sometimes you would give us courage . . .

When Mother asked Father, Wasn't that so? Father answered, Without a doubt. I looked at Father then. Was that true? Were our appetites not just frightening but also something that gave him courage? Unlike my perked-up mother, my heart felt heavier. It was a shock to me to hear that in his youthful days, our appetites had frightened him. For the first time, I thought about Father's boyhood, his youth, and his early adulthood. What he must've felt when he lost his parents to a disease within two days of each other, when he lived through the war, when he married Mother without ever having seen her face, when Eldest Brother was born. I tried to think of his years living as the eldest son of a household after his older brothers died, but it was difficult. Not a single photograph was left from that time of Father's life. All I knew about it was from the Father in Aunt's memories or Mother's stories.

This was also when I realized I had never, until that moment, regarded Father as an individual person in his own right. Being so used to having regarded him as a farmer, part of a generation that lived through war, or someone who raises cows, I was vague on the details of Father as an individual and hadn't even tried to find out more. His occasional grumblings of resentment toward his father for never having sent him to school suddenly weighed on my heart. As each of his children entered school, moved up in grades, and eventually left home for university, what had been on Father's mind?

Had he ever had a day without dread or fear?

I realized another thing as I read the musty letters I had discovered inside the wooden chest in the abandoned house full of cobwebs. That the reason why I never felt from Father what might be called patriarchal pressure, or the reason I felt closer to Father than to Mother was because of the fear of the world Father had hidden inside him. That, fearful of so many things, Father dealt with the world by not saying much. The thing Father said the most was, Got nothing to say. Got nothing to say . . . When something joyful happened, he expressed his feelings with, Got nothing to say, and when something painful happened it was also, Got nothing to say. When he couldn't even say he had nothing to say, Mother would interject as if she were his conscience. Saying, The thing about that, actually . . .

Read this, Seungyeop

Winter is here.

You said it was summer all year where you are so you must not see snow.

They say there's a desert called the Land of Death in that country. I am
sure there's a reason why they call it the Land of Death.

I learned only today.

That Koreans are working there because a large lake was discovered
under the Sahara Desert and they are building a large pipeline to bring up
that water.

To think there is water from 10,000 years ago in the desert is hard to
imagine. It must be a great amount of water. I tried and failed to imagine
how much but it still fills the heart with wonder. They say the land is
mostly desert but if the pipeline is successful does the land turn into
farmland?

It is astounding to think such a large construction is occurring
somewhere in this world.

I was born in this village and lived here only.

When I was younger I went about a lot but it was to search for another
way to live and I had no peace in my heart and that's why I have no
memories of that time.

But I still remember the first time I went to Seoul. Unforgettable.

I realized then that we had to stay in the village if I wanted you all to
finish school and survive. After having you all it seemed to me that
surviving was not everything. I wanted you all to continue with your
studies. That became my goal. I had to make money for that. I bought a
train ticket and went up one night to Seoul where I knew no one because I
figured money gathered where people gathered. There must be a place
that would give me a job. My only thought was that it had to be better
than farming.

That was 1960. Third Brother was born in April of that year. How could a baby's eyes be so bright? Third Brother was like that since birth. On his fourth day he opened his eyes and looked right into mine with those black and bright pupils and my heart jumped. I married before any of my friends. Suddenly I had three sons before turning thirty. Before Honnie was born it made me frightened whenever I saw my three sons together. How could someone like me who has never been to school raise these children properly? The thought was heavy on my heart at night and I would have to sit up.

I had to make money. I thought I would go where money was common. I had to leave this house and do anything it takes to bring home money. Thinking I was going to leave I fixed the roof and the porch and emptied the outhouse.

Maybe you knew what I was up to because you followed me around for all of it.

Calling Father, Father. I still remember. I was scything grass on the dyke next to the railroad when you came home from school carrying your bookbag and calling Father, Father and running into my arms and burying your face in my chest and when I asked what had happened you were panting and said Father you were here and smiled a big smile. After you caught your breath you sat down on the pile of cut grass and told me not to go anywhere.

You knew what I was thinking. You said if I stayed you would do better in school. That you would teach Second math. You said you could not concentrate in school these days. That you were afraid your father would run off somewhere and you kept staring out the window. You said when I wasn't home it was hard to fall asleep. We both sat on the dyke and watched the train pass by on the railroad. You said you would grow up and become a lawyer. That you promised mother that.

You were like that from the beginning.

Since you were little you would stick to me whenever I came back from somewhere. I still remember the first time you said Father to me. Ah . . .

ppa. It's when none of my friends were married. I had married early and I had you who called me Ah . . . ppa. It was strange to me at first. My friends were free and they could go anywhere and do whatever they wanted but after you came into my life that was hard for me. When I wanted to go out with my friends I would unhook your wriggling fingers from my clothes and walk out the gate and you would call Ah . . . ppa, appa . . . and start crying. When you got a little bigger you went Appa, appa and followed me everywhere. When you were starting to walk and I sat on the porch you stumbled out of your room and came next to me and when you could walk better you came down to where I was shoveling manure and went Appa. You called for Appa when you were sitting and you called for Appa when you fell. Once you could walk well you came to whichever room I was in and called out Appa, appa as you followed me wherever I went. When my friends were waiting for me on the riverbank you held my hand and tried to get up with me and grabbed my arm or leg and tried to leave with me. I managed to separate from you and would meet my friends by the bridge or downtown. When you followed me it was nice and also a nuisance. When I shook you off and went out I always felt I could hear you call Appa, appa and I would look around me and far away. It did not feel good having left you behind. Sometimes I left my friends and went back home to see you again.

Father married Mother when he was nineteen.

Those who had fled the South Korean army to hide in the mountains would come down to the village not just to steal food but also to kidnap women. Mother was born in Nungmweh, a mountain village near the Galjae Pass. As unmarried women kept getting kidnapped into the mountains, my mother's brother decided he needed to marry off his sister, and my father happened to catch his eye. After some consideration, he arranged for his younger sister and my father to be wed. Born in Nungmweh, Mother walked far past Iseoleoji down a winding path away from Jinsan-ri soon after turning seventeen to come to this house and wed Father.

—Without ever having seen his face.

Mother occasionally said this with a sigh as if she couldn't believe she'd done such a thing. I couldn't believe it, either. How was that possible? My uncle introduced my father to my maternal grandmother as a diligent, unpretentious man who had lost his parents at a young age and was managing to get by with one ox. The only thing on my grandmother's mind was to hide Mother, who was conspicuously tall, from the marauding mountain people, and she quickly made arrangements.

My maternal uncle and father were friends and also worked together. They transported wood cut down by woodcutters on an ox-led wheelbarrow to the lumberyard and split the profits. Father had an ox and uncle knew woodcutters. Father's ox worked a plow by day and dragged a wheelbarrow by night. Woodcutting was forbidden, which meant fines or even jail time if they were ever caught. Which was why it mostly happened in the night.

—That poor ox dragged so much wood it almost fell back . . .

Whenever Father spoke of his first ox, his expression turned sorrowful as if the ox were right in front of him.

—I've sinned so much. Worked it to death in the day, and then dragged it around at night so it couldn't sleep . . .

On one of these nights, coming back from offloading another load of lumber, my uncle mentioned the idea of marriage between my father and his sister. Father didn't pay him much heed, but Aunt took the proposal to heart. Her first thought was that if Father had a wife, she would take on the housework, and that would make the household more presentable. My uncle said his sister was still young but very steadfast and grounded. That whatever household she ended up in, she would raise it from the ashes. Anxious that the mountain people hiding away from the South Korean army would kidnap his sister, he said he could let my father sneak a look at her, and this was how Father got to see Mother once before marrying her.

At nineteen years old, Father hid in the bamboo grove behind the hut where my mother's family lived and saw Mother. An innocent seventeen year old at the time, Mother was in the backyard of the hut, opening an earthen jar and about to ladle some soy sauce into a sauce dish when she saw a white cloud reflected on the surface of the sauce. My seventeen-year-old mother looked up at the sky to see the actual white cloud. It was beautiful. She sang a song. Here comes a young lady in spring, wearing her new clothes . . . She hummed the parts she didn't know the lyrics of and sang the parts she knew. A white cloud for her veil and wearing dew pearls on her shoes. As her suntanned face sang this song, Father listened quietly in the bamboo grove. When the wind passed through the grove her voice became distant, which is why he wished the wind would stop. When the singing stopped, Father sneaked another look at her. Mother was staring up at the sky fleeced with white clouds, saying something to it. Silence was all around. Mother, she was saying to the sky. Mother. Mother, I don't want to get married. The nineteen-year-old boy hiding in the bamboo grove heard this lament and grew anxious. He wanted to come out of the grove and take Mother to see his ox. He wanted to take her to the field he planned to buy once he had saved enough money. He wanted to tell her how he had pierced the septum of his ox and hung the nose ring and how obediently that ox followed him about. He wanted to tell her how much rice and barley a double crop of the fields he wanted to buy would yield. His face turned hot with the prospect of telling her.

The back of my hand was itching; the flesh between the thumb and index finger was swollen. Small insects had crawled out of the pile of letters when I took them out of the chest, and they must've bitten me. Suddenly conscious of the itchiness made it unbearable, and I raised my hand to put some saliva on it when I stopped. This was something my father would do. Whether he was bitten by leeches, got stung by a bee that had wandered into the cattle pen, or got welts from whacking the grasses in the cemetery, he would apply saliva to the affected area. A habit since childhood—first aid before first aid. Even when I told him he needed to sterilize the area and go to a hospital, he stuck with his habits.

After fanning the letters to shake off any bugs hiding in the creases, I opened the next letter.

For the eyes of my father,

I hope this letter finds you well.

Winter should be coming soon where you are, and the preparations must keep you busy. You will need to repaper the windows, and more than anything else, make enough kimchi to last the season. Will Mother do two hundred heads of cabbage this year as well? I remember the rows and rows of cabbages she would harvest from the vegetable patch. She would haul them onto a cart and wash them and salt them . . . Kimchi-making looked like a whole construction site. I still remember how surprised my wife was when Mother sent us a large amount of kimchi the first winter we were married. Mother always said, Eldest Brother loves kimchi . . . Thanks to this, we would have plenty of aged kimchi up until summer and have kimchi stew whenever we wanted.

As you've said, Father, there is no winter here. No winter, and therefore no snow. It's hard to imagine when you're from a country like Korea that has four distinct seasons, but it's equally hard for people in this country to imagine snow falling.

There are also very few places in the world where it snows as much as it does in J—. Talking about snow makes me think of the winter days I spent as a child. Once the snow begins to fall there, it falls for days. The snow you swept into a pile by the well would be so big that it didn't even all melt until well into spring. But thanks to you, Father, we never had to worry about there being too much snow. It would all be swept by the time we woke up the next morning. When it was too much to sweep with a broom, you watched it come down for a while and then stomped down a three-pronged path through it first. One to the well, one to the outhouse, and one out the gate. I still remember those three paths in the snow. Not to mention the sight of you sweeping and sweeping the snow as it continued to fall. One winter dawn, I saw you were sweeping by yourself and went outside to help you, but you said I would catch a cold, that I should go back inside. Go back, you said, it's too cold.

Thinking of that now in this hot country is like feeling a cool breeze on the nape of my neck.

The three-pronged path you made in the snow is as clear in my memory as the cover of a Christmas card. My younger siblings, up much later, would go to the outhouse and the well and wash their faces and go to school. On days there was too much snow, you would clear a path from the gate to the main road, just wide enough for a person to walk . . .

In the winter, Father would sweep the snow as soon as it started falling. Snowflakes would pile up in his hair and then on his eyebrows. Not pausing to brush off, Father continued to bend over and make paths through the whiteness that had descended overnight. Just so that in the morning we could walk down those paths. When we woke and looked out into the courtyard, the three-pronged path would be there in the courtyard no matter how much snow had fallen. I had forgotten about this path until now, and Eldest Brother's large handwriting felt like they were breaking into snowflakes and scattering away.

I saw Father failing to spare the rod just once. Perhaps it was because it was just once, but I never fail to remember that happening. And when I do, the memory turns itself into words. Often, at that.

When Third Brother failed his high school entrance exams and ran away from home, Father let go of all work on the fields and searched high and low for him. If anyone ever mentioned they'd seen him, he would run there no matter how far it was. The late admission exams were about to be held, but when it looked like Father might not find him in time, he grew ill from exhaustion. Third Brother had astonishingly made it all the way to Muju. At the mention of someone saying they had spotted a boy who looked a lot like Third Brother hanging out with a group of delinquent boys, Father bolted upright from his sickbed and went straight there. He nabbed Third Brother from a bunch of older boys who had grown their hair long, wore silly wide pants, and slouched around with their hands in their pockets. Father brought him home on a winter night.

—Let's eat.

Sitting across from Third Brother who hadn't been home for a long time, Father mixed his rice into his stew. Too nervous to eat, Third Brother put his spoon down but Father told him to eat up. Third Brother, sitting across from a father who didn't berate him or say a word, ate ravenously. Eldest Brother sat at his desk in the small room and didn't come out. After he was finished, Father took down something wrapped in newspaper from the top of the wardrobe and said to Third Brother, Let's go, and led the way. Worried, Mother followed suit, and so did I, clutching Mother's hand. The snow that had started to fall at sunset was deep by then. Father walked on the snow, followed by Third Brother, and then Mother and me. Life is full of the unimaginable. The newspaper-wrapped bundle was a bunch of wooden sticks. Father took Third Brother into the abandoned house and locked the door. Until that moment, Father had never even raised his voice at us, much less used a rod, which was why not even Mother could've imagined Father would break every single one of those sticks whipping Third Brother. It also must've been unimaginable for Father that Third Brother would fail his high school entrance exam. To him, Third Brother was good at everything, so much so it was hard to decide what his future should be. Every teacher in school wanted him for something. The music teacher wanted him to be a percussionist in the school band, and the volleyball coach wanted him to become a volleyball player. He was also a top student who never placed below first in his class—and to think that students who had placed lower had managed to be successful where he had failed. Perhaps it was that last, very unimaginable situation that had been so unacceptable to him and made him run away. Mother gripped the locked door and pleaded with Father that he mustn't hurt the boy when he was about to sit for late admissions, and I was so surprised at this side of Father I'd never seen before that I fell on my behind in the snow-covered yard, bawling my eyes out.

—You ran away because you failed some silly test?

Third Brother tried to hold back his tears as he took the blows.

—Keep throwing your life away whenever you fail from now on.

—. . .

—Will you leave again?

The morning Third Brother limped to Jeonju to sit for the late admission exams, the snow fell heavily. Father woke up even earlier and swept the courtyard clean. All the way to the bus stop where Third Brother would take the bus. Father warmed Third Brother's shoes in front of the kiln, wrapped Third Brother's neck in a woolen scarf, and put gloves on his hands. In a low voice, Father said, It's all right if you fail the exam. If it doesn't work out, you can try again next year, so come home right after. Third Brother limped on board the bus. From his window seat, he bowed to Father, who stood next to the road.

Listening to the torrential rain—now as rough as falling rain could ever sound—I shook off bugs that were hiding in the folds of Father's next letter. I hadn't been bitten again, but I felt itchy all over.

Father's letters, which had been short at the beginning of Eldest Brother's posting, were growing longer and longer. They now filled one whole side of the paper and continued on the reverse.

I left home while you were at school.

I knew I couldn't leave if I saw your face.

I rode the night train to Seoul and got off at Seoul Station. I left at 9:00 p.m. and it was dawn when I arrived. You asked at your university graduation if that was my first time in Seoul, and the reason I could not answer you was because I had been to Seoul when I was younger. I never told anyone what happened then.

I got off at Seoul Station and went to the bathroom and was shocked. Beggars were sleeping on newspapers in the bathrooms. The smell of waste was so bad that I covered my nose. I thought Seoul would be different, but Seoul Station was full of the kind of people who lived under the bridge in J—. The benches in the waiting area were full of people sleeping with newspapers for blankets. I tried not to gag as I used the toilet and came out to the station plaza where at that hour disabled veterans had their stumped limbs out as they begged for money. Seoul was disappointing. I had come to shake off my poverty but Seoul that dawn was a shabbier mess than anywhere else I had known. I stood there not knowing what to do when the sun rose. In the weak light I saw the clock tower I had only heard about and behind it the sight of Namsan Mountain. The faraway sight reassured me a little. I looked closely at the people who pulled wheelbarrows with tires. Because I needed work as well. The wheelbarrows were piled so high with vegetables and whatnot that they looked ready to fall over so I helped one of them who was having a hard time. The people whipping by on bicycles at Seoul Station Plaza made me think Seoul may not be that different from other places. I saw people taking down bags from the train and putting them onto rickshaws. I looked closely at the rickshaw drivers. Because I may have to become one of them.

The company you joined later has a tall building in front of Seoul Station that blocks the view of Namsan Mountain. I think this was before that building was built.

A man and a woman who looked like a married couple had parked their cart and were selling cooked eggs in square bread. It could not cover the smell of something rotting. But I was curious how much they made selling that. I tried to forget my hunger. There was some money in my pocket but I was not going to spend it unless I had earned some. It was the only way I could survive.

I had thought that wherever there were many people there would always be work but now that I was in a city where I did not know anyone, it was hard to even take a single step.

On the first day I wandered. I crossed the street from Seoul Station and walked down into the city. Later I learned that place was Myeongdong and Namdaemun Market. There were more people than buildings. Many selling things but also gangs of children and disabled veterans sitting on the street. Of course I was as pitiful in their eyes as they were in mine. I walked in the crowd all day and went into a place that sold agar in soybean broth and had a bowl and said I had no money but I would do any work they asked. Because I did not want to spend money on days I made none. It also felt like I needed to talk to someone and make friends if I ever were to survive there. That was the hardest part for me. The owner looked at me and asked if I was from the country and I said yes and she said in rough times such as these one could at least save their own lives by living quietly in the country and in any case they did not have work to give me but if I wanted work I should try the store over there and when I went to where she gestured it was a small banchan and rice eatery deep in the market. The eatery had a sign that had the name of our town J— in it. It was lunchtime and the place was so full of market people that when I stepped in and helped them serve the banchan plates they were so busy the owner did not even ask who I was and allowed me to work there until the end of the day. Later she asked me where I was from. I said J— and the owner looked at her sign and must have thought I was lying to her to get a job but I said it was true and that I was from Kkettari. She said, Kkettari? Everyone called our neighborhood Kkettari. Kkettari was a name only the people who lived there knew so the owner finally believed me.

All who leave home and live in other parts are lonely.

The eatery owner was not strictly from J— but hearing I was from there made him welcome me like a guest and asked me if I had a place to sleep. When he was younger he had moved to Ipam in search of Cha Cheonja and built a house there but left J— when Cha Cheonja died and the Japanese colonial authorities forcibly dissolved the movement. Unlike when he moved to Ipam he no longer had any money, and at first he went about with some gang until getting his act together and came into Namdaemun Market. Business wasn't good at first but he remembered in J— how he cooked cutlassfish over small potatoes and sold that and it became very successful. He had moved to J— for Cha Cheonja and thanks to the braised cutlassfish he learned from the people there he made enough money to send his daughter to university.

You like braised cutlassfish with small potatoes in it so you should know how good it is.

Usually you put sliced turnip but turnip is scarce when potatoes start coming in so we used potatoes instead. The market people loved this braised cutlassfish and they kept bringing other people to his place for lunch and soon people had to get in line for that dish.

In Seoul there is a place called Jonggak and a big Buddhist temple called Jogyesa. He suggested we visit it later. After Bocheonism's main worship hall was destroyed in Ipam, its remains were used to construct Jogyesa. He asked me if I knew the Shibiljeon building's materials were brought from Baekdusan Mountain and I said I had been there. He put the chairs together to make a bed and let me sleep there. That was my first night in Seoul.

I slept until the smell of braised cutlassfish woke me. Since that place made braised cutlassfish all day without a break it always smelled of it. I could not fall back to sleep. I went outside the store. It was dawn but the lights were on in the market and people were walking quickly about which made my steps quicken as well. Even at that hour the ragpickers were picking up litter and the shoeshiners were shining shoes and the newspaper boys were running by. People carried cabbages or rolls of fabric stacked high on their backs. Watching the people move busily about made me think I must live diligently as well. I may have no job now but I should find work here and make money and no matter what else I would send my children to university and I felt confident then that I could do it.

Despite this confidence, Father bought his return ticket to J— a mere two months after he had arrived in Seoul.

In the letter Father wrote to Eldest Brother, he said he had returned to J— and regretted it later when he sent him on his own to Seoul. *Even when the protesters were dragging the statue of the president through the streets with rope and even when it was like there was another war I could stand it*, Father had written. Puzzled, I tried reading between the lines. Something had happened that had made Father return to J— despite being able to withstand a Seoul that looked like it had gone back into war, but I could not tell what that was. All Father wrote was that he regretted not holding on to his life in Seoul, the one he was so determined to make despite the things that were going down, because if he'd done so, it would've been easier to support Eldest brother when he himself made it to the capital.

I read the letter from the top once more. Father had endured life in Seoul under war-like conditions, but something had still made him return to J—. What was it?

What Father witnessed, mere days after arriving in Seoul, were bullets being shot at students as young as thirteen or fourteen. The eatery's owner had a daughter in college. A daughter who would come to the eatery after classes and roll up her sleeves to help. On the stove where the braised cutlassfish would be cooked during the lunch rush she had left a hastily scrawled note:

> If I say I am going to the protests, you will try to lock me in a room, which is why I have no choice but to leave you with this letter. They are stealing our votes right before our eyes, and if we do not resist, there will never be an end to these farcical elections. This is our greatest obstacle to achieving democracy. I must stand with my friends in the struggle. Even if you cannot understand me, please forgive me, and take care of yourselves.

The eatery owner became so distraught over this note that he closed up shop and grabbed Father's hand, begging him to come downtown with him. That he was old and his eyesight might fail him in identifying his daughter. As he followed the eatery owner, Father was swept into the protest crowd on Sejongno. It wasn't just students there. Father stood with the eatery owner and listened to the university students read aloud their proclamations. The students shouted their slogans and began to march forth. *Redo the vote*—Father didn't understand the slogans. Never having seen so many young people in one place, he felt like he had stepped into another world. Somewhere on this street he had never heard of before, protestors and police clashed. Tear gas exploded. Father grabbed the trunk of one of the gingko trees lining the street and fell below it. The loud bangs muffled his hearing. People kept scattering and gathering; he had no idea where the eatery owner had gone. They separated when the bullets began to fire, trying to take cover and losing each other in the melee. This is the presidential residence I'd only heard about, thought Father when he passed it. Otherwise, why would they have shot into a crowd of their own citizens? It had begun as a student protest but soon, people everywhere were joining in. People who had previously stood on the sidewalks, cheering on the protestors but not participating themselves. Under the gingko tree, Father watched as the sound of the bullets actually made more people gather, not fewer. He thought he needed to save himself and retreat. That he needed to return home. The thought of his third child, a newborn no doubt wrapped in a blanket, crossed his mind. Not to mention the worried face of his eldest child who had begged him not to go anywhere. The second child, who was good at doing what he was told, was probably feeding the dog. Father listened to the sound of guns firing and ran in the opposite direction. Thinking he hadn't survived a war in order to die here. He had to get out of there and go back home safely.

He had to go back home.

That was his slogan in that moment. Even when he could barely keep his eyes open from the tear gas, he ran away from the protest. And he witnessed the guns shooting at the scattering people, frightened out of their minds. Thugs wielding chains and pieces of lumber striking the heads of students. As he ran in the other direction and into an alley, he stopped. Because the woman surrounded by the lumber-wielding thugs looked like the eatery owner's daughter. She had said she'd join the struggle with her friends, so why was she alone and surrounded by those evil-looking men? The daughter was so frightened she was backing away and stumbled to the ground. Father shouted at the passing crowd, Look over there! But no one heard him. Whether the young woman was being ganged upon or not, the crowd only moved forward. All thoughts of going back home disappeared as Father ran towards the woman and shouted, Hey, Darae!

—What the hell are you doing here!

The thugs with their weapons stared at Father.

—Her name is Darae, and she's my younger sister . . . What are you all doing here?

He got the eatery owner's daughter to her feet and slapped her in the face.

—What did I tell you! It's wild out here today, I told you to stay put at home. Are you deaf!

Shouting at her all the way, he roughly dragged her by the wrist into an alley lined with hair salons as the thugs left with their weapons, grumbling and cursing, She's that bastard's little sister? That little—

Father wrote that it felt as if he had fallen into the depths of hell.

For the eyes of my father,
I hope this letter finds you well.

The construction company you mentioned in a previous letter about the irrigation wells isn't our company but one called the Dong Ah Consortium.

As you mentioned, it was the largest civil engineering project in world history. It's still going on.

The project involves bringing up water from an underground lake and changing the deserts of this country into arable farmland. At first, everyone said this was nonsensical. That it was a dream. The leader here, a man named Gaddafi, put out a contract for this nonsensical project to the whole world and our company was one of the bidders. We had a whole separate task force for this bid, but we failed. Well, it was a competition between some of the biggest construction companies in the world so we didn't have high hopes, but the fact that a Korean company ended up winning made our failure especially noticeable.

Father.
While our company did lose the bid, it is a proud thing that a Korean company will build this irrigation system in the middle of the desert. The stories of the Dong Ah people have gone down in legend. The total cost of the construction was 2.9 billion US dollars. They were overjoyed at winning just a large bid but devastated at the work environment. It was, as you put it in your letters, a land of death, and the only construction materials

available were water and cement and gravel, which meant everything else had to be procured and the first stage alone needed 246,000 water pipes, an unimaginable amount. In the end, Dong Ah built a factory here to build those pipes, as none of that could be procured in Libya.

It was not a task our company undertook, but the Sahara irrigation project set many astonishing records.

Dong Ah has finished the first stage of their project and has moved on to the second. Once this is over, they will have six times the farmland South Korea has. An extraordinary project.

Father.

I learned for the first time that you were in Seoul during 4.19 through your letter.

It was something that happened when I was a child and read about later in books, which is why it never seemed real to me, but I was astounded that you were there in person.

But Father.

Was the name of the eatery owner's daughter really Darae?

I was surprised that she should have the same name as Mother.

You said you'd seen hell and come home feeling like a failure, but you don't know how happy I was when I saw you again. That was the longest you had ever left home. You were in Seoul during that time. I had no idea. Whenever you left home, I could not fall asleep. Mother looked so desperate and my siblings looked even younger than they were. When you weren't there, I would get up from sleep to go and lock the gates. I was afraid because Mother would keep them open to other dangers just in case you should come home during the night.

Father.

I am to leave Tripoli soon.

I've been posted to work on-site of the construction, a 500 km strip of land between Ajdabiya and Tobruk. Tobruk was a battleground during the Second World War, and landmines are still being uncovered there. Father, there used to be a Nazi general named Rommel. He is a key figure in that war. The first movie I ever saw in a theater was about the life of General Rommel. He was loyal to Hitler, and he won every battle here, even in this desert land. But for conspiring in an assassination plot against Hitler, he is given the option of guaranteed safety for his family if he commits suicide in a forest near his house. An unforgettable story, and they say Tobruk is where he had many victories. Someday, when I can sit down with you again, I shall tell you more. Apparently, cars there still drive over the occasional landmine, leading to flat tires. There shall be 100 Korean workers there, 600 from Thailand, and 400 from Bangladesh. My job there will be to safely feed them, shelter them, distribute their pay, and run the infirmary. Human resources management, in other words.

There will be more conflicts than here in Tripoli, but since there are many people there, I suspect there will be much to learn as well. More than anything else, both my body and mind will be busy, which means time will fly by.

And Father.

Before I switch workplaces, I shall be given about twenty days' leave in Seoul. There have been vacation days given before, but they were just a week, too short to go in and out of Seoul, but I am coming this time. The thought of seeing you and Mother after a year and a half's absence makes my heart soar. My second child in Seoul will turn two. Having left him before he could speak, I wonder how tall he's grown and how much he could speak now. According to the photographs my wife and Honnie occasionally send me, he's already going out into the playground to play, and the cassette tapes how he's speaking a few words. In the last one, my second said, Father, hello, and that astonished me. I'm sure my wife had him do it but he also sang me a song. It starts with, Hello, we meet again, which made me laugh. My wife says he says the words, Hello, we meet again, quite often. Thinking of going home makes me wonder if this was how you felt when you left and came back to us, and that makes me miss you all the more.

Father.

These days, I wonder what present I should buy my second when I go back on my break. Because this is the first time I am getting him a present. He likes model airplanes so I'm thinking of getting those for him, but I'm not sure if I can get them here. There isn't anything made here that a three-year-old boy would like. I remember a winter night when you came home after being away for so long. Mother made all of us except me sleep in the little room together. Because it was winter, mostly. Only two kilns would need kindling if we slept together. It was after autumn harvests and into early winter, and you had come home with a tin of cookies, a kind I had never seen before. The rustling woke everyone up and we all ate the cookies that night. There were also cakes filled with creams and sweet bean paste. Mother got a separate plate for me. Mother was always like that. If there was a bunch of grapes, she would take half of it and say, This is Eldest Brother's, don't touch it . . . It's embarrassing to think of this now, but back then I considered it natural this should be so, and my siblings complain about such favoritism to this day. Honnie occasionally says to me, Isn't it hard being the eldest? But think of how Mother would give you the biggest peach, the juiciest ear of corn, the first serving of stew . . . Just think of this as paying back all that. Back then, I wondered where you had bought such a delicious thing.

I also want to give my children a memorable present . . .

You may not know this, but even when you weren't home, Mother would leave a covered bowl of rice for you wrapped in the hot spot on the floor. And kept the gates unlocked. On windy nights, she used heavy rocks as doorstops. Mother probably did not know how I would occasionally lock these doors. There were nights such as those. When I'd suddenly feel anxious about our family's safety and had to do something as the eldest son.

Please send Mother my regards. She never takes care of herself and does all sorts of hard work, I am always worried about her.

I shall talk to you soon.

September 4, 1991

Your son, Seungyeop

The things that Eldest Brother remembers.

After Father let go of his shop at the edge of the village, he often went away during times when farming was at rest. When this happened, Aunt would tell Mother it was because he was so used to roaming and hiding during the war years, and Mother would tell us Father went away to make money. I think Mother was right. Father never came home empty-handed. He always brought things like a new radio or bicycle. The new bicycle always went to Eldest Brother. The old one would go to Second Brother, then to Third Brother, and so on. By the time I inherited the old bike, it would be junk. The patches on the tires looked like stains. The joy of having a bicycle of my own, despite the ragged appearance. This was how at one time we had seven bicycles standing in a row in the courtyard of our house in J—. Only Mother, who didn't know how to ride one, had no bicycle.

Second Brother taught me how to ride.

Father had asked him to teach me. He held on to the back until I could find my balance. Second Brother, who had never seen a girl my age ride a bicycle in the neighborhood, said to Father, Should Honnie ride a bike? Father said, She should learn if she wants to go to middle school.

—But the girls' middle school uniform is a skirt, Father.

Father considered Second Brother's words for a moment until replying, But she should still learn to ride a bike. Being too short for it, I used a step to get on the mount and Second Brother held the back and gave the signal: Let's go! Instead of going, I fell over. I fell over so many times that I still have a clear physical memory of the falls. My left knee got scraped, and just when it would get better, my right knee got scraped. Both of my knees bled and scabbed over. I did not get any better. The moment Second Brother let go of the bike, I lost my balance and fell. As Second Brother gave up on me, he said to Father, it's no use. Honnie has absolutely no reflexes.

Father, who had been watching me, said the ability to ride a bicycle was a skill I could take into adulthood. What a useful and dependable skill it is, he said. That I should keep only one foot on the pedal and the other ready to stand on if I should topple. That there was nothing to it, all I had to do was find my balance. Father held on to me as we took a turn around the courtyard. When I smiled, Father said, Fun, isn't it? I nodded, and Father said, That's it. If you don't fear falling and have fun instead, you could pick it up quickly. Even if you fall, I'm here to catch you. And if you touch the ground with your foot before you fall, you won't hurt yourself and the bike won't topple. When I kept falling regardless of his advice, he said it was because the seat was too high and it wasn't my fault. That the world was getting better every day and someday we'll have adjustable seats on bicycles. That, nevertheless, I will grow to fit the bicycle anyway. Father told me to press down on the pedals because he was holding me in the back, so I did. The bike went forward and the wind touched my face. Not knowing Father had let go of the bike, I pedaled my way around the courtyard, right to where Father was standing at the starting point. Father had his arms up and was waving them in the air. The laughter that exploded from my mouth. Father and I went to the bridge with the bicycle. I stepped on the pedals, and the bike jumped forward. The more I pedaled, the more I went forward. As I got used to riding on my own, Father jogged next to me on the bridge, which I must've traversed at least twenty times that day. And like Father said, I never forgot how to ride a bike. I rode my bike to town as a middle school student, and even now, if I happen to see a bike somewhere, I get on it and put my feet on the pedals. Even despite not getting on one for two or three years, I step on the pedals and the bike goes forward.

On late nights when Father came back, I would hear them talking to each other in the night. Mother would ask where he'd been this time, and he'd say he went to Gunsan and took a boat to Janghang and did some smelting work there, or some other time he'd say he spent a season in Taebaek with a young man named Hachul who lived next to Aunt's house.

Read this, Seungyeop

How far the road back after your leave must be.
    I am sure you are finding it hard to work again.

    What worries you must've had leaving your children behind and getting on the plane.
    I remember something from long ago.
    One year I had gone to the cow market in Gwangju where I helped negotiate some sales. I had spent several months doing that and returned to find you in your neat middle school uniform coming home by bicycle. The sight of you made my heart swell with pride.
    How had this baby grown so big?
    You were as tall as I was and steadfast. I decided I should stay home from now on.
    I remember when I first took you to the baths in town.
    Your firm strength as you scrubbed my back was good but also made me determined I should do my best to set a good example. That was the winter when my heart stopped wandering.
    Even when I did not know how a father to such a big child should be.

How heavy your heart must have been to leave your children behind to work in that faraway land.

I am sorry I cannot be a strength to you at this time.

I thought my yearning would ease if I saw you but now I only want to see you again.

Nothing more I would want.

As long as you are healthy somewhere under this sky.

Ah, and Seungyeop.

You asked if the eatery owner's daughter was named Darae and I did not answer.

I did not know her name at the time. I needed a name and your mother's came out of my mouth. Darae. How long has it been since I have ever written her name like this? Your maternal uncle's name was Muhru.

Later I learned the eatery owner's daughter was named Soonok. Kim Soonok. And she asked me the same thing. Who was Darae.

All in the past.

Nothing more I would want.

As long as you are healthy somewhere under this sky.

January 19, 1991

Your father

The shortest letter Father had written was about me. He was so anxious that he hadn't bothered with his usual greeting.

Read this, Seungyeop.

I have a question.

Does Honnie smoke?

I saw her smoking a cigarette in the backyard by the taro the other day.
I was so surprised my heart is still beating fast. I hope I am mistaken.

I don't know what to do about it. I am pretending I saw nothing
for now.

Did you know about Honnie smoking?

One summer day when nothing was happening in the city, I had come down to J— with some books. I had finished reading all of them. The sun was beating down and I was tired of looking at the flowering plants in the courtyard. Father had come back in for some errands and tossed his jacket on the porch before going back out. There was a cigarette carton sticking out of his jacket. I sat with my legs dangling off the porch and stared at the carton for a while before taking out a cigarette. I grabbed a matchbox and glanced around before going behind the house. Father was from the countryside. He couldn't have imagined a daughter of his would ever smoke. The structure of the house was the same back then, which means you could walk around the whole structure. The backyard had a lush growth of green, umbrella-like taro leaves the size of my palm. I crouched by them and put the cigarette to my mouth. Listening carefully to make sure no one was there, I lit a match. Into the damp air of the summer afternoon came the scent of sulfur. I wasn't interested in smoking. When friends in Seoul smoked, I hated how the smell got on my clothes. The reason I took a cigarette and crouched by the taro was—it vexes me to say this—the weariness of summer days. It was the year I had finished writing a novel and was feeling bereft. Is this all there is, a tiny voice kept whispering to me. Is this all there is to living, all there is to it . . .

For months and years I thought of that day. If I hadn't realized it was my daughter's birthday, if I hadn't driven my car to the cram school unlike our usual times, if I hadn't parked my car across the crosswalk and waited for my daughter to come out, if I hadn't spotted her, turned on the interior light, lowered the passenger-side window, and called out to her, then she would not have come running toward me without looking both ways. Whenever I think of that moment, I rage at myself, my blood freezes over and then it boils, and I can't get a grip on my own thoughts. The entire world fills with the sound of a truck braking to stop and then falls into an empty vacuum. Then one day I find myself thinking, Is this all there is to it . . . As I look down at the world. The moment I feel this, despair threatens to split my vertebrae in half. Because the events of that day seem like punishment for my prematurely bereft feelings. That day long ago I was about to light the cigarette in my mouth when for some reason I looked toward the side yard and locked eyes with Father. The flame in my hand, the cigarette between my lips.

Father hesitated. I thought he'd seen me, but he turned and went back the way he came. The cigarette was still in my mouth, the flame in my hand. No chance of making an excuse. I threw the cigarette and match into the taro and bowed my head, sweating with fear. Rather than face Father again, I wanted to make a run for it, my books and things be damned. Expecting a scolding, I timidly sat down at the dinner table but Father didn't say a word. Not the next day or the day after that, to this very day. To think he had never spoken a word of it to me but had frantically written to Eldest Brother overseas. If Father had scolded me about how women should not smoke, I may have become a smoker then and there. A human chimney, even.

But Father said nothing, and I never touched another cigarette again.

The rain showed no sign of abating. I had a longstanding habit of checking the weather app on my phone every morning. It had said nothing about rain that dawn. But look at it come down now. The time indicated it was past lunch and almost three. Had Father managed to meet up with his gukak friends? I was about to call him when it occurred to me I should leave the abandoned house first, and I put the letters back in the wooden chest. But then I was stumped. Should I put the chest back on that shelf?

What of these stacks of dusty deliveries? The sight of the boxes made my heart heavy. They told a story of how Father had been spending his time in the country. Through the rain, I thought I could hear the gate to the cattle pen creak, and I made my way through the spiderwebs and looked out the door. Apparently spiders were hard at work while I had been reading the letters, the space between the boxes and the door was already hanging with new webs. Already? There were two insects already caught in those new webs, unmoving.

Someone had pushed open the pen door, trying to get out of the rain in a hurry, but had stopped at the open door of the abandoned house and was standing there.

Father. In the same clothes he'd been wearing when he set out this morning. I had no chance to say anything before our eyes met, my hands still holding the wooden chest. Just like that moment by the taro years ago with the cigarette in my mouth about to be lit. Father looked down at what I was holding; he himself carried the delivery box I had left in the shed. The box was already wet from the rain. The sight of me carrying the box made an expression of abandonment flash by on his face. I lost my grip on the box and it fell—at the same time, the box Father was holding fell as well. Inside the room, the letters inside the wooden chest spilled onto the dusty floor, some knocking the cobwebs in their motion, some landing on the other delivery boxes. Rain splashed on the box Father had dropped. It was clear he had tried to hide the box here as soon as he had seen it in the shed. Father had no umbrella, and the rain had made a fold in the middle of his hat.

—You're here.

Father's words were awkward.

—I just happened to . . .

I said it like someone who had been caught snooping around Father's secrets.

—I'll clean this up, Dad.

My consternation had inadvertently made me say Dad instead of Father.

—Go inside, I'll do it.

At night, I woke when I caught a whiff of smoke.

Out of habit, I looked toward Father's bed first. He wasn't in it. I sat up and called out, Father? and then went into the master bedroom, the bathroom, the kitchen, the laundry room behind the kitchen, back to the living room, and then opened the door to the little room. Father wasn't there, just the smell of a fire. I went to the window, opened the curtains, and looked out into the courtyard. The trees were swaying in the rain and the gate was shut.

Father?

I called out for him in the rain. An empty echo returned. The smell of fire made me worried, and I went out the front door. Despite the rain, the smell of smoke hit my face. It was coming from the shed. Holding onto the front door, I stared at the shed where there was a little blaze going. The rain kept trying to take out the fire, and Father was standing there fanning the flames, throwing something into it. I squinted through the falling rain, trying to see what he was burning. Letters. Eldest Brother's letters? Out of surprise, I was about to call out to him, but I stopped. There was no hesitation as he tossed the letters into the fire. Each page he held up to the flame until it caught. Even if his fingers must've gotten hot. Hours before, when he had told me to go back inside the house, his voice had a firmness I had never heard before. He strode into the house and I came out into the rain and was putting the wet box into the room when I glimpsed Father putting some letters into his pocket instead of the wooden chest. He must've sensed I was watching because he turned away from me and told me to go back inside the house.

I shut the front door and leaned on it, staring through the dark at Father. I felt my daughter come up next to me and say, Mom, what's Grandfather burning? We leaned against the door and watched Father. The rain thudded down. Father didn't realize I was watching him burn the letters. It wasn't just the sound of the rain. Even if the front door had slammed shut, Father wouldn't have heard it. He was that intent on burning those letters.

What letters were these, that he had to squirrel away and burn them in the middle of the night?

Thinking I knew nothing about my father made the door feel very cold against my back, and an unexpected loneliness flooded me. At daybreak, I went to the shed where Father had burned the letters. There was a pile of ashes. What letters had he burned? My foot sifted through the ashes and then I sat down. In there was a fragment of an envelope. I stretched out my hand and picked up this charred fragment, examining it carefully. The address was burned and unrecognizable. I squinted. The letters I could just about make out spelled Soonok. Soonok? That eatery owner's daughter? She used to write to Father? I sat there holding the envelope fragment, the pile of ashes by my feet.

CHAPTER 4

TALKING ABOUT HIM

SECOND SON

You told me to talk about Father; I thought about it a lot these past few days. It made me realize how seldom it was that I'd thought about him. It's strange. I have a lot of stories about Mother and things I want to say about her, but the thought of talking about Father gives me pause. What exactly is this feeling? Like the words won't come out. I kept going over the list of seven questions you sent me. Especially the seventh question. *What would you like to do with Father?* I was surprised. There should be no hesitation in answering this question but my head immediately turned into a sealed tin can. Come to think of it, I don't think I've done anything these past few years that I had wanted to do with Father. I think it all began when we started taking turns going to J— for the weekend. I don't think we would've made up that system if our parents were in good health. The more I think about it, the more I see how that was the point Father stopped suggesting we do things together and just went along with whatever we told him to do. Oh wait, there was one thing. We went to the cemetery on the mountain together. Father used to go there even outside of the holidays, trimming the grass and cleaning the tombstones. Like he was going out for a run every morning. I don't think we could ever separate him from that mountain. We all know how much time he spends taking care of it ever since the last of us left home. He would ride his bike there, and later, his motorcycle. If we couldn't get a hold of him on the phone, we assumed he was out on the mountain. Do you remember how he would ask us permission to take a portion of our wedding money to take care of the cemetery? You know how we've never heard him ask us for money, ever, which made us answer yes in a daze, and Mother would scold Father, saying we were just about to start our new lives and he should let us have all our wedding money. Father used those funds to harden the dirt on the burial mounds and plant new grass and replace old tombstones. I assumed he just happened to like that mountain a lot, but maybe it was a kind of ritual for him. Ever since we left his home, Father would visit the cemetery before the rice fields whenever there was a typhoon warning.

I feel sad, suddenly.

Because it occurs to me that Father must not have visited the mountain for a while now. When I stayed in J—, he would often ask, Want to go to the mountain? But there will come a day when I won't be able to hear that. Is getting worse the only thing that's left to him? I couldn't always say yes to him. That's just life. Things you wouldn't even remember once they've made your life hell make you go, Let's go some other time. I said that to him a lot. It's not like we had to walk there like we used to—there's a road that goes by it now and it wouldn't take so long, but I didn't have time even for that. All right, Father would say, and the disappointment on his face makes me feel even sorrier now. He didn't have anything else to look forward to apart from going to that mountain, and I remember him choosing his clothes carefully and going in his best outfit. Even in the summers he wore socks and a hat. When we got in the car, his face just filled with enthusiasm, like we were on our way to a picnic. In the car, he told us stories about the olden days. His memories would be so detailed, I asked him every time, You can remember all that, Father? He always seemed a bit excited to be going to the cemetery for ancestral rites. He would get ready and stand in the courtyard calling out each of our names, making sure none of us weaseled our way out of it. Even Mother, who wanted to stay behind and clean up the jesa mess in the kitchen . . . I remember our uncle and cousins and all of us walking in front of him as if he were herding us out to the mountain. I'd be chatting away with my cousins and look back to see him lagging a little behind us, lost in thought.

I keep talking about other things. In any case, it felt so absurd I had never thought of what I wanted to do together with Father until you asked me, that I felt sad. I'd actually taken them for drives when it was my turn to come to J— and we went to Naesosa Temple and everything, but after a while, Mother and Father didn't say anything and simply looked out the window. At least Mother would say things like The flowers are blooming or The roads are the same here, but Father just gazed off into the distance. He didn't seem to care what was outside that window. I was going to record my answers to you so I turned on the voice memo app on my phone, but I ended up just clearing my throat and the words refused to come, which is why I'm writing it down. But this isn't any easier. Maybe I should try speaking again?

I heard I got measles not even a month after I was born. That it was so contagious, I needed to be quarantined. Are there still kids who get measles these days? It's not that common, right? They say there were many kids getting it and even dying from it in those days. It was especially fatal in cases occurring before the first birthday because the immune system was too fragile. With little red dots covering my body, a high fever, and so much crying that my throat had closed, Aunt took me from Mother and put me in the small room. Not even on the hot spot. Putting babies in the cold spot meant to start thinking of the child as dead.

Think of your firstborn! Aunt was said to have wrapped me in a blanket and placed me away from the hot spot and guarded the door to the small room so no one could enter. I'm sure she stood guard there in case Eldest

Brother should stumble in. Two days later, Mother lifted the blanket from my face and saw me quietly looking back at her. My birthday is in July so it must've been the middle of summer. I heard it was Father who took me to the hospital while I was burning up in the middle of the hottest days of the year. It was near a jesa date, which meant Father had come home; as soon as he saw what was happening, he pushed Aunt away and carried me all the way to the hospital in his arms in the middle of the night. I was so little that my neck wasn't even strong enough to hold up my head.

It all happened before I was a month old, so I have no memory of it. And that's why I imagine it instead. Thinking of being a baby lying alone on a cold floor makes me feel a strange loneliness. Sometimes I imagine being too hot and dehydrated to cry, being rocked by a large shadow as it carries me through the night. Father arrived at the hospital and kicked the door until someone opened it. Aunt tells me often that that was how I survived. That if it wasn't for Father, I'd be dead. Honestly, it makes me feel weird whenever she tells that story. To think of abandoning a sick child for two whole days. As a child, the story scared me and angered me and I wanted to shout, You wanted me to die! Think of what it's like to be sandwiched between two strong-willed siblings. I learned a long time ago that the best way to not let a situation escalate was to avoid inserting myself into it. The moment the second child shares his opinion on a matter, opposing sides are created. Whenever there was some conflict among all of us, it only seemed to stress Mother. Which was why I kept checking up on Eldest Brother's pride and Third Brother's feelings. Still, when Aunt told me that story again about Father running through the night with me in his arms, I had to ask why she didn't think of taking me to the hospital sooner. Her answer was anticlimactic. I'd worked up so much courage to ask that question and risk the peace, but all she said was that in those days, children with measles were rarely hospitalized. That there was little thought to treating them and it was all about isolating them before they could infect other children, that it was common to leave them alone in a room. That they would say the child was haunted and would hang notices on the gates telling people not to enter the house. They say measles were even more frightening than hohwan or mahmah. I looked up these words: "hohwan" means a tiger running off with you in its jaws, and "mahmah" means smallpox. She was saying measles were scarier than tigers or an even worse contagious disease; I couldn't understand her reasoning.

There is no way a newborn baby could survive two days of neglect. Measles or not, if a child is sick, they need to be taken to a hospital. But to wrap them in a blanket and leave them to die alone? Would it have been better never to have heard this story growing up? It makes me think this is why I'm so sensitive to cold and prone to thoughts that I'm all alone in this world. What would've happened to me if Father hadn't shown up? That's the first thing I think about when I think about Father. I have no memory of the incident itself, but having heard about it from Aunt and Mother, I consider it my first memory of him.

There's another feeling that comes up when I think of Father. I wasn't sure if I should tell you this but I decided to be honest with you, this being a kind of interview. I sometimes resent Father. Resent him? I'm sorry if this surprises you. Resenting the man who saved my life by carrying me to safety in the middle of the night . . . I know, right? The feeling deepest in my heart when it comes to Father, though, is resentment. I don't really know what to call so I call it resentment, but it's not because I resent anything Father did. That would be absurd, considering Father's character. I think it's because the house kind of revolved around Eldest Brother. These days no one cares about birth order, but in Father's day, the eldest son had so many responsibilities, which made it natural for him to depend on Eldest Brother so much. You probably don't remember, but he took Eldest Brother everywhere he went. You might consider Father a living history of Korean people-movers. He carried Eldest Brother in a cart, then a bike, then a motorcycle. Weird, right? That Eldest Brother and I are three years apart but I still remember him riding on the back of Father's bicycle. Get on, Father would say, and Eldest Brother got on. Even when Father hadn't specified who. Father, whenever he arrived home, would always look around the house first. All of us knew the person he was looking for was Eldest Brother. He was always looking for him. When Father spoke to me, it was usually about Eldest Brother. Is your hyeong back from school? Where is your hyeong? Did your hyeong go to school? Does your hyeong know? That kind of thing. Growing up like that, I found myself telling Father Hyeong got top grades in his class, Hyeong needs a hat, Hyeong's bike has a flat, Hyeong is bad at running . . . Eldest Brother is a really bad runner. He would always end up last in any race by the time he got to the fifty-meter mark. I knew he would come in last on Sports Day, and I just wanted to warn Father beforehand. I thought that would be important to him. That he was prepared for disappointment. Because I didn't like it when Father was disappointed by hyeong, either.

I just took out a can of beer from the fridge. My throat was parched. I read over what I just wrote. What am I trying to say with all of this? I'm laughing at myself right now.

This resentment I hold for Father deep in my heart is probably the same emotion any second child feels for their parents. Of course, nowadays people hardly have more than two children, so the feelings of a second child are probably less of a thing. They say that only an eldest son could understand the world of an eldest son. Well, the same could be said for second children. How could I possible explain it all? It'll only get long-winded, but let's just say the world of the second child is a thing. Anyway, Father always put hyeong first. Mother, too. It was so natural for them to do so that even I put him first. I'm sure Eldest Brother found it hard as well. He was likely pressured to act with utmost propriety at all times. He probably heard the mantra that the eldest has to do well if other siblings are to succeed as well. He must've heard how he sets the tone for all of us until he was at least nineteen, which makes me feel bad for him. That's not all. Since I ended up in the Army Academy, I didn't live with Eldest Brother in Seoul, but Third Brother and you moved in with him, and Father repeatedly said you two to think of Eldest Brother as your father now. I didn't think much of it at first, but the weight of that must've been awful for Eldest Brother. He was just nineteen himself. I think I kept thinking of Eldest Brother as an adult despite his being only three years older because of the way Father treated him. When I was entering elementary school, Father brought me before Eldest Brother and asked him to teach Hongie math and writing. That was the start of it, and anything that had to do with school, I did through Eldest Brother. At first, I wondered what another child, who was only three years older than me, would know, but there was no one else I could turn to, which was why I asked him about homework and got it looked over by him and later showed him my report cards. Eldest Brother tattled on me, telling Father my grades were full of Mi's and Yang's. They had that Su, Wu, Mi, Yang, Ga grading system back then, if you remember. Father would only say, As long as they're not Ga's. He was always a man of few words, and when it came to school, his words were even fewer. He never showed up at parent-teacher conferences. Even in situations where he was supposed to, only Mother would show up. I wonder what school was to Father. The only time he would come was Sports Day in the fall. They set up shades on the sports field and invited parents to watch. That was why I had to warn him about Eldest Brother's running. Because I didn't want him to feel disappointed on the only day he came to our school. And at the same time I would be thinking, There's one thing I'm good at, at least . . . That lack inside me, making itself known.

Not that I have anything against Father or Eldest Brother. Especially the times when Father would tell me to ask Eldest Brother instead. I would ask Eldest Brother, and he gave me good answers. Eventually, I simply asked him on my own. I was depending on him more and more. There was no need to worry about or decide things on my own because of him. Eldest Brother will figure it out, I'd think, and take a step back. I'm still doing that. All a part of the world of the second child. But sometimes, I do feel left out. When you and him and Third Brother and Ippy talk about our childhood, it makes the four of you seem like a collective unit. When Third Brother would say, And then Eldest Brother . . . Or when you or Ippy would say, That's when Eldest Brother . . . I would go as silent as Father. The four of you share a time that I do not know about. They're not even beautiful or happy memories you share, either, just days of being poor and anxious and struggling, but I was still jealous. Having been separated from all of you for so long, I had nothing to add to your stories.

I do remember this, though. How strange, the things we do remember. You've probably forgotten it, but you were telling a story one time: We were living in Garibong-dong in Seoul, and you were visiting us, Hongie oppa, and you bought us hotteok from a hotteok place in front of the train station. They were so delicious . . . Until you told that story, I had completely forgotten it, but your words immediately brought the memory back to me. I was a cadet at the Academy. I think I used to visit the room where you and Eldest Brother were living on days when school was out. Just the thought of visiting Seoul was so exciting that I would shine the buttons on my cadet uniform so thoroughly that I could see them glow in my reflection on the train window. Just having someplace in Seoul I could go to was wonderful. I was so proud to have family in Seoul—siblings no less. So proud I was, buying a Metro Line 1 ticket upon arriving at Seoul Station to where you two were living. I bought hotteok hot off the grill at the subway station and went to your address, but the door was locked. The night was falling but no one came. I waited there for Eldest Brother or you or anyone to appear, and when it got dark, I walked around a bit. The gate itself seemed to be always open. People kept going in and out. That was when I first saw locked doors along a corridor. Were there really rooms behind each door? I'd never seen an interior structure like that before, and I couldn't imagine it. Where was everyone, and why were all these rooms locked? I remember thinking that. To the left of the gate was a shed stacked with coal briquettes, to the right a communal bathroom, and there was a stairway leading up to the roof, which I checked out. There were some earthen jars and some laundry drying on a clothesline. I walked around the washing to the edge of the roof and saw the chimneys of the factories soaring before me. They were holding up the starry sky. It was night, but white smoke was obscuring the stars, like the day. Was this the Seoul my siblings were living in? The excitement I'd felt on the train settled down, and I looked down at the city. I could see people pouring out of the subway station I'd come from, and I came downstairs but your door was still locked. The hotteok was cold now. I took out a pen from my uniform pocket and wrote *Second Brother was here* on the hotteok envelope. I waited a long time after and followed my previous route in reverse out of the alley, took the subway to Seoul Station, and bought a ticket to J—.

It was dawn when I arrived there.

When I told Father I'd been to Seoul, he asked how Eldest Brother had been doing. I told him I had wanted to visit but Eldest Brother had told me not to come, so I hadn't gone. I told Father not to go as well, unless he was invited by Eldest Brother. As I ate the meal Mother made for me, I thought about the hotteok I had left in front of your locked door. The sugary filling must've congealed and the crispiness gone soggy by now, I thought. And years later, you mentioned that hotteok in the middle of a casual conversation. That the hotteok I had left you guys—which would've been cold as ice, seeing as I left around midnight—was so delicious.

So. I see they were delicious.

Whenever our family, Eldest Brother, Third Brother, you, and Ippy talked about those days, I would keep my mouth shut and think about the cold hotteok I left at the locked door—where no one came even as I waited until midnight. Would you understand if I told you I was jealous of the four people who shared that time, who only needed one word to prompt a Right? Back then, that was the time . . . See? This is what I mean when I say the world of the second child is so hard to explain.

Eldest Brother's circumstances did not improve. In fact, now that Third Brother was in college and you moved in as well, they'd grown more strained. Father had never even visited him; Eldest Brother refused to let him come. Do you remember, after years of being told to stay away, when Father bought a ticket to Seoul without telling anyone and popped in on you? He sat in that room for a while, not saying anything, and then went to a cousin's in the Heukseok-dong. He told me later he'd gone there determined to collect on some money he had loaned him ten years ago. To give to Eldest Brother, you see. Father walked through the unfamiliar streets and managed to find the cousin's house, but he never got to even mention the money and just came back to J—. At the cousin's house, he saw there were seven people living in one room. His cousin was not there, and his cousin's wife was lying in bed sick. There was no heating or food, so Father went to the coal seller in that neighborhood he had never been to in his life and had coal briquettes delivered to the cousin's house and dropped by the rice seller to arrange a rice delivery for them. I was staying at our house in J— at the time, and I saw Father come back with the most devastated expression on his face and take straight to bed. He asked me, looking exhausted and sad, to help hyeong if I could. My whole life I'd heard Ask your hyeong or Do as your hyeong says. The moment I heard him say for the first time, Help your hyeong, my knees buckled.

I remember how surprised Father was when I told him I wanted to go to Maritime University.

Even then he asked, Did you talk to your hyeong about it? When I said I hadn't, he became very disconcerted. When he asked me what I would do after university, I became disconcerted myself. To be honest, I didn't know what one could do with a degree from there, either. But I didn't want Father to get the upper hand; I told him I'd become a sailor.

—Sailor? You'll get on a boat?

Father then asked, Why? Why do you want to be on a boat? And I had nothing to say to that.

—It's not about getting on a boat, Father. I can be a ship's captain if I graduate from there.

I still don't know to this day. Do people really become captains after they graduate from Maritime University? Father had never tried to stop me from doing something before. This whole thing with going to Korea Maritime University was also a part of the world of the second child. I wanted to go where they had the cheapest tuition and immediate employment after graduation. My high school teacher had recommended Korea Maritime University. It was a national institution, which meant it was almost free, and there was a dormitory on campus. I looked it up and learned it was in Busan. It used to be Jinhae Maritime College affiliated with the Ministry of Transportation and then it moved affiliation to the Ministry of Defense, changing its name to Korea Maritime University, and then later to the Korea Maritime and Ocean University.

In the middle of some conversation we were having, Ippy once asked, We used to be poor? That was surprising. You and I are six years apart and she and I nine years, so I suppose being almost ten years apart means we experienced that time of our lives very differently, but Ippy honestly seemed to think we had never been poor. It's thanks to our parents that she feels that way. Think about Father. Remember what he would do in the first days of winter? Carry home a load of fur-lined shoes and thermal underwear on the back of his bike and spread them out on the porch. Each member of the family had a set in their own size. So what, you might say, but this was a big deal. Back then, there were still kids who were too poor to have a packed lunch so they drank tap water at lunchtime instead. Whenever all the kids of the neighborhood were lined up along a sunny wall in the winter, the only ones who wore new fur-lined shoes every year were us. When I opened the shoe closet at the end of the school day, the only noticeably new shoes among the sixty-something pairs were always mine. Which is why kids would occasionally steal them.

But however Ippy felt at the time, our family was actually poor. Father had a dream of sending all six children to college on just farming—how could we not be poor? Eldest Brother was working as a civil servant in a district office by day and attending college by night, which is why I couldn't ask to be sent to a regular university. The world of the second child. Where I am not allowed to think only of myself, where I've got to look every which way at all times.

It's still like that for me to this day. There was that time our parents came to Seoul for a family event. They would go to Eldest Brother's house whenever they came up. It's not like anyone said they should—that just became the rule. Eldest Brother took that for granted, and our parents seemed to as well. Especially Father. Even when we had all established our own families, his attitude never changed when it came to that. We also took it for granted that when our parents visited Seoul, we gathered at Eldest Brother's house. That's not all. Father found it very awkward staying at any of his other children's houses. If any of us happened to move, he would come to visit, to see the new place, but he would stay at Eldest Brother's. If Eldest Brother didn't come to get him, he would anxiously ask one of us to take him to hyeong's place. Whenever hyeong moved, Father would always ask, Is it near Seoul Station? Because to Father, Seoul meant Seoul Station. It was very important to Father whether Eldest Brother's house was near or far from Seoul Station.

I applied to Korea Maritime University and failed to get in. What now? Having never thought of an alternate plan before, I sincerely didn't know what to do. I did find an opportunity to apply for the Academy . . . At first, I got ready to go on a backpacking trip around the country on my bike. Father was worried about my plans and said my bike was too old and it was dangerous. He was probably concerned about a son going on a trip after having failed an exam as well. The only trips we had ever taken were our class trips in school, so a backpacking trip on a bike was a strange proposition for him. He couldn't even ask me to talk to Eldest Brother because he was in Seoul. I was adamant. You know how all of us outgrew him in height once we reached middle school. As I bustled about checking my tires and getting a map and a pair of binoculars, he stood there uncertain of what to do and looked very small to me. As I left the house, Father followed me and put an envelope into my back pocket. When I rode out of J— and rested a bit before entering the mountain paths to Sunchang, I opened the envelope. Inside was a letter saying, Don't starve. There was also a crumpled bill. I remember having a bowl of jajangmyeon in Sunchang and paying with that bill. Nowadays you see bike paths everywhere, but back then you had to use the main roads, many of them unpaved. Whenever someone working in the fields would look up to see my bicycle rolling by them, I felt a bit guilty. Here they were, too busy with work to even look up, and here I was distracting them with my leisure. Riding along the mountain roads meant basically pushing the bike up, but once I parked at the peaks, the vistas I saw moved my soul. The thick trees, the valleys, the birdsong, the whooshing of the wind . . . Immersing yourself in nature washes away so many things. At the very least, you stop blaming other people. You assume there was a reason for things that don't work out. You feel your heart grow bigger.

My backpacking trip ended just four days in. Because my head was shaven per high school regulation, I was accused of being a North Korean military spy. It's funny to think about now, but spies were a serious thing back then. I graduated high school in 1976, and you remember what happened that summer. It happened around my birthday; two American officers trimming poplar branches at the Joint Security Area of Panmunjeom were axe-murdered by North Korean soldiers. An American aircraft carrier and bomber squad were dispatched, and the poplar in question was cut down—a whole mess. Father thought war was about to begin and he bought boxes of instant ramyeon—you know how he'd ask us why we paid good money to eat such garbage—and hid them away in the earthen pots in case of an emergency. Thankfully, the North expressed their regrets and the situation de-escalated, but the national mood that year was so tense. Remember how we used to train for catching North Korean spies in grade school? There were anti-communist slogans posted everywhere. In the name of raising anti-communism awareness, there were village drills where we were made to pretend a spy had infiltrated our community and we had to report them. And those posters about how to spot a spy. Anyone who looked like they'd come down from the mountain early in the morning with mud on their shoes, anyone wearing a cap who keeps looking around or doesn't know the price of things in a store . . . There were rewards for catching spies, which made my friends and I join in the spy-catching drills with special fervor. Dok Goseong, Shin Younggyun, Jang Donghui, Huh Janggang. These were the kinds of characters they'd present. A North Korean spy contacting a relative in the South and leading them to praise the North and enter the North with them, but the Southern relative convincing the Northern spy to confess instead—cliché situations like that.

My appearance must've been exactly like the spies those posters warned us about. Dragging around an old bike, wearing a cap, taking out a pair of binoculars once in a while and gazing at the mountains. Someone must've gotten suspicious and reported me to the police. Once they arrested me, they found a map and red marks all over that map, so you can imagine how that helped my case. I didn't even get that far from J——. I'd been checking the route to Gwangju when the police nabbed me. Later, I heard the police in J—— were notified as well, and they sent plainclothes police officers to our house. They burst through the gates and went up on the porch with their shoes on and searched every inch of our house. It's ridiculous and laughable and disgusting to think of now, but back then, it was just normal.

Father eventually came down to Damyang Police Station to fetch me. He had a stack of photographs and documents proving I wasn't a North Korean spy but his son who had just graduated high school. He even brought my school ID, notebooks, and bookbag. Father said I was not a spy but his second son, my name was Hong . . . I still remember what he said. That I was so kind and considerate of my mother's workload that I practically raised my sisters on my back, that I was almost too considerate as I tried to not get underfoot at home and strived to keep the peace among my siblings often at my own expense—so how could I be a spy of all things? I had applied to Korea Maritime University because it offered low tuition fees and I was on this trip trying to clear my mind after being rejected, what kind of a spy was that? He pleaded my case with such clarity and conviction, and I had never seen him speak so much in one go. Father had known everything all along. Why I had applied to Korea Maritime University, and all the uncertainness in the world of the second child.

As we came out of the police station, Father looked at me with my head bowed and my bicycle and said, Now that you can't continue your trip, why don't you give your father a ride home? He had been in such a rush to get to me that he'd taken a taxi all the way from Damyang. It would take a whole day to bike from Damyang to our house in J—, but it was night by the time the police let me go, and we had to spend a night there if we were to bike back. We found an inn nestled in a thick bamboo grove and Father said, Let's go take a bath, and so we went to the bathhouse attached to the inn. At the entrance we got our locker keys and towels, and when we got inside, there was a framed photograph of the president hanging on the wall. Was this the bathhouse owner's politics? The sight of the president solemnly looking down at naked people made me laugh. Father had a reason why he asked me to the baths. We soaked in the big pool with the hot water, which relaxed me. In the steamy washing area, Father scrubbed my back and I scrubbed his. Father wasn't just shorter than me, his back was also narrower. Having seen the stub of his right index finger all my life I was used to it, but in the bathhouse, I saw he also had a deep scar on his right elbow, stitching scars below his neck, a burn near his knee . . . soaping and scrubbing his scars felt sad. I think I made a silent vow then to never bring suffering to him for any reason. This was probably the only trip Father and I ever made together, just the us of two. At night, we sat on the raised platform in the inn's yard and drank beer. We'd been sitting there silently looking at the stars when I suggested we have some beer. Father said beer was expensive and we should drink soju instead, but I insisted we drink beer and I would pay. Remember Father and his shop when he soaked beer bottles in cold water in the summer? Because we didn't have refrigerators back then. One very hot day, I'd gone to the shop to see Father and saw someone from town who was an acquaintance of his come with his friend and order beers. Father took a bottle out of the water, opened it for them, and placed it with two glasses before them. His shirt was sticking to his back from the sweat. His forehead and neck were also beaded with sweat. The two customers poured the beer and clinked glasses, and I thought, as a child, How nice it would be if Father could cool down with some beer, too. I think that thought made me forget why I had come to the store in the first place. It pained me to watch Father not drinking and just looking at them drink. How cold could that unrefrigerated beer even be, but I felt like Father was the only one standing there in the sun. Someday, I'm going to buy Father a nice cold beer, I thought—and I remembered that thought that day in Sunchang. It wasn't even summer but late spring. Father had no idea about any of this, of course. Because I insisted on it, he ordered beer. I poured it into his glass and the sound of it made me feel so good. Father asked me to drink as well and ordered another glass, and he poured some for me. There was a pear tree by the wall of the yard and whenever a breeze blew, pear flower petals dropped on the platform.

Father drank his beer and said, Hey, Hong-ah.

—Why do you have so many thoughts in your head?

—Me, Father?

—Do what you want to do in life. Stop caring what others think.

—. . .

—My wish is if there's something you want to do with your life, you do it.

—And what did you want to do, Father?

—. . .

—Was there something you wanted to do?

—I wanted to go backpacking on a bicycle like you, things like that.

Like you . . . He laughed. Father wanted to go on a backpacking trip, too? I was surprised and fascinated at the same time. Father said he even had someone he'd wanted to travel far away with. The things Father said to me that night were so unlike the father I knew that I couldn't imagine where these stories had come from. I'd never imagined his sojourns away from home to be anything like travel; I'd assumed he'd gone to make money somewhere. And it was the truth. I guess it's a bit strange. That we think of how nice it would be to go off on a trip somewhere and have a change of scenery, but we never imagine Father would be the same. Father drank his beer and asked, What's the date?

—It's almost May, Father. April 29.

Father sighed. He must've been exhausted from that day's events as he was drunk from just one glass of beer. If you want to live a good life, he said, you must study hard. You don't want to live like your father, do you? I didn't answer Father as I gazed at the bamboo grove along the garden walls. Father said, I've regretted that all my life. I don't know why I didn't ask him why, in that moment. Father said the only way out of poor country living was one thing, and that was to go to university. That this was the only path out of a harsh life of farming. Perhaps it was from taking a hot bath and drinking that beer, but he also spoke of his time in Seoul. I learned about it for the first time then. That there was a place called Namdaemun in Seoul, and deep in the market there was a braised cutlassfish place and he had worked there. That the owner had lived in Ipam and was good to him. That he had later been accused of being a communist spy and the eatery had been put out of business. I asked, A communist spy? Father said he hadn't been the kind of person who would do that. The owner's college-student daughter occasionally held meetings with her friends in the eatery, and that had brought about some misunderstanding. Just as it had happened to me, he pointed out, all for taking a little trip on a bicycle. The daughter was a good person and she would come to the eatery after classes, roll up her sleeves, and help out with the work. Father told me she was someone who studied a lot. That this young scholar would show him around Seoul after the eatery closed for the night. The width of Sejongno Street, how steep the paths were on Namsan Mountain . . . Father knew the environs of Namdaemun like the back of his hand. He walked Myeongdong at night with this student. That they rode the trams. Father said he was, in truth, disappointed in Seoul back then. It shocked him how dirty it was. He was also surprised at how people were lined up to buy something that looked like boiled pigs' feed to him. He rode the tram with the young woman to the end of the line in Mapo and there were shacks upon shacks there, with children playing naked by the tram tracks. He visited the Miari neighborhood as well and it was filled with fortunetelling houses, which made him wonder at how horrible Seoul was. The slums lining Cheonggyecheon Stream and the dirty waters of that stream made him wonder if Seoul was also a poor place. But Father said he once went into a teahouse and drank coffee with her. Father drinking coffee? He was telling me all sorts of things he'd never told anyone, but that's the silly detail I was struck by: Father drank coffee with a college student? In Jangchung-dong, the two of them were together watching the crowds pull down the statue of the president who stepped down. At one time, he saw the young scholar coming down a hill that had lots of theaters with her friends, chatting and laughing. That she passed him without acknowledging him. That she had met eyes with him but ignored him as she chatted with her friends. That just the night before they had walked through Namdaemun Market together, but she avoided his gaze before her friends. Because I was stupid, I asked him, Why did she do that? Father said the only thing he could teach her was how to ride a bicycle. They dragged the bike up Namsan Mountain at night and he taught her, and once she could zip around in it, she said they should take the bike and go far away from there.

—Why didn't you leave with her?

—I couldn't.

—Why not?

—I had to come home.

Father stared at the bit of foam in his beer cup and smiled an empty smile. I sometimes think about that moment. Me asking, Why not? And him replying, I had to come home. The way he looked then. I miss the father who could easily pedal the bike with me riding in the back. Now I was bigger than Father. I put him on the back and was tired just half an hour later, and when I suggested we hitch a ride with a passing truck, he switched with me. It's hard for me now to reconcile the man who pedaled me on a bicycle all the way to J— that day is the same man who is now so weak that he needs a cane to walk.

If only Father were strong enough to ride a bicycle again. I would love to go on a biking trip with Father. Even for just one day. We wouldn't need maps anymore—we've got phones and navigation. Binoculars would still be handy. I'm sure no one is going to report passing strangers with binoculars as spies anymore. I loved how Father looked when he had his buk drum in front of him and sang his traditional sori narrative song as he struck it . . . *The mountain here, the mountain there* . . . It looked like Father's only joy. Sometimes, Father sat alone in a room and sang the entire Sacheolga from beginning to end, and that broke my heart. Because he had to give up all that talent and energy. According to Mother, the longest Father was away from home was his time in Seoul, and when he came back, it was with the buk. He always brought something back with him that the countryfolk had never seen before, but that time, the only thing he had with him was the buk. Will we ever put his buk on the back of a bicycle and go to Damyang? Will that inn still be there? If that bamboo grove still stands, I want to move that raised platform to the edge of it and film Father playing the buk, singing Sacheolga. *The mountain here, the mountain there, the flowers bloom, it must be spring. Spring found us, but the world is still filled with sorrow* . . . I wish I could hear him like before, singing his heart out.

Do you think that day will ever come?

JUNG DARAE

Don't know what you want me to say. Didn't expect to leave your father behind and stay in Seoul for so long. Hard to believe you're at home down there, even when I call you. Thank you. If you'd come when I was there, I could've made you the bird's egg red bean soup and sweet potato sprout kimchi you like so much. Feels like I'm all healed up but as soon as the hospital discharged me, Third Brother brought me to his house and wouldn't let me go home. All your siblings are determined not to send me back. Me being here makes everyone visit. Let me go home . . . The moment I say that, everyone says, Not yet. First they tell me I needed to come back for a follow-up in two weeks and who was going to drive me up again, that I'd be doing them a favor if I stayed. Two weeks later and the follow-up is done, they tell me I need to come back in a month and that's why your siblings didn't let me go . . . A month later they say they've booked a full-body checkup for me and that's the new excuse. It's not uncomfortable here. More than anything else, your father doesn't wake me at night. But being comfortable isn't everything. I need to tend to the vegetables, go to the senior community center. Your sister-in-law makes breakfast and we eat it and Third Brother goes to work and your sister-in-law also has her work and I sit or stand about in the empty house.

You should know by now how your father disappears somewhere in the middle of the night? He's hiding. Who knows what memory troubles him so. It's been a while now. Maybe after his stroke. That year the youngest went to college, he had five strokes. I thought I would lose him then. When that year passed, he started having strange dreams and moving his arms and legs and shouting himself awake and going off somewhere to hide. In the morning he remembers nothing. First he thought I was joking with him because he couldn't remember. Told me again and again not to tell you all . . . Your father's disease back then was something no one had heard of and it makes you shake like you're have a seizure and have moments of strength where you push others. Your aunt said people may misunderstand and spread rumors that it's epilepsy and told us not to say anything. Aunt's words made me think it would be bad for all of you when you marry, which is why I said nothing about your father getting up and hiding in the night. The new medicine made him not have strokes, which was something to be grateful for, and the thrashing in his sleep and hiding and not remembering were just those times, so I didn't say anything . . . And now you know what only I know. You must've been surprised. I was. Waking up, your father gone, thinking he went to the bathroom but him not coming back, I'd go out and call, Honnie's father, Honnie's father . . . Your father was hiding under the porch, and when he saw me, he put a finger to his mouth telling me to be quiet and run away . . . That was the first time. I still feel the surprise I felt then. He didn't remember hiding under the porch come morning. Once, he hid in one of the big jars in the yard and when I went round and round the house calling for him, I fell and scraped my knee and it bled, and your father came out of the jar and shouted what was I doing here, I needed to flee at once, he would hold them back if I escaped from the small gate. I was so afraid. Let's go to the hospital, I said in the morning, or I will tell the children, and we went but they found nothing. It could've been the side-effects from the stroke medication because it's something that fixes tiny calcified bits on your father's brain and prevents them from floating in the fluid. But if we stopped the medication, it would dislodge and block the arteries . . . We couldn't stop the medication. We took many brain scans without you knowing. But then he would get better . . . As the years passed he grew weaker and it happened less, and I accepted things as they were . . . But now you've learned what is happening. That's why I never stayed more than two or three days with any of you in Seoul, and why I made excuses about feeding the dogs. Don't be alarmed—just make sure he gets an IV in the morning. He's knackered the next day from running around and hiding, right? Go to the Lim Cheolsu Clinic downtown. There's a shot they give him. It's 30,000 won, 50,000 won, or 70,000 won—get him the best one. Then he'll be better for a few days.

Even when I do nothing, the night comes and the morning comes. When I was young, I never had enough sleep and I fell asleep as soon as my back hit the bed, but now that I have time to sleep, I feel awake all the time. Your father used to ask why I was so sleepy, that someone could carry me off and I wouldn't know it, but now I hear everything because I can't sleep. Third Brother waking up at dawn and creaking open the door to go exercise, your sister-in-law washing her hands in the bathroom. Your sister-in-law's heart hasn't changed since she was young. Having an old woman take up a room for so long must be hard for her but she never lets it show. When she goes out for Bible study she asks, Mother, is there anything you would like to eat? I'll get it for you on the way back. Since there's nothing for me to do, there's nothing I want to eat. Sometimes, I open the front door, look outside, and think about stepping out, but it occurs to me that once I shut this door, I wouldn't be able to open it again, so I quietly close it. I don't think I can live in an apartment. Even opening and closing a door is so complicated. All the buildings look the same and I'm lost. I open the door and look at the elevator and stairs. Never been on an elevator on my own, it scares me. Since walking is hard without my walker, I can't use the stairs, which means I can't go outside. *There's nothing out there anyway*, I think as I shut the door, but why do I find myself opening it again and wondering the same thing the next day? There's nothing to do so I lie down and sleep and wake up and sleep and wake up and think about how useless I've become. Not feeling so good these days about having lived for so long. Want to go home. More so knowing you're there. My daughter, home after so many years. You always liked your father more than me. You'd go, Really? I did? If I say that to your face. Not saying it because I resent you. What's to resent? When it's so true you loved him and listened to everything he said since you were a child. Lots of daughters and fathers don't talk much but you get along with him and that's fortunate.

Last winter there was a pain in my stomach whenever I ate something. Went into town for medicine and that didn't work so the clinic by the bank took an X-ray. At first the doctor said it was nothing and that old people don't digest so well and it's natural to get little aches here and there. Don't know when doctors started saying just the most obvious things. He said, If you can't digest something, chew thirty times, don't lie down right after eating, walk at least half an hour a day, laugh loudly or clap your hands . . . That kind of thing. None of it helped. Only annoyed me. We tried their medicine and the things Ippy sent us, but I didn't get better so we took another stomach X-ray and they said something was in my stomach and I needed to go to the hospital. Now you tell me to go to a hospital? They wouldn't tell me what was wrong no matter what. Something about needing me to come with a guardian. A guardian . . . Your father is an old man with two more years of life lived than me and if they don't tell me then they surely won't tell him, which is why I told Third Brother who calls me every morning. I think Third Brother cares so much for us because we put the character for filial piety, Hyo, in his name. Always calling your father when he gets to work. Even when there's nothing much to say. Did you sleep well? How is Mother? Don't catch a cold . . . Things like that. Sometimes we might have somewhere to go in the morning but we'd get there late because of his call. The temper Third Brother has, the way he turns as meek as a lamb when he calls your father . . . The dental work your father is getting now is thanks to Third Brother. He was in high school. That man from Soseong got drunk and started talking about the war and mocking your father for cutting off his finger because he didn't want to fight. They got into a fight and two of your father's teeth broke. Third Brother was at home, and we knew with his temper, he would drag the Soseong man out and demand he apologize to your father so we decided to keep it a secret. Your father lived all this time with broken teeth. After I mentioned it to Third Brother yesterday he was so surprised I had to calm him down. Didn't he say something to you? Does Third Brother's company know he calls your father every morning? If I were the company owner, I would charge him for those calls. Third Brother calling us every morning makes secrets impossible to keep. Whenever your father or I end up in a hospital, Third Brother makes sure you all know about it.

This was when your father would go into the mountains and fields to shoot birds. Handling shotguns required tests and classes you had to sit through. That man had never sat a test in his life, but he breezed through it all. You must remember. There was a shotgun in the house for a while. Why is this in the house? you children would say. It's dangerous, get rid of it, and he would take it away like he was going to do so but bring it back later. All the wild boars in the mountains kept breeding, which is why the municipality loaned out guns sometimes for people to shoot them. Not that your father ever brought home a boar. Boar, what a thought . . . he never even brought home a pheasant. The most he would say to that was, What's the point of shooting some bird? Then what's the point of going out with the gun? Saying you've got to catch birds and leaving with a gun and then coming home empty-handed saying what's the point. One time, he was out with his gun when that Geumsan man met him on the road and asked to see his gun and said, You don't have bullets in here, right? And he pulled the trigger. Your father had no time to stop him, that man just pulled the trigger. That bullet meant for some bird or boar ended up in your father's thigh. Still shocks me to think about. Your aunt almost killed that Geumsan man that day. You know how she is. Think of how much she cares for your father and what this news would've done to her. Saying something like, If my brother's legs are hurt because of this, I will rip off that Geumsan man's two legs myself . . . Such a character, your aunt. She never spoke to that Geumsan man again until the day she died. Even when your father continued being friends with him. Look at his right leg. That scar from his surgery back then is still there. And his lack of strength in that leg is also because of that accident.

On the way to the hospital to get the bullet removed, he told me not to tell any of you. That if it were good news, it would be fine, but you had your busy lives in Seoul, and in truth, that was how I felt as well. At some point, Let's not tell the children, that was the thing we would say to each other most often. We hid the fact for as long as we could but after a few days of me picking up the phone, Third Brother asked to talk to Father, which is why I told him he was out and he asked where, and he asked so many questions that I had to tell him. Of all the things to hide from him, he shouted, how could we hide this . . . Got scolded so by Third Brother. This is what it's like being scolded by your child. The feeling was odd but also reassuring at the same time. So, after the doctor told me to get a guardian, he came down to J——, met with him, and he explained I had a small bump and it was not serious and they could remove it with an endoscopy. That he would speak to all of you in Seoul and set a date and all I had to do was come to Seoul then. He told me it wasn't surgery but a procedure. Ate nothing the day before, got an examination at the hospital and they did the anesthesia but it didn't take. They were afraid of using too much of it because I was old but when I didn't doze off they used more and it still didn't work. I could hear everything and feel something come through my mouth and whip around in my stomach and it hurt so bad . . . They do endoscopies in the countryside that didn't hurt but the doctor at this fancy hospital in Seoul did so badly I pushed him away. We need to calm her down, they were saying, and Ippy came in and took my hand and said, Umma, I know it hurts but we have to get it over with quickly. If you resist, it'll only be prolonged. Lying there distraught I asked her, Do I have a serious disease? No, she said, you have a polyp the size of a grain of sand, we just have to remove it. Polyp, I wondered what that was, but Ippy said it was nothing and my stomach was just sensitive and since they were removing something it would be strange if I hadn't felt anything at all. Think of how it was when you had me, she said. This is like picking a booger, don't you think? She almost made me laugh. Ippy can really talk. I'll be just outside the door, she said. Don't worry about anything and listen to the doctor and get it over with so we can see you again. Only when Ippy said that could I be still and do what the doctor told me. With my eyes shut, I let them kill me or save me or do what they will. When my eyes opened again there were people lying in beds all over the place. My insides hurt bad and I felt dizzy and someone next to me was being wheeled away so I asked, Where am I? You're in recovery, was the answer. That's when I realized I had gone under and woken up. Jung Darae's guardian, please come to recovery, I heard, and Ippy appeared saying, Umma. That word—guardian—summoning Ippy. Ah, that child, Ippy, is the guardian of me, Jung Darae. It was all over. They said the procedure went well. Two more days inpatient, and come back in a week for a checkup. After, when I was going to go home, they said I was to get a full checkup in two weeks and I thought I would go home after that, but then . . . they wouldn't let me go. The polyp or whatever had been removed, so I kept asking whoever visited to take me home, but last Sunday I heard Eldest Brother and the youngest talking. After lunch, I was lying down when I heard their voices, they thought I was asleep. The thing they took out from my stomach, it was a four-centimeter-long tumor. The youngest said if it were 1 cm larger, the endoscopy wouldn't have worked. That they had to be careful and make sure. Me, cancer? The strength left my body. You've all tried to fool me, saying it wasn't cancer but some kind of blemish, and I was fooled. The youngest said there was no way I could be sent away in my condition. Me, cancer. Of course. Otherwise, why would've I been in pain every time I ate something, pain like being turned inside out. Thank goodness it could be taken out by endoscopy, and maybe that was because of my age. They were talking to Ippy, saying cancer cells grow slowly in aged bodies and we needed to stay vigilant. Eldest Brother saying, Poor Mother . . . Talking in low voices like they were in a conspiracy.

In the morning before he went to work, Third Brother said, Mother, Honnie wants to listen to your stories about Father. Here's a recording device you can speak to all day. If there's anything you want to say to her, say it. I'll turn it on like this, and when you want it to stop, see? Press this, he said before leaving the house.

If I had known what was inside me was cancer, I wouldn't have let them touch me. Touching it makes it spread more, and I've seen those who suffer because of it. How many years have I lived? Don't want to spend what's left going in and out of hospitals. My one wish is to not be a burden to you all and to live at home without a fuss. Maybe this is greed, too. Wanted your father to go before me as well, but that's not something I get to choose for myself. After hearing what they said, there were a few days of me going, It's cancer? But after a few days I began thinking, So what? I'll be wherever you tell me to be. What else can I do. There's one regret. I should've taught your father how to cook for himself when he's alone. Making food isn't as hard as it used to be in the old days and all you have to do is wash the rice and press a button, but I didn't even show him that. How to make tomato juice, that kind of thing, but I didn't want to for some reason. He would've picked it up immediately if I had.

There were two times I was astonished by your father, and one was when he brought the cultivator home. Its parts were all over the place and it needed assembly, why on earth did he buy it and bring that upon himself, but your father spread a mat in the courtyard and looked at the instructions this way and that and built the cultivator in one day, telling me to come out and look. I didn't show it then, but I was impressed. The body and wheels and the place you put your bags had all been separate and he had put it together and taken it apart when it didn't work and looked at the instructions again and there it was, perfectly assembled. Could hardly believe it. Such skills, that man. You know I'm not good at putting things together. Even the jars, they're all crooked because I can't keep them straight in line. Can't even put the lids on properly. Whenever your father makes me upset about something, I think back to when he built that cultivator and called me outside to look. That's not all. I had never seen him drive one of those things before, but he looked in a book and did this and that and not too long after, he drove out the gate in it. So proud of him. Your father, that's the kind of person he is. Nowadays he can't even buy a train ticket on the internet or whatever it's called, but every new kind of farming tool in this neighborhood, your father was the first to try and put together and drive, you know. The rice planter, tractor, your father was always first, and others followed. Which is why ten years ago, when your father wanted to learn how to drive, I got you to tell him to give up. You said, Well, even if he learns how to drive, how will he get a license, anyway? At that age? But I knew. Your father would've got his license on his first try . . . Maybe the written test would've been hard. You listened and got him to give up but I regretted it later. It would've been nice for him to have driven a car in this lifetime, why did I have to be so afraid for him?

Another thing your father astonished me with was when he would leave. Your aunt didn't know what he did, either. He never told us he was leaving when he left. Or where he was going. The white envelope on the corner of the shed with the rice pot was how I knew. Yellow sometimes, white on occasion, but when your father wouldn't come home at night and I went to the shed and looked up, there would be an envelope. Money inside, to use while he was gone. Not a lot. But we led a country life, so we could be frugal. Still, there was enough to send you all to school and also cover an emergency.

One time, there was lots of money in the envelope. It was shocking. The amount was so much, I thought he might never come back—I took it to your aunt and threw it at her and screamed and cried at her to find him and bring him back. There had been many letters then. The face he had reading those letters, I had never seen that face before. Me asking who they were from and him mumbling some nonsense made me suspicious, the letters coming every once in a while just as I was about to forget them was suspicious, and the letters disappearing no matter how much I searched for them later was also suspicious.

One time, before the letters, I was washing cabbages by the well when someone creaked open the gate and peered through it. Who is it? I asked, and she had been about to enter but quickly stepped back. Wondering who it was, I wiped my hands on my clothes and went out to the gate, and there was a face I had never seen in either village or town. A straight skirt coming down to her knees and an indigo jacket with a yellow blouse under it. I still remember her. When I asked who she was looking for, she said she'd moved to Ipam and said your father's name and that she was wondering if he lived here and was passing through. Ipam is an hour's walk from here. J— would not be somewhere to pass through, and this obvious lie made me ask her again and again, But who are you? And she wouldn't give me her name, only saying she met your father in Seoul and he'd been a great help to her.

Seoul?

I remembered that Seoul was when he had stayed away from me the longest. The longest, but unlike the other times, there was no money or shoes or bicycle, no gifts of new city things for the children. And how he brought back, strangely, a buk drum and bukchae drumstick. It was the first time he'd brought home something useless for the children. Not to mention him lying in bed for two weeks after coming back.

Told her the children's father wasn't home and asked her name again so I could tell him later. She tried to go and I grabbed her arm. Tell me your name so I can tell him. Only then did she say, Kim Soonok. A kind face she had until that moment, but then it turned cold and she said, Tell him Kim Soonok was here. At sunset, your father came through the gate and I said, Who is Kim Soonok? He almost fell off his bike. Just from the name. She said she moved to Ipam? He said Soonok-ssi's father had been a follower of Cha Cheonja and had lived in Ipam before going up to Seoul, was imprisoned for something and couldn't stay there, so he had come back down to Ipam. Never mind Soonok's father, I said. Who is this Soonok? He clammed up. I had never heard him call anyone ssi in his life, much less a woman. She said you helped her? Your father said nothing. He can't lie, you see. After that, I would be working and suddenly remember how he respectfully referred to her as Soonok-ssi and it would bother me. Soonok-ssi? The more I thought about it, the more things in my head got tangled and I couldn't work. And here was the envelope with more money than it had ever contained, making me remember right away, Soonok-ssi. That pale face, dark eyes, the calves under her skirt. It felt like lightning striking. The fear that swept me up made me run to your aunt. The only person who can drag him back was her, that was my thinking. Your aunt was very strong. She must've heard something beforehand, too. About some man who had made lots of money in Seoul with a braised cutlassfish eatery and had come back to Ipam completely broke. His daughter, a college student, was accused of being a communist sympathizer and had to quit her school and go to prison, which is why her father quickly sold off the place and came down to Ipam to hide her, but then she had run away somewhere. I didn't check, but that daughter and this woman, they had to be the same person. You know it's a small village, everyone knows how many puppies a neighbor's dog had in a litter. Your aunt, after ten days of him leaving, really did bring your father back. She never told us where she had found him, she took that secret to her grave. A fierce one, she was.

That evening, I came back from the fields and there was your father sitting on the porch next to your aunt. Neither of them was speaking, just sitting, so I took the towel off my head and sat under the persimmon tree.

Your aunt suddenly stood up, her movements creating a cold breeze.

—If you want to see me dead, do as you please.

You know what she was like when she was angry. Tweaking and fiddling with her clothes or the front knot of her tunic. She was wearing baggy pantaloons, not even a skirt, but she gathered and smoothed out the folds, shot your father a cold look, and marched out the gate. Never had I seen her give your Father such a cold look. Your father shouted, Sister! And he rose for a moment, but then just collapsed again onto the porch. I got up from beneath the persimmon tree, got the white envelope he'd left me, and threw it at him.

—I don't need this!

After saying this in an angry voice, I marched away like your aunt into the kitchen. It was evening and I needed to make dinner, so I went to the shed to get rice and the well for water and the patch for vegetables and was busy doing this and that, but your father still sat there on the porch. Then Eldest Brother came from home and went, Father, and sat down next to him. Father and son, just sitting there saying nothing. Then Second Brother came and sat with them because they were there, then Third Brother . . . I don't know where you were then. It was dark everywhere. I set the table and brought it out to the porch. Eldest Brother said, Eat, Father, and then he replied, All right . . . And he sat down at the table. We had dinner like nothing had happened. The smell of the doenjang stew, the sound of spoons and chopsticks were making me cry. So close I was to leaving your father and that house in that moment, doing what he had tried to do.

From that day on, your father has never left our home without telling me first.

When I would visit Seoul to see you and call him at home, your father would say, Stay as long as you want, but his voice has no strength like a cow that's sick and can't eat and is sitting with its legs curled in the pen. Later, your aunt would tell me his shoulders slouched like someone who knew nothing of happiness in this world, then he would take his buk drum and start playing it. Your father's skill at the drum is just as good as any artist's. No one in this region can play it as well. And his singing. You fall into it. Not sure of this, but that drum was the first time he ever spent money on himself. It's probably been by his side longer than I have. Must have it repaired when I get back. Isn't the leather in the bottom part wearing thin? It is very surprising to me your father could survive for so long without me. Well, I suppose you're there. When your aunt was alive and brought his meals when I wasn't there, she often found he hadn't touched his previous meal. That made my heart drop to my stomach. If your father hid somewhere in the night and no one was there to look for him, he could be missing all night, which is why I said I was in such a hurry to go back home and feed the dogs. When it was your father who took care of the dogs better than me.

Ever since your father stopping leaving, he became a fine farmer. Nowadays, there are empty fields everywhere and no one grows anything anymore but back then, it was different. Once your father put his mind to it, there wasn't a patch of land that wasn't pushing up peas or zucchinis. Studied up on a lot on rice varieties, he did. Back then rice was scarce, we were importing rice, we sacrificed taste for yield. The really delicious native rice like Maekjo, all of them went extinct during the Japanese occupation. Did I just say Maekjo? Can't believe I still remember the name of that variety—looks like I'm not dead yet. The Agriculture Promotion Agency or something developed a lot of varieties. Your father listened to them carefully and was the first to try their ideas. Tried the new varieties in the seedbeds, saw which fell sick and which laid down and died in the monsoons or a typhoon. The ones that survived were the best. I remember when the Tongil variety appeared. No one liked it. Just didn't taste good. But the popular varieties were weak against blight so the policy was to plant the Tongil variety. This was when people didn't have enough to eat and the government cared more about yield size than taste. Even if it wasn't profitable, we wanted at least to be self-sufficient in our rice, and the Tongil variety promised us that. It makes me laugh. When we were soaking the seed rice, the civil servants would visit and look into the bowls and take out whatever wasn't Tongil and replace it. Scandalous they could do such a thing, but back then, we just accepted it.

How I hated that Tongil variety. No stickiness to it, frittering everywhere and making me think I used too little water. No sweetness when you chewed it, no flavor at all. So whenever your father soaked those seeds I dumped them out and replaced them, but those Agency people would come along and switch them to Tongil. I switched them back after they left, but your father switched them again to Tongil and we had a big row. Man of few words as he is, he still won that argument. When I said the stalks were too short he said it helped them against wind. When I mentioned he preferred sticky rice to nonsticky grains, he said he preferred nonsticky now, and when I said all the grains drop off when I scythe it he said the Tongil variety still yielded three times the harvest . . . I couldn't win. Nothing your father said was false. The Tongil stalks were so short you might wonder if the growth is stunted, but they really were strong against typhoons. More so, the yield was much higher than the previous varieties. Maybe our rice worries stopped with the Tongil variety. Not that I was wrong. The rice still tasted like nothing. But it was the beginning of big rice harvests. So tasteless they came up with more varieties, and your father was the first to try them out and tell the neighbors. So many varieties: Manseok, Taebaek, Yongju, Namyeong, Hwaseong . . . Not a single one he didn't try. Later when we all had enough to eat, people started caring more about taste than yield, and your father looked for tasty varieties. For something more delicious than that, what do you call it, Koshihikari, your father said. He thought about nothing but rice back then. Your father wished we had developed our native varieties, that we would've come up with the perfect variety for our country. But we stayed a colony for too long and those were lost forever.

My thinking is that it isn't people who do the farming. They say a single fruit takes the care of eighty-eight hands. The heavens must allow a proper harvest, or else your efforts will be washed away in the rain. Then there's the certification when you sell it. From Special to Non-certifiable, but even a Grade 2 certification makes you so mad you can't sleep at night. But you've got to accept it anyway for the money, and when they give you the date, you've got to have your rice dried and gathered and packed again. Doing all that gives you no time to even stand up straight. Your father often received Special certifications. Even when everyone else's rice died in a drought or was blown away by a hurricane, he got at least Grade 2. And prizes for his farming. The good harvest awards he won can fill up a wall if we hung them. Think of all the houses that farm. How precious it is to win an award out of all of them! You think it's easy? The judging is serious business. Even the same rice paddy can have a good yield side and a bad yield side. The farmer being judged tries to show only the good side and hide the bad. It's a lot of push and pull. The judge looks at the nominated rice paddy and rules out the very good and very bad sides and tries to get the average. They mark it with rope and count the number of stalks and panicles and even the grains. They calculate the total yield through that; it's so thorough. Quite an achievement to win. When I hang one of his big harvest prizes, he takes them down and we fight about it. Even if my name isn't on them, I still was part of growing the rice so it's my achievement, too, but your father refuses to listen to me. Your father liked the prize money, but the prize itself he thought, What's the point of this? He said prizes were things they gave out in schools, he hung all of the prizes Eldest Brother won, even the perfect attendance certificates . . . Come to think of it, you weren't so clever at school so there weren't any of yours to hang, not even for perfect attendance? Because you were late all the time and three tardies counted as an absence? Were you the only one of the children who never won an award in school? No award to hang on the wall back then, no picture with your graduation cap to hang now . . .

Your father once scolded me about Ippy, when she was in the second grade. Don't remember exactly but that was about the time. All foggy now. Maybe I'll forget such things one day? Thinking I will only forget things now makes me feel empty. What will remain once I forget everything? You leave this life with nothing in your hands, they say, and they're right. It was fall. Harvest time, meaning we worked in the fields until dark. Came home one evening and saw Ippy had made dinner. Even used the grinder on the barley to make the rice soft. Don't know if Ippy remembers but it must've been the first time she made rice and it tasted wonderful. Chopped chili on the enamelware and cooked the braised anchovies in rice water and seasoned it with soy sauce very nicely. Surprised, I asked Ippy, How did you do this? You were three whole years older than Ippy and knew nothing of cooking, but here was your younger sister making a meal. Thinking I would be tired at night after working in the fields, she had tried her hand at it. It was such a treat to come home after a hard day's work to make dinner and then smell rice being cooked. The rice with a little barley mixed in came out so well that my bent back straightened and I felt like I'd been given a big present.

Everything lit up and I felt so much happiness as I said, How wonderful, you made dinner . . . There I was, hugging her for joy when your Father gets angry at me. For making the little one make dinner. Make her? She did it on her own! Ippy, after all her trouble, wasn't praised but scolded by your father: Don't ever cook again! You hadn't come home yet at this point. I said, What's wrong with you? The little one was only doing a kind deed for her mother . . . Your father demanded I don't make the children cook, that they were too young. Couldn't believe what he was saying. Meanwhile, the little one is crying her eyes out . . . So her cooking is asking too much, but me cooking after a hard day's work is all right, is that what he meant? I shot this back at him, and he was quiet and said later that he was sorry. That he had suddenly remembered how your aunt had worked so hard to cook their meals every day and he had blurted out the wrong thing. I think that watching Ippy cook made him think of your aunt and he was afraid she would end up like her. Anyway, I could never ask Ippy to put the rice on again, after all that fuss. And if he hates his daughter cooking so much, why doesn't he do it himself? Should've taught him to cook his own meals even when I wasn't there but I didn't. You know your Father can cook all kinds of things. When you were all little and spring was coming, and we were starved for heavy food over the winter, he would go to the town and get a load of pork ribs from the butcher, marinate them, set up a fire in a brazier under the persimmon tree and set a wide grill over it and cook the ribs for you children to eat. Made gukbab rice stew with kimchi and ribs thrown in. Or boiled them until the bone broth turned nice and white and the taste was perfect. But your father can't make rice. He can't set the water right. Not like we're doing it in iron pots over the kiln but he still can't do it. A strange thing. When the pressure cookers came out, the person who used them first was me. No idea what they were; it was your father who brought one home. What a clever invention it is. The rice you get from it—just sticky enough. But let's say they're tricky to use with their lids and their water levels and all that. The electric rice cookers they have nowadays just ask you to soak the rice and press a button and you're done. But your father can't do the soaking. Or maybe it's not that he can't—he won't do it. Don't you think so? This is the man who can put a cultivator together in one day. Men can be really useless. They don't know how freeing it would be to make your own food. No need to worry about irritating your wife for a meal, no need to eat when you don't want to . . . Well, if I'd taught your father how to make rice, your aunt would've run me out of the house.

No cooking, your father, but a diligent farmer he was. Holding the lines up so the rice gets planted straight and singing to the planters so they would feel lighter in their hearts, going out with a shovel before anyone had risen, even before the sun, to irrigate the fields, and such a kind man that even in the fields of people he fought with over water he would pick up their stray rice panicles, and in the winters after the harvest he would clean those farming implements until they shone and go out early late winter before everyone else watching for spring, and in the summers scything the grass to make compost. Going all the way to Gochang for good earth to pour on his fields, which were so well-turned that anyone passing would think, It's that Nungmweh man's field . . . They knew his work at first sight.

PARK MULEUNG

Who are you again?
Who?
Oh . . .
What's in the box?
Books?
Your father told me to bring those to me? But I can hardly see with my eyes now let alone read. How is your father? It's been a while since I last saw him. Not sick, is he? I used to see him at least once a month. Didn't know his daughter would come looking for me. I heard he had a writer daughter, is that you? If it is, he must be very happy right now. It pained him that he never got to see you often.

How should I address you? We've just met, I can't just call you by your name. *You there* is a little rude, but *writer-seonsaeng* is awkward on my tongue. Can I just call you *my friend*? I call everyone younger than me that.

You want me to use the informal form?

Oh, I can't do that. We've only just met and you're a writer-seonsaeng to boot. If you don't like being called *my friend*, don't worry too much about it because I've a feeling we won't ever meet again. Maybe it's because I've read your books, but you don't seem like a stranger to me. Did you know that? Your father talks a lot about you. Even when I act indifferent about them, he always brings me your books when they're published. Some are autographed, do you remember? Well, I suppose you autograph your books all the time. Why that face? Ah, so you do remember. See, if you really want to remember, you can. He brought autographed copies almost every time. You couldn't have thought to do that yourself; your father must've asked you to do it. I'm sure as you signed, you wondered from time to time, Who is this man?

Ah . . . I'm sorry for laughing. I just remembered something from long ago. I'd asked him what his daughter did for a living. Your father said you were someone who wrote letters. So I thought you were a calligrapher. You know, who rubs inkstones with ink and dips a brush into it to write. I thought, His second daughter is a pharmacist but his eldest girl is a calligrapher, how odd. I'm not such a man of the world, you see. I have never seen a female calligrapher and couldn't imagine what one would look like. But I took your father at his word, misunderstanding and all, until one day, your father brought over a newspaper folded up in his back pocket and spread it in front of me. Saying his daughter was in the paper. And that was you, to my surprise.

—You mean, this is your daughter?

He said yes. The newspaper was a local one, published in J—. You being from here, the reporter kept asking you about your childhood memories of J—. About school, your teachers, being a child, your parents who still lived here . . . You hated doing that interview, right? The questions were banal, but your answers were also pedestrian, uninspired. Something about suffering bug bites in a storage shed to read your books. The interviewer asked why you read in there, and you said it was because you had so many siblings that the only way to read in peace was to go to the shed.

After my body became like this, I spent my life reading everything in sight.

Now even reading is hard for me and I stopped a few years ago, but at one time I subscribed to three newspapers in the middle of this mountain village. I felt bad they had to deliver just one paper all the way up here every day, so I ended up subscribing to all three they offered. It's not wrong to say my only joy in life was reading the papers. Tomorrow meant new papers would be delivered. Sometimes I'd wake up in the middle of the night and yearn for the sun to rise because of the papers. I saw you several times in them, my friend. But the one your father brought me wasn't a national daily but a local paper. After he showed it to me, he folded it carefully and put it back in his pocket. So I told him, Your eldest daughter is not a calligrapher but a writer. So the next time anyone asks, he should call you a writer. He had no idea what I was getting at, but he did keep bringing me your new books. Maybe he thought they would help because I was always reading something, or that I understood you on some level he couldn't. I don't think your father reads your books. I said to him, You can always take it a few pages at a time. Shouldn't you read the books your own daughter wrote? He said reading your books made him feel you were getting further away from him. That you sounded like you were lying. That he never knew you to be a liar, but when he read your work, he felt you were lying a lot. I said that wasn't lying, that was being imaginative. Did I say the right thing?

Oh, you think I've got lots of books?

Your father brought them to me whenever I asked. He started bringing me books when he brought some of yours over. I asked him what all this was, and he said his daughter was going overseas for a couple of years and was moving out of her old place, and that she had sent over two truckloads of books for safekeeping. That all her books in Seoul were now in J——. He brought a box of them to me. When I read them I'd come across references to other books, which I'd write down and ask your father to get for me, and he'd pass them on to a bookstore in town. A few days later he would pick them up and bring them here, and twenty years of that led to this pile.

Don't just stand there, come over here and sit down. You see how I can't walk. Putting the prosthetics on is a chore. Is it strange to say that since the war, it's just been me in my life and the cat that goes in and out? It's one cat but the latest of scores of generations. Each one has a kitten here and after a while the mother disappears and another kitten appears and so on. Cats with stumpy tails, sometimes with six toes. Sometimes the yard would be full of them, but I guess there was never enough to eat around here for them and eventually there will only be a couple that stick around. With my body being like this, I wondered what I could do with myself. There wasn't much except to read. And even my eyesight has limits. All I can see is down to there. After the war, people would say to me—a Gwagyodong man upon hearing someone was from Jangseong or lived in Jangseong would ask, Have you seen Park Muleung? The mention of my name would make them go, Ah . . . This man from Gwagyo-dong, he was looking for me. Your father—I heard many times he searched for me. But he didn't visit me himself. Well, I would've done the same. I'm alive, as you see, all he had to do was come. And because I was in the same state as I am in now, I couldn't go see him myself. I knew he wanted to know what had happened to me and I also knew why he couldn't bring himself to come to me. Because that's how I felt, too. That if I were your father it would've been the same. It's all because of the war. Thinking of that makes me wonder what will be left after I die. They say you've got to live in a way so that you will have the least regrets. Does that apply to people like me as well? Some people, you see, their destinies are decided by their times and situations . . . What is there to think about, in my case? That

I shouldn't be swept away by a current without at least thinking about the current? What's the point of knowing the current . . . when there's nothing I can change. I understand what your father felt in the years he'd ask after me but did not see me. He was in the current; there's nothing I can say to that. But one year, he suddenly came to my door with his third son who was a college student. And both your father and I were so old that it wasn't a problem at all. It was even silly to think about all the years spent not seeing each other. All I said when he showed up was, You're here. Like I hadn't been aware until that moment that I'd been expecting him all this time. That I'd been waiting for him. I sound like I'm talking about someone else. But there are just some things you realize much later on. When I saw your father again, it didn't feel like I'd missed him or I was glad to see him, it felt like a knot was being untied.

Who is this third son?
How should I know?
You'd know better if anything.
If he's the third son he must be your third eldest brother.
What a terrible world we lived in back then. Me and your father, having survived a war where we could have died on any given day, used to think no matter how bad the world got afterward, it wouldn't get as bad as that. This attitude will never change for us. What use is it to tell young people that now. The coup d'état gave power to a president who ruled for the next twenty years almost, and I thought he would be president forever, but then his underling shot him with a gun. I think your brother was brought to me right after that. Something about a state of emergency, universities were closed, and gatherings of over five people were forbidden. His son was going to a university in Seoul, I think. Chased by something all the way home, and your father brought him here. The son could barely unbend his back. Forehead creased like he was in pain, but still a handsome young man. Taller than your father. Think of such a man almost being carried here by your father on his back. Twenty years since our paths split

in the chaos of the war, but it was like we'd been together yesterday and the day before. Like before, your father called me hyeong, and without further preamble asked me to take care of his son for a bit. No, to be precise, to hide him. His hothead of a son with no fear of anything in this world had made trouble, was caught, then tortured, beaten until his back was injured, and was on the run and sure he would never survive if he were caught again.

How is he doing these days?

I asked him what his crime was, and the young man said he'd been protesting. The son lived with me here for about half a year. Later he told me he hadn't come home on his own. When he was on the run, he had hidden in the university campus. Not knowing his father would come all the way there looking for him. While surreptitiously passing out fliers on campus, he had spotted your father looking around the campus and was trying to jump over the wall dividing the school and the old palace when he fell and the fliers scattered, and your father caught him in the mess. That son told me all kinds of news I never read about in any of my papers. That someplace called Namyeong-dong in Seoul was full of college students caught protesting and tortured. That he had been beaten there, injuring his back, and falling from that wall hadn't helped, which is how your father managed to force him to come home. Every morning your father carried a metal lunchbox packed with rice and stew and ban-chan on his bike and brought it here. Once every four days he brought salt and heated up a sack of it to put on his son's back. He must've heard someone say heated salt was good for the back. I don't think it's that effective, but it's the strangest thing. Nowadays when my back feels stiff, I find myself heating up salt. Father and son never exchanged a word. Your father didn't so much as open his mouth in front of him. When the son tried to speak, your father would get up and leave. I asked him once why he wouldn't talk to his son, and he told me that your brother was too big for his britches to be reasoned with. That listening to him talk made his rage flare up, ready to burst out of him. That not listening to his son was the only way he could stand the situation. The war had passed, and this time would pass, too, and until then, all he was going to think about was keeping his son alive.

But why do you want to know about your father and me?

Ah . . . You're a writer.

You're gathering material, aren't you?

Then what?

You want to know your father?

What?

Your father suffers from insomnia?

Well, it's good to see you here like this. I don't know when the last time was I saw another person. I called 1-1-9 the other day. You don't have to look around—nothing was burning. I didn't call because of a fire. They say the fastest way to get someone to appear around here is by dialing 1-1-9. I'd do it more often if they didn't bring the fire truck, but it makes me feel bad when they drive it out all this way. Yesterday had been a month since I'd spoken to someone. I couldn't stand it, so I called. I told the firefighter, let's eat jajangmyeon noodles, my treat. Who knew we could get jajangmyeon delivered all the way out here now. We sat right where you're standing now, eating jajangmyeon. Not to mention sweet and sour pork. The young firefighter had sauce all over his grinning mouth, and he left, admonishing me to never make such a call again. I told him to come closer so I could wipe the sauce off his face but he just left. He even paid for the noodles. That was yesterday and now you're here, so if I see someone tomorrow that's three days in a row I've spoken to someone. Can you believe my luck?

I met your father before the war began.

The Railway Office was hiring railroad track repair trainees. Applications accepted at the J— Station office. It wasn't my dream or anything to become a railway man. And it wasn't even administrative work; it involved checking the rails when the trains weren't passing through, tightening couplings, fixing what was broken, temporary work. Your father and I did not get along. I had an older brother whose school fees so overwhelmed my father that he did not want me to follow in my brother's bookish footsteps. At the time I was young and didn't want to listen to my father, and so I went to the station as soon as I saw that job opening. To put in my application and take the written test. As it was hard to live off farming at the time, there were many applicants. At the station offices there was a young man, almost a boy, standing by himself outside. It was your father. I could tell he had taken some care with his clothes. White shirt tucked into black trousers. A manila envelope in his hand. I figured he had come for his application form like me, but he was still standing there by the time I had come back out. And then he started following me. I figured we simply happened to be going in the same direction but I had an odd feeling about him, and after a while I turned around and demanded, What do you want from me? He asked if we could fill in our application forms together. He was so desperate I couldn't bring myself to say no. I had to fill mine out, anyway. There wasn't anywhere to sit so we went back to the station. Sitting uncomfortably in the smelly waiting room seats, your father called me Muleung hyeong. When asked how he knew my name, he replied how could he not know the smartest person in J—. I was the smartest person in J—? I liked the sound of that. I really wanted to study, you know. If it weren't for my father I would've left this place, spent the war elsewhere, and my life would've turned out completely different. My farmer father was worried that I would get scholarly notions in my head like my brother. He couldn't afford to send us both to school so he made sure I would never dream of getting an education. Your brother studying is enough, you have to stay at home and take on the family work. That's the refrain I heard nonstop since I was a child. My father took me down to the rice paddies for weeding and then sent me up to the mountains until sunset to gather wood. Furious, I would open a book right in front of him and read every day. When he told me to gather wood, I took my axe to the mountains, hit a tree hard enough to make a loud sound he could hear, and then sat down to read. Even when we had to go into town on the oxcart, I made a point of sitting up straight and reading a book the whole way. Even with the rattling of the oxcart. That must've been where your father got the idea. Because every time he saw me, I was reading a book—he mistook me for a smart person. Even as we were filling out the applications, I realized that your father was an excellent writer of classical Chinese characters. When I complimented him, he said he had learned from his father. He could read Hangul but found it difficult to decipher, so I read out the form to him many times and helped him fill in the blanks. Anyway, we had submitted our forms and were on our way home when your father then said he would do anything I asked him to if only I helped him with the written test.

Help him with the written test?

We didn't know what would be on the test, much less study for it, which made me laugh, and his face turned red. But he said, Muleung hyeong, you read many books and studied a lot, you must be able to predict what's on the test. He begged me so much that I relented. It was like seeing myself begging in front of my father. And until he made that proposal, I hadn't even thought of trying to predict what was on the test; it was good thinking on his part. How refreshing it was to have someone begging me to study, not begging me to drink.

Why do you keep standing there by that tree?

Is it because of the way I look? I know I look repulsive but . . . You're too far away for me to talk to you about your father. The tree next to you is a bokjagi. Have you heard of it? Also known as a three-flowered maple. The trees growing by the bokjagi are Japanese Judas trees. You're a writer, you should see the bokjagi and Judas leaves turn sometime. If not here, then elsewhere. My body is so mangled that I've done nothing but read and listen all these years, but I have never read a writer describe the way bokjagi and Judas trees turn their leaves. It makes me think writers are quite lazy. How overwhelmingly beautiful it is when bokjagi leaves turn. Summer is the hardest season for me. I can't go anywhere and it makes me want to die, but I always tell myself to stick around to see the leaves turn one more time . . . That's how pretty they are. Their reds are as sparkly as baby birds' eyes. Incomparable to other trees in the fall. You're a writer; you really should see them in the forest in season. Even if you weren't a writer, anyone gazing upon bokjagi leaves in the fall or breathing in the sweet scent of the trees would be freed—if only in that moment—of whatever ails them. The bokjagi trees are discernable from a distance. They have this blinding shine. Like they're showing off how they're bokjagi. People say it's a supercilious tree. What does "supercilious" mean? A writer, asking me this question? I guess the dictionary definition is, to act superior to others. We say bokjagi is supercilious because it's so prideful and it knows it, I suppose. The tree next to it is a Judas tree and it grows well anywhere and quickly. The leaves turn five colors—such exceptional beauty. You smell it before its beauty catches your eye. I don't know how to describe its scent. You're the writer; you smell it and try your hand at it. That sweet smell as the leaves change color, it seeps into the air around it, and one finds oneself following the scent with their eyes to the Judas.

Are you really going to keep standing there? And here I am, unable to get up . . .

Your father was full of passion for learning. His eyes shone at the prospect of that nothing of a test. Taking in every single thing I said and making it his, I could barely keep up. He took an hour and a half every morning walking all the way here. To the exact spot where you're standing. We put a table on the platform there, put our heads together, and studied what we could. He always brought something with him when he came. Like a potato or an egg . . . Speaking of potatoes and eggs! He was always putting things in my house. Like his third son to hide, twenty years after I had last seen him, although later I heard that since your father learned that I lived here, he would come up to the house from time to time. After the harvests he would leave rice, a sack of potatoes, meat wrapped in newspaper on holidays, thermal underwear and thick gloves in the winters . . . I thought it was some relative who had taken pity on me, and it was only much later that I learned it was your father. When his third son was here, he brought thermals and fur-lined shoes for his son as well, and that's when I figured it out. Because there were no other thermals left for me that year. It had been your father all this time. It took that long! We studied, but back then I didn't know much about the world, either. All I could do was what your father suggested, to simply try to predict what kind of questions they would ask, but he was so grateful for even that tenuous thing. He never came empty-handed. Even if it was a few sweet potatoes. He was so studious that when I couldn't think of anything more to study, he asked if it was because he hadn't been a good student, that he would do his best . . . Well. Despite our efforts, the war began even before we could take the test, and our studies were for naught. Do you think we would've become railway men if it hadn't been for the war? If you look out that way, you'll see the trains passing toward Cheonan. Life is strange. If it weren't for the war it would've been some other unimaginable current that swept us away. And our lives, they would look very different from how they look now.

It happened in Galje.

Maybe it's called Noryeong now. Every place has its stories but there are still rumors about the ghosts that haunt Galje, that's how many people died there. Look. That's Ibamsan Mountain and that's Bangjangsan Mountain. They're rough mountains, the partisans hid there and went from valley to valley killing countless people. Peasants with no power were killed by this side, by that side. The only thing that ordinary people had wanted to do by crossing the Galjae Pass was to go about their business, but the ones in hiding didn't want their whereabouts to be known, they'd kill whoever passed and then tossed the bodies into the valley. Those partisans really did some damage to our army. Because neither side wanted to give up the pass. It's the boundary that divides the North and South Jeolla provinces, the only way into the south . . . If the Southern army had lost the Galjae Pass to the partisans, their pathway south would be blocked, which is why the fighting was so desperate.

What?
Did you say Cha Wuhyuk?
How do you know that man?
Your father told you about him?
I think you mean Ilhyuk.

He was no ordinary man. Born in Hongseong, or was it Gimje? Some called him the bastard child of Cha Cheonja. Unforgettable, he was. We were in the middle of a war but it was Cha Ilhyuk who let us hear music. In the year after the war had broken out, around spring, the partisans were holding strong in the Galjae Pass. Cha Ilhyuk was on the opposite side, directing the police. My father, who had refused to send me to school, was the village head. What we'd call the mayor now. How could he have known his elder son in the city of C—, whom he had thought was diligently studying, was a commie? The partisans marched around with bamboo spears and wooden bats and dragged even the village children up the mountains for re-education, but they always left me alone—I thought it was because my father was the village head. Later, I learned it was my brother's doing. The upper hand changed constantly in the war. The people training their beady eyes at the villagers could be partisans, then the army, then when the partisans won back the territory, they would massacre anyone who had collaborated with the army. And when the army was in power they would mow down whoever had helped the partisans . . . the valley of Galjae was a horrific place. It's funny to think about now, but since my brother was on the left, my father tried to play both sides by enlisting me in Cha Ilhyuk's police force.

How could that be possible?

Nothing was impossible back then. You could graduate from middle school and get a job as a schoolteacher.

This was also during the student soldier uprisings.

That's how I became part of Cha Ilhyuk's regiment and fought in the battles at Galjae. Your father was about to be conscripted, which was why he couldn't sleep in his own house and had to live in hiding. When he was desperate, he came to me. And when I said I'd become part of Cha Ilhyuk's police force, he begged me to get him in it. But he had lost his trigger finger, putting it out of the question. Instead, I put him up in a shed not too close to the house and got him food. But your father kept circling the regiment. He followed us. Even in the mountains when we'd stay up all night in the winds and rain, he was hiding close by. Even when I found him and tried to convince him to leave, he kept saying this was safer than hiding in the shed. Then one day, our regiment was tasked with saving a touring actors' troupe.

What, you say? Actors touring in a war?

I'm telling you, it's absurd to think about now, but back then it really happened. Maybe because we needed music more than ever in a war. For morale, and to ease our worries for a spell. What was that troupe called? I can't remember, but back then there was a famous troupe that everyone wanted to see. A tragic actress nicknamed the "Queen of Tears." She was the troupe leader. And there was Go Boksu, Hwang Geumshim . . . People like that were performing in it; they were very famous. But I've forgotten the name of the troupe. Some bird or something. Their shows were epic. It was a wasteland of an era, and when the troupe was in town, people gathered like rainclouds. Our neighbors would be dying, and we were spending each moment in fear of what the day would bring—by the end of each song, the audience was an ocean of tears. That troupe had finished performing in Gwangju and were on their way to Jeonju through Galjae when they were ambushed by the partisans. If it weren't for Cha Ilhyuk, the troupe would've been massacred or dragged away somewhere. And if they'd been dragged away . . . After Cha Ilhyuk's counterattack, the partisans retreated into the mountains. And making his way through the shaking performers, who a moment ago were convinced they were going to die, Cha Ilhyuk went right up to the troupe leader, the Queen of Tears herself, and asked if they could put on a show. A show, when just moments ago, bullets had been flying past their noses. Can you imagine? Despite their consternation, Cha Ilhyuk kept pleading his case. Well, he was smiling at the time, but it was more of a command. Quite an eccentric, he was. A flaring temper, but also an eloquent and concise speaker, and I've seen no one match his wit. Getting rid of the partisans was his mission, and you know, Hwaeomsa Temple itself, the very famous temple in South Jeolla Province, he was the one who saved it. Partisans hid away in the mountains, and when summer came and the foliage made it difficult to spot them, an order came down to burn all dwellings and temples in the mountains. I don't know if he was Buddhist, but Cha Ilhyuk seemed to want to protect Hwaeomsa. He had his regiment take the gates and doors off Hwaeomsa and burn them near the main building. And since there were no doors, he reasoned there were no places for the partisans to hide from bullets, and left. He accomplished his mission, and at the same time guarded what needed to be guarded.

When the troupe was concerned about how they were to perform under such circumstances, Cha stopped being polite and practically begged them to raise the morale of his men who didn't know if they were going to survive from one moment to the next. Watching such a tough guy be so sincere perplexed his men and some of them had to suppress their laughter. But his sincerity worked. And that's how a musical performance was held in the valley where bullets had whistled through moments before. *I cried as I came and cried as I left, if you do not understand my tragic fate, who shall?* Hwang Geumshim's voice echoed through the valley. You won't believe me, but it's true. The men started singing along one by one, and the mountains were full of the sound of the stream and singing. *You who must know, you who should know, why do you pretend to not know?* Lyrics that had not even the slightest to do with war, ringing in the hills. They say retreated partisans heard and sang along from afar—yes, all of this really happened. This song,

I can still sing it to this day. I find myself, after all these years, singing it from time to time. A song only I sing and hear, heavy with the frost of regret. Why did people of the same blood kill each other and point guns at each other and bury each other in hastily dug pits? These were people who would've fought in the resistance side by side during the Japanese occupation. We couldn't continue singing along. In the middle of the performance, the partisans attacked. The fighting started again. Those players who had been so scared at the thought of performing in the beginning sang on through the whole battle.

I made this cutting board. And that's a wooden pillow. These are cubes. You can put them in pillowcases and get rid of smells. This is a cypress steamer basket. A bit complicated to make, but fun. The cutting board and pillow are old, but I've just started on this steamer. Restaurants use it to steam food. You line it with mung bean sprouts and put some brisket on top along with a few greens. Who knew cypress wood could be used in this way? It was your father's idea to make something like this. Saying I needed to make a living somehow. So I followed his advice and that's how I've survived. In the very beginning, your father brought me a cypress block from a lumbermill and told me I should try making a cutting board from it. I still remember the first time I did. The scent of it got stronger when it was wet, so I'd soak it and put it by my pillow . . . I spent many years sitting here and cutting cypress planks and sanding them. Your father connected me to a store in town that would sell them. Cutting boards was how I started but when I got really interested in it, he got me some other things I could make as well. Neck pillows, wooden pillows—he took all of it to the store in town and brought me back the money. Cypress doesn't burn well. Which is good, but it doesn't cut easily either, making it difficult to carve. Which is why people avoid it, even back when wood was rare, but now the material is a point of pride. Ever since they found out how resistant to germs it is. The world won't settle. It changes according to need. Of course it does. How meaningless it is to have convictions.

In this new battle, our side won handily. We did have more ammunition than the partisans. It was clear when the partisans left behind their dead that they were about to give up Galjae and retreat permanently. Our morale was never higher. In the mountains one day, we cooked chickens, made rice balls, and drank alcohol. There were few days when we could eat so well. Thinking of your father hiding in the woods, I smuggled out my share of the chicken and rice balls to give to your father. Since he was hungry, I was going to drop them off as quickly as possible, when before I could even get to him I was captured by the partisans. They grabbed the food from my hands and ate them up as quick as lightning. I think they were deserters. I had no way of knowing how long they had been starving, but judging by how fast they ate up that food, I became afraid they'd eat me as well. They held a gun up to my head and demanded to know who I was bringing food to in the middle of the night. I told them I was afraid my food would be taken by the other men and so I was looking for a place to eat alone. They didn't fall for my awkward lie. The gun moved to my throat. I wonder now if it had any bullets in it . . . When killing, there are many ways to save bullets. It wasn't a standoff situation; there was no reason to waste a bullet on someone who was running somewhere with a bag of rice and chicken . . . But that only occurred to me later. In the moment, I thought I would die that day. Your father, who had been watching us from the forest, couldn't bear to stay hidden any longer and bolted out of the foliage. He had no other choice. They were heading to where he had been hiding. And that's how we became prisoners of war. They tied our hands behind our backs and linked us with a rope as they dragged us through the night forest. We walked for such a long time that I didn't know where we were. Tripping on the trail, getting torn by branches, following the terrain down as well as up. There was no way to tell where we were going. But at some point, I began to smell a terrifying stench. The ones urging us on with guns to our backs were the first to block their noses and take a step back. I realized immediately it was the smell of rotting corpses. There had been rumors that the people from Uchi-ri or Namchang Village had been massacred by the partisans, their bodies were piled up in pits. And I had heard the news that my own brother had been executed there. Devastated, my father and I stuffed our feet into our shoes and set out to find him. It was the same smell that had assaulted my nose at the time. The police were keeping watch during the day, so we had to hide nearby until it got dark. When night fell, I followed my father to the valley where the corpses were said to be, but the darkness made it impossible to see in front of us. Birds flew up from the bush wherever we moved, and as we made our way, we were terrified we would be discovered—anyway, that was the smell from back then. As soon as I realized this, I couldn't take another step forward. The fear was one thing, but I couldn't stand the smell. My father, determined to find my brother's body, made his way through the stench to the valley but I couldn't follow him. Mucus flowed from my eyes, my nose, my ears, everywhere I had holes. I kept wiping my face with my sleeve. How could I forget that smell? Behind us I could hear the partisans whispering about this being the place they had dug pits. Where they had executed scores of people who they accused of cooperating with the militias, throwing them into the pits after. Sometimes they didn't bother with pits, and they tossed the bodies into the ravine. I knew what a blessing the darkness of the night was, that it was only the smell I was dealing with and not the sight. This amount of stench meant the bodies would be unrecognizable as people—they were just bones tossed aside. They may have covered up the bodies with dirt to prevent the dead from being recognized, but there was nothing they could do about the smell. I just collapsed on the spot. Your father, too. Despite not having eaten anything in a long time, he leaned against a tree in the dark and kept vomiting.

The smell of vomit was refreshing compared to the stench from the valley. Neither of us could walk anymore in that smell no matter how much they force us. And they could no longer walk because we couldn't. There were three bastards who had taken us prisoner, and one of them told your father to run toward the smell. That if he did, he would let him live. Still vomiting, your father kept looking for me in the dark until one of them threatened to kill him if he didn't run now. The valley was full of trees and rocks and inclines. It wasn't the kind of terrain you could run on. As they watched him stumble in the dark, one of them untied me and put a gun in my hand. Telling me to shoot your father who was running into the valley. The other two bastards had their guns trained at me. I said to them, If you shoot, your location will be exposed. That made them hesitate. I didn't, telling them right away that I was under the command of Captain Cha Ilhyuk. That he and his men were close by. Cha Ilhyuk? they said. I thought I had them for a moment, but then one of them said they didn't believe me, and ordered me to shoot your father. When I continued to refuse, they told your father to come back. Threatening to kill me if he didn't. He was far off by now; there was no way he would return. But in a little while, there he was, limping toward us again. A war where it was kill or be killed, but there was still a bit of naïveté and innocence left in the world, I suppose. I had told them Cha Ilhyuk was close by because I wanted to persuade them. You see, Cha Ilhyuk was a little different from the other militia leaders at the time. He was acclaimed for having killed many partisans, but killing wasn't all he did. Cha often converted partisan deserters to fight for the other side. He was quite the orator behind the megaphone. And he actually followed through on his promises. He even buried fallen partisans, observing their proper rites. Which is why his name spread quickly among them. There was a belief that if they could meet him in person, they might survive. Which is why I mentioned I was one of Cha's men. Seeing as they didn't shoot us when they could've, I realized they weren't interested in killing us. If I could convince them and return to the regiment, all five of our lives could be saved. But when your father came back, they tied my hands behind my back again and gave the gun to your father. Ordering him to shoot me. In the dark, your father said he couldn't fire a gun, and showed them his maimed hand. What a twilight comedy that was. One of them came up to me and slammed the butt of his rifle against my head. I was beaten up so badly, I went in and out of consciousness. When I fell, another bastard kicked me, and I felt like I was about to throw up a lung. Covered in blood, I could hear them tell your father to roll me down into the valley. That if he didn't, they would shoot him.

What do you think your father did then? Did he push me down into the valley filled with corpses below as they ordered? I don't know. The only thing I remember was that I was more frightened of the smell coming from below than any threat they can make. The smell made me half lose consciousness, not helped by the beating I'd received. But no matter how tattered my body became, I kept inwardly shouting, Anything but being thrown down there. Then—*click*—blackout. My consciousness ended. It was my father who found me among the corpses in that valley. He couldn't find my brother back before, but he could find me. Through the name he had tattooed on my shoulder when he sent me into Cha Ilhyuk's regiment. He had it tattooed when he'd failed to find my brother among the corpses. And that's how he could drag me out of that mountain of corpses that overflowed the pit in the valley, but I wonder if that was a good thing in the end; my bleeding body was half gangrenous by then, which is why they had to amputate my legs.

I learned of the place Vosnon in France from one of the books in the first batch your father brought me. Did you know that I've read almost all of your books? He kept swapping boxes of them whenever I finished one until he said there were no more from your library I hadn't read.

Have you ever been to Vosnon?

Never?

Where is it, you say?

You really don't know?

How surprising. After I read that book from your own shelf, I became so curious about that village and used to yearn to visit it. I wondered what kind of place it could be that two such people could live like that there. But you don't know Vosnon at all? I thought you'd know since the book was yours. Do you remember it, the one written by Gorz? A thin book, but it made me think many thoughts. I'm guessing Vosnon is a little country village like this one. Gorz was eighty-three and Dorine, his wife, was a year younger at eighty-two, and the two of them died lying side by side in their bedroom in Vosnon. The book said neither had wanted to die alone—that the world had been shocked by their choice. I hadn't known anything about them until then. The first I'd heard of them was because of the will they left, asking to be buried in the yard of the house in Vosnon where they had lived together for twenty years. I still can't forget that will. There was a time when I yearned to know all about this couple who asked to be buried together. I learned that Gorz was a Jewish man from Austria, a philosopher and journalist who had deeply analyzed capitalism, socialism, and environmentalism, and that Dorine was an even more accomplished intellectual. Every life has a period where we settle down. They had such an era, too. They had settled in France and were at the peak of their intellectual powers when Dorine contracted a serious disease from spinal surgery. Ah, you seem to be remembering what I'm talking about. Yes. What fascinates me is the life Gorz chose after he learned of his wife's illness. No one can make such a choice easily. To give up his entire career. To leave Paris for Vosnon with his wife. They decided to ride out her sickness there. For twenty-three years, Gorz lived a new life in Vosnon, taking care of his wife. He looked up alternative therapies for her, cultivated organic vegetables so she could have a better diet, and became an environmentalist. Environmentalism wasn't just a theory to him, it was a way of life. Gorz had gone out to the countryside for Dorine, but he says it was he who gained time and space to think, if anything. To concentrate on what is truly fundamental. He wrote to his wife that no matter how much he thought about it, the only truly fundamental thing was to be with her. I realized, reading that, if I had never known war and just lived my life the way I wanted to, that would've been it. The first lines of a letter Gorz wrote Dorine a year before they left this world together read like this:

You will be eighty-two soon. You're six centimeters shorter than before, and weigh only forty-five kilos. But you are still seductive, and elegant, and beautiful. We have been together for fifty-eight years, but now more than ever before, I love you.

Are these lines too beautiful for someone as useless as me to know by heart? Their life in Vosnon didn't always go smoothly. The first house they lived in was built for meditation to aid Dorine's treatment. But unexpectedly, a nuclear power plant went up nearby, which meant they had to move. They bought an old house, set up a new fence, and planted trees in the grass. We planted 200 trees today, he wrote. They let in hungry and sick stray cats, giving them food and care. Thankfully, Dorine's condition improved somewhat, allowing them to take the occasional, manageable trip. Manageable trips, mind you. They couldn't travel far. Because Dorine's disease gave her headaches and full-body pain while driving. Through all this, Gorz, with Dorine's encouragement, continued to write. That was their life in Vosnon. Concentrating on each other and being true to each other. Do you remember their will? Its last line, and the last line of the book, is that the world was empty and they did not want to live any longer. That the two of them were one, and they hoped neither would have to survive without the other. The whole time I read that book was a blessing to me. After I read their will, your books that your father brought me became much more interesting to me than the papers. Books pushed away the long and stifling hours ahead of me. I've never actually seen the bookshelf in the small room of your house, but I've read every book in it. It was a time of pure pleasure for me in this little country village. I'm so happy I could thank you for it now. I'm curious, the books about fishing and birdkeeping . . . Why did you buy those books? One of the boxes your father brought was full of books like that. Even about raising terrapins. I read those, too. They were underlined a lot. Why did you underline them? I could never figure it out.

What?

Oh, they were research for your own writing?

Really? Ah . . . I see now. Reading the books you've written, I was distracted by an error here and there. One of your earlier works, I think, had a scene where a character sprinkles lily seed. But lilies are grown from bulbs.

You plant bulbs, not seeds. I'm not nitpicking, I'm just saying those are the kind of things that tend to ruin the reading experience. I wondered if you only liked lilies and never grew them yourself. What? You read a book so you could write about lilies? So I guess you also have a story with terrapins? Anyway, reading soothes me. Would you understand it if I told you that reading enabled me to accept myself? I could understand humanity through books. How weak we are, and also how strong we are. How endlessly good, and yet endlessly violent. People for whom things did not turn out the way they wanted, who fought unhappiness all their lives—they leave a trace of themselves. Traces of having endured unspeakable situations. I wonder if my act of reading was a search for such traces.

My eyes ache nowadays, so I can't read anymore. The last thing I managed to read recently was an interview with the pianist Kun-Woo Paik. He lives in Paris but apparently came to Korea to play Schumann at a concert. I don't know much about Schumann, but he is said to have lived a very complicated life, one filled with bitterness. Paik said he didn't understand those emotions when he was young, that it made him avoid Schumann. But now he could understand why Schumann had packed his bags and checked himself into a mental hospital. I read that part several times. Wondering what kind of a person Schumann must've been, checking himself into a hospital like that. Paik, who had said he had lately come to understand Schumann, was alone. His wife who had always accompanied him on tour wasn't by his side. I had a sudden urge to go to Paik's Schumann performance because at least I can still hear music . . . but I can't go. My eyes are bad, but of course my ears aren't much better. I shall become totally deaf soon. It's all right. I can't say it was a good life, but I think I endured it well enough. It was a long road reaching this point of acceptance.

You've listened to me for this long. Can you do me a favor? I heard from your father that you never come to J— anymore. That you had to say goodbye to your daughter, the one who came running to you . . . Your father always lamented how he could do nothing for you then. There was something you said in one of your books. *Life has ambushes.* When I read that, I turned to the flaps of the book, to the photo of your young face, mouth firmly closed and eyes looking off into the distance. I stared at it for a long time. How could such a young person write such a line? There have been ambushes in the times we lived through. There are lives completely comprised of ambushes. Lives where you want to scream to the skies, to the earth, rip out your heart and cry the fates, How could this happen? But nothing comes out of your mouth . . . But to live through it, that is human. Your father wanted to be by your side but you wouldn't let him come, and he was so tortured by that. How worried he was that there was not a word from you, like a dead person. Like recognizes like. I saw it when you first stepped into the yard. That you're someone who has already died before. I know how hard it is to keep living despite this, but the only human friend I have in this life is your father. Please let him be by your side. Endure with him, enjoy the sunlight with him, pick fruit with him, sweep the snow with him, all of that. Tell him your stories and listen to him tell his. What else is there to do for each other.

I do have one more favor to ask. Be honest. From the moment you came to this house, didn't you think there was a fearsome stench in the air? Why didn't you say so? Did you think it was coming from me? Well, I suppose I am made mostly of smell by now. Do you see, though, not the bokjagi tree next to you but the tree over there right before you turn the corner toward the backyard . . . that one? That's a cypress. Go look at what's under it. You'll find a yellow cat with white spots on its back, lying there dead. He was a friend of mine who lived here with me, but he passed away a few days ago. Crossed the forest and jumped the wall and walked across the yard to come all the way to my knee, the only bit of breath by my side, but he's gone on before me. As payment for my stories, please bury him for me. Leaving him like that will attract maggots . . .

Human or animal, death only leaves behind a body to rot and decay. All my life I've suffered from that unforgettable smell. No matter how much time passes, or how the world changes, it's always following me, always by my side, it grates on my soul . . . So please, my friend, bury that pitiful little thing for me before you go.

WHAT THE SON OF THE SON SAID

Aunt.

How is life in J—? I heard you had gone but I only found out today that you were still staying there. Dad told me. It made me wonder if I had been too out of touch with you lately. Did you take the train? If you had called me, I would've driven you. Remember years ago when you had to go to J— and asked me to drive you there? At first I did so with some reluctance, but once we were in the car, I really enjoyed our conversation. All these things from my childhood that I didn't remember . . . I love hearing those stories from you. Especially about poop. I don't know why I find it so hilarious that the thing I was most interested in as a little child was poop. That when I sat on the potty and pooped, I always called Dad. Dad, I pooped! Later, I learned that it was Dad who was in charge of my potty training. He would come and look in the potty and go, Look at that, good job! And I would smile like my cheeks would burst. Maybe that's it. My father is to blame for my early interest in poop. Or should I say, my interest in his interest in my poop. He would worry over the state of my stool and ask me questions about how I felt . . . Dad was checking on my health, you see. I think I just liked to see Dad's big smile when I'd made a good poop. Which was why I kept calling him over after a poop, and why I needed the confirmation of his smile.

How is Grandfather? You remember how Dad used to work in the city of C—. C— and J— were so close together that we went often to see Grandfather. He was pretty young back then. Wearing a leather jacket, hair pomaded, riding a bicycle. Going to Grandfather's house was fun because Grandfather was always willing to listen to me. He took me riding on the back of his bike, buying me Gameboys and soccer balls and that sort of thing. My parents forbade me from playing with video games, but Grandfather said that if all the other kids were playing with them but I wasn't, I would only grow to resent them. This made me think, as a child, that Grandfather was on my side. One time, he saw one of my textbooks had a stain on the cover, so he took all of my books out of my bag and used the thick pages of an old calendar to wrap each of their covers. He even wrote *Nature* or *Math* on the new covers depending on the subject. Saying the covers would keep the books clean. When the semester was over and I took the covers off, they really did look new, so I gave them to my little brother. One time, Mom punished me for something so I left home and took the bus alone to Grandfather's house. Grandfather didn't have a phone at home back then. When he saw that I was alone, he asked me, Did your mother punish you for something? I started crying. Grandfather took me on the back of his bike to the post office in town and called home, reassuring them that I was in J— and everything was all right. What miffed me was that I had come all the way from C— to Grandfather's house in J— on my own but my family hadn't even noticed I had left home. To think that I had run away, and they didn't even know I had run away. That upset me so much that I started crying again in the post office. Grandfather took me on his bike to a Chinese restaurant. I'd never been to one before and had fried dumplings and jjajangmyeon noodles for the first time. Pushing the plates in front of me, Grandfather kept asking, Is it good? Is it good? And I would say, Yes, Grandfather . . . still feeling teary and with jajang sauce all over my face. I remember his voice telling me to eat slower or I would get an upset stomach. Perhaps because it was my first time eating it, I think of Grandfather whenever I have jajangmyeon. Remember that time we went to J— together and took Grandfather to that jajangmyeon place? It bowled me over that the very same Chinese restaurant was still there. You wanted to order him something fancy like ohyang jangyuk steamed pork or stir-fried palbochae vegetables, but Grandfather said jajangmyeon was fine, which seemed to disappoint you. I think at the time I said we should drive down to J— together again, and that was already a few years ago.

Aunt.

My second child was born two days ago. I announced it on the family group chat, so I'm sure you saw it as well. The child must be an impatient one because he arrived two weeks before he was due. Two months before, my wife had felt contractions and was swiftly hospitalized. The doctor said if the contractions continue, they would have to deliver the baby early and told us to stand by, but thankfully things came back to normal within a week of entering the hospital. A premature birth would've meant the baby would've had to have gone straight into an incubator. Because we managed to avoid this scenario, my wife kept talking to the baby in her womb as we drove home from the hospital, Thank you, my darling. Thank you for being patient. And then he was born two weeks early.

Maybe it's because he was born two weeks early?

He's very small. 2.4 kg. Amazing that 2.4 kg can include a head, face, body, hands, and legs. His face is small, too. And that small face has everything: eyes, nose, and a mouth. A newborn with thick hair and clear eyebrows. His wriggly fingers and toes are so tiny that holding his hand makes my hand look as wide as a soccer pitch. Of course a newborn is tiny, you might say . . . But I bet if you saw him, Aunt, you'd think he was small, too. His size made me think back to my first. Was he big? My memories are vague already, but I don't think I've ever considered my first as small, but my second is very small. So small that his every movement seems wrigglier than normal. I just can't stop talking about how small he is.

I was in Hupo and wanted to keep on working a little longer but my wife said she felt the baby was coming, which made me return quickly to Seoul. How could I have left my pregnant wife behind to work in Hupo? I can sense how shocked you would be to read this. Well, things kind of happened that way. Hupo is a harbor on the East Sea—I wonder if you know it? I don't think I've ever heard you talk about it. This was the second time I'd ever been to Hupo. Script work sent me there in the beginning of the year as well. I had finished that work, and this new work was a side job I was doing for an online drama. Knowing I wouldn't be able to work for a long time once the baby was born, I wanted to get it out of the way.

Hupo is the hometown of our producer for the online show as well. His parents run a pension, and that's where we stayed. Seeing how we were behind, the producer told me to concentrate on the work as he left me at the pension and returned to Seoul alone. I wrote three scripts while I was there. I needed to finish two more episodes, but I came back anyway. You might find three complete scripts impressive, but we're talking about episodes that are five to seven minutes long. And they're interconnected, which makes the work much easier. They ought to be going into production by now. That would be great, but you know how it is in my field, things move along fine for a while and then, disaster . . .

I thought about you a lot while I was at Hupo. It's a really nice place to visit and rest. You and I both grew up inland, so the ocean is always new for us. I think I once read something that you wrote where you mentioned that mountains were so familiar to you that you never think you're traveling when you visit one, but when you're by the ocean, you get the feeling that you have come a long way. It's the same for me. Especially when I first went down Route 7, which starts in Sokcho and runs along the ocean. It made me wonder, is this truly the land I was born in? What a beautiful place, right here on our doorstep. Hupo is along that road. Pohang, Yeongdeok, Uljin—don't those town names make you think of saury fish? When I mention Hupo on the phone with friends, they ask me where it is. People don't know the place. Hupo is under Uljin, and it's a relatively prosperous fishing town. Some houses have two cars. A truck or an old car to go into town or to the harbor, and the jeep to go into Uljin or Yeongdeok. There's a passenger terminal at Hupo Harbor, and you can take a ferry from there to Ulleungdo Island. You can go to Ulleungdo Island for work, maybe, but it's not the kind of place you can visit on a whim. Writing this makes me think that once the second child is old enough, I should take him to Hupo and Ulleungdo. Like Father when he took me to Namdo Island after I was discharged from the military.

The eastern shore is generally beaches, but Hupo has both village and ocean, which gives it the look of a true fishing village. It's far from Seoul, which is probably why it's so quiet and peaceful. There are beaches everywhere, too, so it is great for walking or jogging by the ocean. My producer's mother runs a pension that's right by the beach. You don't have to make special plans to go down there, all you have to do is step outside and there it is. I imagine you walking toward the rocks every morning and then again at sunset. The water is so clear . . . You'll feel free from all your burdens. And the food is to die for. My producer's mother can really cook a delicious meal. To the point where you've got to make an effort every day not to eat so much. The cook's skills aside, it's the fresh flatfish and red snow crab that really makes the meal . . . Everything you like, Aunt, they have in Hupo. Which is why I was reminded of you so much. Since I was staying there for a while, I got to know some of the people who lived there and their stories made me think of you. Lots of stories that I wished we were listening to together. They say there are lots of rich people in Hupo, but not too many young people. Like many other places in Korea, the boats would be idle if it weren't for workers from overseas. The youth have left for Seoul, and all that's left are the old people. Even when many own their own boats now and their catch is so bounteous that it's perfectly possible to make your own fortune. There was so much work available; I briefly wondered if I should move down there. Most of the boaters of Hupo were from Indonesia. The scenery there was so impressive I wanted to capture it on film, and I got to know the Indonesian workers and ate with them and helped them work. They're a bit darker-skinned, very modest, and around twenty-five to thirty-five years old in age. They told me they send money back home every month. Occasionally they visit their families in Indonesia, and it makes their footsteps heavy as they have to leave their children behind again—the little ones growing bigger every year. When I ask them if they miss their children, they grin and look out at the ocean. One of these new friends is a thirty-five year old, and he said he'd been in Hupo for seven years now. His Korean is so fluent that sometimes the villagers ask him to interpret for them when dealing with other Indonesians. We became friends quickly, and he proudly told me how he bought a house and land in Indonesia with the money he had made in Hupo. That he was going to work a few more years and expand his land. That he's going to go back and farm that land. He told me the names of all the grains and fruits of the crops he was going to grow . . . He said that on the land his wife had bought, she was growing palm trees. I guess it's the same everywhere—when a crop does well, you can't get your crop's worth when you sell. He was worried that the palm market wasn't doing too well, and they wouldn't get their investment's worth. Being his friend made me see a different side of his situation, that he wasn't a poor laborer from an impoverished country. And that only a few decades ago, our fathers were the same as him. I still remember when we all went to the airport to see off Eldest Uncle on his posting in Libya. The people who gave me the warmest welcome when I went back to Hupo were the Indonesians. I was as happy as if I were reuniting with family after a long absence. It made me feel guilty that they'd slipped out of my mind when I'd gone back to my busy life in Seoul. And I wondered if I could shine a light on their story as well. I hope I can make a film about Hupo someday. We had our meals together and I chatted with them whenever we had the time. We differ in many ways. When Koreans reach a certain level of comfort, we put a lot of planning into our children's education, but Indonesians are more concerned with buying houses or land. They're mostly hands-off with their children's education . . . That struck me as an interesting difference.

I don't know if I would be able to do this, but I hope I get to travel a lot with my children. I still remember the trip I got to take with my dad after I was discharged from the military. I really enjoyed that time. To the point where I think about it every time I travel. A couple of days ago, I picked up my second child and went to the bank. To set up an installment savings plan so I could buy a camper by the time she's six or seven. We can barely get by, but to be saving for a camper . . . It was such a ridiculous situation that I didn't even tell my wife, but once I came back from the bank,

I felt less anxious about it. I thought about how that trip with my dad had come about. Dad was the one who had asked me to go on a trip with him as soon as I'd finished military service. The day I left the army, Dad drove up to the regiment gates. That feeling of freedom I felt as we took turns driving to Namdo Island. Yeosu, Mokpo, Haenam, Gangjin, Goheung . . . We changed hotels every night and went to the beach, the temples, and we ate clams, octopus . . . I loved it. A week flew by like it was a day. It was the first time Father and I treated each other as adults. Father asked questions about my college major, which was digital media studies: what job could I get with that? Being a bit naïve, I said I was more interested in going into film rather than some corporation. That I wanted to continue my studies in film. That everything I was learning in digital media studies was relevant to filmmaking—I think I got all excited as I blabbered on about this. He must've understood only half the things I was talking about, but he said, You should do what you want to do. Later, I thought he must've been under some strain because of me and my little brother. I was going to school for digital media studies, whatever it was, and my brother was studying for art school. The monthly fee for his preparatory classes was almost as high as Dad's salary. But he still sat by me on a potato patch by the sea at night, smoking with me and drinking beer . . .

On the last leg of that trip, we visited Grandfather's house. Because Dad suggested we drop in on J— on the last day and treat Grandfather and Grandmother to the hot springs. That Grandfather liked immersing himself in the hot waters there. When we got to J—, Grandfather told us that Grandmother had gone to Naejangsan Mountain with friends. It was her regular lunch club where the women ate namul wild vegetable banchan together, so Grandfather had stayed behind. A little regretful of having missed Grandmother, we took Grandfather to the hot springs near Byeonsan, anyway. I drove, and somewhere along the way, Grandfather handed Dad an envelope. When Dad saw that the envelope was full of money, he waved his hands in front of him, refusing to accept. I watched them fight about it through the rearview mirror. Grandfather was so adamant that Dad ended up shouting at him, Why are you doing this! But Grandfather refused to back down.

—It's from the rice harvest.

—. . .

—It's because your father didn't do anything for you.

—. . .

—You went to a military academy because I couldn't afford your tuition!

—. . .

—Since I couldn't pay then, pay Dongie's tuition with this here.

My tuition?

Grandfather, who was never a man of many words, had suddenly mentioned my tuition, and the envelope immediately became my business. It was hard watching them through the back mirror as I drove. Their pushing the envelope toward each other stopped and there was a heavy silence. For the rest of the ride, Grandfather stared out of the window on his side and Dad stared out of the other. *Why do they have to be so stubborn?* I thought. They continued to not speak to each other when we arrived at the hot springs and entered the warm water. But Dad did scrub Grandfather's back thoroughly. Saying, Father, you've lost so much weight. He scrubbed it for a long time, so I scrubbed Dad's. I'm not sure if Dad paid my tuition the next semester with the money Grandfather gave him, but in any case, the sight of the two of them arguing in the back seat is clear in my memory.

I remember when I got married. Even you, Aunt, were worried about me when I announced it. It was the first time you ever expressed concern about me. Because no matter what I got myself into, you always told me, I'm sure you'll do well. But when I mentioned I was getting married, you gave me a long look. How are you going to manage? You didn't say it out loud, but you were saying those words—if you know what I mean. At the time, I had just three short films to my name and no regular income, and to think that I was getting married . . . and to think despite all that, I did get married and become the father of two children. I wonder if I'm just foolhardy, you know? Recklessly getting into marriage, having two children. My wife will be displeased to hear this. I met her while shooting a short film, so she knows all about the industry. She likes what I do and believes in me and has faith that tomorrow will be better than today—I can't tell you how wonderful that is. It's why I married her, although who knows why she married me . . . I never got up the courage to ask. You know, Aunt, that my eldest has quite an appetite. He can finish a whole apple on his own and several slices of cheese . . . Some children have to be chased around the house because they don't want to eat, but we've never had to. Watching him eat even gives us an appetite. When it was just my wife and me, a single fried chicken was enough. Sometimes, we couldn't even finish that. But with the child growing, one wasn't enough. When he asks for fried chicken for dinner, I wonder whether we should order two. Once, we ordered one chicken and I ate a single piece and pretended someone had called me outside. I walked around the neighborhood before going back home. When will I be able to order two chickens without feeling it is a strain, I wonder . . . I suppose I should work harder and earn as much as I can. See? I'm a father already.

Around the time I got married, Grandfather had been admitted into an orthopedics hospital in Gangnam for surgery on his leg. I went to see him then. When there was no one else but the two of us in his room, he gestured for me to approach. I did, assuming he was going to tell me something, but then he squeezed a check into my palm. He said, I can't give any of the other children anything, but you take this and don't tell anyone. He then lay there on his hospital bed and closed his eyes. He wouldn't open them, probably afraid I would try to refuse. When I walked out of the hospital and looked at the check, I saw it was issued from J— Nonghyup Bank for the sum of one million won. He'd been coming to Seoul for surgery, but he took the time to drop by the bank to get a check for me because I was getting married. Even now, despite my repeated assurances that I'm earning a living, he tries to give me money. I think he's trying to protect my pride by doing it as secretively as possible, even if all his efforts are so touchingly transparent.

So, Aunt.

Remember a couple of days ago when I sent you a photo of me holding the baby and you texted, What's up with your expression? I looked at the photo again and saw it showed how I feel these days. The worries of a man who has become the father of two children. People look at the photo and see the baby, but you're the only one who saw me—it made me embarrassed. But Aunt, when we had our firstborn, what was happening didn't have a chance to sink in because time passed so quickly. When my wife first told me she was pregnant, I was honestly a little overwhelmed and thought, *What am I going to do now?* To my wife I blurted out, What? Can you imagine telling your husband you're going to have a baby for the first time and all he could say was, What? Seeing my wife's tears well up made me come to my senses. Thinking of that moment makes the hairs on the back of my head stand on end. I feel terrible for having hurt my wife, even inadvertently.

When our first was finally born, the nurse took me to the nursery. They were squirming in their bassinets, yellow tags on their thin red wrists, and the nurse put on rubber gloves and pointed to the baby's different features. Here you see the hair is clean, he has eyes, a nose, and a mouth. She unclenched his fist and said, See? Five fingers, one, two, three, four, five . . . You see he's a boy child, yes? She touched each of his little red toes saying, Here we have his toes, one, two, three, four, five . . . See? As the baby was being presented to his father as having arrived safely and whole into the world, he shook his fists and feet and began to cry with rage. As you can see, the nurse said, his cry is very loud and clear, right? I kept answering, Yes, yes, yes, and my heart felt ready to burst. The nurse's words seemed to fall right into my heart. Yes, my child's hair was clean, his eyes, nose, and mouth were intact, his fingers and toes had arrived to us safely. All the things I took for granted, the nurse was telling me to really observe—look, here it is—and I realized, these were not things to be taken for granted. He could've been blind in one eye, or missing a toe, but he had come to me safe and sound. My eyes had welled up so much by then that as the baby kicked the air, some of my own tears fell.

It's so different, having two children instead of one. Now I really feel I've become a father, and the sight of the newborn makes me anxious about the future. Sometimes my heart just aches and aches. Yesterday, the older one, having had his mother taken from him by his new brother, came to my room to read and fell asleep with his hand on his forehead and his legs all twisted up. Just like his grandfather when he takes a nap. Dad also sleeps like this, and my wife informs me that I do as well. What funny things we pass on to our children, I thought, which then made me wonder, How on earth am I going to raise this child? And the future turned dark again. I don't know what to do. But whatever it is, I need to do it well . . .

Remember how some time ago, you mentioned that a publisher you knew had set up a new media division and they were creating video content for new books and authors and that it wasn't so far from what I did and I should think about applying? You must've been extremely careful when you brought that up with me, but all I said was, I only wanted to make films. That I was going to survive in this space no matter what. And wasn't I so dramatic when I said that to you? The answer came out with such confidence, before I had even thought about what you said, and you answered, All right . . . I remember you looking at me then. Nothing has changed about how I feel since then, but if I were to be asked that question again now, I don't think I would give such an abrupt, rebellious answer.

My first has grown a lot. I was worried about how he would cope with getting less attention because of the baby, but funnily enough, he immediately began acting like a proper older brother. No one taught him to do so, but he will stroke the baby's head, get a bottle for his mother when the baby cries, rock him to sleep, read him picture books, and tuck him into his blankets. And then he goes to the bathroom. It's stressful, apparently, being an older sibling at such a young age. After having everyone pay attention to him, he seems to be experiencing a bit of shock and loss that everyone seems interested in the baby now. But he doesn't let it show. He just goes in and out of the bathroom. When my wife tells him, Come over here and give me a hug, he normally would've run right into her arms—but now he glances at the baby. Do you feel left out? Don't keep it in, we tell him. If you want to say something to us, just say it. Nothing, he replies. Nothing, nothing . . . It gives me a strange feeling to see him like that. I find myself murmuring, I'll make it through this, too . . . As if it isn't me raising him but him raising me. Long ago, that sight in the rearview mirror while I drove, of Dad and Grandfather fighting about the envelope of money, back then I wondered—why were they making such a fuss? But now I think I know what they were feeling, and I feel a stinging in my nose.

Aunt.

I've said so many things here. The family seems to be very careful about giving you news of my second child being born. But I want to celebrate with you the safe arrival of my baby with clean hair, intact eyes, a nose, a mouth, ten fingers and toes—we can do that, right, Aunt?

CHAPTER 5

ON THE VERGE
OF GOODBYE

To the south, the rains had flooded the rivers so much that cattle had swum up to the roof of their cowshed. It was that kind of summer. Father stared at the sight of cattle being rescued by cranes on TV and mumbled to himself, Those cows are going to hurt their stomachs if they handle them like that . . . The summer was passing.

These past few years when I hadn't visited J—, I tended to lose things. Objects I had carried in my own hands failed to make it safely home. Slippers I'd bought at a shoe store, oysters from the fishmonger, reams of paper I'd paid for at the stationery store because I had run out of printer paper—I had no idea where I'd left these items. By the time I'd come home, my hands were empty. I would clench and unclench my hands, then turn on the water and wash them for a long time. The day I realized I had only one spare key left to my front door, my only means of entering the house, I took that key to a key cutter in our neighborhood. A shop so narrow it didn't warrant a front door, just a long space fading into the back. The key cutter looked at me over his glasses and asked if all was well. Did he know me? I was suddenly aware of how I must look. Unwashed hair, the neck of my shirt stretched into an oval, sneakers with the heels folded in . . . *I should've washed my face at least.* Smiling instead of answering, I asked him how long it would take and he said twenty to thirty minutes. So I said I'd come back, took a walk around the neighborhood, and when I got back to him, he said my key was French and had such intricate grooves that it was hard to lift a good impression from it to copy it easily. Was the lock on my door from France? As I stood there disconcerted, the man said the lock was probably chosen for this very reason and asked if I'd rather have a keypad installed. When my daughter and I went out together, she always found her front door key first when we returned. What would you do without me? That's what she'd say as she slid her key into the lock. How I longed for that moment, standing in front of the door with my daughter. I asked the key cutter if he could fashion a new key anyway and he said it would take time but it was possible. I asked him to make the same key, even if it took a little more time. He said it would be 40,000 won per key and 240,000 won for the whole job, and did I still want to do it? I thought, 40,000 for a key? A bit much, but if I wanted to keep using the lock, I had no other choice. But I did ask him to only make five copies in that case, took out 100,000 won from my wallet to pay him a deposit, and gave him my phone number. Because I'd given him my only key to work with, I had to leave the front door unlocked whenever I wanted to go somewhere. As soon as I received his message to come collect the keys, I paid the balance and came home gripping my bag tight, afraid I would lose my only means of locking my front door. I tested each key as soon as I arrived—none of the new keys worked. Not a single one of the five. I tried three times with each key. When I went back to the key cutter and told him the keys didn't work, he insisted I was wrong. That he had been a key cutter in this same spot for the past twenty years, and no one had ever not been able to open a door with his keys. I stood outside the window of his store and he was inside. With the glass partition between us, I kept telling him I had tried three times to unlock the door and he kept insisting that was impossible. He furiously asked me what would I do if he went to my house himself and the keys worked. But I can't open it, I said, and we went to my house together. He couldn't open my door with his keys either. He took the original key and the copies from me again and messaged me two days later telling me to collect the new keys, but the same thing happened. When I went to his store and informed him the new keys still didn't work, the man shoved his money out his window and muttered, Fucking bitch. I refused to believe my ears at first but the words themselves refused to stop lingering in my ears: Fucking bitch. I'd paid him 200,000 won all in 10,000 won bills but all he gave me through the hole of the transparent partition were three 50,000 won bills. My nose was starting to bleed. You owe me 50,000 won more, I said as calmly as I could, trying to still my beating heart, and the man replied there had been five keys each at 30,000 won each so 150,000 won was correct. I said he had told me was 40,000 won per key. Behind the man, the countless locks and keys hanging on their nails seemed to be shouting back at me. I never should've tried to get my money back from him. All I'd wanted was to get my original key back and maybe ask him to try one more time, but the moment he said, Fucking bitch, my offer froze in my mouth. His complaints about everything he had had to go through to find the right keys fell on unhearing ears. I calmly explained our previous situation that had led to this one. How he had said it was 150,000 won to install a keypad instead. That copying five keys at 40,000 won each would be more expensive. Did he forget I'd insisted on copying the keys anyway, despite this? The man listened, then suddenly turned violent, jumping out of his store and shouting, When did I ever say that? I thought he was going to grab me by the throat. He screamed I was a novelist who was so used to lying that I could do it with a straight face—the whole world knew I was such an evil liar that my daughter had paid for it by getting into an accident. Passersby glanced at us as they moved on. Someone who had been across the street waiting for the crosswalk signal walked right up to us to watch. My heart was pounding in my ears and my ears were turning red, and I felt my mind fill with darkness. In my hand were the keys the man had cut, the ones that couldn't open my front door. I threw them on the ground and shouted, Why don't you go back inside and cut keys for the rest of your life! I might as well have gathered in my hand the blood from my bleeding nose and thrown it in his face. I shoved him aside and pushed past the whispering crowd, and as I walked away I found myself repeating, Father! Oh, Father. The words I'd spat out at the key cutter man were piercing my heart. Often the things I said to others would come back to me and make me sit right up in the dark. As I rubbed my face, my roughened palms scratched my cheeks.

I wrote these words sitting right next to Father, and I don't want to erase them. I'm erasing some words as I go, but it is my hope that there would be some words that remain despite their erasure.

It was the night of the first typhoon. The rain pounded on the roof like it was determined to rip it to shreds. I spread my bedding on the floor next to Father's bed and fell asleep, but later woke up from the sound of the wind and rain and was staring up at the ceiling. The wind, whenever it swept in or out, would shake the gate outside, snap off the camellia branches in the front yard, and fell the taro in the backyard, the sounds making their way to my ears. Afraid of waking Father, I didn't dare move— at some point, he sat up in bed and was silent for a while. He looked in my direction and carefully tried to get out of the bed. I could tell he was try- ing not to wake me. I sat up and said, Father, you're awake. Don't you want to go back to sleep . . . Father was opening the cabinet under the televi- sion. I turned on the lights. Father, his eyes suddenly overstimulated by the lights, blinked as he kept rummaging through that cabinet. He must've been having trouble finding whatever he was looking for because he started taking out all the contents and putting them out on the floor. Flip-cap pill- boxes, containers for batteries, puzzle pieces brought by my sister. Simple puzzles Father had trouble with if even two pieces were missing, so my sister suggested I take out just one. Father thrust his hand deeper into the cabinet and took out a rectangular bundle wrapped in white cotton. The four corners of the cotton wrapping were tied together in a knot. Father untied the knot, and from there emerged old, yellowed books tied together with yellow string. The *Sohak*, an elementary ethics primer for children from the Joseon Dynasty. Through the light falling from the ceiling bulb, I could clearly read the title written in Chinese characters. Its cover was well-handled, smudged and shining with use at the same time.

—The *Sohak*.

—. . .

—You kept this book all this time?

Father rubbed his face with his hands. Life sprouts in the spring, grows in the summer, ripens in the fall, and is harvested in the winter, this is the unchanging rule . . . Father could recite this book perfectly. Whenever he struggled to remember where he had put things, I would tell him, Try to remember, and he would say, After these tasks, if one still has strength, one must recite poetry and read books and learn music through song and dance and avoid straying from the rightful path . . . As he rummaged, he would mumble the *Sohak* just loud enough so I could hear. This was his way of reassuring me he was all right, but sadly, he would never find the things he was looking for. From the pages of that book he had read to tatters, he took out some papers and a folded piece of paper. An old letter. The same stationery Father had used to write to Eldest Brother in Libya, only very yellowed from age. On it were the names from Eldest Brother to the youngest and their birthdays and birth times. I gazed at his handwriting. A mix of Chinese characters and Hangul. Eldest Brother was born in the evening, Second Brother in the middle of the day, Third Brother early evening, me the fourth during myoshi, meaning dawn. My sister's birthday was the eighth day of Lunar April, Buddha's birthday. Inshi, so around first light. I looked closely at the youngest's name. That's when I learned the "ik" syllable in his name was 益, the symbol that means additional. Who knew when he wrote this, but simply imagining him bent over and carefully writing these names and dates down made my heart ache.

—Just remembered I put this here.

Another document Father had taken out was a deed for some land in Daeheung-ri.

—A land deed?

—The mountain where you can look down to the place where Cha Cheonja had built his worship hall, saying it would be the origin of a new world.

—. . . ?

—Bought it when that mountain was cheap . . . Knew there were many people ruined by Cha Cheonja, but there wasn't much else for me to put my heart into . . .

I could hear echoes of Aunt's voice from my childhood in Father's voice as he said this. Aunt had told me the people who used to come to see Cha Cheonja, dreaming of a new world, were so numerous they were like clouds. The Donghak Revolution defeated, the country stolen, no one to lean on . . . That's what she had said. Father folded the letter-writing paper and land deed and wedged them inside the *Sohak* once more.

—A useless thing I did.

A mere mumble. I stared at Father. He wasn't the kind of person who expected anything for free. When one didn't sow seeds in the spring, there would be nothing to harvest in the fall—that's what he believed. Father had been scrupulous enough to carefully put every hoe, every scythe in its rightful place his whole life. Had he had this other side all this time?

Since that night, Father would call me to his side to show me things. Here's this, he would say, revealing four Nonghyup bankbooks hidden in the back of a picture frame, or staring into the well in the backyard after having removed the cover. When I approached him he said, There's still water coming up here, and bade me to look. The deep well was full of water, just like he said. Even when no one drank from the well, the water had silently pooled and was reflecting the sky above. Father said, Don't fill in the well even after I am dead. To hear him say it was all right to rebuild the house but to never to fill the well felt like he was passing on the well to me. His words *after I am dead* upset me so much that I countered, Don't say these things to me, say them to Eldest Brother. To which he replied, Watching you made me think you hold things precious even when they have become useless . . . Another time, Father was standing in the master bedroom with the wardrobe opened, holding a winter coat. One he wore from the beginning of winter to spring, pure wool and very old. The elbows were worn so he'd sewn leather patches. He said, It was such a warm coat . . . The moldy coat in his hands, he looked distressed. I took the coat from him and said, It's all right, Father, I'll ask the dry cleaners to save it. His face brightened. He said, The dry cleaners? Wait. He took out a paper bag from the wardrobe. When had he put it there? When you enter the town, he said, there's a dry cleaner there and right next to it is Oong at the frame shop. Give this to him. Father said that he had met Oong earlier and his hair was falling out and would appreciate it. Oong? How long since I'd heard that name. When I thought of him, it was the sign that said "Oongie's Calf" that came to mind. And how Father had shown Oong how to cut and plane the wood and guided Oong's hands in engraving the letters.

As I stood waiting for the bus to take me to town, I looked inside the paper bag and saw four hats. Father's hats, one for each season of the year. After dropping off his coat at the dry cleaner's, I saw that Oong indeed had a frame shop next door. The glass had the words *Custom Frames* painted in blue letters and it was closed. I peered inside. Vintage-looking empty frames, drawings and photographs of dogs, acrylic frames with machine embroidery. The frames had cards with their measurements—5×7, 6×8, 8×10—beneath them. The thought of Oong making a living with such a neat store gladdened my heart. Oong, who would scare me by sticking cooked birds at me, Oong who wouldn't listen to anyone except my father. Oong who would take naps on the roof. I couldn't imagine that same Oong having aged and balding. Now Oong was going to wear Father's hats. I hung the paper bag on the locked door. For a moment I wondered if

I should write a note, but he would probably recognize the hats were from Father at first glance, so I only made sure the bag wouldn't slip off the handle.

Before going to the dry cleaner's, I had simply assumed Father was airing out some of his clothes, but when I got back to the house, I saw an oil drum in the middle of the courtyard and a pile of Father's clothes burning inside. Shocked at his clothes going up in flames in the manner of the trifles one usually burns in an oil drum, I kept calling out, Father, Father! He only stared at the smoke and finally opened his mouth saying, They're done being worn. All I could do was stand by his side. The smell of burning clothes permeated the entire house. As he looked into the flames, Father said, Remember Nakcheon? I asked, You mean Mr. Nakcheon? Father said, I don't know where that man is now. Father told me that ever since Mr. Nakcheon had disappeared, he had tried to find him so he could help him get a welfare benefits card, but there was not a trace of him anywhere. He went wherever there was even the slightest mention of someone like him, but in the end, he couldn't find him. Hon-ah, Father said in a weary voice, if you hear Nakcheon died somewhere, you must gather his remains and arrange funeral rites. Me? Father looked back at me. Why, can't you do it? Well, I said, you can do it yourself, Father. Father sighed. If I'm still alive then . . . His voice trailed off and he patted my shoulder. Look, he said, it's because there's a thing that should've been done that hasn't been done, and I've a feeling you'd understand . . . I couldn't answer Father. He told me that Mr. Nakcheon had left his cow with us, and when he did the math, it was only right we hold his funeral as compensation. That way, he said, we don't leave debt behind. On another sunny day, Father put some alcohol on a rag and cleaned the leather of his drum and its round stainless steel ornaments one by one until they shone. He neatly trimmed the split ends of the bukchae drumstick and oiled the wood many times over. On another day, he went downtown with me and stopped in front of a watch store by the five-way intersection and took off his watch to hand to the store owner, telling him it was his most precious watch that needed its insides cleaned—and also a new battery. The owner examined it and said it was a good watch, quite expensive. Father said he didn't know, that it had been a gift from his son and he only took care not to lose it. When we returned home, Father didn't put the cleaned watch back on his wrist but into a Ziplock bag and found the box it had come in on some shelf. I said, You didn't know where the fan you held in your hand yesterday is, but here you are finding the box for your watch? Father said that when Third Brother failed his high-level civil servant exams for the third time, he had cried as he entered a corporation instead. Father said that he had wanted to purge the injustices of my generation in his. Third Brother, who was now the closest to Father, had fought with him the most when we were young. All the things I could never say to Father, he poured out onto him mercilessly. That's wrong, Father, that is the old way. You have to change, Father . . . Perhaps Father took his ox to the protest because of Third Brother's influence. Father placed his watch inside the old, dusty box. All summer, he took care of his things. From the abandoned house next to the cattle pen, he took out the delivery boxes one by one and spread them out on the vegetable patch with the lids open, telling Isak to take what he wanted. Isak took in the knife sets and frying pans and mesh laundry pouches, his eyes widening, and said, But these are all brand new! The supplements and other stuff that were past their sell-by date were ripped open and buried in the field. As for the pots and silverware sets that were left over . . . I put the plates into the basket set and moved them to Mother's kitchen and asked Father why he had ordered all these things. Because, he mumbled, when I thought of your daughter I wanted to see her so much and felt empty . . . I was so astonished at this that I took a step back. The boxes of cleaning tools and various rust removers, I gave to a store near the village. Father's store had long disappeared and a pedestrian bridge had been erected in its place. Father took out the lenses in his sunglasses, wiped the frames down to their lens grooves before putting them away, and saved just one pair of shoes for each season while sorting out the things to burn. That day when I had discovered the wooden chest—whose letters had Father been burning? As I helped Father burn his extra shoes, I asked him but he did not reply. The doctor had told me to make as much conversation with him as possible. That letting him speak of the things he had buried in his heart was a kind of therapy, and making Father talk about them would alleviate his symptoms. When I asked again, several times, Whose letters did you burn, Father? He replied, Kim Soonok's letters. Who is Kim Soonok? Father didn't answer as he emptied the sprinkler on the smoldering embers. But Father, who is this Kim Soonok to be sending you letters? Father put down the sprinkler and gave me an unreadable look. Had Kim Soonok's letters been hidden among Eldest Brother's missives? If I'd known, I would've read them first. Father, please tell me about Kim Soonok. I'll listen to anything you have to say. But Father was still silent. Father, what was in those letters that you had to burn them? He said, If we had lived in a better world, she would've had a good life . . . Here was Father, thinking the same thought about Kim Soonok that I had thought about him. People who would've had a good life had they lived in a better world. Father's face was full of sadness. I couldn't bring myself to ask him any more questions. For two days, the smell of burning shoes lingered in the air.

Father talked to me at breakfast.

—The rain came until dawn?

—It rained in the night but stopped at dawn. They say a typhoon will come tomorrow.

—How many typhoons have we had this year already?

—I know, right?

Typhoons normally came after summer passed and Chuseok was imminent, but this was already our fourth typhoon. Last night, I woke up at the sound of the relentless rain and struggled to go back to sleep. Whenever I turned on my side, I looked up at Father in his bed. Whether because of the Korean medicinal supplements my sister had sent or his fatigue from watching the news for too long while worried about the state of the ancestral cemetery, he didn't wake up once throughout the clamor of the rain. After another summer night of rain and strong wind, Father insisted on visiting the mountain where our cemetery was, and I followed him. This wasn't something unusual for him, apparently. Sections of the road were blocked by mud avalanches from nearby hills. On the news, the banks downriver had overflowed and the people fled their deluged homes while chickens and ducks and dogs tried to keep their heads above water. But the mountain cemetery, for which my Father was the caretaker, was all right. I watched Father as he trimmed the turf and picked up the leaves that had tumbled all the way to the grave markers. I had a good impression of Father's days during typhoon season.

—Last spring there wasn't rain for over fifty days but now there's so much of it. It's useless in the fields.

—. . .

—Isak is going to have a bad harvest because of these typhoons.

—. . .

—That family rice paddy I tended—it's Isak's job now.

—. . .

—Because everyone else has left.

—. . .

—At least Isak is here that the family paddy is tended. Who knows what will happen after him.

—. . .

—All the persimmons have dropped.

Only at this last comment did I break my silence and say, I see. Father's calm voice worrying about the rains that were of no use to farming, the typhoons, Isak, and even the persimmons made it seem like nothing was the matter at all. When he talked about the persimmons falling in the wind, he added, Your mother likes persimmons so much . . . A summer where Father and I would take a stroll around the neighborhood after a rain and see piles of unripe persimmons fallen by the trees. J— had many persimmon groves, three or four trees growing at each house. In my childhood when snacks were scarce, children would gaze up at the persimmon trees waiting for the fruit to ripen. The trees would revive in the spring and sprout leaves, and as the persimmon blossoms bloomed and fell, the children would gather under the trees and pick up the blossoms to eat. The sweet taste of persimmon blossoms spreading in their mouths. Girls would string them into bracelets and necklaces and wear them until they were hungry and eat them. No doubt I was always among these children, me with my hair cut short just past my ears. Persimmons weren't the only thing to perish in the winds and rain. But Father was concerned particularly for them because of a subconscious memory. As the summer rain and wind made unripe persimmons fall, the children would put them in a small earthen jar in saltwater to wait for the tartness to steep away and take them out to eat one by one. Sometimes, a big persimmon would fall before autumn, and the children would race to be the one to pick it up. The persimmon trees at our house were called wide persimmon trees. They didn't always produce fruit, but when they did, they were indeed larger and flatter. If I ever happened to find a persimmon ripening on one of those trees, I would visit it every day. I would open my eyes in the morning and inspect the tree first thing to make sure the fruit hadn't fallen in the night. Every winter, after harvest, we had a designated persimmon-picking day. Father would split the ends of some long bamboo poles and hand one to each of my older brothers. He himself climbed the branches and tossed down the fruit to my mother and me, waiting below. Our basins filled quickly. The bounty of wide persimmons glowing orange in my eyes would make my heart full. I felt like we'd become rich. Mother cut some and dried them as well as the peels in a colander, and put the rest in an earthen jar, handing them out as they ripened to us children as a treat. Those long winter nights we would chew on dried persimmon peels. The last thing we did on persimmon-picking day was to leave some for the magpies. When my brothers, who were having fun picking the persimmons using the split ends of their poles, would try picking the fruit on the topmost branches, Father would tell them to stop.

—Leave those for the magpies.

·Who knows if the fruit left on those high branches were really eaten by magpies, but Father's words have stayed with me through the years. This childhood memory was probably the reason I planted a persimmon tree when I moved into a house with a yard for the first time. The first time I picked fruit from that tree, my daughter was with me. When she fretted about the fruit on the top branches we were leaving behind, I'd say, Let's leave those for the magpies.

It was a quiet morning. We had shared only a few words when Father's face suddenly filled with concern as he said, Maybe it's because of the rain but I didn't hear your aunt's footsteps this dawn. My chopsticks hovered over my breakfast as I stared silently at Father.

—Maybe she's sick?

Still not replying, I placed a piece of soy sauce-braised beef on his spoon. Now that Father had completed his dental treatment, he could chew meat again.

—Please finish your meal, Father. We can go see Aunt after.

Father put the spoon with the beef into his mouth. Nowadays, he only asked after people who weren't with us anymore. Most often Aunt or Chammie the parrot. Two days ago, he had sat up in the middle of breakfast and asked me why I hadn't brought my daughter with me.

Every morning without fail, Third Brother would call Father after breakfast. On other mornings, Father would already be sitting by the phone and waiting, but today he was dressed and wearing his hat, standing by the front door and waiting for me to hurry.

—You should take Third Brother's call first, Father.

But Father stood still at the door. When his eyes met mine, I gestured to the phone. Only then did he understand and went to sit on the edge of the bed. As soon as he did so, the phone rang. He picked up.

—Father, it's your third.

—. . .

—Did you sleep well?

Father held the receiver against his ear. Even standing a few steps away, I could hear Third Brother going, Father? Father? After a moment, Father lowered the receiver.

—The connection must've broken. I couldn't hear a thing.

I took the receiver he had handed me. Third Brother's voice kept saying, Father, Father? Can you hear me? I held out the receiver to Father.

—It's working.

Father only gazed at the receiver, but perhaps he was not interested in talking to Third Brother, so he didn't take it from me. As I couldn't stand like that forever, I held up the receiver to my own ear and answered, Oppa.

—Why isn't Father saying anything?

Not knowing what to say about Father, who was sitting on the edge of his bed with his head bowed, I hesitated for a moment before glancing at the bathroom door.

—He had to go to the bathroom.

—Oh . . .

—Are you at work?

—Yes . . . Is Father all right?

—He's fine.

—Sorry to put you through so much trouble.

—It's all right, oppa. Go back to work.

—I'll call tomorrow then.

—OK.

I hung up and sat down next to Father.

—What's wrong, Father?

—. . .

—You don't want to talk to oppa?

As Father said nothing, I slid down to sit on the floor next to him. My hand snaked up to hold his, which was resting on his knee. I weaved my fingers into his and the stub of his index finger stuck up in the air. I ran a finger over it. Father was startled and tried to extricate his hand, but as I held on, he soon gave up and sighed. We sat like that for a long time.

—Do you want to talk to Mother? I can connect you.

—No.

—You don't want to talk to Mother, either?

—I do.

—Then I'll connect you.

—No.

—Why not, Father?

—Can't hear.

—. . . ?

Having apparently forgotten that he had wanted to go out with me, Father pulled his hand away and lay down on the bed.

—Weren't we on our way out? We can go now.

Father sat up at that. Had he forgotten we were supposed to go to Aunt's house?

—Where? The cemetery in the mountain?

—All right, Father, we'll go there. But what did you mean by you not hearing anything?

—Can't hear the phone.

I stared at Father. Can't hear the phone? Father had talked to Third Brother the day before, not to mention his call with Mother in the evening. He had told Third Brother to watch out for other cars when he drove and if he couldn't quit smoking to at least cut down to three cigarettes a day and to not drink at home. His calls with Mother mostly involved her talking to him for long stretches. Her voice as it leaked over the receiver had lively tones while Father mostly replied listlessly and then said something about learning how to use a rice cooker from Honnie. That even if Honnie went back to Seoul, he would be able to make rice for himself and she shouldn't worry but concentrate on getting better so she could come back soon. After Mother had hung up with him, she had called me separately and asked, You taught your Father how to use the rice cooker? Well, I replied, it's a useful thing to know how to do. Mother raised her voice. Why did you do something no one told you to do? It was the only thing he's never had to do on his own . . . I wanted to spare him at least that little thing. There was a stubbornness in Mother's voice. How many years had it been since Mother had said exactly what she meant to me? Ever since I stopped visiting J—, she walked on eggshells around me. We never said what was on our minds and just exchanged banalities instead, like, How are you doing, Be careful not to catch a cold, Have you eaten, Good night . . . But even then we were careful my daughter was never mentioned. I listened to her for a while and then said, Umma . . . making rice and all that, it's no big deal. All you have to do is let it sit in the water for a bit and then press the button. Father should know how to do that much himself. Mother said, All right . . . that's no big deal, your mother did it her whole life! And she hung up. I had no idea why our conversation had taken such a turn, but it felt like Mother was talking to me like before without being overly cautious of my feelings. Normally when I annoy her and she hangs up on me, it's my turn to call her up and finish our talk, but I didn't call her. Even more annoyed, Mother ended up calling me instead and said, You hurt my feelings, so why didn't you call me back? Dragged back into the argument, I replied, Because you were going to call me anyway. Mother hung up, and I tried calling her again but she didn't pick up. That was only yesterday.

—When did you start not hearing the phone?

—A few days ago . . .

—But how did you listen the other times? You were on the phone just yesterday.

—Well . . . They say what they always say, so I just say yes to everything and then say what I want to say.

Not knowing he wasn't able to hear on the phone, I had chased him around for days with the cell phone we had provided for him because he'd left it behind. I'd delivered it to the village community center and slid it into his pocket at the vegetable patch next to the cattle pen where he was picking Mother's eggplants. A few days ago, when the rain had stopped,

I'd taken it to the gukakwon at J— where he'd gone. Father was sitting among the other musicians with his buk, his bukchae in hand, staring at me. You can't leave this behind, we have to be able to reach you, I said to him in a nagging voice. I slipped it into his shirt pocket and left the gukakwon, standing stupidly for a while in the sun before walking slowly out of J— alone. Realizing the gukakwon Father frequented was near my old middle school, I was walking toward it when a student on a bike shouted, Out of the way! Out of the way! and as I quickly moved to the side and he passed, he looked back and shouted, Sorry about that, my bell is broken! He was gone like the wind. I stared in the direction he had disappeared in. Thoughts of my own childhood, of going to school on my bike. My knee tensed, remembering how I once fell from my bike and scraped my knee. The drops of blood on my wound. It didn't heal quickly and there was an inflammation; every time it touched water, the healing scab would flare up again. I remembered Father's hands applying ointment. Telling me, when I said I wanted to give up the bike, how riding it was a skill I could learn once and use for the rest of my life. Because I learned to ride it back then, I can still ride the bicycle to this day. The front gate of the middle school I used to bike to had been altered and I didn't know how to enter the grounds. I simply stood there, looked through the fence, and turned away. There had been a long flowerbed here and a bell next to the teachers' offices, and bells ringing to signal the beginning and end of class. Who had rung that bell? After leaving this place, I still thought of it every time I heard the sound of bells. Crossing Charles Bridge in Prague, that cathedral with the blindingly beautiful stained glasses—even the bell I heard there made me think of this country middle school. If I could enter this school again, I would see if the bell hanging in the redbrick belltower was still there. And whether the wisteria grove behind the main building where the students and faculty parked their bikes still stood. I liked the shade of that grove with its purple blossoms. Reading on the benches below them. Things I had forgotten all these years. I've changed so much, and surely so have the places I had left behind. I didn't feel like looking for the new front gate so

I walked away and wandered the streets of J— until I found myself on the Daeheungri Bridge. I stood where I had inadvertently turned away from the sight of my father wearily walking in my direction, looking smaller than I'd ever seen him, and stared down below. The water, swollen up from the recent rains, was crashing along. I stood for a while and took a step back. The white water seemed to charge at me and demand, Are you going to keep living as you have? My heart did a flip and fear washed over me. For the first time since coming to J—, my daughter's face rose clearly in my mind. For the past few years I had not come to J—, I couldn't remember her face properly. Her face, when I imagined her turning to me and running toward me, would blur in my mind. Afraid that I would permanently blur her face as a defense against my suffering, I had her name engraved next to ours on the address tablet by our door. Beginning with the picture of the lizard I found in a sketchbook she had used as a child, I took sculpture classes to learn how to turn her drawings into engravings and hung the copy of the lizard next to our door as well. The more I obsessed over the things she had left behind, the more her face blurred. It frightened me that I would forget her face forever, and I would get up in the middle of the night and stare at photos of her on my laptop. That my daughter's face, which refused to show in my dreams, would appear in the foam of the river flowing through J—. My daughter, I am here, I'm right here . . . The foam frothed and churned, but her face was as clear as ever. It seemed like she was trying to raise herself from the current, calling for her umma, but she disappeared. On my way home, I changed my mind and turned to the gukakwon where Father had gone to play his buk. Having expected me to be home by now, Father discovered me in the gukakwon corridor and said, Honnie? I ran to him and linked my arm to his. That was three days ago.

The first time I realized how torturous it was to be unable to fall asleep was on an eight-hour flight to Helsinki. My book was being published there, and I'd been invited to the launch. Saying it was the first time a

Korean book had been translated into Finnish, the editor handed me a copy of the book that I gazed at with bleary eyes. This book I'd written but could not read a single sentence of seemed to stare back at me. The book and I thus met each other for the first time in this awkward way. My eyes, already exhausted from being unable to sleep on the plane, became increasingly bloodshot as I failed to fall asleep the whole time I was there. It was because of the white nights. I learned only then that the country had white nights from the end of May to mid-July. White nights. Just as the term implies, darkness did not descend during night hours and it remained light out. I'd read or heard about it and seen it in movies, but who knew I'd encounter them myself? In that unfamiliar city, I lay down in my hotel to sleep, but it all felt so odd I would sit up. I had no idea what was the matter. Trying to calm my nerves, I flicked open a curtain to distract myself. It was day outside, not night. The clock said it was 11:00 p.m. Why was it so bright? I stood by the window and stared down at the street. Had something happened? The sight of the white street allowed my brain to conjecture, Maybe it's daylight savings time. But even past midnight and up to 2:00 a.m., it remained light out. At 3:00 a.m., 4:00 a.m., 5:00 a.m.—still light out. The white night kept me awake. Even with the melatonin and Advil PM that I'd brought with me to beat jetlag, I couldn't fall asleep. It was the same the next night when I had learned about white nights. I closed the black-out curtains that blocked out the light. Even when I clipped the curtains together so there was no crack for the light to seep through, sleep refused to come. I lay on the bed, and the second I thought about how it was light out, sleep escaped me. Getting up, I would open the curtains a crack and peer out again. The white street and the strange white buildings, the street-lights, the closed restaurants and storefronts—they all looked like they were part of a dream. A night with no darkness. The more one tries not to think about something, the more one thinks about it. Just as the more one tries to forget, the more one remembers. If only not thinking was as easy as bidding oneself not to think, but the only way to not think about some-thing is to think about it until there is nothing more to think about. Just like things are forgotten when it is their time to be forgotten. I tried hard not to think it was bright outside, but the more I did, the stronger my impression that it was bright outside became. I'd napped easily during the day, and writing and reading have often made me flip my nights and days before, so why was I finding it so hard to fall asleep during white nights? When I came back from the events my Finnish publisher had prepared for me, my feet were swollen. Even as I felt tired enough to fall asleep as soon as my head hit the pillow, my mind remained as clear as ever. No matter how much I told myself I needed to sleep, that I needed rest if I wanted to survive the next day's events, it was useless. The week I was there, my eyes remained bloodshot the whole time. I would hurriedly look away if I found myself meeting someone else's gaze. Lack of sleep kept making me stumble. I gripped the bannisters as I climbed stairs, dizzy from the effort. I had migraines so intense that I felt my skull would split. On the fifth day, I could barely hear what people were saying to me. My cognitive abilities dropped so much that I couldn't understand the questions I was being asked by interviewers. I realized how precious it was to be able to work during the day and sleep at night. And how wonderful it was that darkness descended at night. Eating lunch, I kept dropping my utensils. This was the first time I was being published there, and in that country, I was a new writer. Who would come to visit such a writer at a bookstore event? But by the time I sat down at the seat prepared for me, the chairs would be filled, with the overflow audience sitting on the floor. I once dozed off for a moment while reading from my work. But the people paid attention to me to an alarming degree. Even in that second I nodded off, they assumed the pause was necessary for the rhythm of my reading. These readers from another country, of another language and culture and society have gathered here because of my book, I have to pull myself together—I kept telling myself this as I fought against fatigue. There were moments when their rapt attention would awaken me. Like the time I immersed myself in the reading so much I felt something was healing in my heart, and the reading and talk that had been scheduled to last for an hour went on for two. Afterward, I felt so dizzy I thought my eyes would pop out. I dozed off during a dinner I could not get myself out of, and it was 11:00 p.m. by the time I got to my room.

—When will it get dark?

I kept asking my Finnish editor this as if she were responsible for ending the white nights. My tone begged her to put a stop to them. Her answer was apologetic, despite the fact that it wasn't something she needed to apologize for.

—At least the sun sets here. In the east, the sun is still up after midnight. At 1:00 a.m. even.

How could the sun be up at 1:00 a.m.? How do the people there fall asleep? I couldn't even wash my face at the end of the day. I was afraid the moment I dipped my hands in cold water to splash on my face that sleep would flee. I secured the blackout curtains shut again and climbed into bed. Despite my extreme fatigue, the light of the world outside lingered behind my eyelids. Why am I like this? I might die if I don't sleep—I mumbled, as I spread a blanket on the bathroom floor and lay on that, trying to see if the cold tiles would help. Nothing worked. Where was it darkest in this room? I contemplated the space under the bed. It was too low for my body. The wardrobe? I slipped into it and closed the door, thinking of Father. This was around the time my sister had told me Father had a sleeping disorder. I hadn't thought too much of it. My sister explained it was like he was asleep but his brain was wide awake—I thought this was mere metaphor. Something to do with Father's cerebral infarction. But that sleeping disorder I had dismissed came back to haunt me in the white nights. A vision of the audience listening carefully to what I was saying flashed through my mind. An audience that could understand me only through an interpreter, still listening to every word I said. Inside the wardrobe, my face burned with shame—had I ever tried to listen to Father as intently? People of a foreign land had generously lent me their ears, but I couldn't even listen to my own Father. Father's sadness and suffering were remembered only in Father's own brain, I realized. Only when I'd come to an unfamiliar country and had the minor inconvenience of not being able to fall asleep, crawling into a wardrobe as a last resort, had I thought back to Father's sleep disorder and what that would actually be like. When I told a friend I was going to Finland, she told me the country had over 200,000 lakes. That numbers-wise, there was a lake for every four households. That there were endless stretches of coniferous forest and white birches, and I'd be able to see the lakes sparkling among them from the plane. But my lack of sleep made me unable to visit the granite church right next to my hotel, let alone a lake. In the wardrobe of a hotel in a country where it did not turn dark at night, I mumbled, Father, did you sleep well last night? As soon as my last event was done, I flew right back to Seoul. All I could think of was falling asleep.

Ever since coming down to J—, I'd been asking Father every morning, Did you sleep well last night? Father nodded for the most part. Even after the night he had been crouching in the shed, he had nodded at my question. Even as his sleeping disorder worsened, he gave the same nod. When he was young, Father would come through the front gate exhausted and dark from the sun, eat dinner with all of us, and fall asleep in the early evening. That Father could fall so deeply asleep in this house made the place seem like the safest refuge from the world. But here was Father unable to sleep as deeply now, wandering the house like a sleepwalker, unbeknownst to him, until he was fainting from fatigue. My sister begged Father to come to Seoul with her, but he refused. Saying that they were inconveniencing their children by having them take care of their mother, that at least one of them had to stay behind. When I said he needed to go to Seoul to get a more precise diagnosis and specialized treatment, Father, very rarely for him, became angry.

—You're treating me like a patient just because I can't get a little sleep?

—. . .

I said if he was so averse to visiting Seoul for his treatment, we should go to a major hospital in a nearby city, the provincial capital where Father's old hospital was. When people in J— got sick, the Jesus Hospital was where they went for more intensive treatment, which is how I know it's still the biggest hospital in that city. When I suggested this, my sister said that the hospital wasn't like it used to be and I should take him to the university hospital that bore the name of the provincial capital instead. There was a university hospital there? My sister said, You didn't know? You should take more interest in the affairs of your home region, she said with a laugh. When I asked her how I would know the affairs of that city when I barely kept up with news of J—, she replied, But unni, you seem to be familiar with what's what in Manhattan? Things like the location of Chelsea Market and that bakery called Emily's or Amy's or whatever? I mumbled, I'm just saying. Had I really said those things to her? I said to Father, Why don't we think of it as going on a trip, not as going to a hospital? I nagged him so much about it that he finally agreed on the condition we did not tell the rest of the family.

—What's wrong with telling them?

—Don't want them to worry.

There was nothing I could say to that. Since I myself had prevented Father from visiting me all this time, and for the same reason.

The streets of the capital were so changed that when we got off the bus, I stood confused for a moment before Father said, Let's get a taxi there, and led the way. As I stared out at the very changed streets of the city, Father said things like, That's Jeondong Cathedral, and that's the new hanok village. As he explained the sights, Father really seemed like someone on an outing. Despite having booked an appointment, we had to wait for two hours before his sleeping disorder test was administered. I had to write down Father's symptoms in detail on a chart beforehand, and I called my sister to help. I couldn't fill out the questionnaire on my own. There were things only those who lived with him could answer, and I called Mother for those, feeling lost. According to Mother, he had started to get up in the middle of the night thirty years ago, his violent sleep-talking started twenty years ago, and even the walking about the yard at night and entering the shed had been going on for fifteen years.

—Why didn't you say anything about this sooner?

—You're the only one who didn't know . . .

I had already realized I knew very little about Father, but it was disconcerting that I knew so little I couldn't fill out a doctor's questionnaire about him on my own. Father didn't care whether he slept well or not, but it was a serious matter. Once the evaluation was over and I returned to the city four days later to hear the results, the doctor looked at Father's chart for a long time before telling me that Father's body wanted to rest but a part of his brain was refusing to, a similar diagnosis as the doctor in J—. But this new doctor mentioned that his disorder had been neglected for so long that Father was also experiencing depression. And anxiety, and panic attacks. That it was meaningless at this point to determine which had come first. If we had caught it at the onset we could've tried to determine whether the sleep disorder came from his depression, anxiety, or panic attacks or the other way around, but the symptoms were too intertwined now for that to matter. It was not something that could be treated in a short period of time, and he would need to be an inpatient.

—But what caused all this?

The doctor could not give me a precise answer. I'm sure it was a silly question. Just as everyone had a different past, everyone had a different reason for not being able to fall asleep.

Ever since our trip to the university hospital, my thoughts about Father turned darker and I kept imagining the insides of his brain. I sat with my laptop at the table in the middle of the night and studied the walnut-shaped brain, its structures like the frontal lobe, the pineal gland, and the cerebrum where memories were stored. What did Father's brain remember? What was it he couldn't forget that made him so unable to fall asleep? Did Father's brain know he cried frequently? Like the doctor in J—, the new doctor also recommended psychiatric therapy. Saying at Father's age, a lack of sleep could lead to dramatically compromised immunity and increased likelihood of dementia. He tried to connect me to a therapist in the hospital but I declined for the interim. Who knew how Father would accept such news? When I sent Father's prescription to my sister and asked her if Father would comply with therapy, she was skeptical. It was something she herself had insisted Father undertake for a long time and had gone so far as to take him to a psychiatrist, but he had refused to say anything to the doctor.

—You did that? Why didn't you tell me?

Here I was again, asking her the same question I asked Mother.

—I'm sure you wouldn't have remembered if I told you, but I did tell you, unni.

There was nothing I could say to that. What had I been like that my Mother would say I was the last to know, that my sister would say I wouldn't have remembered even if she told me?

Even as I stayed in J—, my siblings would take turns visiting from Seoul on the weekends, aside from Third Brother's family who was taking care of Mother. When they were here, Father not only slept better but he became more energetic. Even as he chided them for coming when they were so busy with their lives, his face had an expression of peace like never before. Especially when the youngest visited; he even smiled. When the youngest said he was coming, I asked him to drop by my study and dig up the photo of me wearing a graduation cap. He found it and as he hung it in the empty spot meant for my photo, he asked me why I hadn't brought it myself when it had existed and was even framed all this time. I made some inadequate excuse about having forgotten it and left the room. It felt awkward standing next to Father who was gazing happily at the graduation photos on the wall as if they were an old photo album. While the youngest was there, he helped Father mend the house. They fixed the gate that wouldn't close properly and replaced the broken door handle to the shed. Getting rid of the wire fence around the doghouse that was no longer used took the better part of a whole weekend. After every job, the youngest would say, What's next, Father? And Father would take him to the wall connected to the small gate where the stones had fallen out. When the youngest was going back, Father saw him out to the main road.

—Oh Father, you'll follow me all the way to the train station at this point.

Even as the youngest bade him to go home, Father stood with him until his taxi arrived. The youngest lowered the taxi window and said, Please go in now, Father, and Father bent over and reached out with his wizened hand and stroked the youngest's hair, saying, Goodbye. He stood there even after the taxi had disappeared from view and returned home with his shoulders slumped. More than anyone else, it was the youngest whose departure made the house seem deathly silent. It made me guess how silent it would've been each Sunday evening for my mother and father after their children had departed. Once the youngest was gone and Father and I were left alone together, Father tested the door they had fixed together and tugged the shed's new door handle, mumbling to himself how all he'd done as a father was put him to work all weekend. He was also different when it was the youngest's turn to have visited. He kept wanting to make sure he had gotten home safely. He must be on the train now, he must've arrived by now, did he arrive safely . . . But when I texted the youngest, telling him to call Father because he seemed worried about him, Father would simply say, That's fine then, and hang up. I asked the youngest, Why is it with you that he's so worried? The youngest said it was because Father had always seen him off.

—Seen you off where?

—The train station. Ever since I left home for university. Even in the middle of the night, two in the morning . . . He always saw me off. Adjusting my coat, retying my scarf, rebuttoning my collar. Little things, nuna, but it made me feel so odd, you know? He'd buy a platform ticket and see me off from there until he couldn't see me anymore. It made me feel like he's always by my side, and it sometimes makes me call out, Father! Just like that. Especially when I'm faced with something difficult, I just call out for him . . . Father, help me . . . before I realize I'm even doing it. He used to see me off at the station until recently, but he can't do that anymore . . .

When Eldest Brother, who was retired, said he was coming, Father came back from town and handed me a takeout meal of steamed carp simmered with dried radish leaves, saying it was Eldest Brother's favorite dish. Three portions. Did Eldest Brother like steamed carp? After our meal, Father got up from the table to go to the courtyard and Eldest Brother followed without being asked. The two walked round and round the house, traversing its backyard, side yard, and courtyard, talking until late at night. Eldest Brother, who had left J— at a young age, and Father, still kept up this habit of circling the house whenever he visited. When I heard Father laugh on occasion, I marveled that Father knew how to laugh at all, and looked out at the two men as they passed the small room's window. I could hear snatches of their conversation where I also made an appearance. Father was saying, Honnie listens to you so you should tell her she must go back home, and Eldest Brother replied, She's staying because she feels it's no trouble, so let her stay. Eldest Brother had his arm around Father's waist as he told him some long story. After Father went to sleep, I told Eldest Brother that I'd read their letters to each other and Eldest Brother smiled and said, He still has those? That at no other time in his life had he ever written so many letters. Not knowing I'd been listening to their conversation as they circled the house, Eldest Brother asked me if I'd been away from my home in Seoul for too long and that he was willing to take over looking after Father for a while. When I said, I'll stay until umma comes back, Eldest Brother gave me a thoughtful look.

Until umma comes back. The words made my eyes tear up and I cleared my throat, turning my gaze to the graduation photos on the wall. From the once-empty space, the photograph of me stared back at me. Was it possible to go back to how things were? Mother was having stomach troubles and had to be readmitted. My siblings and I decided not to tell Mother of her worsened condition and acted like it was all just an extension of her previous treatments. Even in her own ignorance, Mother urged me not to tell Father that she had been readmitted to a hospital. Throughout late spring and summer, our family kept telling each other things that we urged not to tell each other.

One night, Father came down from his bed and shook me awake as I lay on the floor.

—Hon, you've got to make a run for it!

Father seemed to hide me from a presence outside the door as he kept shouting.

—I'll stay here and distract that, you've got to get out of here!

He was practically pushing me. His fear was so great he was trembling, but he kept flailing his arms against a phantom threat against me. I hugged him from the back. Father struggled, but I held him tighter. It's a dream, Father, it's not real . . . The tighter I held him, the weaker he became. It's nothing, Father. The night will pass and the morning will come and it'll be all right. I let him out of my grip and stroked his thin back. When he lay down again on his bed, I stroked his chest and sang to him. As he fell back asleep he said with a faint voice, Don't tell your mother. I sang the children's song about the child waiting for his mother to return from oyster-picking . . . Father drifted to sleep. Why on Earth did I think of this sad song about a child living on an island as a lullaby? On another night, Father suddenly sat up in bed and ran out the front door before I could stop him. By the time I caught up to him, he had fallen by the garden wall. When I approached him and shook his shoulder in the dark, Father said, Why am I here . . . I helped him, bewildered, from the yard of the empty house next door to our kitchen and discovered Father had shattered a toenail and was trailing spots of blood. There were dried leaves in his hair, and his clothes were soiled with earth from the garden. What he said as I took out the first-aid box and sterilized his wound was to not tell Mother. What are you, I said, Admiral Yi Sunsin? That I have to tell Mother you did not fall in battle? Despite the obvious pain in his toe, Father laughed. All these admonitions to not tell each other things. My siblings telling each other not to tell Mother about her worsened condition, and Father telling me not to tell Mother about shattering his toenail.

When Eldest Brother went back on the night train on Sunday, he sent me a long chat message divided into several chunks. He must've written them all the way to Suseo Station near Seoul where he disembarked.

He wrote about how reassuring it was that I was watching over the house while Mother was gone, but he was worried about me. That our parents had aged so much it wasn't possible for them to age anymore, but the trains still ran on their rails, the rice still ripened in the fields, and the white herons still flew up from the reeds by the river. That going out for walks with Father meant avoiding the roads with cars and following the dykes along the fields, which meant the dog watching guard in a cattle pen would run out and bark at them.

I knew one large black dog living in a cattle pen built on a rice paddy. It barked but not in a menacing way, and Father said he knew the dog. I asked Father why the dog lived there and he said it was to guard the cattle. It was already odd to see a pen in the middle of a field, but a dog guarding it? When we first walked by, I asked him whose cattle pen it was and Father said this used to be the man from Wolseong's field but he didn't know who owned it now. Whenever I asked Father to go on a walk together, he got out leftovers like cooked mackerel from the refrigerator and put them in a Ziplock bag to empty into the dog's bowl when we passed it. Which was probably why the dog, surrounded by cattle all day, would run out to see Father as soon as he heard his footsteps, pulling at the rope that tied it to the pen. I felt sorry that he couldn't stray too far from the pen because of that rope. From up close, his eyes were filled with gladness. It must've been the same dog that barked at Eldest Brother.

Eldest Brother's messages continued.

A sunbae of mine once suggested that when I retire, I should go down to my childhood home and spend a couple of weeks there. I forgot about this advice. Yesterday, I kept remembering it. I'd wondered if retirement would really make much of a difference. I've never stayed for two weeks straight like my sunbae had suggested, but I still went often because our parents were still there. But yesterday, I suddenly understood. Since retirement, whenever there was family business in J— like a wedding, I'd attend and then leave for Seoul as quickly as possible. I wondered if I'd been in denial about having retired. Or perhaps it was all the busy habits I'd picked up in Seoul since leaving J—.

The habits that have fused to my body from having left J— at twenty and worked for fifty years as a civil servant and a conglomerate employee. Rising at 6:00 a.m., supplements instead of breakfast, arriving at work by 7:30. I grew up in the countryside and wasn't used to the rhythms of the city. Which is why I always set aside time to prepare myself for things. In the beginning, when I had an appointment, I would visit the place the day before to make sure I knew how to get there on time. I wanted to at least never be late. That's how I survived the city and corporate life. Work began at nine, but I got to the office every morning at 7:30 and often finished the day's work by 9:00 a.m. I had set my own starting time of 7:30, but never set an ending time. That was my work life.

Even in retirement, I keep getting up at six. My sunbaes who had retired before me set up an office space, and I showed up there at 7:30 every morning like I was going to work. Even when the first thing I had to do there was watering the plants, I did it. I don't know what's going to happen in the future, but so far, I have lunch with friends almost every day, and, well, who knows how long this will last but I also teach twice a week, and I do some consulting work for the old company.

The past fifty years were not easy. I don't think I ever spent more than four days in a row at the J— house since leaving. It was that kind of life. Always chasing the next thing, day after day, week after week, then a month, then a year . . . Time just flowed by.

Actually, no; a few years ago, Father was having a hard summer and was taken to a Seoul hospital in an ambulance, and thankfully he got better after three weeks and I took him down to J— where I spent a few days with him. None of the other children could get out of work, so I used up my vacation days to help him. So much rain on that day. I was going to drive but ended up taking the train. Such a strange feeling to be retired and sitting next to my old, sick father on the train, taking him home. When I supported him on his way to the bathroom on the train, or when I stuck a straw in a water bottle so he could sip, there were moments where I felt such loneliness. Not long after the train left Seoul Station, Father drifted to sleep and his head rested on my shoulder. I could feel my heart, which I'd thought had hardened through and through, crack. That wasn't the only thing that made me feel bereft. I thought about the things I had done for the first time. Leaving home for the first time at twenty, holding my civil servant exam certification in my hands, working as a civil servant in the day and going to night school, my first night at my posting in Libya—all those feelings were rising from my deepest self that I'd hardened in order to survive in my own way.

I was bringing my father home from the hospital into the house I had left fifty years ago when Mother came out the front door, calling my name. Normally she would've run out, but this time she only called my name and leaned on the doorframe. I wonder how father and son looked to her then.

My plan had been to leave for Seoul straight away, but we got to talking and it became dark, and I was about to leave the next day when I saw how Father was finding his new medicine harder to take than his usual medication so I decided to stay a day longer. But then I followed Mother to her Eastern medicine doctor where I saw how swollen her feet were, and I couldn't bear to leave her behind with her feet like that . . . I ended up staying a week.

Last night, sleeping in the small room, I couldn't sleep for thinking of you. It felt like I had saddled you with the duty I should be undertaking. But here I am again, returning to Seoul. To meet an old friend I had already rescheduled with four times. I couldn't sleep so I took a walk in the village. I listened to the sound of the water flowing in the irrigation ditches dug by the Irrigation Association, the river of stars in the dark night sky, the rice panicles brushing against each other in the wind. I thought about the old days. You know, how I followed Father around as a little boy, afraid he would leave again. People kept emphasizing how I was the eldest son, ever since I was very small. That the eldest son had to act like an eldest son. That if my younger siblings went astray, it was my responsibility to lead them back to the rightful path. I'd heard it to death, even before entering school. To tell you the truth, it was a lot of pressure. The thought of ruining everyone if I faltered was enough to make me sit up straight from a slouch. When our young father left home, I wondered what would happen if he never returned, what I would have to do as the eldest son . . . I was frightened. Even when I knew he would leave home because there was no money to be made in a small country village. Thinking about those days makes something squirm in the pit of my stomach. Our aunt, who is no longer with us, once took me to see him where he was living. It was one of those seasons where cold winds seemed to blow into our house every day, and Aunt showed up at school and took my hand saying, Let's go bring your father home. I had no idea then where we went but I now think it was somewhere in Iksan. There was a small rental room by the train station. Aunt pounded the door and a woman appeared. That was the first time I saw a woman wearing a pretty hairband and not a towel on her head. The black hair that cascaded to her shoulders made her face look almost white. She was so surprised to see us that she took a step back. I remember seeing through the door a blanket with a flower pattern. A pair of bokjori strainers hanging on the wall. Aunt, who had marched all the way to that room with a handful of her skirt bunched up in her fist, calmed down a bit as she took a long and hard look at the woman. When I squeezed Aunt's hand, she glanced at me and turned to the woman saying in a loud voice, Are you Kim Soonok? What do you think you're doing, an educated woman like you . . . Perhaps unsatisfied with just words, Aunt grabbed the pot cooking on the coal briquette stove and flung it to the floor. There was braised cutlassfish cooking in that pot, the only pot I could see in that room. The red broth of the cutlassfish splattered even on my face. Aunt said, I'll be taking my younger brother home so don't you wait for him, and we were coming out of that room when we saw Father walking up the alley to the building. Aunt stood in his path and said, It's time to go home now, but Father pushed her aside and kept trying to go up to the room where the woman stood. I called out, Father! and grabbed his arm and looked up to him pleadingly. Father kept saying he was only going to say goodbye, but Aunt refused to let him. I couldn't hold her hand. There were red blisters from the heat of the pot she had overturned. When Father was examining her hand, I said to him that if he came home with us, I would do anything he asked me to from now on and never go against his wishes. I'd forgotten all about that until last night. That promise I made to Father. I'd said it because I worried about what I would be burdened with, the eldest son, if I lost Father. That train we took to leave the village was still running on those same tracks last night. Walking around the village at night made me feel like I'd come home after having finished some job. That I had come to report all was well. But the person whom I should report to, our mother, was sick in Seoul, and Father couldn't even ride a bicycle anymore. Even though I'm retired myself, it's hard to accept this is who we are now.

When I left J— fifty years ago, all I thought about was my future. The future I needed to achieve. Have I achieved it now? The thought made me lonely. Coming home to J— reminds me of my roots. The sight of the old woman selling her basket of beans in the market by the train station makes all of my ambitions seem futile. Where else but J— would I have these realizations. J— makes me think of getting up to go to work at 6:00 a.m. despite my retirement. I was a workaholic my entire life. What am I so afraid of that I can't rest even in retirement? I wonder if you remember that boy Gaphyun. It was J— that made me remember him and his mute parents. He spoke for them when he was as young as seven. Remember how he would show up with his parents when they needed to say something? I was friends with him for years. I think his having to speak for his parents made him a quiet boy. I could talk to him because he was very good at keeping secrets. When he became a young man, he took his parents to New Zealand. Why New Zealand, I asked him, and he said he thought its natural environment would be good for his parents. That was the only reason he chose New Zealand. Walking in the fields last night made me think I had never seen him make so much as a grimace when he lived here. I held on to my memory of him as I consoled myself. That I shouldn't be afraid of taking care of my parents. But my heart is still heavy. I'm writing all this because I don't know how to carry such heaviness in my heart, but I'm not doing it because I expect a reply. Am I not old enough to know that the things that happen to everyone else can and will happen to me? And the memory of my friend who left for a faraway country with his mute parents gave me much courage.

Watching you last night made me remember something from a long time ago that you probably don't know about. Remember when you published your second book? It was Father's sixtieth birthday, and you gave him your new book as a present. Father came to Seoul a few days later. There was that big bookstore in Jongno that's no longer there. You were signing books there that day. Father got off at Seoul

Station and called me. Saying he wanted to go to Jongno Bookstore. That Honnie was signing books there and he wanted to see for himself. It was a hoot to hear the words Jongno Bookstore come out of his mouth. I met him under the clock tower at Seoul Station and we went to Jongno. I think the event was on the fifth floor. Father hid and watched you signing copies, surrounded by piles of your own books. He kept ducking under the display stands when you looked up, and I was about to burst out laughing at the sight when he covered my mouth, and I saw tears in his eyes. After the signing was over, Father bought every single one of your books on the display stand save one and took them down to J—. Am I not the one who's retired? I'll come down again next week and stay with Father, you go back home and return to your work. Because surely that's what Father wants for you.

It must've been the day of the second typhoon. Worried about the roof every time the wind blew, Father suddenly began rummaging through drawers. He found a new year's card with a picture of two nests resting on a wintry branch. A new year's card? I wondered what he was up to as I glanced at the card and then at him. When did he even buy this? He sat down on the floor and stared at the blank inner page for a long time before writing *Muleung hyeong* at the top. Maybe bending over hurt his back, so he lay on his stomach like a boy doing his homework without a desk. I stood by him and watched as he wrote lying down, curious as to what he would write in a new year's card in the middle of the summer. The closed windows rattled in their frames. It made me think the roof might actually be blown away. Father paused for a long time, pen in hand, before continuing to write: *This is the last new year's card I shall send to you in this world. I often cannot remember things. Next year, I might forget what a new year's card is.* Father wrote phonetically, spelling words wrong. *We are now old enough for anything to happen.* Behind him, I regarded the misspellings in that sentence. *My heart feels like it can accept anything but my body can no longer do anything. Thank you for not asking me what happened in the valley at Galjae when we met again.* He almost bore a hole through the card with his stare. Father bent his stub of an index finger against his pen to write the final sentences. *I pushed you, hyeong, into the valley below. All these years, I often wondered what you would have done to me if the gun had been aimed at your head and not mine. When it was light, I wailed like a wolf as I looked for you in the valley, but I couldn't find you. When I learned you were alive, hyeong, I swore an oath on my own rice fields. That I would take care of you for life. But here I am writing this new year's card and realizing such oaths are nothing but a mote of dust. Thank you for being my lifelong friend even when you knew everything.*

Father handed me the card. Asking me to mail it when it began to snow, before the new year.

They said we needed to reduce his stress as much as possible but I had no idea what exactly stressed him out. The best I could do was prevent him from taking his daytime naps by taking him out for walks. I made sure he took the medicine my sister sent him and went to the market to buy seaweed, which was supposed to be good for sleep according to the internet. But I couldn't find any, and after a futile search through the market, I came home empty-handed. Whenever Father rose from sleep and went to the bathroom and locked the door or crouched down in a corner of the laundry room, I recorded the date and time in a notebook. To determine his cycles. I kept breaking into a sweat whenever I discovered him wandering off and hiding somewhere, but at some point I became used to it. Father, crouching and alone, looked just like a frightened and neglected little boy.

—What are you doing, Father, come out of there.

When I held out my hand to him, he would obligingly take it and be led to bed again where I would cover him with his blanket. One summer night, sticky from the heat, he talked in his sleep as he flailed his arms. Father was piteously calling out for someone. I listened hard, trying to catch the name, but the words were muffled. I grabbed his flailing hand and held on as he continued to mumble in words I couldn't make out. Perhaps it wasn't a name but a scream. Because Father suddenly bolted upright and ran for the sliding door, almost making it outside to the courtyard.

One year, it was spring. I was gazing at the pheasant's-eye flowers sprouting up through the earth at dawn and suddenly decided to visit my daughter, throwing the door open and hiking up the mountain. My daughter was no more, but the pheasant's-eye flowers still bloomed, and I kept eating my meals—it was intolerable. The frozen hiking paths had melted into mud in the spring. I kept climbing upward at first, but soon got off the path to sit on a rock until the sun rose. I sat for a long time. Caught hostage to this life by the fact that in this house in J—, my elderly parents were still living.

At first I would shake Father as I told him it was just a dream and he needed to wake up, but after a few times of this, I began to simply make him lie down again and stroked his chest whispering to him, This is nothing, everything will be fine in the morning, Father . . . I missed his strength that saw him through the heaviest trials of life. The father who could barely stand, but could still hide his wounds. I was tall for my age in elementary school. In fourth grade, I was as tall as a middle schooler. My height always put me in the very front of the parade number on Sports Day in the fall. The student in the front had to memorize the path of the parade, which meant I had to practice the route before every Sports Day, going home alone after the sun had set. I may have been taller than most sixth-graders but I was only a fourth-grader. The hilly road home after hours was always scary. The moon was scary in the sky, and the rustling of the forest made me think it was rushing up at me, which made me run toward home but stop when it sounded like my very footsteps were after me, and I collapsed on the ground. When I told Father to please talk to the teacher to take me out of parade practice because I was too afraid of coming home alone in the dark, Father came to pick me up on his bike every evening after practice. He'd come from the fields and smelled of rice stalks and sweat. One time, I came out the school gates expecting to see him, but he wasn't there. After waiting for him, I had no choice but to make my way through the hills alone again and I suddenly remembered the cemetery. I felt tears coming and my legs shaking. Willing my exhausted legs to move, I ran home as fast as I could. I kept remembering the ghost stories the other children had told me, especially the one about the baby ghost, which I felt was running alongside me. No matter how much I ran, I didn't seem to get any nearer to home and I felt like I was running in place. I was crying and running like that when I saw Father running up a steep incline, panting. The realization that it was my father rushing toward me in the dark made me shout, Father! and I collapsed. I was crying loudly with my legs stretched out on that gravely road. His panting voice explaining how he was late because someone had borrowed his bicycle without asking and he had been looking for it everywhere. In his mere presence, all my fears melted away. Even when the clouds swallowed the moon and the road darkened, I wasn't afraid. The dark shadows swayed in the forest, but I felt nothing. That moment, a wild beast darted away in surprise and I hid myself behind Father. In that moment, Father's presence was enough to dispel the most all-consuming fear. I would miss that moment from my childhood. I was now by Father's side but I couldn't dispel any of his fears, not even in the slightest. Father would suddenly get up from bed and look for a hiding place or talk in his sleep saying, Don't do this to me, or run away in the night like someone was after him. One time, he tripped on a threshold and fell asleep on the floor. After a night of disrupted sleep, he couldn't remember what he had done at all. You don't remember? I used to ask, but no longer did. I didn't want him to suffer twice over a night he couldn't remember. It occurred to me that maybe it was a blessing in disguise that he couldn't.

Having apparently forgotten about walking to the mountain cemetery, Father took off his hat and held it out to me. Meaning, I should hang it. He was in danger of napping like that and ruining his night's sleep.

—Shall we take a stroll through the neighborhood?

Father silently put the hat he had handed to me back on.

—Do you need your sunglasses?

—People will make fun.

—Who will? That Kim Soonok lady?

He laughed, and I laughed with him. The sunglasses were wiped clean and in a box under Father's bed. Ever since Father spoke Kim Soonok's name to me, I deliberately mentioned her in front of him a few times. When he refused to eat I would say, Now what would Ms. Kim Soonok say about that? He seemed affronted at first, but now he just laughed it off. I was simply joking in hopes that he'd be free of her name, but Father seemed genuinely displeased at my speaking her name so freely, like now. I said, Well, Father, if you tell me about her, I'll stop saying her name then, to which Father mumbled, But I didn't even say goodbye to her . . .

Because Father had ended up lying down again with those words, our walk happened nearer to sunset. We went out the side gate and walked toward the dykes and Father glanced at the cattle pen.

—It's useless now, we ought to knock it down . . .

He pushed open the cattle pen gate and peered inside for a long time before saying, Are those four-o'clock seeds? In a corner of Mother's vegetable patch, where the flowers had bloomed and fallen, were black four-o'clock seeds. How bold they look, he said in a low voice. That seeds hardened around now. That the heavenly bamboo in the yard will soon show its round, red fruit and I should watch out for them. A few days ago, Father had picked the red fruit on the boxthorn where its purple flowers had fallen and trimmed off the new branches touching the ground. But those are new growths, I'd said by his side. Father said the lower branches had to be trimmed for the nutrients to reach the whole plant. Was that true? We came to an old woman of the village sitting on a platform in the shade of a nettle tree by the dykes, scraping at the insides of an old pumpkin. When this granny from Naechon looked up at us, Father spoke to her.

—What are you working on?

—Can't see I'm digging out a pumpkin? You want some pumpkin bumuri before you go?

Father smiled.

—If I want something to eat, I should make it myself.

—You think I'll die soon?

—How should I know?

—I'm sick of living but they won't take me.

—It's not up to us, is it?

—You should be happy. The old gentleman fixed his teeth so they're nice and strong.

Perhaps embarrassed, Father closed his mouth.

—But dye your hair. Who knows when it's your time, do you want to have white hair when you go?

—Dye, yes.

—Be clean and ready always. So you can go anytime.

—Yes.

—That old gentleman came to take me away in my dream last night, but I remembered the lid was open on a jar in the yard and when I came back from closing it he was gone and I couldn't follow him.

By that old gentleman, Naechon granny meant her late husband.

—See Honnie's mother before you go.

—When is that?

Father bowed his head.

—The next time the old gentleman comes I'm going with him jar lid or not, so if she wants to see me, she better come home soon.

—All right.

—Winter solstice means we need to make the bird-egg tteok for the red bean soup together. Think she'll be home by then?

Father couldn't answer and looked at me instead. Of course she will, I answered for him hastily. Apparently, my mother still made red bean soup with Naechon Grandmother for the winter solstice. The women of the village observed all of the lunar calendar rituals. On Samjitnal they made red bean tteok, on Daeboreum five-grain rice and namul vegetable banchan. On midsummer Yudu they boiled white rice into a chicken porridge and shared that among them. Mother and Naechon grandma collaborated on the winter solstice soup. Probably because the boiling and crushing of the beans and ripping each bud of tteok and rolling it into a bird's egg shape between their palms took a lot of time and effort. That soup they took turns making in our kitchen cauldron one year, her cauldron the next.

—Well, I suppose I might be the one who's gone by then.

—Say goodbye if you go. Don't leave without a word like the Wolseong man.

After listening patiently, I pulled at Father's arm so we could continue. Whenever we bumped into other villagers on our walks, their conversations always ended up like this. Words appropriate for people who might never meet again, spoken in the most casual manner. When Father was done with his dental work, Wanglim grandpa who we met on the street bade Father to sink his teeth into as much meat as possible before he died. Father replied that he would. The speaker and listener of such words were always very casual. Chogang grandpa who lived by the dykes once came up slowly to the garden wall and put something on it, asking me as I stood in the yard, Your father home? When I told him he was getting physical therapy in town he said, I see . . . He turned and slowly walked back to the dykes. He'd left some antique nickel bowls and 60,000 won in cash on the garden wall. In the evening, I told Father that Chogang grandpa had left him some dishes and money, and Father stared at the money in the bowl and said, He must be on his way soon. I said, Excuse me? Father said calmly, He's paying me back for some money he owed me a long time ago. He must be getting ready to die . . . In my own walks about the neighborhood, I would get the feeling that the only people remaining here were the elderly. There were yards lush with grass but an old person sitting alone on the maru porch. Some houses were completely empty save for a couple of dogs lying under the porch, and the trees of the empty houses were heavy with birds. They emitted sharp cries as they flitted from tree to tree, it was deafening. Surely they weren't singing, but fighting. The dogs barked up at the aerial battles. A thought—that there were more dogs and birds living here than humans. It wasn't just dogs and birds; once, I saw a deer come down all the way to the railroad tracks. There was even a boar that had come down from the mountain to the fields. It didn't run away from me but looked right into my eyes. This must've been a common occurrence as there was a sign posted by the path up the hills about how to deal with boars. Do not shout, make no sudden movements, and look into the eyes of the boar as you slowly walk away. Do not throw stones or engage in other threatening behavior. If you sense danger, hide behind a tree or nearby rock. The old grannies I ran into from time to time seemed to be unafraid of boars and deaf to bird noises as they had no expression on their faces. I couldn't recognize most of them. Hello, I said to one the other day, and when I passed her, I could feel her staring at the back of my head. In the mountains right before the path turned steep, I once came across some old women coming down from the other direction. They had canes and their thin white hair was in a bun, and despite the summer they must've felt cold because they wore sweaters—three or four of them in all—including the granny I couldn't recognize from before. Was it because of the sunlight? The glow of their white hair made me think they weren't people of this world. Not to mention how fragile they looked, ready to shatter in the grip of a hug, and yet their sunken eyes still sparkled. One of them knew who I was at first glance. Aren't you that bookworm of a daughter of that man from Nungmweh? "Bookworm" was my nickname from childhood. It wasn't as if we had enough books in our house back then to justify such a nickname. For the life of me, I couldn't remember who the granny recognized me was, and the best I could do was to say, How have you been . . . My voice trailed off. A granny next to her said, Who's this child again? She licked her dry lips. You know, the eldest daughter of the Nungmweh man. Going off to the shed to stick her nose in a book ever since she was as small as a bean. Now she's a writer, said the granny from the other day. Another granny said, Ah, that one. They were like ghosts in the sunlight as they gathered around me and their faces frowned sympathetically, chattering away.

—Don't be sad for too long.

—We wandered all this time ourselves.

—Everyone has to wander a bit before they go, that's what living in this world is.

The grannies came close to me and held my hands and rubbed my shoulders and stroked my hair and back. Their fingers were like wintry branches but their touch on my head and shoulders and back was gentle. In the middle of my hike, surrounded by these grannies, I was unexpectedly being consoled. I felt something scarred and pitted within me start to become more malleable. My cheeks, roughed by the grazing of my own palms night after night, were softening under their caresses. The grannies who had surrounded me and comforted me said, Wonder if we'll ever meet again—whatever you're here for, I hope you find it and come back again soon, and they turned and slowly went down the path I had come before.

I hope you find it and come back. If it weren't for these words spoken in dry and split voices lingering in my ears, I would've thought I'd just hallucinated or walked out of a dream. I felt the heavy grip of a rough and large hand loosen its grip on me, and the feeling of a black stone door of a grave being rolled away from before my eyes as I moved forward, the strength returning to my legs as I walked home. That was a few days ago.

—Father, it's Isak.

We had left Naechon grandma behind and were walking toward the Irrigation Association road when we saw Isak coming out of a plastic greenhouse. Father raised his head and looked at him. Isak saw us and called out, Where are you off to? Father didn't answer and his gaze moved to the new combine harvester parked in front of the greenhouse instead. Behind it stood the rice planter and cultivator.

Isak noticed him looking.

—These are new. We're going to harvest using them beginning this year.

—And your old tools?

—No one wanted to buy them, even at a markdown. Gishik in Samsan-ri said he wanted them, so I sent them off.

—They weren't bought that long ago . . .

—Machines get old in just two or three years. Just when you pay one off, the next model comes out . . .

—Nonghyup doesn't let you rent them? How does one person afford all this?

—I keep asking them, but they haven't been listening so far.

—Ask Mayor Lee, he'll listen to you.

—I did, but . . .

He couldn't hear the phone, but he could hear Isak well enough. I watched Father converse with him for a while.

—Wind and rain expected again. Careful the typhoon doesn't take too much.

Isak said a leopard had come down from the mountain and entered the greenhouse with an eye on one of the chickens, but the dog had chased it away. Boars were a familiar sight nowadays but a leopard cat was a first. He told us to watch out for them hiding behind the dykes. Father listened but said nothing in response to Isak. Isak then said, Nuna . . . I looked up at him, and he said his wife had two questions for me. I had never met Isak's wife. Two whole questions? I smiled. Yes, my wife says she's written something and was hoping you would read it and tell her your thoughts. What? I was as surprised as if I'd accidentally swallowed an ice cube. Someone in this village was writing? I'd heard his wife was from Vietnam, she was a writer? I asked Isak, What's the other thing? Well, said Isak, she wanted to know if "sobbing" was crying or if it meant one is near tears. Isak said his wife spoke Korean better than he did now, but she had remarked that there were words only people who were born here could understand. Is that true, nuna? Isak's face was very serious, and I told him I was out for a walk with my father now and we should talk more later. We were about to leave when Father said, Isak-ah, and turned toward the harvester. Isak, who was about to hop on it, stopped in his tracks. Father said, You can do the procurement without me here, right? His voice was clear. Why? said Isak. You're going somewhere? Father turned and looked at me. I shook my head no. Isak said, Then you must help me out again this year as well. When Father didn't answer, Isak started ripping off the plastic wrapping on the new harvester and said again, Where are you off to? Father mumbled, too low for Isak to hear, How is anyone to know where we're going? and turned and went up the path on top of the Irrigation Association dyke.

As we walked on the fields beyond the railroad tracks, two trains passed by. True to what Isak had said, wild animals were expanding their range as we saw several deer drinking from the irrigation ditches that reflected the colors of the sunset. They leaped in surprise each time and rushed into the rice, eliciting a sigh from Father. On the old tree fallen against the dyke, the light of the setting sun glowed on the old bark. It was the tree we used to hang the rope for tug-of-war when we were done with the game during First Full-Moon Day. After harvests, the villagers would gather to twist leftover straw into new rope for tug-of-war. That straw rope was so thick that children could balance themselves on it. The palms of my hands itched at the thought of the rope. At tug-of-war, everyone from children to the elderly participated, and my hands remembered the feeling of the rope slipping through my grasp. The winning side was said to have a good harvest, so the losing side would ask the winners for a segment of the rope to hang on this tree, and the villagers would give it a glance every time they passed. But now there was no one who would play tug-of-war now, and the tree the rope would've hung from was laying on its side. My gaze followed its form until something made my eyes open wide. The roots must be touching the ditch. The tree was still alive, and the new branches of the tree near the roots were even thick and fresh. Sitting by a branch were two deer that had come down from the mountains. It wasn't my first time seeing the tree since coming to J—, but I hadn't noticed it was alive until now. Father, I said, there are deer. I pointed to them. Father silently stared at the fallen but alive tree and the deer before saying, The things that should live in the mountains are coming down to the village. They have their own turf wars. So many of them these days, they keep coming down. Eating all the potatoes and sweet potatoes, can't plant them anymore. The boars dig them up before they can get too big. Last year, Isak planted some mountain berry or blueberry or whatever but the deer ate them all . . . Father sighed. Well, they've got to eat, too. I asked, Then the mountain patches are all empty? No one plants anything there? Father dragged his feet. He said, The short things get eaten by the animals and the tall things aren't profitable . . . It's why we'd planted plums in our mountain patch. Lots of fruit but no one to pick it. They fall and we leave it there and it's all fertilizer for the next year and there's even more fruit then. Must have a strong flavor—not even the birds peck at them. Father said he wanted to rest and sat down on the dyke by the train tracks and looked out at the rice paddies. The wind tipped the edge of his hat. As he looked around us, his face was bathed in the red light of the sunset. When was the last time he'd seen such a sunset? The edges of the fields in the end of summer turning red from it? Father stared at the evening clouds that were pink and red and yellow as if they'd rolled in watercolors before flying through the sky. He then turned his gaze to the riverbank where he'd brought his calf to feed, the dykes where people had planted beans to grow as much food as they could, and the Irrigation Association road Father had stood on holding a shovel night and day during droughts so he could direct the smallest trickle of water to his crops. The deer weren't only in the branches of the old tree. Another deer in the fields had been hiding and now skipped to another field. I stretched out my hand and held Father's. The light of the sunset that seeped into his wrinkles flowed to my own hand. I lived, he said, never knowing a day like this would come. That people would have fields but didn't plant sweet potatoes, that they had rice paddies but couldn't plant rice . . . Father's low voice was drowned out by the third passing train.

On the way back, we chose the route along the dyke to the edge of the village and into the paved road. Our house was at the center of town, which meant we needed to walk through the alleys to reach it. Walking home as a child during cold winter sunsets, I would smell the rice cooking from each house, hear the children playing in the snow, and overhear the ruckus of adults trying to defuse a fight at a neighbor's. But now the path was so quiet I had to ask Father a question.

—How is Gochang ajeh who lives in that house?

Father turned to look at the place I was pointing at.

—He's dead.

We made a turn and I asked again.

—And Gobu ajeh?

—Dead.

I asked at each turn of the alley.

—Dosan ajeh?

—Dead.

—Soseong ajeh?

—Dead.

—Haman ajeh?

—He's dead.

Calm as ever, Father spoke the words, Dead, Dead, He's dead . . . By the end of the list of dead people, we had reached our house. Father stopped at the gate. A humid wind glanced off our faces. My forehead was cold from the realization that each of the elders in the houses in the alley coming down from the road were dead when Father started to walk again, mumbling, Come to think of it, they're all dead now. Only I'm alive and clinging to you.

Father, who I thought would sleep deeper having walked more than other days—who had gone to bed right after dinner and even snored—woke up around 11:00 p.m. and sat up in bed before calling out, Hon-ah!

—Will you turn the light on?

I'd brought the desk lamp from the small room to the kitchen table where I was sitting in front of my laptop screen. From there I could see Father's bed in the living room through the glass in the doors. Father had a habit of falling asleep with the television on. One of the things the doctor said was to not let him do this, so I would wait until he fell asleep before turning it off. Having noticed Father was awake and sitting up for a while, it was only when he called to me that I closed my laptop and went up to him, turning on the nightlight by his bed.

—Turn that on as well.

Father was pointing to the living room light switch. Why did he want that? I wondered, but I did as he asked and turned the night light off. The suddenly bright lights made me blink. Two buttons were undone on Father's pajama top. Would you like a glass of water, Father? He sat in silence for a long time, not answering. Then, he asked in a low voice, When are you leaving?

—You must leave soon.

—. . .

—I must send you away, but I've liked having you here so much.

—. . .

—But you must leave.

—. . .

I rubbed my eyes and looked at Father again. His white hair flattened from the pillow, a face parched dry of any moisture, bold veins running over the backs of his hands. Just a few days ago, the sight of him surprised me so much I heard a thud in my own heart, but now he looked more like himself.

—Will you write down some things for me?

I glanced at the clock. It was almost midnight.

—It's late, Father. How about we go to sleep and do that tomorrow?

—We have to do it while I remember.

The afternoon had been gray but no rain had come. We'd been relieved the morning's typhoon forecast had not come to pass, but the sound of the wind was getting louder and we began hearing big drips of raindrops. Perhaps this was what had awakened Father.

—It's raining, Father.

I'd said it to distract him, but Father repeated, Write something down for me. I brought over my laptop from the kitchen table, created a new file, and readied myself to type Father's words. His low voice mixed with the heavy patter of the rain. Father would pause from time to time, as if listening to the rain, before continuing to speak once more.

To my first, Seungyeop, I leave my coat and the letters in the wooden chest. It is a good coat I wore for many years since you bought it for me with your first paycheck since leaving home at such a young age. I regret telling your younger siblings to think of you as their father. How heavy your shoulders must've been for it. You took half of a burden that should've been all mine to bear. You were always the firm ground beneath my feet.

To my second, Hongie, I leave my buk and bukchae. I've fixed the buk and cleaned the bukchae as well. It warmed my heart that you always protected what I held dear. It was wonderful when you took me to the National Theater in Seoul's Jangchung-dong. Thanks to your gift of the sound system, my ears have had many happy hours.

To my third, I leave my watch and a bottle of whiskey. The whiskey is called Royal Salute. Having won the highest quality ranking for my harvest several years in a row, I bought it to celebrate and forgot I had it until now. You shouldn't have paid for my dental work—that was your mistake. I wanted to do that. Knowing how fiery you are, I was grateful every time you listened to your older brothers.

The new bicycle in the shed is yours . . . Father's voice trailed off as he looked at me writing down what he was saying with my computer on my lap. I shouldn't say yours, said Father, fix it for me.

To my fourth, Honnie, I leave my new bicycle. I bought it thinking I would ride with you together but three years have passed since . . . . He must mean the bicycle wrapped in plastic by mother's refrigerator in the shed. Father said, I bought the bicycle and waited for you. When you came I wanted to breathe in the fresh air as we rode, but it is too late now. Father spoke as if I weren't right in front of him. Hon, whenever you walk alone at night, I am always sitting on your left shoulder. Do not fear the dark.

To my fifth, Ippy, I leave my sunglasses. You gave them to me as a gift for my birthday, and thanks to my wearing them everywhere since, they say I've avoided cataracts. You've worked so hard to provide medicine for me and your mother. Everyone I meet says I've lived this long because I've got a pharmacist for a daughter, and they're right. Your touch has always been the warmest.

To my sixth, the youngest, I leave the task of dismantling the cattle pen. I tried to do it myself, but I don't have the strength. Dismantle it, and the field it stands on is left for you. You were about to graduate high school when I fell ill several times. Despite your college entrance exam studies, you were the one to take me to the hospital and keep your brothers in Seoul informed, and you still got into college. Thank you for that.

To Honnie's mother, Jung Darae, I leave my bankbook.

Father stopped for a moment, bowed his head, and said he was sorry it wasn't a lot of money—I briefly fought the urge to not type this part. But these were Father's words, and I suppressed my compulsion to interfere to the point my hands were shaking. Jung Darae, you only showed me the fruit of life. How hard it was for you to give me only the fruit. I am sorry and thankful. I regret all the times I failed to say how wide a shade you cast, Jung Darae. It was my fault to stoke your ire by not answering you when you spoke. You might think it was because I thought little of you, but that is not it. It's because I was unable to be next to you more when we were young, and the guilt plagued me so, forgive me. Typing up Father's words, I flinched. All the words I had hesitated to write because of cowardice, because of sudden awkwardness, were slowly flowing out of Father's dry lips. How I had once spat out that I don't expect understanding and therefore no forgiveness either, even when I was clearly in the wrong. I hope I had never said such things to my daughter. Father said, My awe-inspiring children . . . I couldn't bear to type that. My laptop kept slipping from my knees, so I put it up on Father's bed and knelt before it, resting my fingers on the keyboard. Father looked as if he wanted to say more as he stared at the floor. My ears ready to catch every word, I waited silently. Father said something in a small voice but the wind in the courtyard and the rain and the rattling windowpanes drowned him out. I could hear the rustling of the butterbur leaves being blown in the direction of the wind in the backyard. After a long pause, Father said something with some difficulty, but I didn't catch it. What did you say, Father? My hands still on the keyboard, I sat as close to him as possible. What was that? To think how desperately I was putting down his words. Silence flowed between my father and me. The leaves that had fallen from the persimmon trees in the side yard were likely being washed away by the rain. The sound of rainfall mixed with the roaring whisper of the wind whipping through the leaves. Who knew if the drenched leaves had tumbled up to the maru porch? Father, whose head was bowed, finally gathered his strength and his dry lips moved once more.

I lived through it, said Father. Thanks to all of you, I lived.

PHOTO BY LEE BYUNG RYUL

ABOUT THE AUTHOR

Kyung-Sook Shin is one of South Korea's most widely read and acclaimed novelists. She has been awarded the Manhae Grand Prize for Literature, the Dong-in Literary Award, the Man Asian Literary Prize, and many others. Shin is the author of eight novels, eight short story collections, and three essay collections, including the *New York Times* bestseller *Please Look After Mom*, which has been published in more than forty countries.

ABOUT THE TRANSLATOR

Anton Hur was double-longlisted and shortlisted for the 2022 International Booker Prize and has worked on several of Kyung-Sook Shin's books. He lives in Seoul.

It takes a village to get from a manuscript to the printed book in your hands. The team at Astra House would like to thank everyone who helped to publish *I Went to See My Father*.

PUBLISHER
Ben Schrank

EDITORIAL
Alessandra Bastagli
Rola Harb

CONTRACTS
Stella Iselin

PUBLICITY
Rachael Small
Alexis Nowicki

MARKETING
Tiffany Gonzalez
Sarah Christensen Fu
Jordan Snowden

SALES
Jack W. Perry

DESIGN
Jacket: Rodrigo Corral Studio
Interior: Richard Oriolo

PRODUCTION
Lisa Taylor
Elizabeth Koehler

MANAGING EDITORIAL
Alisa Trager
Olivia Dontsov

COMPOSITION
Westchester Publishing Services

ABOUT ASTRA HOUSE

Astra House is dedicated to publishing authors across genres and from around the world. We value works that are authentic, ask new questions, present counter-narratives and original thinking, challenge our assumptions, and broaden and deepen our understanding of the world. Our mission is to advocate for authors who experience their subject deeply and personally, and who have a strong point of view; writers who represent multifaceted expressions of intellectual thought and personal experience, and who can introduce readers to new perspectives about their everyday lives as well as the lives of others.